Conjunctions

Part Five of

Changels Genesis

by Peter King

Peter King Publishing
Wellington, New Zealand

Conjunctions
Part five of Changels Genesis
Copyright Peter King 2015

Cover Image: Justin Ennis "Lightning storm and stars" (Flickr) Creative Commons Licence. Cover Design: Peter King.

Interior design by Peter King.
Interior maps are derived from Google Maps and are under Google copyright.
Typeset in 12 point Georgia. The cover and chapter headings use Exocet Heavy. Type design optimised for remedial and ESOL readers.

Edition 3
First Published 2013
ISBN-13: 978-1-927264-41-6
Fiction
Publisher and Distributor: Peter King Publishing
Wellington, New Zealand

For more information visit http://www.changels.info

SPECIAL NOTE TO READERS

Please be reminded that the author does not recommend this book to children under 13 years. This book contains references to real world violence and sexual behaviour which may disturb young readers.

Dialogue that originates telepathically is rendered in *italics*.

The transition between the narrator's present (in the present tense) and past (in the past or perfect tense) is marked by an elipsis ... centered on an empty line

When the location changes through teleportation ("bending") there is a new line and a '[+]' symbol.

Non-English words have been hyphenated on their first use to expose the syllabic structure and ease pronunciation. The exception is Karearea (falcon) which is always hyphentaed e.g.Ka-rea-rea. Maori words ending in the 'e' have been given a non-standard accent acute (e.g. Tané) for the same reason.

Translations Sam (the narrator) understands are parenthesised e.g kara-kia (prayer). Non-English words are hyphenated to aid pronuncuation.

Changels Genesis is fact based fiction. Facts have been indicated with a superscripted dagger symbol[+] There is a three page fact and fiction section at the end of this part of the story.

THANKS AND ACKNOWLEDGEMENTS

My thanks to Najva Mirhashimi for translating and transliterating some Farsi phrases into English.

I must acknowledge the traditional cultural literary treasures of the Ngapuhi iwi cited in this part of Changels as well as the work of Ngati Toa rangatira Te Rauparaha, whose haka (war chant) is a motif in this book. My object in citing them is not to purloin but to exhibit them.

We are such stuff As dreams are made on, and our little life Is rounded with a sleep

– The Tempest, Act 4, scene 1

Flying to the moon should be more enjoyable than this. Not that I actually *am* flying to the moon. I'm really in a medical evacuation pod somewhere else in the galaxy. But I can see and hear everything my captured speeder senses as it's taken to the alien Administration's moon base aboard a flying saucer.

The connection between me and my speeder (a small, car roof rack capsule sized flying box), never even flickers. Once again the technology of the Fae (historically known on Earth by names like Tuatha De Danaan, Vila, Peri, Kitsune, Patupaiarehe or Faerie or Fairies) is proving to be so much better than the aliens'.

I call my speeder Ka-rea-rea after the fast New Zealand falcon. He's far smaller and more capable than any craft *they* have. If *they* could get into him, they would gain technology the Fae don't want *them* to have.

The small Greys (clones with their dark, unreadable black eyes) at least know better than to get out the power tools and start trying to smash their way into a Fae craft. They must realise that anything as small and powerful as this must contain a lot of energy. And in fact Ka-rea-rea's fuel – a kilo of antimatter – would make a pretty huge explosion if it's released. So instead they're using beam probes to try and see through the diamond lattice hull.

They aren't getting very far. The Fae built it to diffuse any signals sent at it, so their efforts are not helping them. Not that I really care that much. I'm bone-tired. Despite the strange smells, sights and sounds in the alien scout type craft I'm dozing. I've been in survival mode for a week and a half and the stress is simply wearing me down.

A week and a half ago our base under Renwick House (a mansion on remote Aotea island, near Auckland, New Zealand) was compromised. I'd been caught out, flying Ka-rea-rea home from Manila at the time. With the alarms sounding, our leader, Dr Prosperov, and the others had set off the small powergel charges on the compressed natural gas bottles that supplied the kitchen. Then they evacuated to the base before either I, or these little Gray guys had had a chance to get there.

After the fire the house was a ruin, the base in the tunnels below it, collapsed. I'd given it half a day (for them to stop watching the place) while I relaxed on a beach in New Caledonia, then I'd returned home, Sunday night, and teamed up with my girlfriend, Emma Reeves, the only local who knew our secret. We'd snuck into the school office and erased the school's records of us, then hidden Ka-rea-rea in our secret cave by the sea. Knowing the others would be gone for a while, and knowing if I stayed near Emma I'd only endanger her, I'd let myself be taken in by the system: first by Sergeant Smith on Aotea Island, then by Youth Aid. I'd met Detective Constable Sue Williams in my first interview in Auckland with her boss Detective Sergeant Kevin Cooper.

Cooper thought all the missing people at Renwick, including my sister Rewa, Aunt Liz and Grandpop Mike Kahu, had died. Since then I'd rescued Sue twice: first soon after meeting her,

2

when she'd drunkenly taken too many sleeping tablets because her partner, Rachel, had left her; and again, when the alien infiltrator agent, Father Enrico Rocelli, had hypnotised her in her own house.

It was these infiltrators – Die Bruderschaft (The Brotherhood) they called themselves – who had just injured me. Rocelli was one of them. They were a race of aliens who had long infiltrated human society. Normally they did not work with the alien authorities and their clones (who we called "The Administration") which governed Earth for their government ("The Center"). But six months ago we had managed to get the Administration to arrest some of the Bruderschaft in Elan, France in order to stop one of their murderous breeding rituals. Somehow this had backfired as the Administration had now started to use the Bruderschaft to hunt us.

They had almost succeeded in catching me because I had called for help from Dr Prosperov's British lawyer, Sir Michael Hamilton-Smythe. He had dropped everything to help me but the reason was his daughter, Sian, had been held hostage by the Bruderschaft. I had evaded capture with Sue's help, but I knew it was only a matter of time before they caught us both. Deciding to lure them away from Sue I had planned to pretend to fall into their trap which encouraged me to rescue Sian, from the Bruderschaft in a castle in Lichtenstein. My plan was to pretend I was falling into their trap just so I could escape somewhere else. But that plan had changed dramatically when to my huge relief everyone *had* secretly returned. Then we'd decided that instead of pretending to fall into the trap we'd spring it on purpose to find out more about how they had managed to trace us. That was still a mystery and until we knew how it had happened there was no guarantee they couldn't do it again. Somehow one of us (probably Ashley Robinson who came from New Orleans) had been betrayed. Ashley had gone to visit her cousin, Nathan Montgomery, who we projected was a would-be future President of the United States. Someone – probably Nathan himself – had planted a tiny Administration trace on her. That had guided the attack fleet of UFO fighters and a kilometer long UFO carrier toward Aotea island in New Zealand. But the question was, how did *they* even know Nathan – a poor black kid from the poorer 'burbs of Washington DC – was even important? How did *they* know he was in contact with Ashley? And why did *they* suspect Ashley of being in contact with their enemies, the Fae, in the first place?

By this time Sue and me had been placed in a Fae quarantine station somewhere in the Galaxy. From quarantine I'd directed Ka-rea-rea by remote control to Liechtenstein. But from there I'd had to return to Earth personally to act as bait and be seen in the castle.

As expected they had been waiting for me and I had ended up talking to them and learned that the Bruderschaft had more to them than a taste for human blood and marrow. The Bruderschaft had also claimed they were a different species from the usual infiltrators – the Aesir and the Venir – entirely. They were the Iyrin, the Watchers, a synthetic race created by all the humanoid species to watch over us on Earth as a focus of Galactic peace. But the Iyrin blamed our ally, Morganne Queen of Fae, for a flawed gift of near immortality which meant they needed to drink the blood and eat the marrow of young humanoids like themselves. They also had a strange spirit guide, a kind of powerful ghost, which had busted my psychic shield,

4

burning me in the process.

Fortunately their guide met his match in Dr Prosperov's own guide, Lucky, who had got us into contact with the Fae in the first place. I had then teleported back to this Fae quarantine station so I could fly Ka-rea-rea under remote control to rescue Sian. Ka-rea-rea had been captured when UFOs called in by the Bruderschaft leader, Erich Von Streicher to cover his escape, intercepted him, thinking I was still flying inside him.

We were going to let them take Ka-rea-rea back to the moon and my guess was the plan was to then blow him up – making a fifty megaton mess of their darkside moonbase, in revenge for burning down Renwick.

All of this tumbled around in my head like clothes in a dryer making for a strange kind of half dream where I was constantly wondering who I could trust and who was really on my side.

I wasn't properly asleep but I wasn't fully awake when our friend, the Fae engineer, Hekator, telepathically bursts into my thoughts.

"*How are you Sam?*"

"*Sleeping,*" I tell him sleepily.

"*Good,*" and then without a pause of consideration. "*I need you to wake Ka-rea-rea's passive sensors please.*"

Dozily I reconnected. Ka-rea-rea was also asleep. The round cabin inside the Administration saucer, or Scout, where he was locked down, came back. His sensors showed me he was on a bench encased in a series of technical looking rings linked by an upside-down T-shape thing. A control desk being operated by one of the short gray guys with black eyes. They were still trying to get inside him.

"*They have no idea what they are doing,*" Hekator says, a note of amusement in his voice.

I have no idea what they were doing either.

"*So what are they doing?*" I ask.

"*They are trying to use a mind probe on you. It's a kind of telepathic sledgehammer to get you out.*"

"*But I'm not in there.*"

"*No. But, the probe wouldn't work anyway because of Ka-rea-rea's multidimensional antimatter vortex would bend it all over the place. They don't have that technology and it's giving them strange returns. That's good because they can't order you out and they don't know whether you are onboard or not.*"

"*Are they taking Ka-rea-rea to that moonbase we set up the sensors around last year?*" I ask.

"*Yes. I'm picking you up on them as well.*"

The scene inside the Scout didn't change. There was a long pause as Hekator apparently tracked the UFO into the cave in the crater we had surrounded with antennas, hidden in the dust of the moon's surface.

"*OK, I've lost you, you must be inside the moonbase. This will be interesting, we've never done this before.*"

"*Hekator?*" I ask, suddenly feeling sorry for Ka-rea-rea.

"*Yes Sam?*"

"*If we have to destroy Ka-rea-rea, how will he react?*"

"*It'll be fine. Its memory is backed up here. We will reinstall him in your new craft.*"

There's a pause where he reads or guesses my thoughts.

"*A being that has no soul can't really die Sam. Its memory is backed up in a few petabytes and can be reset so it continues to experience being. It won't even notice the missing time. It could be cloned too. Only a being that can change and question its purpose for being can truly die."*

"Oh ... OK, I was just a bit ..."

"Empathy too is linked to having a soul. To use one's imagination is to consider another's being and what it is to be another is not just biochemicals, it is also an attempt to understand how another has chosen their purpose. Only a being able to decide its own purpose can do that. You can, because you can change your purpose if you want to. Ka-rea-rea is a machine given a purpose by us and he can't change it. He has no soul. Perhaps his present incarnation may be most usefully ended quite soon. If so his role will have been useful and that is his reason for being."

He pauses for a moment and then adds.

"Of course, to apply the same logic of usefulness to a being which does have a soul and sets its own purpose is a serious mistake. But look! It seems you are being moved."

It looks like we've docked somehow. The little Gray crewman is joined by a few others. The lower round door opens onto a floor and the bench Ka-rea-rea is on, moves by itself onto it. Then the floor sinks out of the craft about three meters down, smoothly and quickly.

We're in a large, round hangar with a white glowing wall behind the saucer which is now standing on three legs. There are a number of other machines around the saucer of different sizes. It looks like they look after the scout saucer.

"Hekator?"

"Yes?"

"How come we can see this? Why can't they trace us back, like you did when you traced Dr Prosperov's probe on Fae?"

"Good question Sam. It's because of the transceiver

7

inside Ka-rea-rea. *It uses entangled, twin cores linked superdimensionally at string level so we get high information throughput. It's so tiny they can't touch it. But when Control uses a wormhole camera to view a remote location he has to create a dimensional warp by linking two locations in space-time. That requires a huge amount of energy which is why you sometimes see coloured lights in the area, because of the harmonic interference. Although the wormhole is tiny the energy field is much, much bigger, making it easy to detect, enlarge and control. Entanglement works at string levels and so infinitely less energy and it's almost impossible to interfere with.*"

Meanwhile the table holding Ka-rea-rea, complete with rings is being marched by the four small greys to a big round door which unscrews to open just like in a camera. The corridor is also white and quite bare and leads to another round door.

"*I think they will try to convince you to open Ka-rea-rea. They aren't sure of the risks of forcing you so they'll play safe. Even so I don't think it's going to be nice, Sam. They are ruthless. They may threaten people you care about. It would be a bluff, because they don't have anyone, but they may still try to trick you.*"

The second round door opens and they take Ka-rea-rea into a small room. There they stop and wait. It seems weird. Is it some kind of ritual or something? It takes a whole five seconds for my dozy brain to realise why we're waiting – we're in an elevator! It made me feel so dumb.

"*They'll be taking you to a containment bunker,*" Hekator comments.

But that means Ka-rea-rea's explosion wouldn't be so damaging.

"*But why didn't we blow up their hangar?*"

"*Because* you're *meant to be inside, remember?*"

"*If I were inside I'd have blown myself up by now.*"

"*Do you* really *think so?*" he asks doubtfully, "*I think you'd cling to hope that you can talk your way out. And maybe you can.*"

I think about that. It's true. I'm in no hurry to die.

"*But I'm* not *in there and we could have wiped them out, which would serve them right for what they did to Renwick,*" I argue.

"*We would have confirmed their mistrust of the Fae and united the Administration and the Bruderschaft more than they are now. No, we need more information and maybe you can do a little more damage with words than antimatter.*"

"*How?*"

"*Try and create discord.*"

"*How?*"

"*No idea, you'll just have to make it up as you go along.*"

I remember me trying to outwit Sir Michael Hamilton-Smythe, the lawyer they'd turned against us, or the Bruderschaft leader Von Streicher, and gulp. My rep for outwitting adults isn't that great.

"*Man, I hope I don't stuff this up.*"

"*That's why I'm here to help. Just remember why you were planning to make this trip in the first place and pretend nothing changed. You're injured, you're alone and all you have left is the ability to make a big explosion by killing yourself.*"

As always these telepathic conversations are far faster than normal speech.

The elevator door, we had come in by, opens again and the Grays take Ka-rea-rea into a new passage which leads directly to a large door. This opens upwards, revealing itself to be about a meter thick. Behind it is a long, round tunnel about three meters high. As we walk along it the tunnel screws itself up behind us forming a solid seal about ten meters long. We walk to the new door. This opens upwards revealing it too is about a meter thick. The room Ka-rea-rea has been taken to is large, empty and completely dark except for a U-shaped table. Behind the table is a large holodeck showing the Administration's simple silver s-shaped lightning bolt on a black background. Seated at the table are five figures including one I recognise.

The one I know is Inspector Rene Du Croix of Interpol and the French Police. He is the one who arrested many Bruderschaft, including the Bruderschaft pandemic merchant, Dr Clayton Hathaway, six months before at Elan. Du Croix's a straight sort of guy. We had worked with him.

The other two at the table are command biobots. Taller than the short Greys and with slightly larger heads, they still have the same black eyes and gray outer coating. They wear symbols on them alongside lightning bolt tabs which make them look military. Next to Du Croix is a woman-like figure. I can't tell what she is really. She's fat, wearing the cheapest print dress with cheap jewellery, in her forties, with black straight hair, a pudgy, brownish face, ugly makeup and large round earrings. I realise I might have seen her a thousand times before: a supervisor behind counters; in offices; as a nurse or waitress and never noticed. She's perfect for blending into any environment. She wears an unattractive, sour expression which suggests she likes saying "no" to people.

The last figure sits in the centre. He's older with long blond and silver hair, pointed ears, and fierce blue eyes under his shaggy eyebrows. His face suggests he's in his sixties but he's probably

way older. He looks a bit like an old lion. He is certainly one
of the original Aesir, the race which founded the Center, and
spawned the infiltrators and Gray biobots.

He looks like a lord with a silver hair band with a blue glowing
jewel in it – probably some sort of control device. His clothes
are dark blue with the lightning bolt on the collar. It looks like a
kind of business suit rather than a uniform but he reminds me a
bit of a space Sir Michael – obviously important and in charge.
The Grays bring Ka-rea-rea before the U-table, put him down
on a table, and then turn and walk back out again. When they go
the blond guy in the centre looks up like he's only just noticed
Ka-rea-rea and speaks to him in English with a slight British
accent.

"You are Sam Kahu, formerly of the Aotea Island insurgency. Do
you acknowledge this?"

His voice is stern and official.

"*Off you go*," Hekator tells me.

I think of saying 'present' like I'm at school and he's calling the
register but seeing it's a formal occasion, I give them my identity
in Maori, like we'd learned back in Northland. I'm like: you are
the aliens, it's our planet, and I am the only one who should be
here anyway. So I say fiercely:

"Ko Pan-gu-ru Te Maun-ga! (Pan-gu-ru is my mountain)
Ko Ho-ki-an-ga Te awa! (Ho-ki-ang-a is my river)
Ko Nga-pu-he Te i-wi! (Nga-pu-he is the tribe)
Ko Sam Ka-hu ta-ku in-goa! (I am Sam Kahu!)
Tu-hia ki te rang-ey! (Write it in the sky)
Tu-hia ki te when-u-a! (write it in the land!)
Tei-hei Mau-ri Ora !" (Behold there is life!)

The blond man looks at the others.

11

"I'll take that as a 'yes'," he says finally.

"I am Archdeacon Oswald Telarkin, chief administrator for this system," the blond tells me.

"These are Service Commanders twenty one, seventy, thirteen ninety three and twenty one, seventy, thirteen ninety four. We note you claim to be inside a non-terrestrial craft supplied by the Fae rebellion. Please verify this by getting out of the craft."

"Baron Von Streicher asked me to do that too, then he attacked and injured me, so I think I'll stay where I am thanks," I reply.

The Archdeacon looks surprised.

"You are injured?"

"Yes."

"How?"

"Meeting the Baron and his friends earlier."

This is obviously news. Everyone looks curious.

"The Baron told us he was under attack by you and asked that we intercept you."

"Well, they do have a habit of manipulating you don't they?" I jeer.

The Archdeacon ignores my jibe.

"So why did he want to talk to *you*?" he sneers back.

"He wanted to know why the Fae were helping us and I said I didn't really know, and what I did know I wasn't going to tell him."

"And I assume this was when you were injured?" the Archdeacon smiles grimly.

"Yes."

"Where was this meeting?"

"The Castle at Belzer, Lichtenstein."

The Archdeacon looks at Inspector Du Croix who shrugs and nods.

"Who else was present?"

"Father Enrico Rocelli, Mrs Julia Huuygens, Von Streicher, and some dude named Sven who is now also injured. Oh and Sian Hamilton-Smythe who is their prisoner."

Du Croix keeps nodding. The Archdeacon looks to him for comment. His accent is slightly French. He speaks dozens of Earth's languages but he prefers French.

"Eet iz as I suspected Archdeacon."

The Archdeacon gestures to Du Croix to ask a question.

"Did zey ask if you would 'elp Zem?"

"Yes."

"And naturally you said 'no'."

"Of course."

"And 'ow was it you were able to escape, albeit injured?"

"Low cunning I guess."

There's a pause.

"I set the castle on fire before I went in," I explain.

"So you are burned?"

"Yes."

"Is it painful?"

"Yes."

"'Ow painful?"

"Painful enough."

"And this is why you will not come out?"

"Uh-huh."

"And if we leave zhou in zere 'ow long do you zink you will stay?"

"Until I decide there's no hope I guess."

"And zhen?"

"I'll expose a kilo of antimatter and there will be a big hole in the moon. If you attack me the same thing will happen anyway."

The Archdeacon looks concerned at the Commanders who don't seem surprised at all.

"Why did you not do that when you were captured?" the Archdeacon asks.

"I'd rather blow up you than western Austria. It's very pretty."

"Zat is true, but why you didn't detonate in ze 'angar where zhou could do more damage?" Du Croix presses.

"I'd rather not blow myself up at all if I can help it. I'd rather live."

"Then why not get out?"

"Because then I have nothing left, not even the power to destroy myself."

The Inspector and the woman seem disturbed by this but the Commanders' expressions remain the same on their plain, hard-to-read faces.

"How old are you Sam?" the woman asks.

"Fourteen."

"Why do you think we are talking to you?" she checks.

"Because you want me to get out without blowing myself up?"

"Are we are wasting our time?"

"I don't know. I'm hoping we can work something out."

"Tell us how you see yourself coming out of here alive," she seems to be quite used to talking to people my age.

"I dunno. I s'pose I sorta hope you'll let me go."

"Why don't you think that can happen?"

"Because you want my speeder and I won't get out of it."

"Why do you think we want your speeder?" the woman asks, surprised.

"Because Sir Michael wanted it."

"Sir Michael was speaking for himself," the Archdeacon says.

"The craft is not an essential objective."

The Commanders shuffle a bit. I suspect they have a different view.

"So why am I here?" I ask him.

"You cannot be expected to be aware that the entire galactic civilisation maintains a convention against intervention on the worlds of civilisation below level ten. Your world is just entering level four. Therefore the Fae have violated the convention and as Administrator one of my roles is to ensure this does not happen. Given your age we do not regard you as an enemy combatant but as a child soldier who should not be here. We do not hold you responsible for this, so simply wish to return the situation to an acceptable status quo. As such our ultimate goal is to restore you to a normal life for your kind."

That was fancy crappola.

"What does that make Sian Hamilton-Smythe?" I reply.

"She is also a victim of this conflict."

"Why does she have to be a victim of this conflict?"

"In order to bring the Fae insurgency to an end. We needed to secure the assistance of Sir Michael. He was more ... tractable ... when his daughter was taken hostage."

"So now my people are gone and the Fae too, why is she still a hostage?" I ask.

"We are not convinced they *have* gone, and that is another reason for this interview. Are you in contact with the Fae?" The Archdeacon asks.

I'd expected this one and had my act sorted out.

"If I *was*," I say bitterly, "I sure as shit wouldn't be *here* would I?"

"You told Sir Michael you had made contact."

"That was to distract the Policewoman while I was away. Sir Michael knew it was a trick."

"He may have been wrong."

"If I had been in contact I wouldn't have taken on Von Streicher alone and I wouldn't be here."

"Really? Surely, it would have been simpler to just escape. Your actions are not rational for a teenager on the run. We did not understand how Sir Michael's proposed deception could ever work. And yet you did go to the girl's aid, and risked injury, and capture. Either you are very stupid or you have another plan."

"This craft is pretty powerful. I felt fairly sure I could beat them."

"But why expose yourself to the risk? You could simply leave your home island and hide."

"Sir Michael has all my money. If I could get him on side I might have a better chance ..." I paused, that didn't sound strong enough so I go on, "plus I wanted to find out from Von Streicher how you caught us."

"He doesn't know. Besides that information is only useful if you think the Fae will come back."

He was quick this one.

"Yes," I agree.

"So you don't deny that they have, or will return?"

"No. They will come back. Well, I *hope* they will, so I have to plan like they will."

One of the Commanders swivels his scary eyes and looks at the Archdeacon.

"Commander twenty one, seventy, thirteen ninety three reminds us your physical presence here has not been objectively established. You may not actually be speaking to us from inside that craft," the Archdeacon relays.

"Well, sorry. But I'm not so dumb that I'll get out just to prove it. Then you would be able to get me in a second and you'd have everything you wanted. Me and my craft. But as you said I didn't blow up your hangar. If I was just a talking bomb I wouldn't have waited until I was in a blast hardened chamber before detonating would I? And as I said I'd rather not blow myself up at all."

"I am merely pointing out our difficulties in negotiating with a small box, which is potentially a bomb."

"Well, that's your problem. Mine is being in pain, cornered inside an alien base, and cramped inside a small box."

It's amusing, that in reality I *am* in a box. A Fae medical evacuation pod millions of miles away. It certainly made it easier to act my role, although far more comfortable.

"You're doing well Sam. Try and get them on to the subject of the infiltrators. I think you may find a way to create problems for them there," Hekator suggests silently.

"Then what sort of assurances would you need to get out of your craft?" the woman asks.

"Well, I sure as hell won't get out of it anywhere here. It must be on Earth. And I won't get out where you can track me down *afterwards* either. It has to be somewhere busy, that I choose at random, where I can get out and not be grabbed. I suggest you tag my craft and pick it up when I've gone. Then you can have it."

The Archdeacon looks at the Commanders, then at the human-like figures.

"Your proposal has some merit. We will consider it. In the meantime however we have some other questions. In particular

Nathan Montgomery. Why did the young female insurgent Ashley Robinson visit him so frequently?"

"He's her cousin."

"Really? Does she visit all her cousins?"

"You know that's exactly what the Baron asked. And the answer is that Nathan has some pretty big problems and needs a lot of help."

"We find it hard to believe that the extremely secretive Fae alliance gave advanced tools to humans to help their cousins."

"I dunno, my cousins need a lot of help," I smile. "But OK, no they gave us the tools to fight your Iyrin infiltrators. Infiltrators like Baron Von Streicher and Clayton Hathaway who have been here for centuries breaking that convention you mentioned earlier."

"The Iyrin are a failed experiment. They live as exiles in conformance with the convention."

I say nothing. I let a silence build to create doubt. Then I fill it.

"Do the Service commanders know what Von Streicher is really here for?" I ask. "What he told me just a few hours ago?"

The Archdeacon gives nothing away, he ploughs on ignoring me.

"The Baron is a settler who complies with his duties under the Convention. He has the right to settle on this barbaric little world so long as he continues to do so. Now the question of why the Fae sided with your community may never be known but I.."

"Yes it will!" I interrupt.

The Archdeacon wants to continue but he can't ignore this offer.

"I'll tell you. It's not a secret and it's *your* fault, Archdeacon. Inspector Du Croix knows full well the Bruderschaft have never complied with the convention. They have been defying it for a century. Just six months ago he arrested a cell of them."

"But arrest them, I did..." the Inspector interjects.

"For the wrong reasons," I retort.

"Your opinion of our reasons is of no consequence..." the Archdeacon begins, but I interrupt again, shouting over him.

"They are committing high treason against the Center!"

There's a stunned silence. And suddenly it all makes sense.

"And you know what?" I go on. "They aren't the only ones involved in this conspiracy."

"We don't have time for this nonsense..." the Archdeacon sneers. But everyone else is looking at me intently.

"I was trying to figure it out on the way here. Why, I wondered, would the Administration protect Von Streicher? Why stop me rescuing a minor hostage like Sian Hamilton-Smythe? Yes, the Service wants my speeder, but you could have watched and waited for me to get out of it, as sooner or later, I have to. You are right. It has no long term life support system. Instead, Archdeacon you ordered two scouts to interrupt my attack and protect Von Streicher. What that told me is that the Administration's connection to the Bruderschaft is stronger than I thought."

"Your surprise is due to the fact you have no idea what is going on ..." the Archdeacon begins loudly.

"Wrong Archdeacon. Only the Service doesn't know what's going on here under your administration!" I say forcefully.

"Your innuendo ..." the Archdeacon begins, but he is silenced by a glance from the commanders. I continue.

"Von Streicher and the rest of the Iyrin 'settlers' see Earth as a research lab for developing deadly bioweapons completely against the convention. Commanders, this group of Iyrin are making bioweapons from Earth diseases to be targeted at you

Synthetics. Their research centre is Virion Corporation in
Belgium. It was evidence we found of biological attacks on us
humans that convinced the Fae to help us."

I let that sink in. There is total silence. Then I go on.

"If the Iyrin had not attacked we humans I would not have this
craft. The Fae have come to believe that because of *your policy*
of tolerance toward their activities, Archdeacon, the Center has
abandoned the convention anyway!"

There's a short silence. The Archdeacon speaks first.

"Yes, well ... he is fourteen. I think ..."

I ignore him.

"I also suggest you ask the Archdeacon, Commanders. Why he is
actively protecting research serious enough to worry the Fae? If
you look you may also find a small silver skull among his stuff.
That is a weapon like the one that burned me in Lichtenstein."

The Commanders don't move. Nor do the human-like figures or
the Archdeacon. Inspector Du Croix is staring at the Archdeacon
very hard. The woman simply looks surprised. But the
Archdeacon himself, looks surprised, angry and vulnerable all at
once.

"*Sam!*" Hekator says silently. "*You're a genius! He is one of
them!*"

I feel a bit lightheaded with that.

But it isn't over yet. The Archdeacon's furious.

"Commanders, let me assure you any search for a silver skull
would be a complete waste of time. I am not a member of this
group and I am certainly not plotting against our invaluable
Synthetics. I would also remind the prisoner that you toy with
your own life by testing our patience."

"Then why does Von Streicher still hold Sian Hamilton-Smythe?"

"Baron Von Streicher has ... certain ... needs, shall we say, which the girl satisfied. It is not my concern," he says.

"The Fae believed the Administration was ignoring the Convention and encouraging this action as a secret plan against them. Just one and a half hours ago Von Streicher admitted to having just two enemies. One was Queen Morganne of Fae, the other the Synthetics."

I knew I was echoing Du Croix's suspicions at this point and the Inspector was watching the Archdeacon closely. The Commanders too were looking at the Archdeacon in a way I know I would not have liked, had it been me. The Archdeacon knows he's in trouble.

"My policy has been ..."

Suddenly he falls silent as the Commander closest him leaned forward. Then it turns its black, scary eyes on me.

"*What evidence led the Fae to intervene?*" the creature 'asks' telepathically.

I quickly relate the story of Professor Cherensky's experience with the Aids virus including my own brushes with Hathaway and the Bruderschaft which I know the Inspector can verify. When I've finished the Commander turns to the Archdeacon. The Archdeacon looks angrily at the Commander. I can tell they're not friends.

"Very well," he says.

And with that they all vanish.

They had, of course, been holograms. Ka-rea-rea is left alone in a big blast containment chamber.

"*How long do you think they will leave me here?*" I ask Hekator.

"*I think they will test your resolve to see if you are really willing to blow yourself up.*"

"Would it have any effect at all on this place?"
*"Oh yes. Rather foolishly they built this place under their base.
If you detonate their moonbase will collapse into the hole."*
"Do they know that?"
*"I think they can do the math. Anyway you've earned some
sleep. If they come back we'll wake you. In the meantime I
suggest you start a twelve hour countdown on Ka-rea-rea's
outer shell. Your air would start to fail after another 15 hours
anyway. Sleep well Sam. You have done far better than we had
hoped for."*

And with that he leaves me. Millions of miles away my medical
pod is very comfortable. Like a warm bath with blankets and
fresh air. I can see outside where it was the garden again, but
dimly lit as if night time. I drift off thinking about being home in
Hokianga with my sister Rewa, and Aunty Liz.

I sleep deeply, and for quite a while. Seven hours, forty six
minutes to be exact. When I awake I'm still in the medical pod in
the Fae quarantine station. The light outside my box is stronger
now. I can feel something on my wrist. It feels like a spongy
bracelet. It didn't seem to be attached to anything so I open the
pod and get out. My legs feel weak and wobbly. I'm dizzy with
hunger.
The thing on my wrist looks disgusting. There's a pink layer
about a centimeter thick that's gooey and wet with yellowish
tinges. It looks a bit like a mince sponge. On the top of the wrist
is a purple organ about the size of a small leather kidney which
is joined to the pink bit. It has veins and things growing in it
which join to the pink bit. It's no fashion accessory but there's
no pain either.

The angel-like nurse appears suddenly – literally.

"*How are you Sam?*"

"*Hungry and thirsty.*"

"*You had better rejoin the other Earthling. Follow me.*"

The hologram points me to a robe and then leads me through the waterfalls and stuff again until I find Sue sitting alone at a low table, eating.

She makes a sort of noise and runs up to hug me.

"Mmm! ... Sam! ... where have you been?... what have you?... eeeww what is that disgusting thing on your wrist?"

"It's a kinda bandage. I got burned."

"Oh shit! Is it bad? Does it hurt?"

"It is bad but it doesn't hurt. This thing is healing it. I guess it'll die and fall off when it's done. That's what Fae things usually do."

"So what's been happening? I've been bored stiff without you. There's nothing to watch! Nothing to *read*! God even a trashy magazine would be a relief. Even a magazine about ... I dunno ... fishing! You have no idea how boring it is here. You look for anything, *anything* to do."

She's sort of laughing with relief to see me. She's obviously been pretty stressed alone in an alien quarantine station overnight and I can see why.

"Come on, sit down. Eat some of ... whatever this is ... I swear I've put on three kilos eating from pure boredom."

We sit down.

"So what happened? What didja do?"

So I eat and tell Sue all about it. She's a great audience. She gasps, shudders and cheers in all the right places. After half an hour she's up to speed.

"So Dr Prosperov saved you?"

"Yeah ... well it was Lucky really. I have no idea what all that was about."

"Do you think Von Striecher knows his whatever-it-was was beaten by Lucky?" she checks.

"I don't know. I guess he does. I don't really get all that stuff about superdimensional beings. I mean I know ghosts. I've known ghosts all my life but this is something else. It was powerful. I mean if that watch hadn't shielded me my brain would have been mush. We had that with the Bruderschaft in Israel and honestly you couldn't do a thing."

"Do you think they will investigate that Archdeacon guy?"

"I think that was why they stopped the interview. They obviously didn't like him much and liked the suggestion his mismanagment had led to Fae involvement. I think that hurt him more than my accusation he's in with Von Streicher."

"But you do think he *is* in with Von Streicher?" Sue asks.

"It's the only way it makes sense."

"So what happens now? "

"Well, I stay here until they need me again. I guess that will only happen if the Commanders agree to my demand to be released on Earth and I have to walk away from Ka-rea-rea."

"And if they don't?" she asks.

"I guess there'll be a huge explosion on the moon."

"It's a bit spooky thinking that in some alternate reality you might really be there getting ready to kill yourself," she muses. Then she thinks of something and glances at me.

"Would that bother you?" she asks, curiously.

"What?" I ask, confused.

"Death?"

I'm gobsmacked. I can't understand why she wondered.

"Of course! I don't want to die!"

"But you've talked to the dead. Why does it bother you?"

"Because they aren't a whole lot of laughs. Even the gentle ones like Sarah back at Caz and Julia's, they're all sad. Maybe we only get to meet the sad ones, I dunno, maybe the happy ones move on, as they say. I don't know. But it's not something anyone looks forward to, is it?"

"No. Things have to be pretty bad when you want to go there."

There's an awkward pause. Rachel's shadow and Sue's halfhearted attempt at suicide which I had interrupted brushed past the conversation. I say nothing for a while but then neither does she.

"Have you been thinking about her?" I ask finally.

"Yeah. There hasn't been much else to do."

"What were you thinking about?"

"Oh, about the good times, and the bad times ... There seemed to be a lot more bad times than good. She always kept me off balance. I was always running after her. I can't help feeling sorry for myself really."

She looks around.

"Weird eh? I get to go to another planet, or whatever this is, and left by myself all I think about is Rachel and lost love," she tries to laugh.

"Maybe that shows how important it is," I suggest.

Sue sighs.

"Yeah, it does."

I had now eaten some breakfast and felt better.

"What do we do now?" Sue asks.

"Well, I just have to wait until my clock runs out,"

"How long will that be?"

"About four hours."

"Well tell me more background because after eight hours of nothing I'm desperate for something to think about.

"Yeah, OK ... So we found Nathan right?"

"Yep."

"OK, well then we had a bit of drama between Cam and Tarik..."

"Hmmm is it small stuff? Coz if it is, can we skip it?"

"I dunno. It was pretty huge for us ... I mean when you have a small team stuff like that matters. It ripples through everything because when there's only a few of us relationships really matter. Things get really personal and really intense and while I could tell you just about the main points you'd miss out on what was really going down."

"OK, you're right. I get it. Especially seeing we're dealing with a potential betrayal here. I need all that stuff too. Go on ..."

...

CHAPTER FIFTY NINE: A GREATER TREASURE

After Nathan was found in January 2008 Ashley had to go back to Washington in order to officially leave the United States and enter Europe. Ken and Patricia were now very relaxed in each other's company and it was mostly about Ashley getting used to it. They flew through to Frankfurt, Germany and stayed there for a couple of days getting used to the local time.

This time Scotty did not go as well, partly because they didn't have room for him; partly because the twelve hour time difference was too much; but mostly because Zoe said he should stay at Renwick while Ashley got used to Ken and Patricia being an item.

But what it meant was everyone but Ashley got a bit of time off to relax, which we really needed. I suppose if we had known what a year 2008 would be, we would have relaxed even longer. There were certainly times later when we looked back on 2007 as the fun year before things got serious.

While we were relaxing we carried on with our search for Spanish treasure galleons off the Spratley Islands and went swimming on the desert dunes there. Cam was always particularly keen to go. It was in that sea, of course, that pirates had taken her mother, and being psychic she knew for sure her mother was not dead. She somehow hoped to find some clue that might lead her to get her mother back again.

Unfortunately the weather there was not always good. We had got used to checking the aviation weather reports, and storms ruined our plans to go swimming around the Spratley's more than once. But when it came to finding things we had more luck. Our scanners were very powerful. They could detect anything solid under the sand and they could tell the difference between coral and wood or steel. The only problem was telling apart bits of a galleon from bits of an old fishing boat so we had to do quite a lot of underwater checking as well.

We had a lot of dull finds. But we finally had one that made up for all the hours cruising back and forth in a line being bored. It was in deeper water at the end of a run. It was another Galleon down about two hundred meters.

It was sunk in deep mud in the dark, the tops of its timbers sticking up like ribs casting harsh shadows from our bright lights. Compared to the beautiful wreck we had found in the corals of Guam this one looked dead and slightly spooky.

Our problem was the speeders didn't have anything to dig with. We could grab things but it was hard to see how to dig any deeper.

We asked Hekator how we could use the speeders to move tonnes of mud under two hundred meters of water. His answer was embarrassingly simple.

"Bring a rope and pull out it out."

We felt so dumb!

It turned out to be a bit harder than that though because the timbers weren't very strong any more and they snapped. But his point was still pretty clear. This wasn't his problem and he expected us to use our brains and not run to him for answers all the time. So it was Grandpop who thought up the solution. All we needed to do was raid a Filipino construction site for excavator buckets and dozer blades.

That meant late, night time missions because the Philippines was four hours behind us. The cities were too large and busy to pilfer things from but there was still lots of construction in the countryside. So for several nights we dropped silently down from the sky and lifted away steel blades and scoops weighing up to a quarter of a tonne into the night. Then we started to work for hours shoving mud around.

It was difficult work because the speeders would drop the heavy tools if the strain on the grippers was too much. The other problem was the mud and sand swirled everywhere and made it hard to see. After seven days with lack of sleep and being cramped and uncomfortable we were getting snippy. That led to a pretty bad fight between Cam and Tarik.

Cam complained that grovelling in the dirt was probably a waste of time and she'd rather look for her mother. Tarik replied he'd rather look for gold than her mother who had probably forgotten her and become a prostitute anyway. It was a totally dumb thing to say but that was when the fight started and more mean things were said.

Cam was hurt and outraged. She ended up flying off with Tahira and Scotty following her while I stayed behind to calm down Tarik. Tarik spent the first half hour complaining long and loud about Cam who had told him to "eff off and die". Tarik just kept trying to pretend he was being logical. Things still weren't happy when we arrived back home at four in the morning.

Grandpop's response was to ground everyone except Scotty and Ashley. Tarik was sulking and being an arsehole. Cam was hurt and angry while Tahira had been very angry with Tarik too and hadn't been helping things much. But Grandpop said he wasn't going to let us go anywhere or do anything until we had sorted ourselves out.

When Mr Trân found out he was furious and demanded to see Dr Prosperov. Mrs Jones got involved instead and went to see Dr Gursoy. When he heard what Tarik had said Dr Gursoy gave Tarik a real telling off which made him run off in tears. He was out for two hours while we all gathered around Cam. Cam was a mess mostly because she felt betrayed but the girls were clubbing together for a hate-Tarik sesh and that wasn't helping. Finally Grandpop sent me and Scotty out to find him.

Thanks to Scotty's amazing eyes we soon found him hiding in the Fae cave. Tarik was still being an arsehole. He pissed Scott off by being so stubborn so Scott went back to tell the others where he was. I stayed with him.

It took a long, long time to get past Tarik's habit of talking bullshit. Then we had a good long talk about Cam. He admitted he was jealous of her for at least still having the hope that she might see *her* mother alive again. We talked about that. He said he still had nightmares about running back to their flat in London, knowing his mum and sister were alive, thinking that if he could just ran fast enough he might be able to stop the shooting, but his legs were stuck as if he was glued to the road. Then he would hear, and almost, feel the shots and it was like his mother and sister were sucked off the planet by some huge wind, flying past him as he ran, stuck in deep bitumen.

They didn't haunt him like my mum haunted me. All he had was the memory of their bodies, covered in thick black blood, with gore and pieces around the kitchen. He'd seen his dad trying to hide his broken heart and thought that was what *he* had to do too. So he bullshitted everyone by pretending to be clever and cool.

I asked him about Cam. He admitted his problem was he felt a bit hunted by her, and he wasn't sure why she had picked on him. He said if he felt he had a choice he had to admit he really liked her. She was pretty, clever and surprising. He liked the way she saw things. But he didn't really understand what she saw in him because he tried to fake everything all the time.

"Look, mate I'm full of shit, yeah?" he admitted. "*You* know I'm full of shit. *I* know I'm full of shit. But *she* doesn't seem to get it. Know what I mean?" he complained.

"Maybe she sees more," I suggested.

"Yeah but I don't. And *I* ought to know, yeah?" he pointed out.

"Well, all I know is you gotta make it up to her or we'll be grounded forever."

"I know," he said unhappily.

"You know Tahira gave me some hints for getting back onside with Emma when she comes back. Maybe you should try them on Cam," I suggested.

So we thought up a plan, and when we came back we asked for permission to get some stuff. Grandpop okayed it. Tahira wanted to complain that it was unfair she and Cam were grounded but Tarik and me weren't but I gave her a little eyebrow flick to say it was cool and she looked at me with very sharp eyes but said nothing.

[+]

We took a carry bag and first had to go to the US – we chose Washington because we'd got to know it – to get some American money from our gift cards. We bought some chocolates at a place on Wisconsin Avenue and then left for Ho Chi Minh City. Grandpop got Mr Trân and told him what we were doing. At first he was grumpy but as he watched his home country and what Tarik was up to, he cheered up a lot. He started to guide us and we went shopping in the markets where it was before midday. The languages of US currency and English were still pretty well understood and having the suits translate didn't hurt at all. We didn't try to speak Vietnamese which was too hard for us to say easily. I was really impressed with the friendly businesslike manner of the Vietnamese. We haggled a bit because we were expected to, even though we didn't have time to get bargains. We just did it to show we knew what each seller's profit was. An hour and a half before dinner time we came back.

[+]

We gave Mr Trân his ingredients and then Tarik took off to get ready. Everyone else came nervously down to dinner wondering whether the fight was continuing and discovered Mr Trân had put on a Vietnamese banquet. Cam and Tahira came down last, still whispering, apparently not noticing that everyone else was watching them and expecting something to happen.

It did.

I brought in a fabulous silk Chongsam dress, the chocolates and a note for Cam. Then the screens in the café came to life. Tarik was on a beach in this amazing looking bay with these pointy islands sticking up like teeth from the gray satin sea under a dull gray sky. It was famously Vietnam. He was holding cards with writing on them which he replaced in front of him. Mr Trân came out from behind the counter and stood looking up at him.

"I, Tarik Ibrahim Gursoy," read the first card.

"Promise Cam Li Trân," the second said.

"Never again to be," said the third, as Tarik looked down at it.
"Such a humungous arsehole," the fourth read. He looked
embarrassed and abashed. Cam giggled
"To find her mother," read the fifth.
"Wherever she is, or whatever she does," the sixth stated. Tarik
looked serious.
"Whatever it takes," the seventh read.
Cam started to cry.
He replaced the last card.
"Love over gold."
At which everyone began clapping and Cam ran out of the room
crying her eyes out. Tahira was also bawling but got off her chair
and ran off after Cam. I held out the imitation cellphone so
Tarik could hear the response to his show and everyone clapped
louder so he could hear it.
Mr Trân looked very happy and came up to me. I gave him the
cell phone.
"You good boy Tarik. You look later. Come home for dinner
now."
It was interesting seeing Tarik seal up and disappear to a dot like
switching off an old TV set. I hadn't ever seen it like that before.
Somehow it immediately suggested to me another dimension.
Like 2D pictures creating 3D illusions. For some reason that
really struck me. Maybe I was trying not to get too emotional.
Another thing that struck me was how much I liked Mr Trân's
Vietnamese food. It was really good. Tahira came back down,
and picked up Cam's dress and a plate. But it was hard to carry
both and Aunty Liz nudged me to help her. I got to carry the
dress because Tahira didn't trust me not to eat Cam's dinner.
We walked up the stairs together not saying anything, but as

we walked down the hall towards the Trân's apartment Tahira looked at me.

"Did djou zink of zhat?" she asked suspiciously.

"No, I just passed on your advice about Emma," I said. But she wasn't sure, so I went on.

"Tarik got the idea from the movie we saw at Christmas on TV. You know, where the guy is at the door with the other guy's girlfriend."

She nodded, remembering.

"And the last line is from one of his dad's CDs."

We walked on. When we got to the door she put down the tray and took the dress off me. She gave me a shy little glance.

"Per'aps zere's 'ope for boys yet," she shrugged.

And then gestured for me to go away. As I started down the hallway I heard her knock and whisper "iz me". By the time I got to the door into the lounge she'd gone in.

I knew Cam was good looking but when she came out later into the lounge in her new dress I was shocked how stunning she really was. By now Tarik was back and was looking far better than I'd ever seen him before too. He seemed to have dropped his bullshit and although he was still a bit nervous about what people thought about him the hugs – especially from Mariko, had helped. Even despite that nervousness he seemed different. More sure of himself deep down somehow.

That vanished when Cam came into the room. He went red and seemed unable to look at her. I felt sorry for him.

Cam went around everyone and everyone told her how pretty she looked. Finally she came up to Tarik who seemed to find her feet interesting. It was Mariko who broke the ice.

"Rook at her, you idiot!" she shouted.

The adults were all smiling.

Tarik looked up guiltily.

"How do I look?" Cam asked in a tiny voice that barely broke from her.

He looked her over.

"Perfect," he croaked so quietly it was hard to hear, which given there was total silence was surprising. He was bright red.

"Kick him," Mariko shouted at Cam.

Cam looked at her. Mariko winked.

"Kick him!" she nodded again.

So she did. Tarik bore it manfully.

"Hard!" Mariko insisted.

She only had slippers on but the kick obviously hurt because Tarik looked pained as he restrained himself. He was confused.

"Kick him again, harder. Use your training."

Cam did again, giggling a bit, her leg slipping out of the slash in her dress. It hurt a lot. Tarik was outraged by this treatment. He looked furiously at Mariko.

"*Soo* chase her!" Mariko shouted at him.

Tarik looked at Cam. Cam looked at Tarik. Then she grinned stepped out of her slippers and ran, holding her dress so she could get away.

That was something Tarik *could* do. Tarik jumped up and there was a lot of people shouting encouragement to them both and laughing. Tarik chased her around the pool table. Cam couldn't help laughing. She dodged around and then Tarik leapt underneath the pool table. Cam ran off out the door and down the dark hall, her quick bare legs scurrying. Tarik chased after her.

We were all going to chase after them but the adults called us back. After a minute Rewa and Asal couldn't stand it anymore and ran down the hall. They came running back.

"Tarik's pashing Cam!" Rewa shrieked.

Their secret out, Cam came back to her father looking shy and Dr Gursoy went off to see his son. Tahira looked at me, very pleased. Tarik and his dad didn't come back out that night but there was no telling off this time.

Cam got changed and came back out to play pool in her usual jeans. She couldn't help smiling. When her dad went to bed at nine she went too.

"If zhey keessed does zhat mean zhey will get married?" asked Asal when she had gone.

"No, it just means they're going steady," Rewa, the very wise, explained.

Asal didn't know the English so Rewa told her what that meant. Tahira flicked me smiling eyes.

"Ashley is going to be so annoyed she missed this skiner," Scott said joining us.

"Zhou weel av to tell 'er zhen," Tahira almost purred.

Scotty seemed to find that an interesting challenge.

"Oh eet ees so late! We should all go-to-bed," Tahira suddenly announced.

"Especially you!" she added pouncing on Asal.

Asal turned to her mother to complain but Mitra only nodded and half rose. Tahira said something in Persian and Mitra smiled and sat back. Aunty Liz was getting up too.

"Ees Okay Messes Kahu, me and Sam can look after zhem," Tahira told her.

Rewa and Asal were grumpy, but they were tired.

I got Rewa sorted and got into my PJs myself. I switched out the lights and went to my room. I knew Tahira had really wanted to talk but I wasn't sure how she was going to organise it. I waited for half an hour and was just about to give up when my screen announced a call from Tahira. I answered and found her in her PJs as well, lit only by her screen, same as me.

"Hi," I said.

"'ello Sam."

"'sup?"

Tahira puffed her cheeks and blew.

"I ... I per'aps you are ze wrong person..." she said looking embarrassed.

"For what?"

She sighed.

"I ... am I normal?" she asked quickly.

I laughed. She was annoyed.

"What ees so funny?" she asked angrily.

"None of us a normal. It's why we're here," I answered.

"No...no...not ze intuition," she said shaking her head.

"And you know already you are very pretty," I added.

"Not zat either," she said looking irritated. She didn't even smile at the compliment. She *was* tense.

"Well, what do you mean?" I asked.

She thought for a moment.

"No. Sorry! I can't!"

And she switched off. I was left sitting in the dark wondering what *that* was about. Feeling tired I went back to bed. I was almost asleep when my screen came to life again. It was Tahira. I answered.

"What now?" I said grumpily.

"Can you meet me by the 'elicopter shed at one?"

"A.m? Why?" I moaned.

"I 'ave to talk to someone and Ashley ees not 'ere and you ...well, you understand zees better anyway."

"Do I have to?" I asked, knowing the answer.

"Please Sam? For me?"

I sighed.

"Oh, all right then."

"Zank you."

She vanished. I set the alarm and went to bed.

I heard Aunty Liz come in and go to bed. It seemed like only a few minutes later the alarm had started quietly. I slipped out of bed and turned it off, feeling like I'd had no sleep at all. I pulled on my jeans and a hoody, jammed on my trainers and slipped out into the corridor.

There was still a light in the lounge. I wasn't sure whether there was anyone there so I went down the back stairs and out the back door. I ran around the dark side of the house near the garage hearing the scuffing sound of my own shoes on the gravel. The pigs grunted quietly, hearing my footsteps. Then I crossed the drive and tripped through the tussock to the helicopter hangar. I found Tahira sitting by the side of the hangar looking up at the stars. The moon was the smallest sliver.

"Hi," I said crouching down. "What's the problem?"

"It's warm tonight," she replied.

"Yeah," I said, unconvinced this was important.

She got up.

"Walk with me," she instructed.

And she set off along the gravel road towards the lighthouse. I sighed and followed.

For half the way she said nothing.

"Do you zink about Tabika?" she asked.

To be honest I hadn't for ages.

"No. Not really," I admitted.

We walked further.

"I zink about 'er all ze time," she sighed.

"Oh."

That struck me as a little odd. We continued walking as the sea crunched gently on the beach and the moon hung like a faint hook in the sky.

"Do zhou zink Tarik is in love with Cam?" she asked.

I thought about that. It didn't sound likely.

"No. Well, I think he really likes and cares about her ... But *in* love? I dunno."

"So ee is lying to er?" Tahira asked.

"No," I replied hastily. "He's changed a lot today. He ... he ... Oh, I dunno he's somehow stopped hiding. She made him stop shitting everyone. I think he's discovered through her, he doesn't have to hide any more. He really is into her," I ended awkwardly.

"I see," she said, thinking of something else.

And realising I was beginning to probe her thoughts she broke into a run.

"C'mon."

We ran on around the bay. As I caught her up she sped off again, even up the hill and eventually we arrived panting at the foot of the lighthouse. It stood tall, white and mysterious in the still summer's night. Tahira sat down at the base, and I slumped down next to her.

"Remember zhat night?" she said half swallowing a gasp for air.

"Ah-huh," I panted.

We sat for a long time in silence. Listening to the sea and the call of a lonely Ru-ru, or native owl.

"Sam?"

"Yeah?"

"Your aunt was never married was she?"

"No."

"Does she not like men?"

It was as if the question stepped over the doorway of our apartment. Each family was still pretty private behind closed doors. Normally I wouldn't have answered, but I realised it was Tahira I was talking to. Like me she could read minds and probably had.

"No, I don't think so," I answered as evenly as I could, feeling slightly on edge.

"Is she 'appy?"

I thought of Aunty Liz. She never seemed *happy*. She always seemed to be thinking of everyone else but her. Only sometimes when her friends had come by and they'd drunk and sung and partied had I ever see her relax. But it never seemed to last.

"I dunno really," I said. And then because that sounded selfish.

"I worry about it sometimes."

Tahira made a small noise.

"Tahira, what..."

"Did she kiss you?" she interrupted.

"Aunty Liz?" I asked, confused.

"No!" she said impatiently, "Tabika."

"*Oh!*" I said, because finally I saw what this was all about.

"What?" Tahira asked sharply, suspecting what I suspected.

"*You* kissed her, didn't you?" I checked.

"Yes," she said quietly.

"How often?" I wanted to know.

"I don't know. 'ow many times did you kiss her?" she asked back shyly.

"Twice."

"Oh," she said cagily making me think she had kissed Tabika more than that.

"She stopped because she said she needed to be able to think," I admitted.

"Yes," Tahira said, for she had obviously told her the same thing.

"Tahira, we can't kiss those people! It's like a drug! You never want to stop!"

"But Sam I'm a *girl*." Tahira suddenly screamed. "I'm not meant to want to kiss her like *that* at *all*," she cried, and tears started in her eyes.

"I'm not meant to want to *hold* her and … all zhose things … if my *muzzer* knew what I was sinking she would be 'orrified," she said. She was almost shaking.

I said nothing. I wasn't quite sure what to say.

"And zhen Cam kissing Tarik like zhat … and I know Ashley loves Scott. And I see zhem and I see you and you are very nice Sam but … but all I can sink of is '*er*."

She was crying now. Not blubbing, but just tears running down her pretty face.

I got up and sat closer to her with my arm around her and rubbed her back a bit. She put her head on my shoulder, which felt nice. We sat there for a while and then she turned her face to me. I looked at her. And then eyes closed, she kissed me on the mouth.

It felt nice but I knew it was wrong. I was being used in one of her endless schemes and nice as her attention was, it was fake.

I didn't trust her. I let her kiss me but I didn't kiss her back and she pulled back from me, surprised that I wasn't responding. Her pretty eyes flicked open.

"What eez matter? Don't you like me?"

"Why did you do that?" I asked her straight.

She searched my face.

"I thought per'aps you were meant for me like Scott and Ashley and Tarik and Cam and zhat if I kissed you it would be like Tabika but even better."

And now she really did burst into tears and threw her face in her hands.

"I'm 'omosexual. I know it!" she told them.

I hugged her and rubbed her back for a while. Finally I spoke.

"Did Raman tell you that?" I asked.

"No," she whimpered quietly into hands. "They didn't say anything."

"Tahira maybe they couldn't."

"Why not?"

"Because maybe you haven't decided yet. Just calm down."

She remained curled up but she stopped crying and just sat there breathing, letting me rub her back.

"My mother would never understand," she said finally. "She 'as always talked of me marrying a fine man and 'aving children as she did."

"Maybe you will. Maybe you'll meet a Prince who kisses you better than Tabika. Or maybe you won't and you like kissing girls instead. It's OK. You'll find out. Do you really need to decide *now*? We're only thirteen."

She sighed a big shuddering sigh and raised her head. She looked out to sea, thinking.

"Zhou are thinking right, Sam! I don't 'av to decide."

We sat for a while looking at the sea. The warm still night seemed to make it especially easy to sit there, almost as if it was daytime with the lights off.

"And you know whatever your mother thinks, you'll always have us. I can't see how we will not all be best friends for life now," I told her.

She snuck a peek at me and smiled. She was back to just leaking a bit. She took my hand and squeezed it. I squeezed back and let her go as she withdrew it again. Then she sighed and stood up looking happy. I stood up too.

We walked back to Renwick, enjoying the night air. She wished me goodnight and went in the front door. I went in the back. I slipped into the apartment and back into my room. I was just getting back into bed when a shadow appeared at the door.

"Where have you been?" Aunty Liz asked grumpily.

"We had a mission," I lied.

"No you didn't Sam Kahu," she said turning on the light, burning my eyes.

"We know all about your missions. Usually long before you do. There was nothing on tonight. What were you doing?"

"I just went to the kitchen."

"Along the beach with a girl? Who was she? Was it Tahira?"

There was nothing for it. I had to tell her everything. She, of all people would understand. At first she was suspicious but finally she relaxed.

"It's not Tahira you have to worry about me being with," I told her thinking of Emma, but not saying it.

She looked at me very straight. And just for a moment I saw Aunty Liz not as my aunt and foster mother but as a woman. A woman who knew a lot more about Tahira than I did. She got up off the chair she had sat down on while she had listened to me. "You're a good friend Sam Kahu," she told me as she went to the door. She flicked the switch and then in the darkness..

"And a lovely young man," and left me alone, tired and suddenly very sleepy. And a moment later it was another hot, bright blue morning.

The next day was the sunniest we had had for a long time. The sun baked down on a tame blue sea which sloshed about like a dog expecting a walk. Scotty had got up early and gone to Austria, to the villa the Robinsons were staying in. He and Ashley had thrown snowballs at each other and then Ashley had come back here to go swimming.

Cam and Tarik were quite close now and wanted to go to the Spratleys. Grandpop decided they should go together while the rest of us swam. It was a great way for us to chat about them and relax while they spent time together. They wanted to test the equipment we had for working from the speeders in a relatively safe environment.

Tahira and her family were preparing to head to Israel but unlike Ashley there was no particular need for Tahira or Asal to be seen boarding a plane. That meant we could avoid the long flight by bending. But because we wanted to move the speeders Tahira was keen on flying with me the whole way.

Mitra and Soraya were not so sure about this. They didn't mind the suits because they could watch over their daughter and granddaughter and even insist she come home if necessary. But the speeders meant we were on our own.

Alone and together.

They didn't like the idea of a boy and a girl together without a parent to supervise them. Tahira was pissed off about this. Her point was that if she was a boy they wouldn't be so worried. She felt they were suggesting she was a slut. But they said they were just worried that we wouldn't have any protection if anything went wrong.

To put their minds at ease Grandpop said me and Tahira could wear our on-the-ground kit too, and that they could watch us using a netbook like the one Patricia had. They talked around this and with a bit of whining from Tahira and encouragement from Aunty Liz and Patricia they finally agreed. That meant we had two weeks to go because Mitra and Soraya wanted to be in Haifa for the Baha'i New Year.

After Mitra and Soraya landed in Haifa they would hire a car and drive down to Caesarea to open up the villa Dr P had organised. Mariko would bend Aunty Liz, and the two girls there when the Khadems were ready. Finally me and Tahira would fly for four hours from Renwick to the villa.

There were two ways to go. I wanted to fly over the Pacific, but Tahira wanted to fly over the Indian Ocean. Her point was we could fly over Iran and have a look at her homeland. I could tell she wanted to feel in a familiar place again so she could feel more certain of who she was. I agreed on the condition we could stop off in Western Australia for a break. That way we could break up the flight and given the huge size and small population of Western Australia we could be pretty sure we wouldn't have problems being seen.

In the meantime we went back to the Spratleys to keep working our wreck. We spent about thirty hours on the wreck over the next week, digging, moving and sifting mud. We found a lot of broken pottery, and old rotten cloth. But just as we were giving up hope there was a clang on my dozer blade and Cam yelled. "Look! Sam's hit something shiny."

And there it was. A small pile of silver bars glimmering in their broken box. The others pulled them out while I continued scraping with the blade. It took another hour and then we hit the big pile. It was all silver but there was a lot of it. We loaded a treasure box three times until we had cleared it all. Then we went back to digging. Then we struck a level of boxes. We opened one and found it full of silver coins. Tarik counted the boxes. There were seventy three. Each one weighed two and a half tonnes and was worth a million American dollars and Dr P had said the price of silver was rising quickly. That meant we got six million each just for the chests.

We worked for two hours loading silver into treasure chests and bending them home. At the other end they just spilled them into the tank and left them shining sending the boxes back so we could load them again. It was like we needed bulldozers or something. Finally at about six that evening the five of us burst out of the sea into a storm and blasted home feeling tired but happy that we had finished with another huge treasure haul.

The next day we wanted to go back to the Spratley's just to go swimming but Dr Prosperov came down at breakfast.

"Have important news. As you know small aerial support craft have important limitations. In order to minimise transit time and maximise operational time have proposed to Fae council creation of three operations centres for operatives."

"Operations centres to be used for base of aerial vehicle

operations, rest and recovery, storage of supplies, and as transit station for bending in case of suspected bugs. Also to be used as observatory. Hekator wants you to carry out survey of proposed sites. Please to get in suits."

So still eating our breakfast we wandered down to the base and got changed, then came out for the briefing. Dr P and Grandpop were waiting for us. Grandpop had obviously also brought a few pastries because he still had crumbs on his front.

"Fae council have approved creation of three small centres," Dr P began. "Map please, Control?"

The globe appeared floating above the stage. It rotated over the Americas.

"First to be located at Pico da Neblina in northern Brazil. Is one hour's flight to all United States and southern latin nations. Is in northern Amazon rain forest and although is almost ten thousand feet tall was only discovered in 1950s. Has been climbed only few times[†]. Hard to get to through rainforest. As name says is almost always covered in cloud but is too hot for snow. Very few gold panners and some tribes live in area[†]."

"Next..."

The globe spun around to Egypt.

"Is the rocky desert north-east of the Siwa Oasis in western Egypt. Siwa is different to Nile Egypt. Language and customs not same. Siwa is internal tourist destination but not as popular as main Nile places[†]. Exists, suitable remote oasis and rock forms for construction near Libyan border in desert. Area is half hour flight time to London, Basra in Iran, and North Kivu."

"Finally..."

He paused and the globe spun to halfway between India and China.

"Mount Khako-borazi, Burma. Is over nineteen thousand feet high. Mountain very remote and was only climbed in 1996. Area is insecure because of Kachin Independence Army. Tourism in Burma is limited by Myanmar regime and Khakoborazi national park is sparsely populated. Is park for preserving tigers and the animals they eat[†]. However is half hour from all China, all India, Korea to Karachi and Singapore."

"Control has carried out visual survey of potential sites for bases but Hekati is needing survey data. Hekator has sent instruments for surveying sites. While instruments could be deployed by Hekator is best if operatives examine locations. So is need for to visit sites and examine area. Any questions?"

Scotty raised his hand.

"Scott?"

"How long will the centres take to build?"

Dr P shrugged casually.

"Hekati has not said but am guessing based on project here, about two months."

Finding no more questions he went back to his office. Grandpop took over.

"These jobs should be a walk in the park for you guys. I've assigned Cam and Tarik to Mt Khakoborazi, Sam and Tahira to Siwa, and Scotty and Ashley, when she's back, to Pica … uh … Cloud Mountain".

Neither me nor Tahira were that keen on going back to Egypt. The ghosts there were strong and obnoxious and the others' deserted mountains seemed a much better idea. But someone had to go so we bent into a canyon at about midnight local time.

[+]

It was sandy desert within a rocky canyon. It was cold although

we couldn't feel it. There was no moon, just this humungous sky
full of stars. It was very dark. So dark, we used ultrasound to
scan the deep shadows.

We had expected a horde of ghosts to come belting up at
once but the place remained eerily still. It was a low, rocky
depression, complete with wind worn rock bridges and a very
small patch of green at the base of it. A small dog with big ears
gave a short bark, making us jump, and ran off into the dark. I
squashed a scorpion by accident. The suit suggested we radiate
ultra violet light and that lit them up, all blue[†]. There were a
few around but it was only five degrees Celsius so they were
pretty groggy. Tahira found them creepy but in a suit they didn't
bother me.

We found the place Hekati wanted us to check out. We had
to jump up to the cave about ten meters above us, up a small
cliff just a little higher. I cranked up the gravity deflection and
jumped first, and arrived glowing in the cave. There was a small
movement as some small animals scuttled from my glow. But
almost at once I was startled to discover the inside was covered
with drawings.

Tahira jumped up to join me and we walked, glowing, around
the cave that was about five meters wide by two high at the
mouth looking at the little brown figures painted on the wall.
The pictures showed people hunting, and there were all sorts
of animals. Giraffes, elephants and large things we weren't sure
about. It was obvious this cave had last been used a very, very
long time ago. We pressed on to the back and were shocked to
find two shattered skulls at the back of the cave, together with
what looked like old bone splinters.

You might think finding a grave in a cave at midnight in a lonely

desert would be a bit freaky but it was the complete opposite.
Glowing as we did, we felt like future humans finding the resting
place of ancient ones. It was the most gentle and peaceful
feeling and we felt very respectful of this place and our ancient,
ancient ancestors who had been buried there. It was a kind of
connection through thousands and thousands of years and it
made you feel grateful to those people just for surviving. It made
you think about how hard their lives must have been. Shorter,
rougher but more in tune with the world around them, back
when this desert was full of life.

Now that we had found the bones we weren't that keen to see
them chomped up by Hekati's ants and turned into a base.
We sort of felt they deserved to stay where they were. The
instrument Hekator had sent was pretty much like the one we
had used on the meteor sites. We planted it anyway but agreed
we would also see if we could find some other caves.

That turned out to be dead easy. There were hundreds.
Unfortunately they all seemed to be occupied with bones.
By the time we had got to the twentieth cave our feelings of
awe towards the old dead guys were being mixed with a bit of
frustration. And then we found it. The perfect cave.

It was more a crack in the rock about three meters tall and one
and a bit meters wide. Tahira shouted down it with ultrasound
and got a long return meaning it was deep. We lit up our suits
and went in. I went first, because, Tahira was worried about
creepy crawlies. There were some but because it was so cold they
weren't doing much.

The cave turned slightly to the left as we entered and then
widened. We pressed into the dark a bit nervously expecting to
meet some animal or trip some kind of ancient boobytrap and

be crushed by a giant boulder but nothing happened. Instead we found our way into a tunnel which led to a large cavern where stalactites and stalagmites grew and hung.

And then a sound we had never expected to hear in this driest of places. A plonk as a drop of water fell into a pool and the sound echoed in the dark.

We found the pool. It wasn't very big. But what was amazing was that it was there at all. We placed Hekator's sensors and moved them to different locations hoping that this would help. Then deciding we'd found a good site and had enough of looking for more we bent home.

[+]

We were quite excited about our discovery but it turned out we had had the most boring time of all.

Cam and Tarik had found hibernating bears in two of their three caves and Cam had had a nervous time tiptoeing around the big furry animals getting measurements. There was a storm on the mountain with snow filling the sky making the outside white in early morning light. Their third cave was empty although there were small bones in it and an odd pile of branches. They took their measurements and did infrasound shouts to see if anything was further back. Then they went out to see if they could see the sun coming up because the cave faced east. Outside in the snow they found a large footprint which hadn't been there when they arrived. They looked for the owner of the foot but saw nothing in the whirling whiteness on the mountain. They were eighteen thousand feet above sealevel. The air was too thin for most creatures. The print wasn't at all clear and could just as easily have been a bear as a man or even a snow leopard. But we were all thinking "Yeti." Unfortunately Control couldn't help. He'd been focused inside the cave like Cam and Tarik.

Even more mysterious was Scotty and Ashley's encounter. They had arrived on their mountainside in the mist. The whole place was just cloud, cloud and more cloud as Ashley had said. Where they landed was flat with broken rocks but no snow. They could see maybe three meters in front of them but no more through the fog. They set out climbing up a steep rocky slope and climbed about a hundred meters through the rocks to the cave Control had picked. But when they got there they discovered people in it!

A rough camp had been thrown together by three brown men wearing very rough clothes. They were old and lined, probably in their fifties, with dark gray hair and beards and worn looking teeth. They were equipped as miners or gold prospectors. But what freaked out Ashley and Scotty was they couldn't read them. The men showed no surprise at all when two kids with school bags appeared out of the mist and walked into their cave. Scotty and Ashley said they just smiled and offered them a place to sit down. They spoke Portuguese but muttered in a way that it was hard to tell if they were speaking from their mouths.

Control told Scotty and Ashley to leave immediately. They ran out suddenly but the 'men' didn't seem the slightest bit surprised or upset. As they ran down the path a bright light had started to glow in the fog above them and Control had bent them home at once

At debrief Control said we had to expect that the Administration would also have places on Earth for the same reason we wanted them, and it was not too surprising we would tend to choose the same places as we would have the same reasons for choosing them. It was a bit spooky to think that Scott and Ashley had nearly walked right into an Administration base.

We were still getting over that shock when Sarah, the mafia princess, was kidnapped in Israel.

HAIFA REGION

Map data © Google 2016

CHAP+ER SIX+Y: ABDUC+I⊕N

At four in the morning we were woken by Control. It was just starting to get light and Sarah had been kidnapped. We raced downstairs and got changed while Grandpop tried to work out what was going on. As soon as we came out Grandpop sent Scotty out to get Ashley. When he came back about two minutes later Ashley almost undid the bag as it floated on the oil in the jumpstation.

When she was finally able to get out she raced to get changed, yelling "It has been sooo boooring," as she disappeared into the changers.

Control had caught the whole abduction. Grandpop waited until Ashley was back before showing it.

It was The Hague street in Hod HaKarmel, Haifa. The sun was setting in the west out over the Mediterranean. There was a big white van with some large Hebrew writing on it which translated to Israel Electric Corporation parked fifty meters from the house. Two guys in safety gear had set up to work on the power lines. Sarah's big black Mercedes drew up as usual but the garage door didn't open. The bodyguard, Ivan Federov, reversed the car back to the van where the men were working. He had slipped his weapon out but lowered his opposite window casually to talk to the workers – Sarah being in the back, texting as usual. The workers were not Arabs. In fact they looked like Russians. They did a great act of looking dumb and busy with their work, pointing up and down the road explaining what they were doing. Meanwhile another car was coming up the road. Control didn't show us the actual shooting. Suddenly Sarah was screaming and there was blood and gore on the inside of the Mercedes windscreen. The side windows were smashed to tiny, red stained pieces. Federov's almost headless body slumped against the safety belt. The men in the other car got out quickly. The one with the rifle (it wasn't an AK, I knew that much, but it was obviously powerful) in the back covered the electricity workers while the driver got out with a big handgun, and opened the back door of the Merc he was parked opposite and silently waved Sarah to get out.

Sarah sat there screaming, so he reached in and grabbed her roughly by the hair, throwing her out of the car to the road like a doll. She was still in shock, her eyes wide with disbelief as the man picked her up by the throat, held her against the roof of his own car and then slammed her head against it sharply. The rifleman now picked her up and threw her into the backseat and getting in quickly next to her. The driver looked at the stunned linesmen, put his finger to his lips and pointed to show that others were watching, then quickly got in the car – it was a dark blue Audi – and drove off. The whole thing had taken no more than half a minute.

The men who had taken Sarah definitely *were* Arabs. Sarah was slumped between them holding her head, clearly in a lot of pain. There was also a wet patch around her crotch and down her leg where she had pissed herself. The car took off quickly and headed for the motorway down the hill, for the port. The sound of gunfire had brought people into the street, and a crowd gathered around the shot-up Merc and the dead bodyguard. Meanwhile the kidnappers had not panicked. Within ten minutes they had driven through the evening traffic, past the University, into the port area and straight into a large warehouse. The open doors lowered behind them. Inside the neon-lit warehouse were a couple of men standing by a radio thing listening, and a whole lot of cars. The interesting thing was the guy who looked like he was in charge was a heavyset European with dark curly hair. The guy on the radio was Indian. As the Audi pulled in the kidnappers got out quickly dragging Sarah out with them. The heavyset man approached her as the two beside her held her up. He grabbed her face and turned it back and forth inspecting their catch. He nodded and the men dragged her to a Nissan sportscar and bent her over the trunk. They pulled her arms out behind her and put some tiny clear plastic binders over her thumbs and pulled them tight. She was thumbcuffed, screaming and struggling but not getting anywhere. The heavyset man came over and tossed them a ball and a strap. They shoved the ball in her mouth as she screamed and strapped it in place pulling it tight around her head. She coughed and gagged but they just slammed her head down. Then he gave them a black bag which they pulled over her head. They pulled her back up and suddenly one of the men pulled down her pants. It was a bit disgusting as she'd shat herself as well. Then the other man smashed her down on to the trunk again. The guys who'd pulled her pants down came back and threw a bucket of water at her. Then he repeated that. Sarah was shaking uncontrollably as the man held her down exposed. We were all a bit worried what they were going to do but the

heavyset man approached her holding up a syringe. He gave
it a flick and squirted a bit then jabbed it in Sarah's butt. She
flinched but within a few seconds fell limp. The guard tied her
legs with her own belt. Then the men opened the trunk and
shoved and curled Sarah into the space where the spare tyre
usually goes. Then they covered her with a rubber mat and
placed a large suitcase over her.

While this was going on the Arab kidnappers, had checked
out two briefcases filled with golden bars and two crappy little
Mazdas. They carefully looked in the car's trunks, underneath
the seats, underneath the cars, in the hubcaps and in the engine
compartment. Now that the two looking after Sarah were
finished they paired up with the other two men who chose one of
the Mazdas got in and drove out again.

When they'd left two white women came out from a side
office. They were older but not bad looking. They drove out in
the Nissan just a minute after the other two. The Indian man
packed up the radio into a cardboard box and took it outside.
Meanwhile the heavyset man took a petrol container out, picked
up Sarah's dirty pants and threw them into the Audi. Then he
sloshed petrol around the inside of the Audi where the rifle
had been left and then tossed a match into it. The car started
burning fiercely at once. Then he went outside to join the Indian
man in a white VW stationwagon and they drove off leaving the
warehouse to fill with smoke. From arrival to leaving the whole
thing took eight minutes.

Control picked up the two women driving south down highway
two. They seemed surprisingly relaxed for kidnappers, chatting
and laughing together. They drove on as it got darker. Then,
when they reached a place called Caesarea, they turned inland.

They drove for about a quarter of an hour until they came to a place called Umm al-Fahm. It was obviously a poor Arab town. The Nissan stuck out because all the other cars were crap. But the driver obviously knew where she was going because she threaded through the narrow streets and drove into a garage named "Al-Walid Motors," according to the Arabic.

There were a couple of young Arab men waiting for them. They had neat hair and were obviously richer than most of those around them, who seemed to regard them as strangers. They slammed the garage doors closed behind the big Nissan, opened the trunk, pulled out the suitcase and took Sarah's limp body over to an old chest freezer which was sitting beside a grimy wall. The whole place was obviously a workshop. There was grease, rusty tools and pictures of cars under a harsh neon light. They opened the freezer. The motor had been removed and there were small drill holes for air in the back. Inside there was a cut down mattress and they dumped Sarah inside. It was almost big enough to take her stretched out. Then they closed the lid and padlocked it. They put the spare tyre they had into the trunk of the Nissan and opened the door again. The women reversed out and left. The men closed the workshop and disappeared out the back way to the house above the shop.

It was five twenty two in the morning in New Zealand.

Grandpop got up in front of us, coughed and then pulled a face. "Well, that was pretty rugged," he swallowed.

"OK, how is she doing Control?" he asked.

"Sarah is unconscious, heartrate reduced, breathing suppressed. There is a slight increase in carbon monoxide which is concerning. The container she is in is not well enough ventilated and her nose is constricted."

"Will she survive?"

"Probably, but there is a risk of brain damage."

"Well, we can't have that. We need to get that thing off her mouth at least. We also need webs, flies and possibly Cheeky around in the morning. Ashley we also need to move Hooty to be with you so he's synched with night there. So let's see," He stopped to think.

"Tahira could you tend to Sarah. I have a feeling she may have to escape these guys. Take that thing off her face but leave the hood on. Leave something sharp inside the freezer and unlock the padlock. We may need to get her new clothes. Sam, take Cheeky to Umm Al-Fahm and get him set up there somewhere."

"Ashley you're all we've got in the morning so take Hooty and his box, take a suit home and sleep in it. Be ready bright and early to watch the garage. Your morning will be Sarah's. You may want to get a headscarf too."

"Tarik and Cam we need webs and flies on that garage. Scotty go with Sam and explore the town. Scott, Sam, Tarik and Cam? We may need escape routes and hiding places for tomorrow night. Scott. I'll talk to Zoe and Patricia about basing you in Austria. You may end up having a real long day today if we have you with Ashley. Control, do we know where Sarah's dad is?"

"No."

"What's the media saying?"

"They are reporting a shooting but not the kidnap. Some politicians are blaming Hamas. Apparently the workmen have identified a Hamas specialist as the gunman."

"We need to find those two. They didn't look so surprised when whatsisname was shot in front of them. See if you can get their names and addresses we may have to bug them."

"Also Control see if you can find out which detective is being given this case."

"So the question is who has kidnapped Sarah and why? If it's for money they will hang on to her but if it's to get at her dad or grandfather they will have a timeframe. They will probably threaten her more and possibly hurt or kill her. Our job is to make sure she stays safe but does not go straight back to her father. Dr P says in the future we want she spends a lot of time with the Arabs and learns a lot from them. Right now it's hard to see how that could happen, but let's at least make sure Israel's future Prime Minister doesn't die. OK, let's go."

We went to get our animals.

After watching the kidnappers in action we felt a bit scared. They had been well organised and completely ruthless so we weren't so keen to get in their way. At the same time we all felt for Sarah, even though she was a princess. Being brought down that hard and that fast would be tough on anyone.

Cheeky was out, so I had to call him back. He hopped up looking at me curiously, tilting his head. I hoped he'd be all right. He'd be confused by the night time and there would almost certainly be cats about. Still he was relaxed and hopped up so I could put him in my chest pocket.

[+]

We ran down to the jumpstation. A minute later we were standing in Al-Walid Motors under a house in Israel. It was a nice little garage. The tools had a feeling of long use and it smelt of grease and rust and something a bit spicy although I wasn't sure what it was. There was also a smell of cosy fires burning. The ghosts were mostly Arab women who just watched us. It was the middle of winter and quite chilly. The freezer seemed kind of spooky knowing it held a kidnapped fifteen-year-old.

Tarik put Peter the spider in the corner by the phone while Cam released flies and Tahira opened the freezer padlock. I unlocked the tilting garage door. I started to open it but it was sprung which took me by surprise and I lost my grip. It sprang open and made a huge bang. Everyone froze looking at me.

"*Sorry,*" I said.

We all strained, listening for movement upstairs. It was quiet but quick.

"*Let's go!*" I said.

"*You go, I'll hide,*" Tahira said.

We ran out. I felt bad about leaving my partner, Tahira.

Me, Scotty, Tarik, and Cam scattered. A young man appeared at the back of the garage, joined by another. We ran. Tarik and Cam to the south, Scotty and me to the north. The men chased us, so we took off.

The guy chasing us was fast. We knew he had a gun but he had realised we were teens and he thought we were just thieves. He wanted to catch us and terrorise us a bit but not get the Police involved. We ran off into the narrow, winding streets. The smells of food and smoke were everywhere.

"*Split up,*" I said to Scott.

Scott went left, I went right. The guy kept running and went after Scott. Scott also kept running. The man yelled "Qef ya Haraamy! (stop thief!)" but the race through the narrow streets was too fast for anyone to do anything. Scotty would have won the Olympics at that rate. I found a route to join up with Scott, sent it to him, and ran down my road.

The race soon ended. The guy had sprinted three hundred meters through the narrow streets for forty five seconds. He was leaving the garage unguarded. Scott, with the benefit of his suit, had simply outrun him.

"*How are you going Tahira?*" I asked.

"*OK for now. I've got a good spot and I'm blended in.*"

I jogged on and met up with Scott. He was resting against a power pole.

"That guy is fast!" he said out loud as he panted.

"He'll be depressed now that a kid has outrun him," I said, and Scott laughed.

We went back along my route. Cam and Tarik had shaken off their guy quite quickly and Tarik wanted to get back into the garage and get Peter.

"*They're back here now. Back and looking around,*" Tahira reported.

"*They're closing the door, checking the lock, checking the padlock. They're going to sleep down here.*"

"*Shit, sorry guys,*" I said.

I felt like an egg again.

"Tahira, Control can put you *inside* the freezer," Grandpop told her. "Come home we've got some stuff for you," he added.

"*OK.*"

"Tarik you'll have to leave Peter for tonight. You and Cam come home too. I've got other things for you guys. Sam and Scott. Stay there and get Cheeky settled. Look for escape routes. Focus on good places to hide nearby. But start far out and work in. After that chase people will be looking out for kids nicking stuff," he told us.

We started a big circle back to the garage. We both still had our facescreens up and we were in dark colours. There was some light from homes packed close together around us but it was cold so it was some time before we met anyone on the street. It was three older teens with a soccer ball outside chatting. We decided against showing our faces because Scott might be picked on.

We walked up the narrow avenue between the houses while the teens talked and one headed his ball against the wall under a pool of light. The sound of TVs and voices, children and even the distant barking of dogs made us aware this was a living, busy street where everyone knew everyone and the only reason they were mostly inside was because it was the middle of winter here, and fairly cold.

We attracted uncertain looks as we got closer to the teens. When we were about six meters away the oldest one, wearing a hoodie, not unlike our own, called out to us in Arabic.

"Hey, who are you? What are you doing out so late?"

It wasn't unfriendly. It was more big brotherish than anything. I wasn't quite sure what to say, and wished Tarik were around.

"We're going home," Scotty made his suit reply in Arabic. We walked on.

"Who *are* you two? I don't know you! You aren't from around here," the older one said, looking at us suspiciously. They got up. We were starting to pass right by them.

"Hey? Hey! I'm talking to you, squirt!"

"*You know, we need more landing zones,*" Scott said silently.

"*Yeah,*" I agreed as we walked on.

Suddenly someone grabbed my hood and tried to yank it back. Of course it didn't yank, but the sudden pull made me fall back on my butt. This caused a shudder of laughter among the teens. That stopped when I jumped up two meters in the air, glowing slightly to join Scott. The trio looked at each other clearly a bit freaked and suddenly decided to go indoors.

We continued walking, checking out dark corners, alleyways and crevices, our feet soft and padded.

"You could easily run along the roofs here," Scotty pointed out. *"They're so close together."*

We moved quickly and quietly along the alleyways. I didn't really like any of these places for Cheeky. We passed a house in a pool of light where some TV show had everyone quite excited and moved on, in and out of the lamplight.

We met an old man who seemed a bit unsure of himself who said "As-salamu alaykum (Peace be upon you)," as we passed. We didn't know the customary reply "Wa Alaikum Salaam (Upon you be peace)[†]," then.

After a while I decided the best idea was to let Cheeky look around for himself. I took him out of his pouch. He looked around curiously wondering why it was dark, but deciding he would rather stretch his wings, he finally took off. He flew up two stories and disappeared over the roofline.

We continued walking.

"Can you guys find me a landing zone please?" Tahira asked. *"Cam and Tarik are off to the Philippines again and I'd like to be close to Sarah."*

We found her a tiny alleyway barely wide enough to squeeze down. We turned away and a light bomb went off behind us. I noticed movement at a window above us.

"Neighbours," I warned, and the three of us ran off.

"How was she?" I asked Tahira.

"Still drugged, but I got that hideous thing off her face and turned her on her side. It was so squashed I could barely move. Hekator gave us a carbon monoxide absorbent powder which

will absorb the air she breathes out, and we added a bit of extra oxygen to the air. Hekator says she'll be OK for 12 hours but she will have to be strong. It's horrible to be in there. It's like being buried alive. I couldn't stand it."

"I'd lose it," I admitted.

"And you don't mind caves! I wouldn't last five minutes," Scotty agreed.

We walked on for a little while.

"If they threaten her, we may have to stop them doing stuff to her," I said.

"Yeah, I was thinking about that too," Scotty said.

"They have pistols. They seemed very rich, and their accent is not one I know," Tahira said. *"I don't think they live here."*

We walked around for an hour. Cheeky flew about looking around curiously and then flying back to where we were to check on us. It was still early evening when we got back to Al-Walid Motors. I got Cheeky to do a special tour around the place, upstairs and down. Peeking in the window it was clear the two men were not relatives. There was a distance between the old man and woman living there and the two young men who kept their weapons in sight.

Cheeky found a good niche for his nest box. It was on a third storey roof about fifty meters away from the garage. We decided to install it after midnight when more people would be asleep, so we went home.

[+]

To fill in the time we had to deliver colony starter packages to the three caves we'd surveyed.

After the encounter with Administration's biobot gold panners at Pico de Neblina we had also decided on a new location for

65

the Americas. It was an island called Redonda which technically belonged to Antigua and Barbuda but really belonged to a few goats and a lot of seabirds. It was a tall island with old mines on it, set in the Caribbean sea†. It was close to the Eastern US and a bit over halfway from Renwick to Europe.

Unlike the surveys, starting the colonies didn't involve doing much. We just put the insect tubes and a whole heap of sugar in a travel bag and bent to the caves. Then all we had to do was shake out the sugar in the cave and open the insect tubes.

It was pretty amazing seeing these five, tiny insects crawl out of the fluid they were in, open their wings and take off. In a month it would be deadly to enter the cave. A month after that the base would be ready for installing equipment.

[+]

After that we went swimming for a while with Rewa and Asal. They were excited about going to Israel and wanted to practice things like blending in and sneaking. At first I wasn't sure the girls should think about this, but Grandpop said it couldn't hurt, so we played a sneaking game in the bush until lunchtime. They were good at it too. A lot better than we expected.

After that I went back to the rooftop in Umm al Fahm and put Cheeky's nestbox in place. He seemed happy to have it placed in this strange dark place and it was clear he felt more attachment to his nest than he did to me. Once I'd stood back and he'd hopped in and out a couple of times he flew off to explore some more and I bent home.

[+]

We spent the rest of the day flying our speeders back to the Spratleys and loading silver. By five we had got most of the silver and it was time to fly home. We shot out of the clear blue sea into the sky and headed south.

We were almost halfway – just cruising past the Papuan Highlands – when we suddenly started picking up a very strange signal. Then Control started barking orders.

"Administration scout at five o'clock, range ninety seven kilometers, altitude four thousand meters. Restore inertia, vector nor-east, reduce altitude one thousand meters, accelerate to one point four kilometers per second. Disperse to five kilometer radius."

We were at fifteen kilometers altitude and the scout was coming up the mountains behind us. We turned away from the mountains and dove at monstrous speed for the deck. Now we were relying on our warp invisibility field to avoid detection. By getting as low as we could the curve of the Earth would help prevent the scout from seeing us.

So as we went down the scout was climbing up, zooming over us at two kilometers per second, its massive inertialess field broadcasting its presence to us, just as we hoped our antigravity fields were hidden from it.

It was soon at twenty kilometers above, behind a layer of cirrus cloud, barely visible, as a bright star in the sky. For a moment our attention was directed skyward and then it was off zipping away into space. All traces of it vanished. We could finally breathe again.

We turned back to home remaining spread out just in case. We realised now just how vulnerable we were to be jumped, or as we later learned to call it, "bounced" by Administration scouts. It was a good lesson in keeping it real, which was easy to forget with the excitement of flying. It was one we kept in mind as started planning our long range flight to Israel.

The next day an old Ford Transit van showed up early to Al-Walid Motors. Ashley and Scotty (who was now very tired) found a spot on the hillside they could watch from. Control gave them a feed on the men in the valley below so they could start reading them.

Combined with the bugs we began to get a better picture of the whole kidnap operation. This team was Syrian but *their* only links to Hamas were business. The kidnappers thought it had been organised by a rival Ukrainian Mafiya organisation to force Uri Kogan out of a diamonds for arms deal being organised in Belgium.

Now they were organising to demonstrate proof that Sarah was alive and that if Uri didn't cooperate his daughter would suffer. But Ashley and Scott's most important discovery was that the big thing on Hussein and Omar's minds in the morning was being paid on a daily basis.

Every day they dialled into their bank in Abu Dhabi to confirm the overnight transfer. Thanks to Peter the spider's webs, Control intercepted the pitifully slow cellular modem connection when it was made and that showed their payments of US$10,000 each had gone through.

The Transit van took Sarah out of the centre of the town. The flies caught Omar and Hussein giving the Al-Walid's an envelope full of cash. It was clear that they weren't coming back. Instead they drove back towards the motorway exit but then turned up the hill towards a new building area on the ridge which overlooked the motorway to the north, and above the town to the south. Control had managed to get a fly into the van so we had sound and vision the whole way.

Sarah herself was still asleep but her captors were shifting her to a small basement in a small apartment block. It obviously wasn't practical to keep her in a box in a busy garage the whole time. Sooner or later she'd need to eat and stuff, and mean as they were, Omar and Hussein weren't comfortable about taking care of a teenaged girl by themselves. It was women's work. So they had found a group of women willing to do it for them.

They delivered Sarah rolled up in a carpet. The basement room was a concrete hole, barely lit by glass brick windows, so the carpet, tatty as it was, made it look just a little bit homey. There was a crappy single mattress, a table and chairs, and the toilet was pretty filthy.

There were two hard looking women in headscarves, and shawls for guards. They kept their faces covered. The men went out. The women were bored. They talked and fidgeted. One even tried to swat our fly for a while for something to do. Finally the men came back. They had bought a Hebrew paper somewhere and put its front page on top of Sarah's sleeping body and took a picture with their cellphones. Then they left again.

Scotty and Ashley walked across town to where Sarah was being held. Scott was struggling to stay awake and Ashley had to help. They had turned their suits into jeans and hooded jackets but they still stood out badly because they had to show their faces. Control showed everyone noticed them, Scott as much as Ashley. It was pretty clear that me, Tarik and Tahira were going to be the only ones who could walk around there during the day without attracting too much attention. We would still look different, but not completely out of place like Scotty, Ashley and Cam.

By eleven Sarah began to stir. She still had the bag over her head but Tahira had taken off the gag. She began to cry out. The

women told her to shut up. Her complaints brought her a pretty
vicious kick and she lay still crying softly. The women continued
their talk making mean remarks about the girl in their power.
Eventually they fed her, sat her on the loo, and put her back
down again, all without removing the blindfold. A constant
complaint of these guards was that Sarah stank. They called
her names in Arabic and kicked her if she said anything.
Sweethearts they were not. They seemed to really hate Sarah for
some reason and saw this as a chance to make her suffer.

This went on all day. By three in the afternoon Scott said he was
starting to hallucinate. He bent back to Renwick. Ashley bent
back to Austria. So for five hours there was no-one around to
witness Sarah's lonely suffering.

Dr Prosperov was more concerned about two things: Sarah's
mother, and how things were going between the kidnappers and
Uri. So far Sarah's mother Alisha Semovich hadn't appeared
to have reacted to Sarah's kidnapping. Dr P guessed she didn't
know about it. If the kidnapping went ahead as an affair between
gangsters Sarah would probably wind up dead or free within a
week. Neither were the future that led to her future leadership of
Israel.

As he saw it the best solution was for Sarah to escape from the
kidnappers but lose faith in her parent's underworld lives. We
hoped she might be taken in by some of the locals who would
hide her so that nobody would think they had anything to do
with the kidnap. The locals were unlikely to kill Sarah in cold
blood while the kidnappers wouldn't think twice.

But to interrupt the kidnapping operation we needed a lot
more information about it. Finding that out was hard because
Uri Kogan was on the move and specialised in being hard to

find. This was also likely to be slowing down police as well because Kogan was not likely to be open with them about his criminal business dealings. We knew that Ivan Federov's death would not have been missed by Sarah's grandfather Michael Semovich but he was probably on Uri's tail getting him to deal with the kidnappers. So in the end it all came down to Sarah's grandfather, Michael Semovich. He wanted his granddaughter back, he didn't want his daughter to panic, and he would know where her father, Uri Kogan, was.

"Therefore we need to bug Semovich," Dr Prosperov concluded. We decided to start at 1 a.m. local time. That meant 2 p.m. for us. For something to do until 2 p.m. Tarik and Cam went back to the bays in Indonesia where they had been looking for Cam's mother. Me and Tahira decided it was time to harass the slavers who were holding Diana and Elena again.

They were being kept in a smaller hotel in Hungary where they'd been for almost three weeks. It was ten at night there. We knew Diana was scared and depressed and that she hadn't eaten enough. Dr Prosperov wanted the place taken out again.
The problem with this place was that it was tall and in the middle of town. There were three stories and twenty rooms. No sprinkler system and no smoke doors. We decided that the fire needed to start at the top and work down. The fire department would probably bring it under control but all the attention would probably make continued operation of the "hotel" difficult.
Avoiding killing or burning someone was our main concern. We decided being subtle was a waste of time. What we wanted was panic.

"What you need is some smoke grenades," Grandpop decided.

"Where are going to get those?" I asked.

"The local boys'll have them."

He meant the army.

"We just need to find an arsenal. May as well nick any other stuff we might be able to use too."

So Control did a quick search and found a run down Romanian army training camp which relied on concrete bunkers and heavy steel doors as its only security and we bent inside.

By the light of our suits we found ourselves surrounded by boxes and boxes of guns, ammunition and grenades. The place smelt like some guys used it as a toilet sometimes too. It took Grandpop a little while to work out which bombs were which. I picked up a flare pistol but he told me to put it down again. Finally we found the grenades we were looking for. The ones we wanted were the RDG-2 smoke and signaling flares that looked like a cardboard toilet roll core with a screwcap to cover the fuse. They looked pretty cheap and primitive. We loaded them into a box. Then Grandpop told Tahira to take the box to the southern Sahara where we had practiced before going to the moon.

[+]

I had to come get him. Grandpop had got himself a sleeping bag and seemed to be raring to go. So I sealed up Grandpop and bent. Tahira was waiting as normal, sitting on the box full of smoke bombs, looking bored. I arrived and suddenly realised Grandpop was thrashing around like a wild thing. It was hard to open the bag but finally he came out wide-eyed and shaken, gasping for breath.

"Grandpop are you OK? What's the matter," I asked him

He was panting and agitated and got out of the bag like it was full of snakes.

"Christ! That was...that was awful," he said.

He walked around rubbing his neck trying to calm down. Finally the stillness and cold of the night and the sand seemed to calm him. He took a deep breath and shook his head.

"You guys are braver than I thought," he admitted.

After a while he'd settled down enough to teach us how to use the smoke bombs. They were easy-as. You just pulled the string and then the tube started making smoke, slowly at first, then there was a bit of flame and soon there was lots and lots of smoke. Grandpop tried to hang on to one but the smoke made him cough so he tossed it.

We practiced throwing them with our whips and that wasn't so hard either. So after five minutes Grandpop had run out of things to show us. He still seemed a bit scared to get back into the bag though. Finally after talking far too long about fuses he ran out of things to say. He took a deep breath, looked at the bag like it was a large jellyfish he had to wrestle, and then at us.

"Look ... ah ... do you see ..." his eyes looked hunted.

"People who've ..." he coughed. "People who've died," he said with a strangled throat as he swallowed another cough down, "when you use those things?"

"Yes," Tahira shrugged, simply.

I shrugged and nodded.

He swore under his breath, then pulled himself together.

"Right, let's get on with it," he jumped in and pulled it closed. I could see this was how he'd been as a soldier. I grabbed the handle and locked on. I glanced down at his tense face through the window.

"Ready?" I asked.

He gave a stiff nod.

"Go."

And we were gone.

[+]

Of course I had to pull him out of the tank this time. He was stiff and breathing hard which made it harder. Finally I pulled the bag out and helped him climb out of the folds.

"Better you than me, boy," he said looking shocked again.

I wondered what it was that he saw when he passed through the realm of the dead. It clearly scared the snot out of him though. I stepped back and bent.

[+]

I found myself three stories above the street in a small city on an icy, half-meter wide walkway of a narrow slate roof. Tahira was waiting with the box of smoke bombs. I nearly slipped and risked falling to the street below. There was some traffic even though it was freezing cold. I extended my foot claws.

"Uhh so guys, we have to be careful with this so that everyone gets out with the smoke. So what I suggest is that you swing over the side. Smash your way through the window. Size up the situation and make sure everyone can get out before you pull the string. Try to be as scary as you can. OK?"

"Yup," I said.

The top storey windows were just below us, jutting out of the slope of the roof. The problem was it was a very slippery slope and there was nothing much to hold on to with an annoying short two-storey drop that was hard to recover from without bending or glowing. There was too much traffic for wings. Tahira had the best answer.

"Sam, how about you lie down and hold on and I'll hold onto

you and throw in the smoke bombs."

I could tell she didn't want me to see any sex happening. It was a bit because she thought I would be distracted but mostly because she wanted the girls to have their privacy. I almost wanted to argue but I knew she was right.

"OK," I shrugged.

I lay down and let the hairs in my suit cling on to the slate and ice. I extended my whip and Tahira extended hers. Then she took a smoke bomb and a flare from the box, gripped my whip with hers and tugged hard. I slipped a bit. Then I slid a bit over the other side of the roofline so that we were both hanging over the roof ridge, her further down than me. Tahira was pulled slightly up. Realising our roles could end up suddenly reversed if she didn't move quickly she swung over the icy edge, immediately pulling me hard to the ridge.

The two whips held each other well. Tahira was only three slippery meters away and moved around outside the guttering. Then she changed her suit to black. Completely focused she shuffled along outside the window and kicked it in.

There was a brief pause.

"This is no good, it's a girl's room. There's nothing in here."

"Well, they probably live on the top level," I guessed.

"All her stuff is in here. Probably what little money she has too," Tahira said.

"And now her window is smashed," I pointed out.

"Pull me up. I want to rethink this," she thought.

We reeled each other in and were soon standing face to face on the top of the hotel on an icy night in Hungary.

"Let's do the kitchen again. If we do the kitchen and bar the fire will probably be caught before it gets to where the girls live," I

suggested

"But Sam, then everyone upstairs is trapped," Grandpop said. "If the water mains are iced and the fire fighters can't put the fire out the girls – including Diana and Elena die."

Tahira looked frustrated.

"*We can't hurt these girls more! They have awful lives as it is,*" she objected.

"*We could zap the customers,*" I suggested.

"No Sam. That's going to get attention we don't want," said Grandpop.

"*Look Tahira, how about we just set the smoke on the second floor. That will get the fire brigade out anyway and ruin the owners night,*" I said.

She thought about it.

"*Yeah OK.*"

"OK, well, get on with it then," Grandpop said.

So we got back into position and Tahira went back to being a black devil, then she abseiled off the edge of the hotel. She jumped and swung, jumped and swung and then with a smash of glass went through the window.

"*Pig!*" she thought of a man.

She was in there a little while as I moved over and took up a new position. Her whip found mine, hanging over the edge and with a jerk she was jumping again. Then there was another smash.

"*Sam I had to zap one. Can you bring the box down. We may as well do the whole thing from down here.*"

She gave me a landing zone. I got up and got the box. Then I bent to her LZ. I couldn't see a thing. The whole place was filled with white smoke. It took me a moment to realise she was using ultrasound to see. I grabbed some smoke bombs, then closed the

76

box and sent it home. We'd never find it again in this.

People were already beginning to shout "Tüzet! (fire)" in alarm. Tahira was dragging this fat, naked white man out into the corridor which was quickly filling with smoke. I changed my look to match Tahira's and joined her.

I tossed another bomb back along the corridor. Then came back in time to see Tahira kick a door in and toss in another smoke bomb. I dragged the fat man along the corridor heading for the next room. Two adults ran out. The man tripped over the fat man but got up. I went white so they couldn't see me. They staggered past coughing and spluttering. I kicked in the next door with two big kicks, pulled the string fuse with a crack and tossed in another smoke bomb. There were yells of alarm from inside. Then I went back to help Tahira.

"Make sure there's no-one in the smoke guys. It can kill in confined places," Grandpop warned.

We went back through all the rooms. It was kind of fun being unaffected by the smoke and just going about ruining everyone's night. Behind us the whole place was full of screams and shouts as frightened people tried to get out down the stairs. We had to put out a fire in one of the rooms by smothering it. After five minutes we were rewarded by the sound of sirens. It was time to go.

[+]

We arrived back in the tank and waded through the oil to get out. We found Grandpop at the control desk watching the scene from the opposite sides of the road. There were people huddled in bedding and blankets against the cold. The fire fighters were setting up. Some of the owners were talking with police while others were trying to get the girls into cars. The girls were crying and didn't want to go.

We saw Elena and Diana looking scared and worried. They had
no idea anyone was looking out for them and probably wouldn't
have thanked us for getting them thrown out on the street. But
at least this night the threat wasn't beatings and abuse. It was
disaster and confusion. Grandpop waved away the view.

"Useful those smoke bombs," he said, his glasses on the end of
his nose. "We should use them more often."

We waited a while for Cam and Tarik and then returned to Israel
to move Cheeky and recover Peter. That went pretty smoothly.
Cheeky was asleep so moving his box to a new roof was easy.
Tarik called Peter who was so well blended in he didn't see him
until he responded to his pocket beacon. We bent home to get
ready to bug Michael Semovich.

[+]

Control had been over Semovitch's entire mansion to find the
points it was most vulnerable to bugging. The plan focused
on the communications cupboard on the third storey office
level which looked out over the sea. The only problem was
the security system. All the cameras were pointed at normal
approach routes so they were only a small problem. The real
headache was the intrusion detection system which used
ultrasound and would go off if anything moved.

Grandpop decided the best approach was to get Michael to turn
it off himself and the easiest was to do that was to trigger it over
and over until he got so annoyed he turned it off himself.

So from one o'clock in the morning Israel time until three
the alarm went off every ten to twenty minutes as we bent
travel boxes into the private office of one of Israel's richest
and shadiest characters. He was furious and we were killing

ourselves laughing.

Finally he gave up, turned it off, and posted two bodyguards instead. We had to jump them carefully because they had Uzis. Tahira and me went in first and zapped them. Then Cam and Tarik bugged the communications cupboard while we kept watch. Then we hauled the bodyguards onto their bosses couch and desk chair and came home. The whole thing only took five minutes.

[+]

The next target was Sarah's mother's apartment. It's protection was just a secure door and lift system so Cam and Tarik bugged that easily using Peter the spider. The only person we still didn't have was Sarah's father, Uri Kogan, and at that moment Sarah's future depended entirely on what he did.

...

*S*am!" Hekator's thoughts intrude suddenly.
I had just been about to tell Sue more about Israel. We're in one of the rooms in the Fae quarantine station lying on couch bushes.

"*Yeah?*" I reply.

"*The commanders are back.*"

It takes a moment for me to remember that twelve hours ago I had left Ka-rea-rea with a countdown to destruction showing on his hull as Inspector Du Croix and the Administration tried to get me to get out of him and surrender. The twelve hours are nearly up. Now Ka-rea-rea either detonates on the moon base with me supposedly inside him, or they let me go and I have to pretend that I'm still not in contact with the others and that I'm trying to escape the Administration which wants to use me as bait to track down the Fae home planet. I panic a bit at having to act like I've been lying in the box miserably contemplating death for twelve hours.

"*Shit!*"

I glance at Sue. She shrugs and I close my eyes. I feel Sue get up and go past me. Quickly I connect to Ka-rea-rea. It feels weird to be pretending to be inside him now that I wasn't inside the medical coffin any more. I'm trying to get my thoughts together after a long sleep and talk to Sue.

The room has turned back into a meeting room. The table is slightly different now. One commander sits in the centre while Inspector Du Croix and the fat woman sit facing in from each wing. The Archdeacon and the other commander aren't there. If they've arrested him he's in big trouble. The Center interrogates people by getting all the information out of their brains, destructively. It's because the clones don't value individuality at all.

"...*And the purpose of the countdown displayed on the side of the craft,*" the commander finished.

Hekator flashes me the thought that they want to know what the countdown means.

I thought about the situation. I realise if I'm facing blowing myself up I won't be that keen to talk. I've waited for them to talk to me for a long time. I'd make them wait to reply. So I let the silence build up.

"*We would rather you respond voluntarily...*" it adds, meaning that if I don't they would attack.

"It's not hard!" I blurt out. "When the timer runs out I have one hour of air. If you haven't agreed to let me go that's it! I'm not going to die of carbon dioxide OK? What's so hard about that?"

"*Is that regardless of where you are?*"

"No. Obviously if you let me go, I'll stop it."

"*We can, of course, force you from the craft.*"

"Not without it blowing up."

"*I think not. You said you were extracted from your craft in Belzer so we have asked for a demonstration.*"

That worries me. Had they got Von Streicher up here?

The door of the chamber slides up rapidly and Archdeacon

Oswald comes forward from the brightly lit tunnel, blinking uncertainly into the huge dark space looking very small and very nervous. The huge door slides back down behind him and the chamber lights up fully for the first time.

The chamber is a fifty meter cube made from hard looking gray material. A single large symbol which Ka-rea-rea translated as "2" marked the side walls. The Archdeacon looks very small as his footsteps rang across the shiny gray floor toward the table where Ka-rea-rea lay. He must have chosen this as a desperate last measure to avoid reprocessing. The holograms look less solid in the light.

"The Archdeacon has sworn that his links with the settlers are in the interests of the Center. He claims that the group has the ability to determine whether you are indeed inside this craft and neutralise its power supply without breaching the fuel containment field. If this is so it is worth exploring so we have agreed to allow him the opportunity to demonstrate this claimed capability."

"This is serious," Hekator says quietly.

Although Ka-rea-rea is still trussed up in the enclosing ribs of the machine the greys had been using back on the saucer to try and open him, there's nothing physically restraining him at all. I can't see a problem.

"Why?" I ask, and fire my beam at the Archdeacon who collapses on the floor. The silver skull he's carrying clatters out from his limp hands. Then I have Ka-rea-rea smash out of the containing ribs of the machine. I reset the counter on his side to one hour and counting. The chamber goes dark again.

"So you decline to meet the Archdeacon's challenge?" the Commander asks without surprise.

"Yeah, I've already fought that and I'm not going to fight it again for you. Stop wasting time. I will now detonate in fifty nine minutes."

There's a pause as the commander stares at me.

"*We have evacuated the base. You are free to detonate now if you wish,*" the Commander tells me unblinkingly.

"And your bosses are happy to lose this base, and this craft, and the Archdeacon, rather than keep all three and lose me?"

"*We do not believe you are in that craft. We believe you to be in league with the Fae rebellion,*" it says putting its hands together.

"I thought you guys were logical. If your theory was right I'd be laughing. I'd detonate now. I would have already. What difference would it make to me?"

I let that sink in and then continue.

"Unfortunately for me you're wrong. Now I'll give you one hour to save my life, your base and this craft. But I'm getting tired and this injury really hurts and I don't see anything worth hanging around for if you're just going to wait until my air runs out. I will not surrender no matter what."

Inspector Du Croix starts to clap slowly. It makes an empty sound in the huge chamber.

"Bravo, Sam, bravo. You should be in ze movies. But ze game is up. We know you are not inzide zis craft."

There's no way I knew of he could detect me. Hekator didn't either.

"It iz simple. Ze total volume of ze craft is only one point eight cubic meters. Your volume is a third of that. We simply can't believe zere is room for sufficient oxygen stored inside after 12 hours."

I wasn't sure about that. I'd never had oxygen problems in

Ka-rea-rea. Hekator explains.

"Ka-rea-rea uses superconducting high pressure oxygen through the carbon lattice. You could survive for 24 hours before there would be a problem."

I thought for a moment, then reply.

"You are nearly right. At the end of my countdown I'll have one hour left. I can die of carbon dioxide or I can die detonating. If I have to go I prefer taking you out with me."

"Or zhou could get out," he replies.

"And die some other way."

"You would not die my young friend," Du Croix smiles, scratching his neck.

"I don't believe you," I tell him straight. "If you let me go on Earth, then I'll believe you."

There's a long silence. Finally I fill it. I let my voice sound sad, scared and a little pleading.

"Look I *am* all alone. I really don't want to die in a box on the moon. I'm only fourteen! This is my last chance to get away. I'm offering you this speeder. But I won't get out here on the moon for anything. What do you gain from my death? Nothing."

"Your death is of no consequence to us," the commander observes.

"Exactly why I won't get out! But what do you lose? Heaps! Why waste a good base? Why miss out on this speeder? The Fae have deserted me. Dr Prosperov has gone. I have no idea how to reach them. My family has gone. Just let me go back to New Zealand where I belong. I'm no threat to you. Please ... why can't we all get back to where we want to be as you said. Why can't you just tag the speeder and let me go?" I plead.

The commander looks at the others.

"*We will consider your request.*"

And they vanish again.

I fly over to the skull and pick it up with my extendable grippers, fly it over to the table and put it down so I can scan it. There's nothing special about it. It's a skull about the size of a man's fist with silver plating. I wonder if it would be any different if I was really there. Whether the skull would come to life as Von Streicher's had.

"*If the Archdeacon comes to, I would not put it past them to use him as a plant. Make it look as though he's been made prisoner so as to talk to you,*" Hekator warns me.

"*Do you think I'm going to have to detonate?*"

"*No,*" Hekator replies easily.

"*Why not?*"

"*They* want *the deal you're offering. It's exactly what they* do want. *It's why they didn't try and bust into you in space. They just want to make you work for it to make sure you really are in the box.*"

"*And you really think they believe that.*"

"*Yes. They have no other evidence.*"

"*What about the Bruderschaft guide?*"

"*Well, you stopped the demonstration but they probably don't believe in it anyway. Having a purpose programmed into them, and therefore no soul, means the clones are not sensitive to these things.*"

There's a pause.

I have to ask.

"*Hekator, what is that guide anyway?*"

"*It's a superdimensional being that draws power from souls aligned to its way of being. The more that way of life abounds* the stronger it gets. Most of them are fairly diffuse and harmless but sometimes you get ones which have the ability to concentrate energy in our dimensions."

"So they're ghosts?" I ask, confused.

"Not quite, although some may have started that way. They have the ability to think and plan. As you know ghosts can't do that. Dr Prosperov's companion is an example."

"Yeah ... what is Lucky?"

"Your name for that entity doesn't match very well. It is not a fortunate being. It has suffered terrible deprivations. Our fear was that it was made mad from its suffering, and yet remarkably it appears not to be so."

"But what is he?"

"The easiest way to explain it to you is as the ghost of a god."

"How does that work out?" I ask.

"We are not sure. And one of the problems with all these entities is they can only be observed, not studied. If they don't want to help us study them no-one can make them. So they have many secrets of which we can guess only some, and know even less."

It reminded me of Mordecai Ceder, the strange old Jewish psychic I'd met in Haifa. "Listen to God," he always said.

"What about God?" I ask Hekator.

"The ultimate mystery. The more you actually know, the more you realise how little you know."

"But how can you have all these gods and one God?"

"We are all aspects of the conscious universe. Even these gods. Dimensions are spaces of potential being within God. We don't occupy all dimensions. We believe some beings never occupy the dimensions we do but it is hard to prove. Some of these other spaces of potential being are not large, others are bigger *than the dimensions we know. We suspect the fifth is common to all but we don't know. As you know there are more advanced beings than us who are far closer to this than we. Compared to them we are equally primitive."*

He was talking about the strange and terrifying entity, Jibreel or in English, Gabriel, Khadiyeh talked to. But I had more immediate questions.

"If they like my deal how will they get me back to Earth?"

"Ah, that will be tricky. Away from this base they will have less to lose by trying to break Ka-rea-rea."

"Yes, that was what was bothering me."

"You should insist that the Inspector accompanies you. It will reduce the risk of attack while on the way."

"But surely he's going to have some secret counterattack?"

"Probably."

"What do you think I should do with this skull?"

"Make sure it stays behind."

"When do you think they will agree?"

"Not til the last minute. But if the counter gets to zero detonate anyway."

"OK."

I fly over to the skull and with a long burn melt off the silver to a big smoking puddle that flickers flame and runs all over the table. Then with a blast of ultrasound I shatter the sad little bone skull inside to a million pieces. Then I fly over to the Archdeacon. He's still out cold. I sat next to him so I could make sure he stayed that way. Then I withdrew.

Sue's doing some kind of martial arts practice. It's interesting to watch. When she finishes she seemed to come back to the here and now and smiles at over at me.

"It's the only thing I can do. This place is just so boring. What's happening on the moon?"

I tell her quickly about it.

"What about Sir Michael's daughter? What's-her-name, Sian? How can you get her away from the German guy without your speeder?"

"I dunno," I admit. I'd forgotten all about Sian. "I mean I was doing OK until the Archdeacon's scouts jumped me. Now I don't know." I think about it.

"Maybe I should ask Hekator," I suggest.

Sue nods, sitting down.

"*Hekator? What are we doing about Sian Hamilton-Smythe?*"

"*She's in an Austrian hospital. She'll be fine.*"

"*What happened?*"

"*Tahira got Von Streicher as the scouts got you. The vehicle crashed but the passengers were not too badly injured. Von Streicher's still unconscious but Sian is awake and with a bit of help from her 'brother' Scotty who is making a statement to local authorities. Your friends tell me Von Streicher's going to have a hard time explaining himself when he wakes up.*"

It makes me feel proud to be part of such an awesome little team.

"*What else is going on?*"

"*Ashley and Scotty are getting Nathan and his Grandmother away from Washington. Tahira, Tarik and Cam are trying to track down para.no.ID, which is proving difficult. Rewa and Mariko are making sure Emma is safe. The operation to re-establish your new base is progressing. Get them to fly you to near Auckland and then find a highrise carpark. At this point*" *we will have to work out how to return you and Sue to Earth."*

"Then what happens?"

"First you must go through your customs relating to orphans and then you will rejoin the group."

"Why can't I just skip the orphan stuff?"

"Sam, we are trying to convince the Administration that the group no longer exists. As far as they are concerned if you are still alive they will be watching for any sign of contact again."

"What about me?" Sue asks.

I'd forgotten she could overhear us.

"You have been away from Earth for 58 hours. Your choice is to join the group or lose your memory of it."

"What does joining the group mean?"

"It means living by the security codes the others, and Emma Reeves, live by. It means allowing us to monitor you and either living with the others so we can evacuate you or if that is impossible kill you to prevent your being captured."

I gulped. I didn't know that. Sue looks a bit shocked by that.

"How long do I get to think about this?"

"That depends on how the Administration responds to Sam."

"That's not exactly much of a choice," Sue complains.

"Having you here at all is already causing considerable concern," Hekator tells her.

Sue's looking at me nervously sucking her lips. It makes her look a bit stupid.

"Hmm, I have a feeling this could be a pretty serious lifestyle decision," she says.

"I'll let you know when the commanders reply," Hekator tells me, and his telepathic presence left us.

Sue comes over and sits down opposite me, legs out, feet

crossed, leaning back on her arms.

"Was that your cunning plan?" Sue asks nervously.

"What?" I reply, confused.

"To get me to join you?"

"No! I mean, I'd never really thought about it, to be honest. I just wanted you safely away from Rocelli," I admit.

"Really?" Sue asks surprised.

"Yeah ... I mean I like the idea of you joining us, but ... well, to be honest I've spent so much effort on just getting you to believe me I never really thought about you joining."

She just looks thoughtful.

"It'd be pretty wicked if you did though," I add.

Sue smiles.

"I really like you Sam. But I just can't see me doing anything you aren't already doing. I'd just be a spare wheel."

"You wouldn't be a spare wheel Sue. You'd be great."

"Sam, if I stop being useful will they erase my memory?" she asks me nervously. I shrug.

"They might. You have to remember they have millions to protect and I don't think too many of us have visited their quarantine station before," I say.

"So if they erase I won't remember ..."

"Me or anything. They can probably let you remember Rachel is gone though."

"Well, what can I do?" Sue sighs.

I was a bit surprised she took it so easily.

"Is the idea of joining us that bad?" I ask, a little sad that she didn't like the idea at all, and wondering if that meant Aunty Liz must feel the same way.

"Look Sam it's different for you. You're a kid. You have

caregivers. You're used to having adults look after you. I'm an adult. When you are used to deciding things for yourself like where you live, who you want to be with, it's hard to give up that freedom. Sometimes you have to give things up just to stay in charge of your own life."

"Yeah, I guess so," I agree, in a small voice.

"So if they *don't* force you to blow up Ka-rea-rea what will you do?"

"Well, to escape I'd have to go somewhere crowded that I know well enough, like Auckland. But you know this play acting suicide has been making me think the only place I really want to see again is home. My own village in the Hokianga. See all my old school friends. They started high school last year. It's more real to me."

"Won't they be able to track you?"

"In the Hokianga they will, but not in Auckland."

There was a silence. I thought about the place I'd grown up in. I seemed to have left it forever ago now.

"I'd just like to say goodbye. Maybe give them some presents," I say.

"What sort of presents?"

"Oh I dunno. I might get our old neighbours a new boat."

I hadn't thought about this at all, it just popped into my head.

"What sort of boat?" Sue asks.

"A fishing boat."

"How much is a fishing boat?" Sue wonders.

"I dunno. Two, three hundred thousand?"

"Where would you get that from?"

"Sir Michael. It's my money. And he owes me for rescuing Sian."

"How much money have you got Sam?" Sue frowns.

"About 20 million, depending on the gold and silver price. Most of it's in gold and silver."

"Really?" Sue asks, not believing me.

"You saw the treasure!"

"Yeah, but..."

"And I'm paid three times more than you with no living costs. Even Aunty Liz is paid more than you."

"Yeah, OK. Rub it in," Sue says, a bit grumpily.

"It's a fact. You don't earn much."

"Yeah, and money is freedom," she says, sarcastically.

"Well, I dunno, not for us I spose. I mean we have heaps of money and heaps of freedom but it's just a pile of shiny metal really. We sell it sometimes but mostly we keep it because Dr P says the market hasn't peaked yet. But we can't do what we like with it because we'd be traced and we don't buy technology because it's not as good as the stuff we get from the Fae."

"But you can buy your neighbours a boat."

"They've been good to me. Besides I need to go somewhere if the idea is to make the community vanish. If I'm a sole survivor I need a cover story."

"So you don't want to live with Julia and Caz?"

I shake my head.

"I'm not saying they're not nice people but they aren't going to cope with me vanishing all the time. They're rich and comfortable and they're just not open to new things."

There's a pause. Sue's thinking.

"So let me get this straight. After you blow up the moon or come back to Earth, what happens next?" she asks.

"We have to close down the mystery of Renwick House. Otherwise you cops will be on our case, finding out who we were, so when we come back they will know exactly who our next-of-kin are, and then we'll have to hide them too, and that will get pretty tricky, seeing *they* have links into Interpol and stuff."

"Yeah OK, I get that, but what will *you* do?"

"Go to wherever they are, I guess."

"No, if you *don't* blow up on the moon and get dropped in Auckland. *Then* what do you do? If you're going to pretend the others are still missing you have to go back into the system, don't you? There *is* no where else."

That's true. I hadn't thought about that. I've been too excited about getting back to Rewa and Aunty Liz and Grandpop again.

"Umm…I dunno," I admit. "And I wouldn't have Ka-rea-rea either to take off to America either."

In fact I'd be more at risk than ever while I had to pretend I was an orphan. Maybe *they* were thinking they could still capture both Ka-rea-rea and me after all, if they gave me enough line. Like landing a stroppy fish.

"So, maybe you *should* go back to Julia and Caz," Sue suggests.

"But they won't cope with me vanishing to the new base, wherever it is," I point out.

"No, you're right."

"Maybe you could adopt me for a while?" I suggest, hopefully.

"No Sam, it doesn't work like that. I can't adopt you. The judge won't have it. And they might wipe my memory of you. Technically Sir Michael's still got guardianship of you anyway."

I had been hoping I could forget about all this painful legal stuff. It just pissed me off.

"But maybe you could be like Emma…know of us but…"

"Sam, I've already been hypnotised once. I'm starting think

I'd be safer having my memory wiped and being out of this altogether."

"Uhh, maybe ..."

"What do you mean 'maybe'?" she asks grumpily.

"Well, unlike Emma *they* actually know who *you* are. They might still try it on. So one day it'll be bright lights on a lonely road and Bam! You'd be brain leached to make sure there's nothing left."

"*What*!? So basically I'm screwed then?" Sue complains, looking very worried.

She's scared. I've over-done it.

"I don't know. Maybe. Maybe they'll just try hypnosis again. Sorry, I shouldn't have scared you."

Sue sighs.

"But what you're saying is now *they* know I'm with you I'm in deep, if I don't go on, I'm setting myself up for little gray men, or priests in black, or whatever else they have, to come get me."

"If your memory's wiped you won't remember to worry about it," I remind her, to be fair.

"Yeah, but I worry about it *now* !"

She takes a deep breath and rests her chin onto her palm, thinking. I don't want to interrupt and leave her alone. It's a few minutes before she speaks again.

"Oh! I don't know! On the other hand it's not like I have a whole lot of laughs to look forward to when this is over either! There's the house, which isn't that amazing, it's just what I can afford. No girlfriend. That's going to be bloody depressing! It's hard to find someone again! Then there's the job. The system's full of bullshit. The judges live on a planet even weirder than this one. The hours are crap and the pay is ... well, it's less than what your

Aunt gets."

She sighs, looking pissed off.

"But you like helping people," I suggest, trying to make her feel better.

"Yeah, I do like helping kids. You can make such a difference."

She bites her lip, thinking, then looks at me like I'd said something.

"Yeah, I know! I know! You guys are helping kids who are in far more trouble to achieve so much more! But I mean I haven't even met Dr Prosperov so I don't even know if your people would want me."

She stops for a moment, then glances at me.

"Don't read my mind!" she snaps. "It's rude. OK, I have to admit I'm just a bit scared of making a commitment. OK? They haven't gone that well for me lately."

Grandpop taught me if you have a fish on a line, don't muck around, gaff it fast.

"What if I bought you a house?"

"*What*?"

"For us to live in for a while. You own, I pay. I probably can't own a house anyway."

"That's bribery."

"So?" I shrug.

"You can't keep throwing your money around."

"Why not. I don't use it. And if Dr P is right precious metals will double so I'm not poor."

"Well hoo-bloody-ray for you. But what do I do?"

"Join us."

"Sam, I appreciate you liking me but I don't know if it's a real offer. It has to come from Dr Prosperov."

That was true. She pauses, then starts again.

"And my other problem is how do I get *out* again? If I join you people it seems to be for life. I'm young I want to have fun. I don't want to settle down."

That wasn't true.

"What was all that with Rachel then?" I point out.

"OK," she admits without even a pause, "Yes, so I *do* want to settle down, but I want to find someone to settle down *with* first."

I knew someone she could settle down with, but I didn't want to say anything.

"And if you're thinking of your Aunt..." she begins.

I'm starting to wonder which of us is the psychic here!

"...Sam you really aren't in a position to play matchmaker. Just because we're both gay doesn't mean we'll like each other. There's loads of dykes who get right up my nose. We're people just like everyone else. We need to make our own choices."

I feel a bit sad about that. I think for a while.

"Everything comes down to you meeting Dr P."

Sue shrugs. "Exactly! That's why I'm here and I think I've been bloody waiting long enough."

I decide I should ask for her.

"*Hey Grandpop? Is there anyone there?*"

"Ja," Gunter came back.

"*Hi Gunter, where's Grandpop?*"

"Fishing."

"*Has he got a boat?*"

"Ja."

"*Where's the base?*"

"I can't tell you until you pass the exit scans. Besides guessing is part of the party Mariko is planning for when you come home. It's more than my life's worth to ruin that," he tells me in his dry German monotone.

"*OK, well is Dr Prosperov around? I need him to talk to the policewoman with me.*"

"Dr Prosperov is still recuperating after rescuing *you*."

"*What?*" I ask, worried.

"It's not so bad, but he needs to rest."

"*Can I talk to Aunty Liz?*"

"Ja, sure. Wait please."

I wait for a while. Then a familiar feeling came over me. It was my Aunt, as comforting as any mum.

"Hi Sam are you OK? How's your hand?"

"*My hand? Oh it's got some weird thing growing on it, but it doesn't hurt. Aunty Liz you know that cop who's been helping me? Do you think she could join us?*"

"I dunno dear, that's up to Dr P. He's the boss."

"*But she's a cop! We need a cop who knows about police stuff. Grandpop used to say that heaps.*"

"Did he?"

"*Yeah.*"

"Well it's still up to Dr P and he's ... well he's been a bit sick."

"*Is he OK?*" I ask, feeling guilty. "*Is Dr Morozov worried?*"

"No, it's OK. Her problem is more Irina being a monkey."

"*Aunty Liz I'd really like you to meet Sue.*"

"I'd like that too Sam. But we're busy at the moment."

"*But I've got to land somewhere on Earth and someone has to meet me.*"

"You're coming here to get a new suit first, Sam. Then, when you ditch Ka-rea-rea, you can bend here and join us."

"*But what about Sue?*"

"Hekator will bring her directly."

"*Oh,*" I said feeling a bit of a doofus.

"*Was anyone going to tell me this?*"

"Hekator's going to give you some instructions but there's a surprise party for you. I'm telling you so you don't ruin it by going off and doing something else."

"*Oh, OK. Who's coming?*"

"That's the surprise. Anyway you still have to ditch Ka-rea-rea somewhere."

"*Yeah.*"

"What's the matter sweetheart?"

"*Do you think I should buy Sue a house?*"

"*What?* No!" she says.

"*Why not?*"

"Sam you don't know where you will be. You don't need a house. You have to be able to let Sue go if she wants to dear. She's not a bug you can put in a jar."

"*What about buying Ed a boat. I was thinking of trying to land back home.*"

"Sam, you don't need to buy *him* anything. He ratted dad out."

"*But aren't they looking after Grandpop's house?*"

"They're meant to be. But they're not doing it very well."

"*So I shouldn't buy them anything?*"

"No. What for?"

"*I just keep wondering what I'm meant to do with all the money.*"

"You just wait ten years Sam Kahu. You'll find something."

Ten years! I can't wait ten years! Even one year was like, forever.

"*Aunty Liz, Sue thinks we're stuck with Dr Prosperov and we can never leave. Is that true?"*

"We can give a month's notice."

"Yeah but ... they'd erase our memories."

"Sam why would we want to leave? Wait til you see the new place. It's kaa-pai. Even nicer than Renwick. And your Grandfather's finally got a boat. He's happy as a pig in poop."

"Are you happy Aunty Liz?" I tried to keep it light but the worry may have come through.

"Sam! Of course I am. Don't worry about me boy. It's happy families here, one big happy wha-nau. But all I need is for my brave Sammy to come home. So give those aliens heaps. After making us burn down our house and all dad's old stuff too you make them suffer. Then come join the party."

"Aw Auntee," I grin. She makes it sound like a game I'm playing, but I also know she means it.

"See you soon, son."

"Seeya Aunty Liz."

Aunty Liz disconnects. Sue's grinning at me.

"What?"

"See Sam! Now *that's* real. All that 'Oh, I'm so rich I think I'll buy that man a yacht,' bullshit you were spinning me. And 'I found a sad puppy policewoman in the psych ward, can I keep her?'"

I go a bit red but I laugh.

"And your Aunt isn't some sad old prune, like the way you tell it. She sounds like she's having a good time. Now that's what I want to hear about. Anyway it sounds like I will finally get to meet Dr Prosperov and frankly after all this boredom, he owes me. So relax. What happens, happens OK? I'm going for a swim."

I feel a bit funny about all that. Here's me up to my neck in intense adult stuff but to be honest I really don't understand adults. I start thinking they have a totally different way of thinking about time to me and the others. Then Hekator bursts back into my thoughts.

"Sam, I think for this next stage I'd like you to manage Ka-rea-rea's escape from the new base. You may need to use your new suit."

"But I haven't been in quarantine long enough. Have I?"

"Not for Fae but you're cleared to visit your new base and get into your new suit. Then you bend to Ka-rea-rea's landing point so you can pretend to get out of him when he arrives."

"But I thought the suit couldn't match my Australian clothes I was wearing."

"It wouldn't have fooled Von Streicher in the same room but from space, they won't notice anything."

"So where do I go after I leave Ka-rea-rea? I mean in the story we're telling."

"You go back to Sue."

"But she isn't there."

"No but she will be. In the story you've been hiding out somewhere."

"Why?"

"To hide from Rocelli. Sir Michael had discovered your new safe house and you wanted Sue safe, remember?"

"Did I?" I ask. I'm getting a bit confused.

"Yes, you actually did Sam. You have been hiding as you would have. OK, it's a bit further away than if you were just driving one of your cars, but you needed to hide. And after Rocelli's attack we wanted to take you both in."

"*Aww yeah.*" I remember.

"*Go back through the scanners to the medical box. It'll remove that dressing as well.*"

"*Why do I need an exit scan?*"

"*It's to compare with the entrance scan to make sure you have nothing growing in you.*"

I open my eyes. The angel-like Fae is waiting. But first I call over to Sue.

"I gotta go. Hekator will be taking you home to your place soon. Then I guess you'll get to meet Dr P. I'll see you in a while."

"Oh, OK," Sue replies. She's happy to be going home.

"See ya!"

"See ya. Give those Discovery Channel aliens hell!" she grins, and dives under.

I follow the 'angel' back to the waterfalls, scanners and stuff. I have to get undressed again but that doesn't bother me around the Fae. It's sort of like they don't count. I get into the pod naked and it feels much better than last time. I just hope there won't be a big welcoming committee at this new base.

I'm kind of excited to be finally arriving at the new base. I wonder a bit what it will be like. I've just got comfy when time seems to slow down, and the colour seems to drain out of everything. My whole field of view folds up and distorts and I have to close my eyes. I'm falling back, unable to move. Falling and spinning. Suddenly, I stop falling back and start falling forward. There's brilliant light all around me. Brilliant light and presences. My mother and my Grandmother. Dozens of people surround me, and slowly begin to fade.

[+]

I open my eyes. My casket is in a small lightning storm inside a shower cabinet. Everything glows, crackles and sparks and then falls still. Suddenly water blasts, followed by a thin blast of air which dries it. The door to the shower cabinet slides upwards quickly.

I look around the six sided room hoping like hell everyone isn't about to jump out and yell "surprise" while I've got no clothes on but everything is quiet. In the middle of the room Gunter is sitting in a cool-looking, wrap-around, white chair surrounded by a transparent screen projected on thin air like a half sphere about him. Around him are some white cube seat-islands. Lazily Gunter gets up and takes a bathrobe from one seat and comes over the casket. He puts it on the outside and then returns to his desk. As he walks away I open the casket and swipe the bathrobe Gunter has left. I put it on noticing the Fae dressing on my wrist has fallen off leaving my skin sensitive and red but mostly healed. Then I head over to Gunter's desk where he's busy watching something.

"What's with the lightning storm?" I ask casually.

"Improved design over der oil tank. If a suit or bag iz bugged zer tag is destroyed on arrival. Much more secure. Come," he says, and gets up.

I follow after Gunter, admiring the gray colour scheme. It seems very serious. We go to a series of poles about as thick as two fists. At the base are white discs. Most of the discs are about a meter wide and two centimeters thick but two are twice that size. Above are holes in the ceiling.

"You stand on zhem und zhey go up like mini lifts," Gunter tells me waving me on with a hand.

I stand on one. Nothing happens.

"You haf to hold the pole," Gunter explains grabbing his. He starts to rise. I copy him and my disc begins to rise too.

"You guyz can slide down zhem like firemen too," Gunter says from his disc.

We pass up through the floor which is about ten centimeters thick.

"Hold on. We keep going up," he tells me.

The floor we pass through is another six sided room. There are four holodecks around the far walls with seats in the middle of the floor.

"We can run four simultaneous briefings now," Gunter points out as we pass up through another floor.

There's a wall with nine holes and nine slides facing me and two entrances on the left and right. The left side is painted blue, the right side pink.

"This is the changer. You'll find it the same."

He hops off the moving disc and I do the same.

"Where are the others?"

"Tryink to find para.no.ID."

"Oh?"

"Yeah, zhey are right in za shit."

"OK."

I pop into the changing room. Tarik and Scotty's clothes are hanging up. I miss them. I slip off the robe again and hop, naked, into the changer.

Gunter is right. The changer is exactly the same. It's comforting to feel the suit attach itself to my body again. It makes me feel so much more protected. At the end I'm shoved out the slot and down the slide. Gunter is waiting for me.

"Za suit is qvite different to your old vun," he says, helping me up and leading me back to the pole lifts.

"As you can see it is zinner and zhere is no schulebag. Za top can hang down from the belt to your thigh or mid calf. You can pull the hood off your head but it seals as normal for bending. When it seals it scans your head for tags."

"Za powerpack is completely new. Zis is why it took so long. It is like your old speeder. It's smaller but also less stable. It uses an antigravity field from the belt and feet instead of gravity deflection so zhere iz no annoying glow. Problem is you experience matter repulsion *inzide* your body so you feel a bit zick ven it is on. Best not to try it after eating like Tarik did. Also zhe field is easily detected by ze Administration so no flying if zhey are around. Za wings are bigger and quieter and zhere are only two – attached at the shoulder blade. Ze uzzers say bend-diving is much, much easier."

"Protection is pretty much za same. Weapons za same, maps and vision za same. The interface is from your old suit. Same diving capability but a bit faster because less drag. You now have varp invisibility as vell – only any use at long range remember. Two extra features: ze index finger squirts a trace glue which contains nanowires so we can track anyzing anywhere and zere is a rear facing eye on hood. Zere is alzo a pszychic counter-shield better zhan ze portable vun zhat burned you. Only problem is you can't use it *and* bend or communicate. It alzo stops your power generation. If you use it Control vill alert eferyone."

"Zis suit can change shape more so you can change clothing styles. You won't all look like schoolkids wherever you go. It allows you to wear suits inside your new speeders which was the main requirement of the design. Anuzzer important feature is lots of pockets and it reminds you what's in zem."

"Finally zis suit grows to fit you. You will never need anuzzer. It is Lana's last creation so we call zem 'Lana's after her.'"

That made me a bit sad.

"Are we having a funeral for her?"

"Ja, a vake in fact."

There's a loud cry from above.

"Sam!"

Rewa flings herself on a pole and slides straight down like she had been sliding down poles all her life. It's one hug I definitely needed!

"Ow you're crushing me," she complains but she's still smiling. I stop crushing her but it's hard to let go. She doesn't seem to want to stop either. Finally we pull apart.

"I had to come see you before you go. I've really missed you big brother."

"I've missed you too sis."

And it was true too, but not in any soppy way. I missed her because she was part of my heart and when she wasn't around I just felt I wasn't at home.

"I'll be back soon," I tell her.

"You better be. Or Mariko said she will hunt you down," she laughs.

"Zat iz no joke," Gunter says, looking worried.

Gunter comes with me. I slide down the pole but he takes a disc. The suit is exactly like my old one to use, but it feels different: lighter and more flexible. We go up to the Control desk.

I have to look like I'm wearing the clothes Sir Michael saw me wearing when I left for Liechtenstein to keep up the story that I'd been stuck in Ka-rea-rea on the moon. As Hekator had said the clothes didn't have to look perfect because *they* would only be watching from space. It was tricky adjusting everything but I think we got it close enough.

"Ready?" Gunter asks.

"Yeah. Where am I going?"

"I don't know. Vere do you want to land Ka-rea-rea?"

"It's got to be under something. So they can't see me appear next to him."

"Right. Somevere vere za bending flash is hidden. Lets haf a look at ze CBD."

The big view projected on nothing comes up looking down on downtown Auckland as if from a helicopter.

"The underground carpark by the town hall?" I suggest pointing at it.

"You von't be able to fly in during za day and it's not open at night. Here...zis is vat you vant. A hotel parking level. Lots of exits into the malls below, fly in after midnight, exit later," Gunter says.

"Perfect. But what's the time?" I ask.

"It's ... vell, it's vun in za afternoon."

"That's a lot of time to wait. I'm going to have to find some other places to visit before I drop Ka-rea-rea. What about my home village?"

Control brought up the village. It was strange looking down on a place I still knew so well. The display was so perfect you felt like you could reach out and touch it. It felt a bit like being God.

But where could I land and bend in? I look at the bush behind Grandpop's house. It looks dark enough.

"Hey Gunter, let's see if I can bend behind Grandpop's old house without too much flash. Sort of there," I suggest, pointing.

The view I had zooms in on where I pointed and fills the whole screen. Then we zoom through the tree canopy and it takes me a little while to work out where we are. There's no-one there so I wonder if we can test the bend a bit better.

"Let's check it out," I suggest. "Watch from above and see if you spot the flash."

"OK."

I go to the cabinet, noticing the Fae casket has gone, step in and seal my facescreen. Then I fold away into nothing and appear in a blaze of light.

[+]

"*How was that?*" I ask, settling down at the foot of a small tree.

"Bad news Sam. Ve saw it clearly. A bright flash in zer dark. But Sam I zink it would be easier if you vait zere and bring Ka-rea-rea to you. Zey haf no idea where you vill choose to land zo zey can't bc watching now. Zey will only be able to vatch once you tell zem vere you want to go."

I thought about it.

"*OK, makes sense. I'll find somewhere to hide here.*"

It feels strange to be back here in this place where I'd played as a little kid for so long. The smells of rotting leaves, sound of water and chirp of the little pi-waka-waka or fantails seem both familiar and strange because of what I'm doing there now. I switch on my suit's blend invisibility and find a comfy bit of creek bed the right size for me to lie in, so that Ka-rea-rea can span the depression and land just over me. I'm completely invisible here. Anyone passing wouldn't notice me until they stepped on me.

"*How long do I have to wait?*" I ask Gunter.

"*Fifteen minutes Sam. It's time to link,*" Hekator interrupts, coming in again.

"*OK.*"

I reconnect with Karearea and the big empty silo. I lie in the
creek, water flowing around me, hearing the sounds of birds
in the bush, and smelling the earth while seeing that dull
bare room. It's strangely restful. But after a while I can't help
thinking that if I had not found Scotty and Ashley in the vault at
Renwick I might really be in Ka-rea-rea inside that awful blast
chamber facing the very scary idea of killing myself. It's an idea
that sits in my stomach making me feel a bit sick and weird.
It's like thinking about my end in a place that is my beginning.
I start to think about my life and realise how young I am. Apart
from the past two years I hadn't done anything much at all and
there was still so much I wanted to do.
I think about Emma and realise how much I want her in my
future. I wonder whether I've really been such a good brother to
Rewa. And I can't help thinking how unfair it would be for me to
die on the moon, miles from my family, all alone and forgotten
by everyone.
It kind of makes me a little angry.
The more I watch the clock ticking away toward the time
when I'd told them I would be forced to kill myself the more
I'm confronted with the question of what I'd really do if I was
waiting to blow myself up, all alone and forgotten.
I pick out the track I'd listened to so many times when I was
flying Ka-rea-rea. It was good for speed. I lift Ka-rea-rea up as
it begins and I blast it out into the empty silo. Then at minus
three minutes thirty seconds I go inertialess and begin to fly Ka-
rea-rea around the inside of the small silo, picking up speed and
preparing to expose the antimatter core as the song ends. If they
want a fifty megatonne bang I will give them one!
Even though I'm really lying in a creek, in the bush I find myself

heading for a very dark place in my soul. Anger, self pity and a desire to lash out combine with a rush toward doom. A will to bring down all those who oppose me.

"Maté (death)," the dark whisper echoes in my brain. I can smell blood, and something deep in my soul feels warm and excited at the idea, like some wolf or something is suddenly licking its chops next to me. I'm so startled by how close this feels I shake my head back under my tree to clear my mind.

The death spiral gets faster and faster so that by two minutes Ka-rea-rea is a whirl of sound and light. The acoustics of the song are dreadful. It just sounds like a jumbled mess. A rage. But I figure if I really was getting set to blow up, I don't think I'd care. Then at minus one minute the silo goes dark and the three holograms reappear.

I keep going. To hell with them. I'm in no mood to stop now. They may have been saying something but I'm not listening.

At minus forty five seconds the exit doors start opening. I begin to slow down but the countdown on Ka-rea-rea's continues. At minus thirty seconds the tunnel is completely open. By minus twenty five seconds I make my last turn and return to face the holograms. I quieten the music as it ends but the countdown continues.

The Commander address me.

"*We agree to your plan. We will mark your craft and let you return to Earth,*" it tells me without any sign of emotion.

I let the countdown run and wait for the fifteen second mark.

"I want to be returned the way I left. Inside a Scout with Inspector Du Croix. You have 12 seconds," I demand.

They glance at each other, silently conferring with ten seconds to go.

"*Agreed,*" the Commander says.

I stop the clock. It shows minus six seconds.

Even though I was on Earth and could still hear the water and birds my breathing was hard, my heart was pounding, and I was sweating heavily. Before they change their minds I turn and fly Ka-rea-rea quickly through the tunnel. I keep thinking they're going to close it but instead they open the elevator doors for me and in I go.

I have a weird feeling of being above everything. I'm so pleased to be alive (even though I was never really at risk) and I'm genuinely happy not to have had to blow up Ka-rea-rea. Unfortunately the lift trip strips me of that. I wait tensely for half a minute and then other doors open and I'm in the corridor which leads back to the hangar. A saucer is waiting for me. Everything looks good except I can't see Du Croix anywhere. They have given me everything I'd asked for except the crucial hostage. I realise this is kind of tricky.

I had threatened to blow myself up, but now I obviously want to survive. Would they risk trying pink light on me now on the assumption I had deactivated the automatic destruction system? It was a fair bet they might try. Another danger was they might do it by taking me into deep space in the scout where an explosion would not cost them much.

I fly past the saucer and out onto the main runway. There are dozens of hangars feeding off of it. I fly into the middle and sit myself down and restart the time with half an hour to run.

In no time a mean-as triangular black-gray Service fighter is hovering over me, its lower dome glowing with a brilliant white-pink light primed to blast me to bits. I reset the clock to 15 minutes to run but it doesn't move an inch. I reset Ka-rea-rea's containment field just in case he really is planning to blast me. Weirdly, though I'm still hiding in the bush, I actually feel a bit scared. I don't know why. I didn't know what would happen if I blew up the Administration's main base on Earth but I couldn't see how it could be good. They would be pissed off and come looking for us. Then a blast of static and ...

"Intruder, return immediately to the designated carriage Scout," the fighter demands using a simple analog AM stereo radio signal. The electronic voice is deliberately harsh and intimidating. But I respond as well as I can.

"I will detonate this craft in 14 minutes and sixteen seconds unless Inspector Du Croix accompanies me on the scout."

"Inspector Du Croix is waiting for you aboard the craft," it informs me.

What a megadoofus!

So feeling like a total turkey I return to the scout to find Du Croix, with a wry smile, hands in the pockets of his camel hair coat, waiting outside. We are loaded into the craft the same way I was unloaded.

Du Croix has been given a reclining chair and sits in it like someone doing something very boring.

"Av you decided where we are taking you?" he asks with someone certain that I have.

"I want to go back to the Hokianga. In Northland, New Zealand. Back to where I'm from."

"Pilot. Please take us to zhat place, wherever it is."

Somewhere on a mezzanine above us in the bright light some little gray guys are piloting us out onto the runway and out the door.

There's a pause which lasts some time. No one says anything.

"I've got you leaving the darkside base. I'm watching for a fighter escort," Hekator tells me. I'm so concentrated on Ka-rea-rea that his voice helps to remind me I am not really on the scout UFO at all, but in Northland already.

"Yes. A fighter has left, trailing the scout."

"Bastards. Thanks Hekator."

The silence continues in the saucer. Du Croix doesn't seem to be all that chatty, which feels awkward. After five minutes I decide to ask him something.

"What will happen to the Archdeacon Oswald?" I ask.

"Ee will be examined," Du Croix says. The words imply a form of questioning coupled with intrusive medical work on his brain.

"What does that mean?"

"It means we want to know zhe extent of zhe conspiracy."

"So you are moving against the Bruderschaft gang?"

"It is not so much a gang as a group of fanatical antisynthetics. Zhey 'av a strong ideology."

"More than that," I say almost to myself.

"'Ow do you mean? 'More zhan zhat'?"

"They have heavy duty spiritual support."

"Ah yes. You are, of course, a fellow believer."

"I've seen it. I've been burnt with it. I'm scared and creeped out by it. I wouldn't underestimate it."

"I would not overestimate it eizzer. Zhey are no match for us."

I start to understand. He knew about them already.

"So you played us off against them?"

"Of course. You enlisted ze Administration for your own objectives to break up ze Bruderschaft bloodbath in Elan. In revenge zey helped locate you and enlisted me to try and capture you two weeks ago. In both cases my objectives are achieved and for zhe moment zer Fae insurgency is suppressed."

"For the moment?"

"Yes. As zhou said, the Fae will return. You will return. We do not yet know what your objectives are but we will find them."

"So you knew the Archdeacon was a traitor?"

"I strongly suspected it. But it does not do to level accusations against an Archdeacon. Who am I? Just a simple policeman. I needed a Service senior commander to be present and I needed someone else to make ze accusation. Preferably someone who 'ad nozzing much to do with me. Who better zhan you?"

"But I'm an enemy! Of course I may try to ruin your operation."

"Which iz what 'e said. But zere were two problems. First, you ad nuzzing to gain. Second, 'e could 'ardly refuse an investigation. And by now I knew where to look. So zanks to you and your friends I av arrested some traitors and stopped a conspiracy and interrupted your insurgency all at very little cost. I use your opposing forces to find balance. In zat way I do not need to exert myself."

"You must have been wetting yourself that I would blow up your moonbase."

Du Croix chuckled.

"Zhe Commanders are convinced you are inside zhat thing Sam. It's the only way they can understand it. If zhey had a drone inside an enemy base zhey would blow it up. It is a simple military calculation. But me, I am different. You want to convince us zhe Fae are gone. That simply confirms to me zhey are already back."

I think for a second.

"Well, I'm not going to make it easy for you now and get out just to prove you wrong."

"No, no, of course not. Besides when we recover zhis craft and it explodes zhey will imagine you 'av booby trapped it when you left."

"So they expect me to booby trap it?"

"I 'av suggested it to avoid calling zhem fools for believing you are inside. Zhat is not a sensible thing to call a Service section commander."

"So if I'm not in here why do you think I didn't detonate it?"

"You want to destroy zhe Bruderschaft but you don't want to arouse the Center. That is not in your interests. It is simply rational."

I can't help being amazed how easily he second guesses us. I decide to shock him.

"By your reckoning I should kill you now for being so clever."

"But you won't."

"Why not?"

"Because I am useful to you."

"Or I'm in the box."

Du Croix chuckles again and shrugs.

"Or you av been in a little box injured and hungry for 26 plus 'ours and to track you will be very easy. No need for a blood 'ound you would smell disgusting," he laughs.

"Tell me about it," I reply wryly.

"But seriously Sam I am sure Dr Prosperov will return if 'e 'asn't already. It may be that a dialogue would not 'urt. Tell Dr Prosperov this when you see 'im."

"And you won't try and catch us?"

"Zat I cannot promise. We will always try to capture the Fae insurgency."

"Why?"

Du Croix shrugs.

"Because we are at war."

"What about?"

"Control. All wars are about control."

"That isn't much of a reason."

"But Sam you are a rebel, you resist control. I am a policeman. I bring control. It is an eternal struggle between chaos and order. You are chaos, I am order. Zhey are mutually exclusive but both 'av zere benefits. Too much chaos and zere is anarchy. Too much order and zere is oppression. Unlike some of my colleagues I take the view zat some chaos is natural and acceptable. My duty is to maintain a workable level of order. Zis may involve some negotiation with ze sources of disorder. So I invite Dr Prosperov to contact me. Will I try and trap 'im? Of course. 'e would be foolish to think otherwise. But is the dialog worth the risk given Interpol's primitive security? *I* think so," he says.

There's a long pause while I think about that. I find his way of thinking strange. He isn't especially interested in winning or losing. All he is concerned about is keeping his work manageable, like mowing the lawn or something. He doesn't want to do too much work but he doesn't want the neighbours on his back either.

Finally he inclines his head, receiving something.

"We are approaching your homeland. We will be zere in a few minutes. It is time to affix the tag."

He reaches into his pocket and pulls out something that looks like a bandage. Then he leans forward, peels the back and rubs it on.

"Do you think that fighter is in range?" I ask Hekator.

115

"I can't tell Sam. I daren't get too close or the wormhole field will be detected and give us away."

Meanwhile Du Croix is talking.

"So Sam. It is time for us to part. We are fifty kilometers up and about two hundred kilometers away from you destination. It is …" he looks at his watch.

"One seventeen in the afternoon, local time. I shall now move aside to open the lower dock. You will proceed down to the airlock and then exit the craft. I must say zank you for your assistance, adieu and bon chance."

And with a smile he slides rapidly aside. The round hole like a camera iris opens suddenly beneath me. Ka-rea-rea falls into a round, white walled space as the iris above closes quickly. Then the second iris, below opens. Kar-rea-rea stops us falling.

We are still inside the saucer fifty kilometers over northern New Zealand. Stretched out below it looks like a perfect satellite picture in a blue sea. I'm still wondering if the fighter will "bounce" me as soon as we exit. I decide to take evasive action immediately.

"Ka-rea-rea, on 'go', drop ten kilometers, go inertialess, random evade pattern, half second phases. OK?"

"Yes Sam."

"Go!"

CHAPTER SIXTY TWO: THE LANDLORD

Ka-rea-rea drops for one second, and begins moving like a little kid drawing fire on a sheet of paper. Every half second Ka-rea-rea randomly changes direction, moving so fast it would have been almost impossible to follow.

Once we've dropped out, the scout goes inertialess too, and disappears at high speed into space. Ka-rea-rea continues whizzing about like a demented bee, or sped-up butterfly, heading toward the ground. If the fighter is there I can't see it, but I'm not taking any chances. Ka-rea-rea is very vulnerable with a tag on him.

I'm making it a bit hard for a fighter, but one could still easily zip up and blast me safe in the knowledge that blowing myself up deliberately is not really option. Not if I didn't want set off a fifty megatonne explosion over little old, nuclear-free New Zealand.

Ka-rea-rea continues the random manoeuvring for another minute but with no sign of fighters I decide to stop and drop instead. So we drop from forty kilometers to one kilometer in under a minute. The distant coastline below zooms up very, very fast and suddenly I'm just hovering over the sea, slightly off the coast, at three thousand feet.

I switch off inertialess and switch on invisibility and zip over

the sea, through the heads, and into Hokianga harbour in two
minutes and twenty seconds.

I stop Ka-rea-rea dead still in the sky, hovering one klick above
my old home town. I still wonder if *they* are keeping an eye on
me.

"*Any sign of the fighter?*" I ask Hekator.

"*No fighter but there's a surveyor one hundred kilometers
above. I think its been put there to keep an eye on you.*"

The cylindrical survey ships are not especially dangerous
but from one hundred kilometers above me they can still see
everything. They don't have the wormhole viewing capability
Control has, but they can scan and magnify in three dimensions.
They can even eavesdrop through windows and off hard
surfaces. I have to be careful. A wrong move now and they would
realise I was never in Ka-rea-rea.

"*If I landed Ka-rea-rea upside down on top of me. Could you
bend a water bomb inside him?*" I ask.

"*A water bomb?*" Hekator asks, confused.

"*A bag of water.*"

"*What for?*"

"*To make it look like I couldn't hold on.*"

Hekator chuckles.

"*Oh! Might be a bit detailed. Especially if it's upside down.
Under trees I don't think they will even be able to see it.*"

"*OK, well, I'll bring him down then.*"

I fly Ka-rea-rea in quite fast, still under warp invisibility field.
That wasn't for the surveyor, of course. *They* knew exactly where
Ka-rea-rea was because of the tag, but a flying box would attract
my old neighbours attention.

I slow him over the bush behind Grandpop's old house and then thread him slowly through a gap in the trees, around and down to settle over the creek where I'm waiting for him.

It feels funny trying to see myself with Ka-rea-rea's sensors. With adaptive camouflage I am incredibly well hidden and I almost missed myself. It was also strange to land over myself because I was seeing from one point of view and felt the box turn upside down and press down over me from another.

I land Ka-rea-rea so that he straddles over me in the creek so that his hatch could open into it. Then I switch off invisibility and have him adopt the look of a log some kid had put there like a bridge. Underneath, I adjust my suit to match the clothes I wore at Auckland airport in front of Sir Michael. The trick to the next bit is to move fast.

I open the hatch on Ka-rea-rea and then roll out from under him as if I'd fallen out. I act holding my hand which isn't hard as it does still sting. Then I sit down at the foot of a tree, just to catch up for a moment. I stay there for a while thinking about the situation.

In theory I'd be wet and a bit smelly. I'd need new clothes. As far as I know all my old clothes are still in my old drawers in our old room at Grandpop's place. I stand up and walk unsteadily back towards Grandpop's old house.

It feels very weird walking back through this extremely familiar bit of bush. It's half past one on Wednesday afternoon back home where I come from. A week ago I'd been in Kevin's car heading toward the Moore's place. Since then I'd flown to Queensland, flown Sue's car around Auckland at night, stayed at the Hotel with Leonora, escaped with Sue to Caz and Julia's, stayed in an alien quarantine station in some distant part of the galaxy, been to Liechtenstein, and negotiated a fake escape from aliens on the moon. It was crazy!

Knowing all this, and coming to the lawn at the back of what still feels like my *real* home, makes me think how insane everything has become since I'd left it. The old house looks like a refuge from this weird world I'd fallen into ever since they'd let Ax out of prison. It seems like a rock of normality in a sea of weirdness – a simple childhood, like my old friends still have.

I stand under the trees, sheltering from the view of the surveyor above me in space, just looking at it. I can't tell if anyone is inside or not. I decide that, in the end I don't have any choice now anyway. I have to go in. I'm committed.

I dash across the back lawn to the back door. The back door window is broken for some reason so I can unlatch the door. I reach in and open it and step inside.

The place smells bad. Beer, cigarettes, dope, everything that reminds me of my father. And something else. I wasn't sure what. It gave me a bad, bad feeling. I feel like I'm small again. I had sorted out my feelings for Ax but to realise that nothing has really changed in the rest of the world and that made me feel I was right back where I had started.

I head down the hall and look into our old room. The place is a shocking mess. It's like a nest. There's a double mattress on the floor covered in quilts, sheets and clothes. Empty bottles around that. It stinks of cigarettes. I go in looking for some sign I'd ever lived here.

There are a few. Old marks I'd made. A little drawing Rewa had done on the wallpaper. But it was all swamped by the pigs who lived there now. Any sense of my childhood had been crapped on by people who just didn't care about ... well, anything by the look of it.

My old drawers are still there, and surprisingly, my clothes are still in them too. Untouched. I pull out an old hoody and track pants. Too small for me now, but I copy them onto my suit. Grandpop and Aunty Liz's old rooms are just as messed up. It's hard to tell if people sleep there, or if they just dump things.

The living room has obviously become party central, and nobody ever cleaned it. The stench of cigarettes, beer and dak is overwhelming. The kitchen, and dining room, up the front, are full of unwashed things.

Nana stands in the passage looking sad. I walk back down toward her. She waits at the end, looking back at me, disappointed. I whisper a "sorry" to her, even though it isn't my fault, and she fades.

The bathroom is the most changed. For a start the bath has gone. In its place is a whole lot of chemical lab equipment, and a portable electric cooker. There're plastic measuring jars and pots as well.

"Sam, don't open your hood. It iz a meth lab und probably contaminated," Gunter warns, quietly.

I knew that already. Grandpop is going to be highly pissed off. Still, there's nothing I can do about it, so I decide to pretend to clean Ka-rea-rea instead.

I go back to the outdoor laundry. It seems a junk pile but I find a bucket and brush. I fill the bucket, and carry it back, slopping water on me, to Ka-rea-rea in the bush.

I set about pretending to clean Ka-rea-rea. It makes sense to do it upside down. I do that for about quarter of an hour thinking about Grandpop's house. My refuge from my father's world. Now polluted by the same people and the same things. It's like everything I had learned, everything even Ax had learned before he died, had been in vain. These people simply didn't respect anything. Not themselves, not anyone else, not anything.

I think about all the cleaning I've done at Renwick and what it means to clean or not clean. Grandpop had always cleaned. His boat and gear; his gun. Aunty Liz cleaned. We kids cleaned too. It meant something. It meant being organised. It meant self-respect. It meant … something. Something about … just not being a slob.

The anger in me was almost beyond my own ability to understand it. Anger that, after all I had been through, here I was back again. Back at my beginning.

"He mea hanga: (This is how is it made):
Ko Papatuanuku te paparahi (The earth is the floor)
Ko nga maunga nga poupou (The mountains are the supports);
Ko te rangi e titiro Ihi nei te tuanui.
(The sky we see above is the roof)"

Finally I stop and stand back. I've been cleaning Ka-rea-rea even though he didn't need it. I tell him to camouflage himself again, close him up and then roll him over the creek.

It's 2:57 p.m. School is nearly finished. I decide to see how things are here now, starting off with Joey and Annie at Ed and Jackie's place next door. I would wait for them on Grandpop's veranda like I had when I'd been sick and had to stay home from school. If I was lucky the slobs who had wrecked Grandpop's house wouldn't be home soon. I walk back to the path and go around to the front and find a not-so-busted chair to sit on. So I sit and I wait.

It's so restful to sit here, listening to the sea and the gulls, watching the light in the trees. It's weird and amazing. Here I am, sitting on a veranda, supposedly just having escaped death on the moon, knowing the alien surveyor is watching a hundred kilometers above, knowing Jackie will be home soon from her job at the school. It sort of made me feel spaced-out.

I make myself comfortable and sit back in Grandpop's old chair. If I'd had his old hat I would have put it over my face the way he used to. Instead I just seal my facescreen and tint it dark. It's nice to lie here with all the familiar sounds around me.

Slowly the spirit of the place seeps into me. It's like a dream from Grandpop's mind, years and years ago ... Nana's in the kitchen, cooking. The girls are playing out the back, by the creek. That little Alan Stephens kid is around again. Such a serious kid. No wonder given what a hopeless family he was from. His mother probably had a client with her. Oh well, gives the kid a chance to get away.

Suddenly Jackie's car arrives next door, rousing me as she pulls into their gravel driveway which runs along their fence. I wake up, and shake my head, peeling back the face screen.

Then I sit up, and watch them. Jackie glances over briefly but doesn't look closely. She grabs her bag, and gets out, calling to the kids to hurry. Annie's in the back. She's taller now, with long skinny legs. She gets out and follows her mum. It's Joey, in his new uniform, who looks over at me, looks away, and then does a double take.

"*Sam?*" he calls.

I grin. It feels like old times. I almost feel a bit teary to see him again.

"Hi Joe. How's things?" I call.

Jackie comes back from the door.

"Sam you better get over here quick!" she calls, anxiously.

"Why?"

"That's the gang house now!"

I get up and walk slowly over toward the fence.

"Sam, come on, quick," Jackie says, glancing fearfully at the road.

I just walk. Joe's standing on the bottom rail of the old gray fence. It's about 1.5 meters tall but by standing on the bottom rail he can see over.

"What are you doing here? Is your Grandpop with you?"

"No."

Jackie looks over with a puzzled look on her face.

"Sam? Are you OK? Wasn't there a fire at that place you were living at? Where's your Aunty Liz?"

"Not sure exactly," I admit vaguely. "I just came to see how you guys are."

Jackie seems to think there's something wrong with me.

"Sam come inside. Have you had anything to eat?"

Actually, not since my Fae breakfast with Sue and I'm hungry.

"No ... I forgot," I say.

"Come over, I'll make you a sandwich," Jackie offers, bribing me away from the old house.

"OK. Thanks."

I go up to the fence and jump over it with one arm.

"Woah!" Joey says, hands to his head, "where did you learn to do that!"

I shrug.

"Where I was living."

We go inside. It's mostly the same as ever. It feels as comfortable as an old shoe. Annie comes out to see me with a question.

"Where's Rewa?"

"With Aunty Liz," I tell her.

"Where's she?" she persists.

"Somewhere safe."

"Where's that?"

"I don't know exactly," I admit.

"How did you get here?"

"Um ..."

I have to think about that. I decide to mention Sue. It seems to make sense. We might have come north to hide her or something. Jackie is listening in to Annie's questions.

"A friend brought me."

"Who?"

"Sue."

"Who's Sue?"

"My friend."

"Is she, like a warden or something?" Joey asks, thinking of Maori wardens.

Jackie comes over with some sandwiches and juice for us.

"No. Sue's a cop."

"Uh ... OK. Where is she?" Joey asks.

"She's ... having a nap."

Jackie's hovering.

"So Sam, the TV news said that everyone was missing after that fire. Have they been found?"

I have to remember *they* are probably listening in.

"No. But they're alive. They just took off somewhere."

"Without you?"

"I didn't want to go."

"But how did the fire start."

"I dunno. But they'll be really pissed off about it when they come back."

"So where are you living now?"

I start to laugh. I feel so bewildered by everything I find it genuinely funny. Maybe the stress is getting to me.

"Sam? What's so funny?"

"Your question. Where do I live? You know, I really don't know. I've been in so many places since the fire. It's getting a bit confusing. I don't even really know where I'm sleeping tonight!"

"Here, of course, dumkopf," Gunter says, gently.

"I still don't know where that is," I reply.

I stop. Everyone's staring at me. Oops! I spoke my thoughts! For a second I'm embarrassed and then it comes to me.

"Nana watches me," I explain to them.

A cold shiver goes around the room. They may think I'm crazy but they've seen me talk to ghosts before, and it scares them. Jackie changes the subject.

"So where is this cop, this Sue Williams then?" she asks.

"Sue? Ah ... I don't know exactly right now... Somewhere ... around," I say vaguely

"Sam, are you sure you're alright? Were you inside your Grandpop's old house?" Jackie asks.

"Yeah. What a dump. Who did that?"

"It's Jason Kingi," Annie jumps in. "He was number two to your dad. Now he's number one."

"Number one what? Pig?"

Annie laughs. Joey doesn't. He just looks annoyed. Jackie looks worried.

"He's even bigger than your dad used to be. And those guys Wiri and John are serious muss as well," Joey tells me.

"Serious wuss more like it. Scared of a vacuum cleaner and dishwashing liquid," I laugh.

Annie thinks this is hysterical. Even Joe cracks a smile. But Jackie is still serious.

"So what have you been doing all these years Sam. What was going on at that place you lived at?" Jackie wants to know.

"Me? Oh. I've been cleaning."

Annie thinks this is funny, but Joe is confused.

"Cleaning?"

"Cleaning Renwick house. I've been cleaning it. It was pretty big ... they paid me. And the others. They paid us to clean it."

"Seriously?"

"Yeah. Seriously. Vacuuming and brass was my job. Me and Tahira."

"Who's Tahira?" Jackie asks.

"My buddy. For cleaning and stuff."

"Did you go to school?" she checks.

"Course."

"And were they into flying saucers?"

"Uhh ... Well sorta."

"What do you mean 'sorta'?"

"Well, some more than others."

Jackie sighs.

"I see."

She didn't, but that didn't matter.

"Hey mum, can we play on the Wii?" Joey asks.

"Why don't we go outside?" I say. "This place is fantastic."

"Sure you can," Jackie tells Joey, ignoring me.

She seemed to prefer to have Joey inside and in sight. That was different too.

"C'mon Sam," Joe says.

He goes over to the screen and switches it on. I wasn't really into games. Tarik had had a Wii but I never used it. I didn't know how to work it. We play for a while but I was more interested in catching up.

"So how's Clive?" I ask.

"He's alright," Joey says, concentrating.

"What's he doing?"

"Being an asshole."

"How?"

"He's dealing at school."

"Drugs?"

"Yeah. Everyone thinks he's cool. Even some of the older kids. He even has a girlfriend."

"Who?"

"Sharleen Fry."

"She's a total ho. You should see her Sam," Annie says.

"He roots her too," Joey whispers. "Mr Burgess caught them."

"That's my cousin," I reply, though I feel a bit put out that he had had sex and I hadn't.

"What about Tipene?"

"They moved. A lot of the old crowd have."

A car pulls into the drive.

"Dad's home!" calls Annie.

Ed comes in and but is headed off by Jackie. She starts muttering about me. I can hear every word because of the suit. She thinks I've run away and need help because I seem a bit crazy. Finally Ed comes in like a big friendly bear. He gives his children hugs. He even hugs me. Annie sits on him and Joey gives him the other Wii controller as I'd given up.

"Sam, hae-re mai, boy, haere mai, long time no see eh? How's everyone?"

"Great. They're probably having a party."

"How's Mike?"

"He's got a boat again..."

"Good on him. Good on him. He needed one. I felt so bad when they burnt Hua Kai."

"It turned out even better than he expected."

"Hey I'm glad. I really am. How's Liz?"

"She's good too."

"Great ... great." he says, thinking that what I said didn't square with the news.

Joey challenges his dad in the game. They play for quite a while. They're concentrating when this car drives up next door.

The car's engine has been adjusted to make it sound loud. It's big, powerful, black, with tinted windows and the base beat of the music is really loud. Ed ignores it. Everyone seems to be trying not to hear the window rattling bass. Then it stops and the men and some girls get out, yelling and laughing loudly. Jackie has started cooking in the kitchen and has her back to me.

I don't know what it is. Maybe it's because I'd just pretended to be ready to commit suicide. Maybe it's because I'd just seen Nana again, looking so sad and abandoned. Or maybe it's the way the Bakers accept this shit, from the men who burnt Grandpop's boat. Whatever it was, a darkness comes over me. I remember how Tahira had gone off at that guy in Balti, and now that I was experiencing it I could appreciate the cold deadly anger that had driven her to punish him.

"Scuse me, just gotta go to the ..." I say softly and get up quietly. I go out towards the loo, but turn out the back door instead. Then I'm gone.

I put my hood up and zip my facemask up. I march around the house, and jump the fence. The anger I had felt before about Grandpop's house has just found its focus. I can hear my heart pounding. The gang guys were just going in as I came up.

The last man in has his girl, who's wearing this white feathery jacket, almost in a headlock with a bottle in his hand. He's drunk. He frowns with annoyance as I approach.

"F____ off kid," John slurs.

The stereo inside the house bursts out with glass rattling loud rap music.

I keep coming.

"I said F____ OFF!" he yells, angry at not being obeyed, and pushing his girl through the door.

I'm up to the veranda. John turns, his face twisted with anger. He can't believe what I'm doing. He's about 1.9 meters tall and he'd cut the arms off his denim jacket because his muscles are so big. I'm less than 1.5 and look small. But my face is blacked out under the hood and behind the screen.

In terms of strength we are about even, but I have way more than strength. I have abilities he can't imagine, and he is on *Kahu* land.

I step forward under the eaves of the veranda heading for the door. He steps forward to grab me, lift, shake and throw me out. Of course he has the advantage of reach.

His hands come out to grab me and I let him start to lift me off my feet. As he lifts me to throw me back I lash out with my feet and kick him hard in the nuts. As if in slow motion I see his eyes bulge with the force of my suit's powerful kick. He's thrown back and hits the door frame as I drop to the ground and recover my balance. He's doubling over in pain so I shoulder charge him up over my shoulders. As I get to the door I shock him and stop, so that he flies past the others in the dining area, and lands in a heap in the passage, hitting his head.

I step into the doorway.

The others are shocked to see a 1.9m tall bro beaten by a 1.5m hooded, faceless shrimp.

"It's time to clean up!" I tell them.

"Who the f____ are you!?" cries the young woman in white feathers who's chewing gum and now looking in astonished horror at her floored boyfriend. I ignore her and point at Wiri in the kitchen. He's no lightweight either.

"*You* are doing the dishes." I order.

He looks at me like I'm a talking cow.

"Clean up!" I yell.

Wiri flinches at the yell, and his eyes widen in fury at my cheek. He grabs a nearby beer bottle and goes to throw it. We don't usually use the beam just to hurt, but I use it now. Just like Tahira, I take no pleasure in his agony as the invisible voltage burns down his nerves searing him from the inside. He screams in spite of himself as his body twitches uncontrollably. I stop and his legs give way.

The girl in the white feathers, named Shayla from my reading, turns from Wiri, back to me, her eyes bulging. Small Shayla might be, but she's staunch. She snatches another bottle off the table and screaming insults, throws it at me, missing so that it smashes on the doorframe.

I shock her down too, and she screams, writhing in agony before falling. That leaves Simone, behind her. She's just wide-eyed with shock and surprise.

For a second there's just the sound of the stereo pounding hate in the background as I eye her. The others on the floor groan and whimper. Simone seems stunned.

"You will *all* clean up this kitchen," I snarl.

Wiri and Shayla are slowly getting up, pale and shaky. Simone grabs a pot scrubber and turns back to me, frightened but hopeful that this device might save her from whatever had happened to the others.

"Get your friends to help or *you* will all suffer," I tell her.

I walk down the passage. I can tell an ambush is coming but I can't use subsonics because of the Surveyor above. There are two of them. Jason has a softball bat in his hand. Hi-né, his woman, has a bottle. They're waiting in the lounge by the door.

"By the spirits of my mother and my grandmother you will learn respect in the house of Kahu!" I say stepping in.

They try to jump me but both are thrown back to the floor by the silent electric shock which jolts their hearts before they can even move. I step past them and zap the stereo which falls silent, smoking slightly.

The whole house seems to be into stunned silence.

"Clean this place up," I say softly, turning to them.

The woman, Hiné, looks up at me. She's older than Shayla or Simone, though not as old as Jackie. She stares up at my blacked out face.

"Who *are* you?" she gasps, clutching her chest.

"The landlord," I tell her.

With a roar of swearwords Jason leaps up again, his eyes bright with fury. It's impressive that he can recover so quickly. He winds up to hit me but my beam shocks him back off his feet, screaming and writhing. I give him five seconds to make my point, which is a very long time in hell. I stop and his head falls back, gasping for breath, clutching his chest.

"I'm losing my patience," I say softly, because I am.

"Clean my grandmother's house!"

Jason glares at me from the floor.

"I'm not your f____ n slave."

I totally lose it.

"Wrong!"

And I burn him again. Five seconds and his screams echo down the passage into the terrified silence of the house. Then I stop, leaving him gasping.

He can't cope and he vomits, in spite of himself, his stomach writhing and shaking. His heartbeat is all over the place. Of course Hiné can't see the invisible beam. All she sees is me glance at Jason and his writhing and shaking on the floor. The terrible pain is inside him and he can't fight it. My voice rising, I make a little speech.

"This is the house of the spirits of my mother and my grandmother! They live here and you *will* honour them," I tell them. I'm furious with their disrespect for Nana and I mean it. I realise I'm breathing hard.

Hiné dashes to Jason who's shocked muscles are shaking uncontrollably.

The suit hasn't automatically stopped me because I'm not enjoying this. Right now I'm reliving a lot of my early childhood and it's not fun.

I'm four.

I'm fourteen.

I'm small.

I'm Robocop.

And these bastards are going to do some cleaning.

"Sam? Iz this necessary?" Gunter asks, bored.

"*Yes*," I tell him, angrily.

Jason's quivering as his insides try to recover from the spasms that wrack him. He's angry but he knows he's beaten. It's in his eyes. It's too much. My ability to burn his nerves and heart without touching him is freaking him out.

"Move!" I demand. "Clean this pigsty! Now!"

Jason tries to get up but falls back on his shaking legs. Hiné helps him. I go back into the passage.

"And if this house is not clean in two hours by my Grandmother's spirit you will never see sunrise again!" I tell them as they stagger out. And I mean it too.

I let them head for the laundry. I head back for the kitchen.

John, who I had kicked when I came in, is sitting in the passage recovering. He wants to get me, but hearing what I did to Jason has made him cautious.

"Get cleaning!" I roar at him suddenly and give him a one second jolt.

The blacked out face, the references to spirits and the incredible pain I'm giving them is freaking them out of their drunken minds. John scuttles out of my way like a big rabbit.

I walk into the kitchen.

I know these men are staunch. They've all been patched. They've all been to prison. They aren't pussies. Normally they'd fight any man, gangster, cop or screw, anywhere, win or lose, until they'd been beaten unconscious if need be. But they had no answer to my hidden face, my talk of spirits and my invisible power to bring agony to their hearts, their nerves and their muscles. They were feeling something they hadn't felt in a very long time. Not since they were four, in the presence of their own gang fathers, like me. Terror.

"Two hours. If it's not clean I will punish you one by one. The laziest one gets it worst. I can read minds and I will know who did least." I say softly.

They start to get busy. They're still drunk and hopeless.

I stand by the door, arms crossed, and watch them.

Ed is cautiously coming up toward the house from the driveway. I turn, unseal my facescreen, and come out onto the verandah, waving. Ed looks amazed to see me standing there. He's far too nervous to come near and hovers by their car – a black resprayed, lowered Ford Falcon with 1995 on the window sticker but with mags and tinted windows. That gives me an idea.

I walk over to their car where Ed's nervously waiting. I smile at him.

"Sam, what's going on?" he asks.

"Oh, I've got them cleaning up Nana's place," I smile. On the opposite side of the car, Ed's mouth falls open and his eyes are wide.

"Well, it's a pigsty. They're lucky Mrs Jones isn't here. She'd give them a *really* hard time," I tell him as I open the car's door with my pinky key.

I reach in, find the hood control, and pop it open. Then I go around the front and open it up, propping it in place.

"Sam? What are you doing?" Ed asks, alarmed.

Wiri runs out of the house.

"Hey what are you? ..." he shouts.

I look down, away from Ed, and seal up the facescreen again, then look around at Wiri. I just stare at him. My faceless hood freaks him out. He goes back inside.

"Ed do you have a screwdriver?" I say over my shoulder as I turn back, unsealing again.

"What?" Ed asks, totally amazed.

He's staring up at the house where nervous faces are watching us from the window. He can't believe what's happening.

"A screwdriver. Philips. eight mil?" I ask.

"Yeah, ah ... maybe."

"Can I borrow it please?"

"What are you doing?" he asks looking into the engine bay.

"Disabling their car."

"What?... you can't do that!" he says gruffly.

"Sure I can, it's easy. It still has a distributor. You take off the distributor cap and ...."

"But Sam it's not your car!" he argues.

"It's not their house. But I want it cleaned and I don't want them driving off."

"But I said they could stay there," Ed says nervously, looking at them.

"I'm not saying they can't. I just want it clean and tidy. Like Nana likes it."

The mention of Nana makes Ed nervous. He knew all about me and the invisibles.

"Look ... ah, Sam, I don't want them coming back at Jackie or the kids eh?"

"Don't worry Ed, they're way too scared of me for that," I tell him grimly, looking him in the eye.

Ed looks into my eyes and he realises he no longer knows me, and he too is afraid.

"Well, yeah … so I'll just look for that screwdriver … eh? he smiles, making an excuse to go home.

"Thanks," I smile sweetly.

He goes back. Then I call after him.

"Actually Ed! Don't bother. I've just remembered Grandpop had one."

He nods and waves, but he can't wait to get back home.

I seal up and turn back to the house. When I get to the door I stop. It's quiet. Too quiet. I reach out for the minds inside. As I suspected …

"Wiri get out from behind the door and put the knife down. John put down the bat. Or I'll set fire to your souls again and the rest can watch you burn all night long as an example," I say quietly.

There's a pause while they think about this.

"OK, if you have to find out the hard way…" I tell them.

They scuttle from their positions and I slam open the door and go inside. They're standing there looking at me. They'd put down the weapons.

"Well? Clean up!" I shout.

They flinch and turn back to work. I turn back to the door, unseal and wave to Joey, who's now watching from the fence. I seal again and turn back to find myself face-to-face with Shayla (the girl with the feathers) who tries to stick a knife in my gut. Shame for her the knifepoint is not harder than diamond.

The knife stays still and the force of her stab means her hand slides off the handle along the blade. She's looking into my eyes expecting to see me die and then looks down, amazed at the blood bursting out from her deeply cut fingers. She drops the knife and bends over her hand crying in pain. The others went to help her. I stop them, stepping forward.

I know these people too well. If I take pity on her for
hurting herself they'd see it as weakness. Instead I pick her
off the ground with one straight arm, shock her to limp
unconsciousness and throw her down the passage like a rag.
This display of supernatural strength and power has all their
eyes on stalks. Their eyes swivel back from Shayla to me. I speak
quietly.

"She might live. The next who tries won't. Now stop wasting
the little time I've given you. Clean like your souls will burn in
the pits of Hell if this place isn't clean by midnight, because I
promise you, I'm nothing compared to what will come after you
if you don't," I tell them.

The word "Hell", my uncanny abilities, and the vicious pain
that had wracked their nerves had made them very scared. The
suggestion there would be worse than me made them even more
worried. They got busy. I walked down to Shayla's limp form.
She was bleeding badly. I held the cuts closed and using my
beam cauterised them. The bleeding stopped.

Ignoring the kitchen crew I walk over to the old drawer
Grandpop had kept his small tools in, find the screwdriver, and
walk out. Outside I unseal my face and go back to the car.

I start working on taking off the distributor cap. I was glad I had
the suit on because I didn't really know what I was doing and
could have zapped myself a few times. Joey watches for a while
and then calls over from the fence.

"Psst Sam?"

"Yeah?"

"Dad says you're making Jason, John and Wiri clean up."

"Yeah."

"F_____ awesome!"

I keep working on the car.

"Did you learn Kung Fu when you were at that place? Can you show me your moves?"

"It's not Kung Fu Joey."

"Well what?"

"It's mind powers, like with the Invisibles? That's what we learned there. That, and a lot of cleaning. The cleaning was important."

I was glad I got to say this because it was something *they* could believe as they picked the sound off the hard surfaces around us. After all *they* use those powers on us so they know it's possible.

"What? Are you shitting me? What powers does cleaning give you?" Joey asks.

"I dunno but all the best soldiers clean. All the Kung fu monks clean. Cleaning is part of discipline. That's why you know those guys are wusses. They aren't disciplined or clean," I say, finally getting the cap off.

I walk around to the drivers seat and try the ignition. Nothing. I go back to the front and close the car's hood, then I walk over to where Joey is.

"See, cleaning that house is something they need to do as much for their souls as my Nana's. Once they get started they'll find it's not hard and it's even fun."

"Cleaning gives you powers and is fun," Joey repeats, thinking about it. I smile. He has no idea.

"Nah. You *are* shitting me," he decides.

"Tahira is fun to clean with," I shrug.

"Why? Do you root her or something?" he asks with a touch of jealousy.

"No," I smile, "We just have a good time cleaning together."

I come over to the fence, and pass him the distributor cap.

"You really are different now, Sam," he says.

"It's my training." I say swinging over the 1.5 meter fence.

"How did they train you?" he asks giving me back the distributor cap.

"We're all psychics. All of us. We have mind control, and body control powers. We learned from Mongolian shamans," I lie.

"Really?" he asks doubtfully.

"Would you go tell those guys over there to clean up the house."

"No way."

"See. I can. It's part of what we learned. Hey let's shoot some baskets."

"Can you levitate the ball in?"

"Nah, not yet."

"OK."

We play basketball outside. A bit later a cop car draws up. Jackie goes out to meet it. The cop, a new one, gets out.

"Why did she have to do that?" I ask myself.

I keep playing with Joey. Finally Jackie and the cop come out the back. The cop is white, small and fairly together-looking bloke. He has a long, open, dish-like face with steady green eyes.

"Ah Sam ... this is Glenn from the police. He just wants to make sure you're OK."

"Hi Sam, how are you today?" he asks in a businesslike way.

"To be honest I'm a bit ... What's the word? ... when you can't think straight because everything keeps changing and you're under a lot of pressure?"

"Stressed-out?" Glenn suggests. He has an English accent. I start reading him. He's used to Wales but Maori are new to him.

"Yeah stressed-out. It's been a busy day."

"So what have you been doing?"

"Oh all sorts. It's really great to kick back and just shoot a few baskets with my mate Joey here."

"I suppose it would be. Sam, look I'm just here to make sure you're OK. Make sure you're looked after."

"I'm always looked after. Sue's looking out for me now."

"DC Sue Williams? Sam, she's been missing since Saturday, Do you know where she is?"

"What's the time? About five?"

"Yes, it's five eleven."

"She should be at home. Give her a call on 0965043608."

The cop got his notepad out and wrote down the number asking me to repeat it.

"Sam who is looking after you now?"

"You mean like who's place will I sleep at tonight?"

"For starters," he nods.

"Sue's I spose."

"And where is that?"

"Auckland."

"Then how will you get here?"

"Same way I got there."

"Which is?"

"Are you going to call Sue? I can't guarantee she'll be there forever."

"In a minute. How did you get here?"

"In my invisible, micro-UFO."

The cop lowers his notepad.

"Don't come the smartarse son," he growls softly, his eyes hard on me.

"I'm not. It's over by the creek. Did you know there's a P-lab next door? It's in the bathroom."

"Sam, for the last time, who is looking after you and where are they now?"

"Right now I'm looking after me, and I'm right here. Did you hear me say there's a P-lab next door?"

"I mean an adult, and I will worry about your P-lab once I know you have an appropriate level of care."

I sigh.

"I'm fine Glenn, I don't need care. I can take care of myself. I've just terrified three patched gang members and their girlfiends into cleaning my grandpop's house and I have an invisible micro UFO which can take me to Auckland in five minutes. The only reason I'm telling you about this is in five seconds you will forget everything I've just said."

"You think so?" the Glenn asks grimly. He thinks I'm a complete arsehole.

"Oh, I know so," I smile.

And I memory-zap the adults and dash off. They'll be phased for about ten seconds and confused for a minute.

"Sam! What's happened to them?" Joey calls after me, confused.

"Mind powers Joe," I yell.

I raise my hood and seal the face. I run, jump the fence, and run again over to Grandpop's house. I run across the veranda and burst in the door. They look terrified.

"We haven't finished yet!" Simone complains.

"You're in luck. I want a good job. You've got 24 hours. But it better be good," I tell them.

"Let's see how you're doing," I add.

I walk through the house. To my surprise they actually are cleaning it. The only downer is Jason, in his room, loading his shotgun.

"Jason? Put the shotgun away," I yell.

But Jason is still pigheaded. He clicks it shut and charges out to get me. It's war. Him or me. For a second my head swims.

Maybe it was because I was at home on our land with my grandmother and my mother and all my other ancestors?

Ka maté (death?)

Maybe it was because Jason, even with his gang patches and his gun, like Ax before him, didn't scare me any more.

Ka maté (death?)

All I knew was that in this place, at this time, with my ancestors behind me, Jason was no match for me. Ka ora (life?)

I *had* changed. I was ready for this. Ka ora (life?)

Time sped up again. Jason leaps through the open door, the shotgun levelled at me, ready to fire. At exactly the same time I zap him and dive on my stomach. He collapses backwards, unconscious, onto his back and the shotgun goes off with a huge bang.

There's smoke and a big hole in the ceiling. Pink insulation rains down. I jump back up. Everyone dashes out behind me. Jason lies crumpled, the shotgun next to him on the floor. Both barrels are smoking. I'm not too sure about shotguns so I just pick it up, click it open and bend the barrel mount at right angles to the butt over my knee. It's very hard steel but I bend it so that it can't close. Then throw it down and turn to look at the others.

"Twenty four hours. Your car's going nowhere. Don't try and run. The hunter who is following after me is not as patient as me. If you give him a reason he will punish you much, much more cruelly."

Then I turn and walk out the back door just as I hear the sound of a man – Constable Glen Higgins – running up to the front

143

door. I walk out the back and then sprint for the bush.

"Sam!" Joey shouts. He's looking over the fence from the Baker's back garden.

I wave and dash into the bush. The surveyor above can see through trees. Quickly I run for Ka-rea-rea and scramble under him in the creek. I get Ka-rea-rea to open and close his hatch while I fold into nothing, bending back to Gunter.

[+]

The lightning dances over me again, then water, then wind and then is still. While I wait I ask Gunter what's happening as I reconnect to Ka-rea-rea.

"The cop is running out of the house after you. How are you? How was that shotgun blast?" Gunter asks me.

"Bracing," I tell him as I switch on Ka-rea-rea's invisibility.

"Du alma (Poor thing)," he replies sarcastically in German. Glenn, the cop, is following my trail and calling for me but he doesn't know the area. Ka-rea-rea lifts off silently. I nose him up toward the canopy of trees just as Glenn comes into the creek clearing. He's well inside two hundred meters so he can see the halo of light, like a faint circular rainbow with a hole, around nothing at all. He watches, gobsmacked as it silently flies out into the sunlight.

Ka-rea-rea flies out from under the trees and lifts up over Ed and Jackie's, rising past the two hundred meter mark. Down below Ed and Jackie are cautiously approaching the old Kahu house with Joe behind them. Then John, Wiri and Simone run out ignoring Ed and Jackie in their terrified rush for their car. But before they get there I zap each of them with another jolt of pain and they fall on their faces on the grass. They look around, still ignoring Ed and Jackie, so I give them another jolt, making them yell. Then, as Ed and Jackie watch in amazement, they jump up and run back inside like spooked sheep. Ed and Jackie, collect up Joey and go back home, shaking their heads and talking. Constable Glenn Higgins comes out of the bush looking confused and a bit shaken before heading for his car. I'm pretty sure not everything will be in his report.

It's time to leave. I've caused enough excitement. I switch to blend, and send Ka-rea-rea inertialess to Auckland in a blur of acceleration.

I get out of the cabinet and come over to Gunter, sitting in the big wrap-around control screen. Gunter puts Ka-rea-rea's view on the big screen and we play with him, sending him scooting around Auckland's skies as the sun begins to set.

There's a movement behind me. Rewa's coming down on the discs followed by the others. One by one they all say "welcome back," and hug me. I put my arm around Rewa. Scott and Tarik pat my back. Ashley and Cam give me big hugs, and Tahira puts her arm around me in a side squeeze. We all watch Ka-rea-rea and talk about how my flying would be interpreted by the Administration from its tags.

"It's a bit sad leaving him like this," Scotty says for all of us. Finally it's dark enough to fly him into the carpark. I zap the security cameras and fly him in. We wonder how we can make it hard for the Administration to steal him. Finally we decide that rather than attach him to a car we'll put him on the roof of a fenced off electrical cabinet. That will make it harder for them to get at him. He folds up and I put him to sleep.

"OK. Now you get to see the new place," Cam says with a smile full of promise.

"Is it better than Renwick?"

"Oh yeah," Tarik says certainly.

"Except zhere's more brass to clean," Tahira adds.

"Where are we?"

"Come and see," they say.

CHAPTER SIXTY THREE: BRAIN WARS

The others start popping out their wings. They're a lot larger than our old wings, stretching from above our heads to our thighs. They unroll and quickly pump themselves up, like a butterfly coming out of its chrysalis.

The wings aren't transparent. The others had chosen colours for them. Ashley's are light purple, Scott's are greeny blue, Tarik's are dull orange, Cam's are pale green and Tahira's are sooty black (I knew who *she's* copying). I choose a dark blue. As they stiffen and spread, the others take to the air. Rewa, who doesn't have her suit on, takes a disc.

The new antigravity field means we don't glow and our wings don't need to beat so hard either. We just fly silently, like huge butterflies. It's a strange feeling. Instead of turning down gravity now we are actively being repelled from the ground. It made flying feel more effortless, even if your insides did float about like skydiving.

The others circle up through the air, leading me through the disc lift holes, just as a shaft of light lights us up, picking us out, and the dust suspended in the air. We're climbing silently past the briefing level, past the changing level, up toward a brilliant light. Riding a disc Rewa beats us to the top easily. The light from above turns out to be a huge glasshouse reflecting the setting sun. It's a dome three storeys high, with two wings extending left and right, each two storeys high. The glasshouse feels warm and is filled with dark green plants, and butterflies of all colours and sizes.

The opening to the disc poles are hidden by plants but we fly over these and come to land on a paved area by the entrance. Outside the dome the lawn stretches about fifty meters to a large three storey house made of stone. It has a central section and two wings like a stone reflection of the glasshouse. In front of this is a glassed-in area one storey tall. In the centre of the lawn is a large, round, fountain with a sculpture of group of six angels about three meters tall. The lawn is surrounded with forest, mostly ferns and taller trees and looks like the bush further up the hill on Aotea. The others look at me seeking my reaction to this even more impressive house than Renwick.

"Wow," I say.

"Welcome to Hastings Hall," Scotty tells me.

"Wow! So where in the world are we?"

"Guess!" grins Ashley.

"No reading!" says Cam.

I walk out onto the lawn. The sky's blue with high cirrus cloud but the air is warm. The sun is in the West. It's late afternoon. I already know it's night in New Zealand so that means its not too far to the west of New Zealand.

It's warmish, but not tropical. There's nothing Asian about this building. It's definitely English. That suggests Australia, or high in the hills of Malaysia? I couldn't imagine Dr P being based in Myanmar/Burma.

The trees are high, but there are mountains in the distance that are higher. They aren't steep, rocky mountains like New

Zealand. These are rounder; older. Australia is my main suspicion – but it's a big continent.

We walk up to the glassed-in area in front of the Hall. It's a big warm swimming pool. I could feel people had been swimming here. Our people most recently. There's a double door with old ironwork suggesting the place goes back about a hundred years. It's been a private home for decades but fallen into disrepair. We go inside. The air is moist and warm.

"Thermal springs," says Tarik, knowing that will confuse me. It does. Deep caves out the back, thermal springs, ferns and mountains. Where *is* this place? We go through the internal door and enter a café like area along the left side. Its windows look out over the pools.

It's quite large. I can see a large modern kitchen in the background. This makes me feel more at home than I had in a week. The idea of breakfasting on Mr Tran's pastries and chatting with the others made me feel more relaxed than I'd been in ages. My whole body seems to sigh with relief. But the others draw me past the staircase that fills the right side and through a large double door.

It isn't really a surprise – I could feel the crowd, as I always can – though the big shout of "surprise!" makes me jump. Everyone was in there waiting for me. The question of where I was had been to distract me from the surprise! Mariko, with her round pregnant tummy, is laughing, blowing on a toy horn, and throwing streamers at me. The others have glasses and are throwing streamers and blowing on toy horns too. There's even a big banner in this ... what is it ... library? ... which reads "Welcome home Sam."

The room is big, long and square. The mezzanine levels on both sides are packed with books. There are shelves along the side, also filled with them. But it's all the people crowded in front of me I want to see. Grandpop is the first to grab me in a huge bear hug, then Aunty Liz and then Rewa again. My sight sorta gets a bit messed up because my eyes are streaming. Everyone hugs me. Even Dr Morozov with bewildered little Irina sucking on a dummy, peeking out from her back pack. Finally I come to Dr Prosperov.

He extends his hand formally. I reach to shake it. Then he draws me into a surprisingly strong, long hug and kisses my cheeks, patting my back. Dr Prosperov draws me aside and steps forward.

"Friends," begins Dr Prosperov.

"*Friends*," he says again – more certainly.

Mrs Jones passes me a glass of coke.

"Sam's return marks end of period of serious loss for our mission. We have lost our home, our base, and saddest of all, our great friend and colleague Lana Vilenskaya."

"All have lost dear possessions. But we are all fortunate to escape with our lives. Even more inspiring has been actions of colleague Sam Kahu. All alone, despite youth, despite limited resources, Sam avoided capture and even managed to help with recovery. Is truly heroic rearguard Sam, and should be applauded. A toast to our valiant rearguard – Sam Kahu!"

"Sam Kahu," they all repeat and toast me. It's funny how all their voices kinda sound individual and a group at the same time – and also how it swells my heart to have them respect me like this. I can't hide that I'm blown away.

And then Dr P starts clapping. Everyone claps. I feel small rather than big. I don't think I've really done anything but cope.

Finally they stop and Dr Prosperov speaks again.

"Please refill your glasses. Nobody heard of Russian making speeches without toasting," Dr Prosperov laughs.

There's a friendly buzz as glasses get topped up. Grandpop passes the coke. Then Dr P begins again.

"Tonight friends, we celebrate life of Lana Vilenskaya, our friendship and survival. We relax. But not too much. We must not forget is much to do. Ten days ago security was breached. Critical question is 'how?' Who tagged Ashley? How much did they know already and how did they know it? Who even knew Nathan was linked to Ashley? When was para.no.ID compromised? How? Before we can again help the others we work to protect we must know how *we* failed. If is next time, might not be so lucky."

He pauses, giving us time to reflect on what he's just said. It is true. We failed. We failed to notice what we had given away about ourselves. But then Dr P starts up again.

"Is said Russians prone to melancholy. Me? I think Russians prone to weather," Dr P smiled. "For while we congratulate Sam and celebrate his return, we must also remember our loss: Lana Vilenskaya."

A sort of serious hush fell over everyone as we remembered her.

"Tonight Fae will conduct special rite for Lana. I have no idea what will happen. Is Fae way to bring Lana home. Doubtless will be special," he shrugs.

"But we must not forget for many years – some hard and terrible years in Soviet Union – Lana lived among us as human being like us," he looks around.

"She gave up life which, as most of us have seen, is very easy compared to ours. No disease, long lifetime, no money, no war.

Is very civilised with no serious suffering on Fae. Much less than we have on our own world. Lana did not need to come here. So why did she?"

Again he pauses. After all I've been through, to be honest, the idea of looking for trouble seems kind of crazy, so I wonder if in some ways she was. She certainly dressed like it.

"I met Lana after she suffered much. Child dead, husband also dead. She was tortured by KGB. Much unfairness, loss and pain. I met her when we travelled among Ken's people on Steppe in Mongolia at end of bitter winter."

He looks out the window at the hedges and roses of the garden. The sky in the west is growing pink.

"I remember am waking early morning. Was dark and very, very cold. Rather than lie in sleeping bag freezing I got up. Got into furs to walk for to improve circulation. Surprised to see Lana already up, watching dawn on Steppe, watching horses playing among snow."

"Naturally am seeking company, so join her. She is watching, face very pink, but with big smile. I make some remark about how cold is weather. But she said, 'cold is our friend because its bite wakes us from indulgence and reminds us to live while we can.' It was first of many things I learn from Lana Vilenskaya. Is something I cannot forget."

"Lana could have lived to please herself. Could have lived without risk with no greater struggle than boredom of how to entertain herself. But she did not see that as living. She saw that as empty existence."

"Am thinking Lana left Fae to live with bite of cold. She is woman who felt deeply. She knew pain. But as she felt so she lived. She loved, she hurt, she gave. Some may feel sorry for her.

I think is mistake. More than anything she chose to feel. Is easy to hide. To protect self is natural. But to seek feeling. Is courage. She chose death and died staring enemies in eye. To me this is not death of martyr but of hero. So to toast. To Lana Vilenskaya, hero of life."

And a lot of people suddenly had wet eyes and couldn't look at one another but everyone repeated all of it. "Lana Vilenskaya, Hero of life."

And that was one very special toast which made everyone a bit quiet afterwards.

"And now Mariko has told me I must, as she says, 'shut up, and let them talk'."

He grins. People turn to one another.

"But," he adds loudly.

"Warning! Is more toasts later," he smiles.

I'm instantly surrounded by the others again so I have to go over the past week over and over again.

But I have to listen too. I learned more about the Fae's home world and the Vimana. It sounded almost unbelievable and if I didn't know them I could have thought all my friends had just gone crazy.

"Worked it out mate?" Tarik asks, sidling up beside me with Cam.

"What?"

"Where you are."

"No."

"Want a clue?" Cam smiled.

"Uh, OK."

"It's more forgotten by the world than even New Zealand."

That sounded a bit unlikely. And I realise that being inside a big library wasn't going to help answer Tarik's question at all. Attracted by this new game Rewa comes over with Asal and Tahira.

"So you wanna see our place and have a tour, big brother?" she asks.

"Yeah OK," I reply and put my arm around her.

So we go back out the way we'd come in but turn up the staircase this time. The stairway is wood and shiny, the carpet is beige, and the walls white. It seems a bit boring for a place where Mariko lives. We turn up, past a window that lets in the evening light. Then I realise something. It's like missing something.

"This place isn't haunted is it?" I ask Tahira.

"Zhe house iz not." Tahira replies.

"What is then?"

"The forest."

"Who by?"

"You'll see."

We turn onto the landing. There's a huge blue and black picture of a figure with yellow dots on it. I knew it was Mariko's answer to the house.

"We're in Australia, aren't we," I realise.

"Ay," smiles Rewa.

"Tasmania … south Tasmania," I guess.

"He got it!" Asal yells down to the others.

They come thundering up the stairs. .

"What's the big secret anyway?" I ask.

"So how did you work it out?" Tarik asks.

"Had to be a few hours from New Zealand because of the position of the sun so that fixed the longitude. Had to be mild, not tropical or desert so that suggested a latitude. Couldn't be northern hemisphere, so it had to be southern. After that you just run out of places. Plus Mariko's picture just said 'Australia'."

"But why Tasmania?"

"Facing south and I dunno ... Dr P likes islands. Why? What's the mystery?" I ask.

"We don't want your friend to know where she's coming," Tarik tells me.

"Who? Sue?"

"Yeah," says Tarik. He looks quite fierce. I'm surprised.

"Why?"

Scotty and Ashley look at each other. Tarik said nothing. Then Cam breaks the awkward silence.

"There's a risk Sam."

"What sort of risk?"

Cam bit her lip. Nobody says anything.

"What? What's the matter?" I want to know.

"Sam, Hekator's found problem with your policewoman," Tahira says.

"What problem. She's clean. She's been in quarantine for two nights. She hasn't got any tags."

"It's not tags, Sam," says Cam, seriously.

"Well, what is it? If it isn't a tag?"

"Dis is hard," Ashley says to herself.

"Someone's gotta tell 'im," Tarik says, determinedly.

"Tell me what?"

"Sam ..." Tahira begins.

"Yeah? What?"

"Your friend Sue has growth in brain. She doesn't know yet," she says gently.

My mind is kind of numb. I can't work out what this means.

"What? What sort of growth?"

"That's just the problem. We don't know yet do we?" Tarik says.

There's a silence as I struggle to understand.

"If natural, is brain cancer," Tahira says.

That sounded bad enough. Tarik goes on.

"If it's not, right? *They* given it her somehow, yeah? It could be growing into a mind tap, or it could be a controller," Tarik says, sniffing.

Now I know why it's important that Sue doesn't know where we were. A mind tap gives *them* access to Sue's brain. If it's based in a memory centre she would be an open book to *them*, just like Sir Michael.

"It's still very small," Ashley says, trying to make me feel better.

"But dere was enough of a difference in her entrance and exit scan to set off da alarms. Dat means its growin' fast."

"So what's going to happen?" I ask.

"Well ... some of 'em want her memory of us erased," says Ashley.

I must have looked upset.

"You gotta look at it from their point of view, right?" Tarik explains. "They 'ave 'ole world to protect. And we gotta improve our security or it's us who'll have no memory, right? "

I think about it for a moment. If it's natural it's growing fast and that can't be good. If it's a tap it might be working already. Maybe Du Croix knew something when he said I wasn't in Ka-rea-rea.

Neither option is good for Sue. I feel guilty that I got her into this mess. If I'd shut up she'd just be a lonesome, lesbian policewoman drinking too much. Now, because of me, she could be facing all the horrors I'd wanted her to avoid."

"Could *they* have got to her Sam?" Cam asks.

"Yeah..." I admit, feeling sick, "they could."

I tell them about Rocelli.

"What does Hekator think?" I ask.

"He thinks you are too attached to her. But he's also keen to operate."

"Operate!" I'm shocked.

"If it's a weapon he wants to study its growth and development," said Scotty. "He wants take the growth out and put it in a simulated brain. His hope is to develop an antibody so he can make a cure."

It sounds gross. Gross and dangerous.

"But can he do that? I mean can he take it out without hurting Sue?"

"Probably," Scotty shrugs.

"*Probably*?"

"It depends what he has to do. But his real problem is Fae law. He's not allowed to operate on anyone without their permission and if he asks *her* the whole point of operating is lost because then *they* know their tap is being removed," Scotty says.

"But if it is a mindtap *they* gave it to her without asking permission so why do we need her permission to take it away again?" I ask.

"It's just Fae laws," Scotty shrugs.

I have an opinion on those laws.

"I want to talk to Hekator," I tell them.

"He's coming tonight," Tarik says.

"Is Sue?"

"Only if he brings her," Tarik says. "And if he does, he'll have operated already. Otherwise he'll leave her in Auckland because

157

he's given her the memory modification treatment."

I feel terrible. I feel like someone should have asked me
something about this, but it's Sue's brain, the Fae's risk, and
Hekator's skills in question. I really have nothing to do with it.

"So if she comes, you must promise not to tell her where we are,
otherwise we might have to evacuate again," Rewa tells me. I can
see she really means it too.

"Don't worry. Security first," I agree.

I still feel depressed that after all that work and effort I've put
into Sue it was possible that tomorrow morning she might not
know me at all.

"You OK Sam?" Ashley asks carefully.

"Yeah ... it's just ... we've been through a lot together ... When I
didn't know if you were coming back, she was ... well, I needed
her," I admit.

They all look at me, surprised.

"Did you *really* think we weren't coming back?" Rewa says,
shocked.

"I didn't *know* ... The relief when I saw you guys at Renwick ... it
was massive," I tell them.

"Aunty Liz was having kittens. She cried every day," Rewa says.

"But for all I knew you hadn't made it, or were gone for good.
That's why I needed Sue."

"Hey man. I'm sorry," Tarik says. He suddenly seems much
gentler. "We've been so into how we don't want to go through
evacuation again, we forgot how bad it must have been to have
no contact at all."

The others are looking at me in a way that's making me feel
embarrassed. I look around.

"So what else does this place have?" I ask, changing the subject.

It reduces the tension which makes everyone feel happier.

Tahira steps up to the door next to her.

"We 'av a gym," Tahira says, opening the door.

I look in. It isn't big but it has cycles, weights, and stuff.

"And a home cinema," says Rewa running next door. She and Ashley open the door. It's small, with four sofas in it. It even has a fridge with soda and ice creams, a coffee machine and a popcorn machine. The flat screen is *enormous*. I'm impressed. We move along to the next door.

"And there's a dance studio," Cam adds.

It has a shiny floor and mirrors. I notice it also has boxing bags and mats. Cam closes the door. We pass a double door.

"Laundry and cleaning," yawns Rewa, who is leading the way. Asal is racing her to be in front.

"And biiiiig lounge," Asal says running ahead. We get to the door and go in. It's reasonably large with a good view out to the mountain over the forest. There's a bar, a pool table, and a lot of sofas. It's a bit like all of our old lounges back at Renwick.

"Without any ghosts," Ashley reminds me.

"And upstairs are the family apartments. C'mon," Rewa says racing ahead of Asal again. We follow them up the stairs at an easy run.

On the top level all the families plus Grandpop are in a row. Rewa takes me into our apartment. The others wait outside to give us space in our own home.

The apartment is pretty much the same as was at Renwick except the view is just the rest of the building. I miss the sea and the lighthouse already, but I notice Cheeky's already been set up in my room. I open up his box. He doesn't exactly go mental to see me but he gives me a cheep. I think he recognises me, but he doesn't move from his nest. I leave him to sleep.

"What are they doing with Buffy?" I ask.

"She's in the greenhouse," Rewa replies.

"What happened to Tricksy and Grunter?"

"Ken and Gunter had to let them go. They must be somewhere on Aotea," she adds.

I suppose the fire would have scared them off pretty quick. The others had left us alone in our own apartment so I could get the feel of it with Rewa.

"It's good you could get all the animals out," I say.

"It was horrible, Sam," Rewa remembers. "Everyone was panicking. Control was demanding we get down into the tunnel as soon as we could and not bring anything. He told us we had to have at least twenty minutes of fire at Renwick or they would put it out. I only just got Mr Nibbles," she says of her old rabbit doll.

"Grandpop only got his pictures of mum and Nana. And the sirens were going whaa-uhh whaa-uhh so loud you couldn't think. No-one wants that to ever happen again. That's why we're so big on security now."

We come out of our apartment and we all go back down the stairs to the library. The light is slowly turning from yellow to blue shadows out in the garden. When we reach the library we discover a whole lot of strangers in white uniforms have arrived. They're unloading trays and trays of food, and bottles of drink from a big VW Transporter van. This is great news because I suddenly realise how hungry I am.

When they leave we all get cheerfully to work filling our plates and pigging out. There's something for everyone. Potato dumplings, rice, Vietnamese soups, green salads, fish cakes, sushi, kebabs, pilaf, lamb and chicken done all sorts or ways, couscous, felafel. After all that weird Fae food, and before that meals grabbed here and there, it's great to be sitting down again with our big family – our whanau – and just enjoying their company, their jokes and table talk.

Even so I can't help thinking of Sue. I keep seeing her unconscious on her bed, in one of her print dresses, as Hekator gets ready to wipe all knowledge of us, and of me. It seems so wrong.

The others read me and try to distract me by telling me how the new suits make flying after dark easier because the don't glow. Even better by controlling the antigravity we can fly much higher and faster than we could under gravity neutralisation.

"It's completely wicked," Tarik grins.

There's a catch however: we have to wait for a while or else our dinner will float around inside us and make us spew.

"And believe me, that's no fun," Tarik admits.

I have to admit that stealthier flying sounds a huge improvement. At Renwick we could never fly for fun because the glow would make us obvious for miles – that, and the amount of buzzing noise our suits made just to get us airborne.

As usual we clean up after dinner ourselves. While I'm helping I ask Gunter something that has been bothering me.

"How come this place is finished. I mean it took ages to get Renwick ready."

Gunter smiles.

"Dr Prosperov started lookink for new bases early last year after you guyz came back from Europe. It was your farter who starded it. Gennady realised that if Renwick vent down ve needed a back-up. He secretly bought a whole bunch of places and Mariko, Hekati and I vorked on some of zhem. I nefer knew exactly vere zey were. Mariko und I vere just gifen plans and photographs. Zere are uzzers. He alvays managed der building. You haf to remember he's uzed to dealing wiz Sofiet style treachery. I don't zink he efen trusts himself sometimes," he smiles.

It was good to know Dr Prosperov was thinking ahead. If he hadn't, coming back would have been a real problem.

After dinner Mariko takes us outside and we light the gas torches and switch off the lights. The lights around the garden are pretty LEDs that vanish into the forest on both sides. The lights on the fountain change in cycles of red orange, green, blue, and purple. Mariko has set up a DJ PC in the glasshouse and there are speakers all around the lawn. The air is warm and the stars are coming out. Mariko starts the music with soft classical piano. Just as a test she cranked it up a bit and the volume was impressive, as was the quality. We go back inside to find the adults coming out. It's a pity I feel so stuffed because it's a good night to fly.

We talk and joke with the music changing from classical to light jazz, and then to light pop until about eight. For all my worries about Sue I'm now more relaxed than I have been for over a week. I can just feel the tension that has been keeping me going, the paranoia about safety, letting go.

It's like, having had to face the possibility of life without this big family of mine, I now appreciate them all the more. I look at them all in turn with fresh eyes. Cam, with her pretty face and surprising, funny comments; Scotty with his earnest, honest stability; Tarik with his quick wit and way of talking crap; Ashley, messy and big hearted; and Tahira, fierce, complicated, and vulnerable all at the same time. I just love knowing we are together again and that was how we belonged. Between walking Patience and carrying Irina, Asal and Rewa are also hanging around. They seem older now. Perhaps it's because they are, but perhaps the evacuation shocked them into realising that they too had a role to play in this strangely different, strangely well-balanced community.

Mariko's music picks up to a light kind of poppy dance music. It makes the adults, who have had a few wines, sway and jiggle a bit. After a while Dr Prosperov and Dr Morozov go, saying they need to put Irina to bed. Bernard takes Patience, who has fallen asleep in Zoe's arms, off to bed too. And when the little ones are safely out of the way Mariko starts the dance tracks.

Of course, we all knew her music. She'd played everything to us when she'd driven Betty. But it wasn't just the tracks – she'd mixed them well too. Cam starts us playing with our suit colours, flashing and flickering, oranges, blues, reds and greens. Scott begins changing himself to different spots and stripes of animals. Ashley mixes up colours and patterns, making purple giraffe and blue zebras, then Tarik discovers anything he sees can be captured as an image, or video clip and put on the suit's outer skin like a walking screen, so he covered himself in pictures of us all. It's a cool trick, and we pass pictures around our bodies. Then as the music gets faster Cam jumps a huge somersault which sets us all off. It's huge fun. We even pick up Rewa and Asal who squeal wildly, and then want more.

As ten arrives the crescent moon rises in the sky behind a veil of high cloud. We all know we want to, but as always it's Tahira who pops her wings first.

"Not so high you can be silhouetted against the moon," is the warning of more than one adult.

Compared to flying in the old suits this is *so* easy. Instead of choosing how much to reduce gravity by, we choose how much to push away from the Earth. You didn't need much.

It felt like falling *up* because everything in your body started floating around. But you can balance lift with falling and drive yourself through the air with your wings. The old suits made flying a bit of a struggle, like a bee, but the new ones make you float like a butterfly.

We rise up from the lawn and fly around Hastings hall. Now I can see it's down a long drive back to the main road that heads west. There's a mountain over the forest to the north-west and we immediately head for it.

As our wings push us through the air our speed rises from about twenty to about sixty kilometers per hour. It feels way faster than the old suits and a bit like flying with Tabika, as we zoom over the treetops. Compared to the speeders it's not exciting but anyone could see just how useful these suits were going to be. We could fit inside the speeders in them and drop out if we had to. Most important we could fly at night, silently and darkly, without the noise and light of the old kindergarten ones.

"These are great!" I tell the others.

"Lana did a good job," Scotty agrees.

Somehow saying Lana's name changes the mood a lot. We reach the mountaintop, land and look around. You can see the sea, and to the east, land on the other side. From my suit I learn that we are in an area called Southport, not far from a small town of the same name. It's at the entrance to a long harbour that leads up to Hobart.

"I think we should get back," says Cam.

For some reason we can all feel it. It's as if we're being summoned. We lift off back into the sky again and fly horizontally out over the forest, gaining altitude as the ground falls away below us. It feels very slow, and I realise that, in fact, at any altitude we're really sitting ducks. I mention it to the others.

"Yeah, normally we would bend down, or up and drop, but we thought we'd let you find that out the same way we did," Tarik says.

We pick up a lot of speed as we begin angling downhill. Soon we're doing a reasonable one hundred and twenty kilometers an hour and buzz the lawn, flashing colours as we come over. It's so easy to land compared to the old suits and we join everyone dancing for a while, around eleven.

Doctor Prosperov has come back outside and is on the side talking to Mrs Jones, Dr Gursoy and Grandpop. Aunty Liz and Soraya are putting Rewa and Asal to bed and Zoe had gone off to watch Patience. Out on the lawn Mariko and Gunter, Bernard, Ken, Patricia, and Mitra are dancing.

It's just about midnight. I'm chatting with the others when presences begin arriving from the forest around us. They're quiet, and discreet. Even a psychic could miss them. They're black as night under the dark forest canopy with dots bright as stars over their bodies. They have brilliant stripes of colour and flicker as if lit by a black fire. The memory of didgeridoo, blocks and chanting rises and swirls around us. It makes me strangely dizzy, like being in a room where the adults are smoking too much weed. I look around. The others are looking as effected as I am. Even Mrs Jones seems to have her eyes closed and is breathing carefully as Mariko's music picks up.

"*Is Mrs Jones getting ready to make them go away*?" I ask the others silently.

"*She can't*," Scotty replies through the suit. "*These spirits are way too powerful. They ignore us, which is probably just as well.*"

"*They're ancient*," Tahira says, quietly. "*They're nearly as old as those ancient graves we found in the desert in Egypt.*"

The strangest thing seemed to be happening as these black spirits gathered. Space and time began to feel different. The window of the sky seemed to flex, and the ground felt strangely distant. It was stronger than the weird feeling I'd had looking at the view with Mr Ceder in Israel. I had only felt something like it once before. In Yemen, in the desert with Khadiyeh, when … well, I still wasn't exactly sure *what* it was that had happened then.

Yet even as the effect started, it stopped, as did the memory of their music. As suddenly and without reason as they had arrived, the black figures melted back into the forest. It seemed as if they had decided that for some reason, maybe the time or the place, they should leave.

Then, suddenly, there's this huge blast of static through the speakers and all the lights went out. There's total silence. Everyone looks at each other in the darkness.

"Shit!" Mariko, swears loudly.

Then, a strange buzzing noise like a power substation. Looking up I suddenly realise the sky is filled with a huge, round, transparent shape bigger than the lawn and way bigger than either the greenhouse or Hastings Hall. It's a Vimana. The transparent invisibility makes it seem like its made of the most perfect glass, and yet, because of its huge size, you can't miss it.

"Children we need Lana now please," Mrs Jones calls.

The others go back towards the hall so I go with them.

"What did Mrs Jones mean?" I ask them.

"We're getting Lana's body. It's in the cool store." Cam says.

"What's she doing in the cool store?" I ask, a bit disgusted.

"Keeping cool," says Tarik.

"But that's where the food is kept," I protest.

"She's in a bag," Cam says softly. "There's no smell."

It still makes me feel a bit ill. Bodies shouldn't be with food. It's just wrong.

"How long has she been there?" I ask as we go through to the kitchen.

"Since we stole her from the morgue last night," Scotty says.

The cool store door swings open and we go in. Lana's body is in a bag lying on a table in the middle. I suddenly feel very sad. Through the clear faceplate she looks like she's just sleeping. Her pale face seems so peaceful, like a princess in a fairy story, except that you knew there's no-one there and she will not wake up again.

We gather around her. For just a moment we all stand there looking at her, thinking about her.

"Thanks Lana," I say out loud, without thinking.

"Salaam Lana," Tahira adds.

"Salaam," Tarik agrees.

"Peace, Lana, and thank you," Ashley says, softly.

"Peace ... and better luck next time," Scotty says.

"Chia tay, Lana," Cam says.

We can feel Lana's presence by her head. She doesn't seem all that unhappy. It's a warm presence, saying goodbye. We each take hold of a strap.

167

"Forward on three," Scott says, in the front, right by the door. "One, two, three."

She sags as we carry her out the door, following her ghost. Through the kitchen, the café, and out past the baths, we come out as the huge Vimana that hangs over us, waiting silently like a huge glass orb in the sky. We walk towards the dark shadow of the fountain where everyone else is waiting, when suddenly four brilliant lights flash in the darkness.

Queen Morganne and her husband Daya (the one with the horns) stand in front of us, lit by a glow that comes from within them. They look magnificent, alien and scary all at the same time. We pause but they beckon us forward. As we approach they step aside revealing two more Fae: a male, who's unusual because he has feathered green legs and birds feet with wings on his back; and a female who has the longest blonde hair, white wings and white feathered legs. They're looking at Lana's face. The female gives a strangled cry and closes her eyes, shaking and sobbing. The male is weeping openly and goes to the female. They hold onto each other for support. And I realise, quite suddenly, that though they look young, these bird-people are actually Lana's parents!

We place Lana on the ground and back out to join the others. Above us, at the centre of the Vimana a brilliant light appears, forming a column down to the body in the bag. Then out of the hole, a spiral of Fae children fly, singing or chanting something in high bright voices, their naked bodies glowing from wingtip to wingtip as they circle. With a jolt I recognise Tabika is one of them.

It's a lovely song. It sounds warm, welcoming, and a little sad. Then, still singing, they land, the light column vanishes and they form a circle around the adults in the centre. As the parents cry and hold onto each other Daya and Morganne hold up their staves, and Lana's bag bursts into huge flames. Then in a kind of slow dance Morganne and Daya circle the body as it burned ferociously while the children dance in the opposite directions on the outside. Above the fire sparks rise high into the darkness. Two flashes flare over by Dr Prosperov. Some new Fae have arrived but the brilliance of the flashes and the fire make it impossible to see who it is in the darkness. Closer to me the fire has started twisting around itself and as we watch it starts spinning faster and faster, rising up like a small fiery tornado. The core is too bright to look at. It's surrounded by dark dust and smoke as it rises into the air as a column of fire getting tighter and brighter.

Then from above the Vimana's light spears the fiery column which now seems to blend into the light column and disperse all the smoke, leaving only dust, still twirling. Slowly the dust began to float *up* swirling around the light up towards Ashanti.

After a while the dust is all gone. Morganne and Daya's dance ends and they stand back so that the parents rise and the children, flying in formation, still singing, circle around them up into a spiral back to the light and disappear. Immediately the light goes out, and Morganne and Daya vanish, leaving us in darkness.

We expect the Vimana to vanish, but it doesn't. It just hovers there, suspended over the house like a kind of mirage. We start to walk over to where Dr Prosperov is when suddenly there are four flashes in the sky above us and four glowing, flying bodies appear above us.

I know who's taken off even as I feel the rush of air as one of us, wings out, leaps into the sky. With savage excitement Tahira is climbing quickly to the Fae. I'm next to take off, followed by the others. It's fantastic to fly so easily the seventy meters up to where the Fae children are beginning to circle under the huge transparent Vimana. Tahira lights up her suit, and we all do the same.

I know it's Tabika she's after. And Tabika actually squeals with pleasure and dives on Tahira, catching her and embracing her in a flurry of feathers. They fall past us as we climb up to the others, then hovering face to face, kiss passionately, both pairs of wings beating strongly.

I can't see Mitra below but I can feel her shock. Then Tabika breaks away and climbs rapidly with Tahira following. I exchange awkward greetings with the two girls and the boy who hovered above. They're all naked and very pretty. One girl has short dark hair like Tabika, and is the same pale blue, while the other boy and girl are black skinned and shiny, silver haired. The two girls have white wings while the boy has black wings like Tabika.

They smile and silently ask my name. In reply they are Hexia, Sheba (the silver haired girl) and Ikarion (the boy). They all kiss me, lightly – even Ikarion (which is not as bad as I had thought it would be).

As always being kissed by Fae makes me feel silly and excited. But it's Tabika who flies up to me and gives me a long kiss that takes my breath away. She turns away to giggle with Hexia (who's her cousin apparently) but I catch a flash of excitement in her eye. I hang there gasping while the others are getting silly too.

We fly around each other in a kind of game of catch. We're all laughing although I can't think why. Tahira's chasing Tabika who's chasing me and I'm chasing Hexia who's chasing Tabika. There's a similar chase going on with Sheba and Ikarion where Scotty and Tarik are chasing Sheba, while Ashley and Cam chase Ikarion, and Sheba chases the girls and Ikarion chases the boys. The only one of us taking this at all seriously is Tahira. The rest of us are laughing like we can't do anything else, but Tahira's following Tabika seems a bit too intense. It doesn't help that Tabika teases her too, pretending to seek my help to keep away from Tahira. Knowing Tahira's heart, as I do, that is not a job I want.

Then the Vimana tells us it's time to go. The goodbye kisses are longer and sweeter than the welcome ones. Last of all are Tabika and Tahira whose kiss is especially passionate. Then Tabika flies after her friends and vanishes into the light.

For a moment the Vimana hangs there, a transparent disc filling the sky. Then, without a sound, it just winks out and is gone. The sky is empty again.

We flutter down to join the others on the ground. With the loss of power the party has ended, leaving just a few left on the lawn. Dr Prosperov, Mrs Jones, Hekator and Hekati.

I feel very tired and need to sleep. I follow the others toward the house but Hekator calls me back. I imagine he disapproves of Sue and has probably given her the injection to erase her memory. I'm a bit anxious about what he will tell me. I'd rather know tomorrow so I don't lie awake thinking about it.

"Sam, we all owe you an apology," Hekator says.

That's an unexpected start.

"We left you alone and vulnerable during the evacuation and you had to find your own support at a stressful time. It's not

171

surprising you latched on to Sue," Hekator tells me.

Uh-oh, this sounds like a build up to 'forget her, she's forgetting you' but he goes on.

"Personally, I wasn't sure about her, but I felt it was better to get her quarantined and checked over rather than leaving her in Auckland where she could be picked up and tapped by the Administration. Unfortunately it appears I was only half right," Hekator grimaces.

"It appears the Administration has a new biotap. We aren't sure how it's administered but my guess would be a nose spray. It grows a mass in the frontal lobe which forms a nano transmitter and conscious interface. Fully formed it means they can read your memories, intentions, everything. We've found one in Sue."

He's looking very serious and I was expecting the worst.

"Sue's transmitter was already working when she was quarantined. Fortunately the interface was only a few days old and still undeveloped. All the transmitter could do was transmit a general brainwave pattern and a very limited amount of sensory data," Hekator says. I nod, so he continues.

"Sue's growth has not yet spread to the visual cortex, conscious or memory centres. But it does mean she was feeding them limited information about her surroundings when she was in the quarantine station. All *they* knew was that Sue was with you somewhere warm, when you were telling them you were alone in a speeder on the moon."

"But is she OK. Is Sue alright?" I ask, impatient to know.

Hekator smiles.

"Yes, Sam. Earlier today the Fae Council overrode the Fae medical ethics court and ordered me to isolate and remove the mindtap for further study. It was a tricky operation using nanobots which had to be done when Sue was in a natural sleep state when Administration monitoring of her brainwaves could be assumed to be reduced."

"First I had to back-up Sue's brain, synapse by synapse which took some time. Then the big risk was switching from natural inputs to synthetic ones without destroying the buds, transmitters or creating a blood clot which could produce a stroke, but I think we got past that OK."

"Is she OK?" I blurt out, neither understanding or caring about the technicalities.

"I think so. The tests seemed normal. But all brains are very delicate so one can never be too sure."

"Where is she now?"

"At home, asleep. She'll wake up a bit disoriented, and it's always best for patients to wake up in a familiar environment." Now I'm sure he'd erased her memory.

"Sam, the old plan of pretending the Renwick house people are still missing is compromised. The Administration know you were with Sue when Ka-rea-rea was in the moonbase and you were pretending to be alone. Now *they* want to use our trick against us by playing along with our deception and tricking *us* into bringing Sue here. Then by using their secret brain tap they would ambush you all again, but this time without any warning. It's quite clever, really."

"So Dr Prosperov and I think the best thing we can do now is play along. We will pretend *not* to have found Sue's mindtap. That will give me time to study its growth and work out a way to cure fully grown ones. We have to assume that is what we will find in Nathan's brain."

"OK," I say, unsure what all this means.

There's a pause. They're looking at me like I should be getting a big fat hint but I'm too tired and I don't see it. I shake my head. "Sorry ... maybe I'm being dumb but what do you want me to do?"

Dr P and Hekator looked at each other. Then at me. I felt I must be very stupid.

"We need the Administration to believe we have *not* discovered their mindtap ..." Hekator began. I interrupt.

"But Sue can't come here, and if the mindtap got to her memories it would tell them everything. So we *must* erase Sue's memory," I guess.

"Well, we *would* if the mindtap were still in Sue's brain. But it isn't. It's in a synthetic brain I control. I can feed it, and therefore *them*, anything I like. But to make it believable I am streaming Sue's experiences from her real brain. I can adapt them before feeding them to the synthetic one with the mindtap. They won't know the difference."

"So what do I do?" I ask.

"That is part of the deception. We need them to think their plan is working and that you are leading her here. We can also use her experience of you telling her about your past to mislead them. When they try to access her memories of what you have told her they will get ones I want them to have."

"But what if Rocelli bugged Sue's house as well? They will know there's a difference," I ask.

"I've swept Sue's hut very thoroughly before I visited it. I haven't found any anomalies to suggest they bugged it. My guess is they realised you were trained to keep moving but still fixated on Sue anyway because you needed some sense of security. I think they wanted to lull us into a false sense of security so they have relied entirely on the most difficult to detect sensor – Sue's brain. Unfortunately for them, the more successful that channel seems to be, the more they will focus on it."

"But … well I'm confused … is Sue not ever coming here, because she'll be pretty annoyed about that, or are we just tricking them into thinking she is?"

My head hurts and I feel so tired.

Dr P smiles at me.

"Sam am agreeing with your proposal that Constable Williams can be very useful means for us to close Renwick House mystery. She is key to the cover story being believed," Dr P says.

"What is the cover story?"

"We say we are all away on superyacht. Except you. You stay to be with Emma Reeves. When we learn of fire at Renwick House we hide in Northland near Mr Kahu's home, and are in hiding from Russian hit team who burned down house. We have contacted you, and allowed policewoman to visit, in order to confirm we are alive, but have prevented police knowing where we are because of risk that Russian hit team has bribed informers in Police."

I know Sue will be impossible if she doesn't meet Dr P soon. I have to make that clear to him.

"Everything she's done has been to meet you, Dr P. But will she really meet anyone? Because I don't know what to tell her if she can't" I ask, confused by all these double crosses.

"She must, if she is to help with plan," Dr P reasons.

"It can be done safely. I will adjust anything that gives away her location. It will focus *their* attention if they think their plan is working," Hekator says.

"However, once we have closed the Renwick House affair we will need to establish whether she joins us on our terms or loses her memory of us," Dr P went on.

"Would you ... Would you hire Sue?" I ask.

He bobs his head weighing it up.

"Has adapted well ... has useful knowledge. If she is interested, why not?"

Even despite being very tired that bit of news was music to my ears. I'm grinning like a crazy man.

"Thanks Dr P! That is just so cool." I tell him. To his surprise I even hug him. Dr P shrugs.

"I think you made decision made for me," he says.

I release him, uncertainly.

"But is good decision," he nods.

"Sam?" Hekator interrupts.

"Yeah?"

"Sue, will need at least twelve hours rest. Her operation was as gentle as possible but it still involved putting things inside her skull. She needs to heal. She won't feel like doing much. Keep that in mind and be gentle," Hekator advises.

"OK, I will."

"And that goes for you too Sam. You've been awake for a very long time. You'd better get some sleep," Hekator smiles.

"Right?" I say vaguely, and then confused. "Where?"

"Back to Sue's hut, it would be best if you are together when she wakes."

"OK."

They stand back a bit, and I realise they mean now.

[+]

So I fold away and arrive in a flash of light a short time later in the familiar spare room. I go into Sue's room. She's still dressed, face down in the pillow. She still has her hair, which surprises me, but she will be a very grumpy bear in the morning. Suddenly a wicked thought occurs to me. I nip into the kitchen and look around. I find her bottle of bourbon and tip out a little into a plastic cup. Then I go into the bathroom and get some cotton swabs. Gently I roll her over and swab bourbon on her dress and skin. It stinks brilliantly. I dribble a little into her mouth then I roll her back and empty out the cup, rinse it and throw the swab out the door and zap it so it burns briefly with a blue glow. With a grin on my face I lie down on my bed and a moment later I wake up.

CHAP+ER SIX+Y F⊕UR: PRELUDES

I wake up in Sue's spare room with a headache to find Sue shaking me. She's frowning and looking grumpy.

"Sam? Sam?"

I groan and turn over hardly able to open my eyes.

"Sam what happened?"

I mumble, "party" and try to wriggle away. My head *really* does hurt and I *really* am tired.

"Sam why do I stink of booze?"

Sue turns me over.

"Wicked party eh," I grin with my eyes shut. I'm really grinning at my evil trickery.

"*What* party?" Sue demands.

"The one we were at," I mumble.

"I wasn't at a party."

I laugh briefly and roll over, eyes still closed.

"Coulda fooled me."

There's silence.

"Where was it?" she asks, worried.

"Spaceship," I murmur like she should know.

"I don't remember a thing."

I snort.

"Not too surprising," I yawn.

She says nothing. I start to drift.

"No, really Sam, nothing. Total blank," she says finally.

I speak with my eyes closed.

"Betcha got a headache? Didja chuck?"

"No ... Well, I don't know ... I *do* have a helluva headache. Maybe I did ... It's really odd."

I just lie there and catch myself snoring. A bit later I hear the shower. I sleep in fits after that. Finally around midday I wake up, a bit worried I've missed something. The whole place is quiet, I wonder if Sue is still there. I get up and look in her bedroom. She's curled up asleep with a book lying open next to her.

I tiptoe into the kitchen looking for some breakfast. There's museli and toast. I choose toast with honey. I'm just making it when Sue staggers out.

"I feel wrecked," she complains.

"Not surprised," I say.

She sits down at the table looking wrecked. I put on the hot water jug for her, then sit down at the table too, with my toast.

"Did I really party last night?" she asks.

I smile. "Yeah. Hard out."

Sue looks worried. "I really don't remember a thing and my body feels fine, no muscle strain or anything."

She thinks for a moment and then asks.

"Nobody would have slipped me anything would they?"

I think about that, spreading the gold clear honey.

"You mean like drugs?" I ask.

"Yeah," Sue asks doubtfully.

"Doubt it ... that's a pretty low thing to do. Why would the Fae do that?"

"Oh, the Fae were there?"

I look at her suddenly. Now I *am* acting.

"Are you serious?"

"Yeah."

I pull a face.

"Yeah, the Fae were there, and the way you were dancing with them I'd have thought you'd remember it."

I feel harsh saying this, but for the moment I don't want her to know she had had her brain messed with by Hekator. That would be too much of a shock and it might give away our tricking the Administration. It was easier to let her think she just had a hangover.

Sue gasps.

"Shit! They haven't decided to erase my memory have they?"

"I don't think so," I say unsure.

I wonder what Hekator is passing on to *them*. But that isn't my problem. My problem is Sue feels wrecked after brain nanosurgery and I can't let her know why yet.

"But you said when they erased Professor Cherensky's memory he was really sick for days."

"Yeah," I admit. She's cleverer than I thought.

"And I'm a wreck."

"Oh."

"Do you think they've started erasing?" she asks, suddenly worried.

"Uhh ... well, can you remember where I'd got up to in telling you about last year?"

"Um ... yeah sure. Sarah Kogan was in a block of flats on the outskirts of Umm al Fahm inland from Caesaria with two nameless Arab bitches, and the Syrian mobsters Omar and

Hussein, but you didn't know yet if her father, Uri, was going to pay the ransom, or do what he was told, or whether Sarah's grandfather, Michael Semenov, would step in or what her mother, Alisha would do when she found out her daughter had been kidnapped. You'd just bugged Alisha and Michael but didn't know where Uri was."

I look at her a bit awed. She has an amazing memory.

"You're *good*," I say, with new respect.

"Yeah but why can't I remember last night?"

"I dunno, maybe they did erase your memory. I can't think why," I shrug.

"I s'pose they wouldn't really tell *you* if you asked, either," she muses.

"No, probably not," I agree, eating toast.

The jug comes to the boil and Sue makes a cup of tea.

"So why are we back here? I thought I was going to meet Prosperov finally," Sue asks.

"They need us to keep to the story that I'm all alone in the world and I've given up Ka-rea-rea."

"And what do I do?"

"Adopt me."

"*What*! But I don't want to. I don't live for you guys! What about *my* job? Where am I meant to have been?"

"We've been in the Hokianga finding the others."

"But I didn't call in. Man! I will be in heaps of trouble."

"You followed a lead and the Renwick survivors would only meet you if you couldn't tell anyone where they are because they are scared of a Russian hit squad with bribed informers inside the Police."

"But I haven't *met* anyone yet!" Sue complains angrily. She

181

fumes silently to herself.

"I'm just being messed around," she says to herself, angrily.
Sue's pissed off. Just like I expected. The headache probably
isn't helping her mood either. I could see her point of view.

"Well, you sort of met them last night," I lie.

"Well, I don't remember doing anything of the sort."

"What do you remember?"

"I got into that coffin thing. It came here. I got out and ... uh.
After that, nothing."

"Nothing? Not arriving on the Vimana, not the party, not
anything?"

She shakes her head, seriously.

It's so tough not being able to tell her that she had had a brain
operation and we're buying time while Hekator studies the
growth so that he can work out how to get the same thing out of
Nathan.

"Well, they must have done something," I admit.

"Great! Just great! I put myself out on a limb with my career,
I play along, and then they stiff me! What am I meant to tell
Kevin? I went to the Hokianga to find them and I did, but I can't
remember any of it? But that's not surprising because some f___
_g aliens erased my memory!"

"Sometimes they have to do things." I say weakly. "You just have
to work on trust," I told her.

"Fat lot of use that is! Why should I trust people who don't keep
their promises?" she asks, pissed off.

"They'll have their reasons. We just need to sit tight," I tell her.

"*Who's on deck*?" I ask silently through my suit.

"Me," replies Grandpop.

"*Can I talk to Hekator please?*"

"I'll see, hang on ..."

Sue hasn't noticed anything. She doesn't have her tiara anymore. She's still got a headache and looks pretty tired.

"So am I meant to go to work or what? And what do I f____g tell them?" she asks sitting down with her tea.

"Well, it's a bit hopeless today, it's lunchtime," I point out.

"Yeah ... and I feel wrecked, I can always just call in sick," she sighs, calming down.

"Maybe you need some lunch," I suggest.

"Mmm ... I don't feel that hungry."

"You know I reckon you've either had a memory erasure or you're just plain sick."

"I can't be sick, I've been in a quarantine station for two nights and you're not sick."

"Well, either way I reckon you need to take it easy and sleep it off," I tell her.

Sue sighs.

"You're right. I feel it's all I can do, anyway."

"Do you want me to tell you more about the kidnapping?"

"Yeah ... It's easier than reading and I always like a good crime story."

"OK ... I ..."

"But not here. Let me lie down. I want to be comfy."

"Sure."

So we go to her room. She props up some pillows and lies down while I sit on a chair by the window.

"*Sam?*" says Hekator.

"*Sue's stroppy. She feels messed around.*"

"*So?*"

"*So it makes it hard for me to manage her. She's an adult, I'm fourteen.*"

"*OK ... When she falls asleep I'll keep the simulated brain asleep and then you wake her up.*"

"*Why?*"

"*So she can meet Dr Prosperov. That way they can talk without the Administration listening in.*"

"*Thanks Hekator.*"

"I'll get Gennady," says Grandpop.

"*Thanks Grandpop.*"

Sue's looking at me.

"Well?"

"Sorry, I was trying to remember exactly what came next."

"And?"

So I begin.

...

The morning after the night when we messed with his intrusion detection system and kept him awake Michael Semovich was too busy to even get mad with his bodyguards (who we'd zapped) for sleeping on the job in his chair. He came upstairs with his cell to his ear at six the next morning, saw the sleeping men and tipped the one in his chair out in the floor and sat down.

On the other side of the world it was after dinner and we were watching (via our bugs) on the TV in the café drinking bedtime hot chocolates with Control putting on subtitles in English. Ashley and Scotty didn't see it because they were in Austria again and hadn't woken up yet.

Michael was on the phone to Uri. While he spoke he switched on his office TVs. The news (in Hebrew) was full of reports of the fighting in the Gaza strip. Neither Semovich nor Kogan had had any demands from Sarah's kidnappers yet and it was upsetting them. Michael was telling Uri he was calling in favours all over the world to find out who was behind this. As far as he saw it, taking Sarah was as much an insult to him as it was to Kogan, and he wasn't going to let whoever had pulled off this little stunt get the better of him.

His suspicions were directed at Semion Mogilevich. He was a tough business rival in his shady world. He doubted if the Hamas connection drawn in the media had anything to do with it. As far as he was concerned someone was making war on his family and anyone who did that was going to get the eye-for-eye treatment.

Uri said he was grateful for his father-in-laws support but begged him not to strike until Sarah was safe. Michael agreed. Uri said he would do whatever was asked to get Sarah back but when she was he would help Michael hunt the kidnappers down. He also asked Michael not to get Alisha involved or things would get too crazy too fast. That was something else the two men agreed on. They speculated the kidnappers were waiting to build up the tension and make their escape better.

Michael pointed out that Uri would have to front up to the Israeli police. He'd already pulled some strings and got Chief Inspector Yigal Gur assigned to the case. He regarded Gur as a practical policeman who wouldn't poke his nose in where it wasn't wanted. Already he had announced that the focus of the inquiry was on finding the murderers of the bodyguard, Ivan Federov, without mentioning the question of the missing girl. They talked about Uri's current deal and in particular the quality of diamonds on offer. Then, running out of anything else to say, they hung up. We were still in our suits and we weren't surprised when Dr Prosperov came down to talk to us.

"Appears Semovich and Kogan wish to keep situation under control. Is probable deal between kidnappers and father could result in either early release or early death of Sarah Kogan. Is therefore necessary to create wider confusion."

"Solution is alert mother, Alisha Semovich, to situation. Is unlikely dramatic personality and mother's concern controlled by men. Means is simple. Mitra will record demand for ten million Israeli Sheckel ransom in Arabic and Control will placed it on Alisha's cellular voice mail system. Idea is to simulate Arab helpers doing own deal. Is expected to complicate situation for all sides."

"Also, Control has traced deposits for Omar and Hussein to Bank Arabia branch in Dubai. Log files show is account in name of Transocean Enterprises PLC Ltd. Tomorrow operation to knock out internet banking channel requires attack on bank's computers. Non-payment of mercenaries will also complicate situation."

"So, is no further need for operations in Israel overnight. Scott and Ashley monitoring Kogan in Belgium. Control to find Gur. Bugs needed on both. Suggest all get sleep."

And he left us to go back to his office.

It was strange not having Scott or Ashley around. We all missed them a lot. I wondered what it would be like when Tahira left to join her family in Israel. There was some nervousness about going to Israel given the battle raging in Gaza between Fatah and Hamas but they were not going to Israel's south. They were flying Emirates from Auckland to Dubai via Brisbane, then

Dubai to Jordan and finally Cyprus Airways direct to Haifa.
They were leaving by plane in a few days and Scott would come
back and fly with Tahira to the Mediterranean. There was still
some discussion suggesting I should fly with them, drop Ka-
rea-rea and then bend back in a sleeping bag. The only question
was whether we needed two or three speeders in the Northern
hemisphere now.

I took Dr P's advice and went to bed early. Rewa was going
to bed too so we chatted for a while. I wondered how Ax's
conversion of the chapel was coming along. We hadn't seen or
heard much from there lately because we were so busy overseas
and just weren't paying attention. Rewa was still excited about
going to Israel. She had been reading websites and looking up
bits of the Bible. She couldn't get over the fact that the Sea of
Galilee and Nazareth were real places she could go, although
Bethlehem and Jerusalem were mixed up in the fighting. She
only really had a Sunday school idea of Israel.

She asked me what it was like. I said I hadn't seen much of it but
what I had seen was interesting. The very old, the new, the rich
on the hillsides, the poor Arab towns. But I warned her in winter
it wasn't warm, even down by the sea. She asked me if there
were ghosts. I said there was no end of them but they were more
confused than anything else. Like sports day when everyone at
school doesn't know where they are meant to be. She went to
bed happy but I found I couldn't sleep.

It was strange. I kept thinking of Mordecai Ceder, the Israeli
holocaust survivor and psychic who I'd met in Haifa.

Listen to God, he'd said.

And somehow I had this weird feeling I was meant to be
somewhere else, doing something else. I paced my room

listening to the sea. It was a warm summer's night and the three-quarter moon was bright on the water. Slowly I got tired and went to bed.

I found myself in a dusty place full of harsh, rocky, red mountains. The sun was golden, lighting the edges of these big hills. It was either dawn or sunset. Beneath a steep slope in a valley by a dry riverbed there were houses which seemed to be made of mud except they were square and three storeys tall, painted in stunning colours and patterns, beneath the steep bank. The shadows were picking out the textures. The yellow light was slanting its way into the cold valleys.

A road ran in front of the house. It wasn't much of a road as there were holes everywhere but the tyre tracks suggested quite a lot of vehicles passed that way. On the other side of the road a small figure dressed all in black was hauling a goat by a rope towards the house. The big nanny goat was stubbornly resisting but not fighting the small person. The goat seemed to want to stay in the bottom of the valley where the merest smudge of green suggested some moisture.

Suddenly there was a rumbling and the black figure froze. Looking up the long valley a blackness had appeared in the distance. It was spreading down the valley like a huge snake winding rapidly through the hills. The small figure was frozen as the wall of black – it was water, black with sand – came closer and closer. Suddenly the figure turned around and looked directly at me although I was not really part of this scene. It was a girl with light brown skin and gray-blue eyes which seemed to see me although I wasn't there and she screamed "Fayadaaaaan," so loudly I woke up.

It was a still, summer night. There were no ghosts in my room.

There was no wind. The sea crunched regularly and gently onto the beach. And yet I could still see that scene as clear as day in my mind's eye. I knew it meant something, but I wasn't sure exactly what. It was two in the morning. There was nothing for it but to go back to sleep.

We all got up early the next morning interested to hear what had happened overnight. Control had tracked Kogan to a hotel room in Belgium where he had met with business associates – all beefy, mean-looking white men in suits. Meanwhile Mitra's message had sparked the fury of Sarah Kogan's mother, Alisha Semovich.

She was scared, but she was also mad. She was furious with her ex, Uri, and with her father, Michael Semovich, for not telling her. She called both of them demanding to know why they hadn't told her about her daughter's kidnapping. They, in turn, were totally confused by her news of a demand in Arabic on her phone, and for payment in Israeli Shekels. They had thought it was a foreign, professional job. Now they were confused. This news suggested local gangsters (who wouldn't normally dare mess with Semovich) were involved and that made Semovich angry. But his immediate problem was his guilt-crazed daughter. Alisha screamed at them, she threatened to expose them, she even threw expensive things around her apartment she was so enraged. Then she decided to get even.

Alisha flew at once to Tel Aviv and demanded to see the Defence Minister, Ehud Barak, because of the 'terrorists' who had kidnapped her daughter. Barak's office told her the Minister was busy with the situation in Gaza and didn't talk about criminal matters. The Minister of Public Security Avi Dichter's office was more diplomatic – given Semovich's connections – but the answer was the same. The Gaza situation was their priority. But with her loud voice Alisha soon found a politician who *was* keen to get involved. Shev Komenski, the outspoken leader of the tiny Russian immigrant dominated "Our Heritage" Party. I didn't know anything about politics in Israel other than what Dr Prosperov and Mordechai Ceder had told me. Apparently Komenski was a former Russian and anti-Arab. He believed that all Israel should be for Jews and Jews alone. As far as he was concerned the million and a half Muslim Arab Israelis should be expelled from the country by force, despite the fact they had lived there for centuries before Israel was a country, simply because they weren't Jewish.

Alisha's story, that her daughter had been taken by Arabs – possibly with connections to Hamas – suited him well. He made sure all the TV cameras were there when he and Alisha met Chief Inspector Gur at four that afternoon. Gur was following up the power line workers descriptions of the killers who were described as Arabs, probably Palestinian. Komenski turned this into the Palestinians generally and by six that evening the whole country knew Sarah Kogan-Semovich was missing and that it was a plot involving Arab kidnappers and "terrorists" who wanted a large ransom.

The TV report had pictures of Sarah looking much younger and more innocent than we had seen her. The Semovichs were described as "successful business people" in the transport and tourism industry who had risen from poverty when they had arrived to make a fortune estimated in the hundreds of millions. The news readers somehow managed to convey the sense that there was more to this than met the eye. Michael

Semovich's neighbours in Caesaria (who looked like mean-as crims themselves) described them as "quiet" and "friendly". Alisha's tearful appeal was mixed with anger directed at "the Arabs who took her". She agreed with Chief Inspector Gur when he said, "Somebody knows something. And others may know these somebodies and are keeping the whereabouts of this child secret. In my book they are as guilty as the kidnappers themselves."

It was a few minutes distraction from the serious news in the south anyway. Unfortunately they all missed the more interesting story: the real kidnappers had finally made a demand.

Uri Kogan called Michael Semovich to say a man calling himself "Laurent" had called him on his cell at three in the afternoon and in French told him his daughter's future depended on him remaining in Belgium for 24 hours. So long as he did that, Sarah would be safe. If Uri didn't, Laurent suggested, Sarah would be exported to the trade in Eastern European girls Uri himself traded in, and it was unlikely he would see her again.

Having to remain in Belgium worried Uri. He was wanted by police in France and by the FBI in the States. He knew if the Belgians invented some reason to arrest him, and then allowed him to be extradited to America, he could end up in prison for a very long time. He was almost sure that was the idea because he was certain he was being watched. And he was right. He was. Scotty picked up the crew watching Kogan while they were distracted by a whiny American girl (Ashley) complaining to her mother in the hotel lobby. The guy playing piano in the lobby was a lookout and there were two others floating around the café. They weren't paying any attention at all to a white boy outside waiting for a bus. If they had known how well he could read minds they wouldn't have been so relaxed.

Scotty tracked down the crew's boss and discovered it was a policeman named Sergeant Olivier Xavier, of the Brussels organised crime unit of the Federal Police. Xavier had discovered there was more chance of living – and living well by criminal standards – by being on both sides of the law than by fighting crime.

We weren't sure whether we were meant to help Uri Kogan escape the Belgian Police or not. But Dr Prosperov decided that our main focus had to stay with Sarah. After all, for Sarah's father this was just a bad day at the office, for Sarah it was all new and terrifying, and it was her survival that was our problem.

So we focused on creating problems in Umm Al Fahm by interfering with the overnight processing of Sarah's Syrian captors' payment and to bugging them as well. Para.no.ID had supplied us with a useful virus to beat security systems and crack passwords but it had to be delivered on a USB data stick. To mess up the payment meant entering the Arabian Bank's data centre, putting the data stick into a server and then using the access it provided to reprogram their computers. Control had already mapped the building's layout. Like you'd expect it was pretty secure against normal entry and there were card swipe doors everywhere.

The data centre was laid out as a series of rows between tall computer cabinets that looked like fridges in a supermarket. At the end of the row was the security control room. Nobody went down to it much except for a couple of uniformed guards

who drank coffee and chatted the night away. The main control
screens for the bank were upstairs where the computer people
worked.

So all we had to do was wait until one of the guards went to the
bathroom, bend in, zap him, take his card, zap his friend, and
take over the control room. Then we could implant the USB
and take over the security system. Once Control had that under
control we could bend into the computer room and crack the
bank's processing computers.

Tahira and me got to do the security guards. Cam and Tarik the
computers. It all went pretty easily at first. The big round guard
with the moustache left the room and went into the stairwell to
the bathroom.

[+]

We bent into the stairwell. He came out of the door and I got
him before he even noticed we were there. We took his access
card and punched in the combo. His mate (a cheery, thinner
looking guy, also with a mo) was leaning back in his chair,
glanced at us and Tahira zapped him so he slumped right where
he was.

I dragged the fat guy into the room, and we shut the door. While
I was arranging fatty in his chair, Tahira put the USB key into
the security system. Now we relaxed. Unfortunately that was
when things got exciting.

The phone rang. We both jumped a bit but then realised we
couldn't possibly answer it, so we sat there and let it ring.
Whoever it was, was not giving up easily.

Two flashes in the aisles told us the security system was broken
and Cam and Tarik had arrived.

"I'm afraid they detected the key, before I locked them out and took control of the computer," Control warned us.

"*Do we go?*" I asked.

"No. But guards are likely to be coming. You will have to keep them out."

We looked at each other. There was nothing else to do but adopt blend camouflage. Cam and Tarik blended their colours too. It made them almost invisible in the low light out among the computer cabinets.

Our guards were propped up in their chairs seemingly asleep. Cam and Tarik were dashing from computer rack to computer rack putting in taps. We were waiting, blended-in lying on the floor, on the wall beside the door. Then came the tap on the glass window of the door we'd expected. More guards.

The new guards outside cautiously opened the lock with their cards. The door was pushed open a little. There was a bit of whispering and a suppressed snort of laughter.

"This will be loud," Grandpop warned us.

It was. The new guards burst in with a huge yell with their pistols drawn. In the silence that followed you could hear everyone's heart beat.

"Look around," said the one in front with a goatee quietly to his mate.

The other one moved in front of the knocked out guards lying in their chairs.

"*I'm good*," Tahira told me, meaning she had the other one in her sights.

"*On two*," I said as I had the first one. "*One, two.*"

Both newcomers crumpled.

"Good work Tahira and Sam," Grandpop said.

We got up and checked their guns. The safeties were off so

we put them on. We dragged them into position and got them comfy. It wasn't much later when Cam and Tarik were finished, so we all bent home.

[+]

"OK, good work guys," Grandpop said in the briefing theatre. "Hussein and Omar won't be paid. But now, just to be really annoying, we want to take their cell phones. They are staying in a room upstairs in this block. They are very disciplined. They don't go out, they don't do anything much but read, smoke, exercise and play chess on their phones. They may even take turns to sleep. What is certain is we'll have to wait until their early morning – our afternoon – to strike. However we may need Buffy so Ashley and Scotty will join Sam and Tahira for the night shift. Cam and Tarik? If you want to go back to searching you can."

"Thanks Mike," said Cam. "You're flying," she told Tarik.

"I'm *always* flying," Tarik complained.

"Well, wear your ground kit too," Cam suggested.

"Yeah OK," he said and went off to the lockers to get ready to fly back to the South China Sea.

That left me and Tahira, as Scotty and Ashley were already in bed.

"*How about we harass Diana's keepers again?*" Tahira grinned wickedly.

"*Oh alright,*" I agreed.

Control briefed us on Diana's situation.

They had moved her to a private house in the mountains near the Hungarian city of Sopol, just across from the Austrian border. She was the maid. She lived separately to her older sister, Elena, under the supervision of a man she had to call "Uncle Vanya". Uncle Vanya kept Elena with eight other girls in the "Guest House" where they "entertained" the "guests" – most of whom were Austrians. Diana's job was to clean up afterwards. Like all the other girls at the "Guest House" Elena was now hooked on heroin. Vanya was a cruel man, but he didn't beat the girls. He just punished them by making them beg for their drugs, and rewarded them by giving them more, making them more hooked than they were before. Control wouldn't let us see what he made them do, but Diana's job was cleaning up all kinds of disgusting stuff.

But worst for little Diana was that she was losing her sister to heroin. Elena looked forward to it. The drug was replacing Diana as the love of her life. And when she got it she was insulated from her horrible world by a dreamy drugged out indifference. It seemed hopeless.

"What can we do?" we asked Grandpop when Control had finished.

"I'd better ask Gennady. The only way I see out of this is if Elena cold turkeys."

"What does that mean?" I wanted to know.

"It means a week or more of living hell for Elena. Heroin fixes itself in your system. Getting clean is like the worst disease you can imagine and all you want is some heroin to make it go away."

I had a nasty suspicion Grandpop wasn't just talking from a book he'd read. He noticed me looking at him questioningly.

"There was a lot of it about in 'Nam," he said quietly.

"But Diana won't be able to help Elena through by herself. She is going to need help."

"But zhey are in mountains. It iz freezing. 'ow can zhey escape? Where can zhey go?" Tahira objected.

"I think this time the answer is going to be the Hungarian authorities. What we need is an honest cop." Grandpop said.

Dr P came down to talk it over with us. Tahira thought he would be willing to sacrifice Elena and was getting ready to fight him over it, but Dr P was relaxed.

"Is correct. Elena is in great danger. Is too early for Diana to lose sister now. Is necessary to assist escape. What is thinking?" Grandpop answered.

"Well, I thought if the drug supply was interrupted and the authorities tipped off, they might be persuaded to rescue the girls."

Dr P rocked his head.

"Interrupted? How interrupted?"

"Car crash of the drug courier. Then the police follow it up."

"Why?"

Grandpop pulled a face.

"No idea," he admitted. Dr P had another suggestion.

"Drugs is good weakness. But suggest no car crash. Police simply trail drug courier to chalet. Then arrest all present. Perhaps tip off local journalist to make sure is no bribe."

Grandpop nodded.

"Operatives should copy owners cell phone sim. Then trace network," Dr P said glancing at us.

"Am guessing four or five in morning is best time."

That meant doing Vanya's phone after stealing Omar and Hussein's phones. So now we had nothing to do until later anyhow.

...

"Sue?" I ask. She has her eyes closed.

"Yeah?" she replies groggily.

"I thought you might be asleep," I explain.

"No ... No ... I'm awake," she replies, but she still has her eyes closed.

I go on.

...

It turned out that Omar and Hussein did sleep in shifts. Hussein watched over Sarah who was tied up asleep while Omar slept upstairs. Hussein played chess on his cell phone and we could assume Omar would probably do the same. That meant if we stole Omar's phone while Hussein watched, Omar would notice not having it when they swapped over. We decided not to bother Scotty and do it the hard way. Tahira volunteered to do cover while I did the job.

[+]

So at three in the morning local time I flashed into the bare little room Omar and Hussein were camped in. Omar was quick. From asleep he had his pistol out in two seconds. But it was still too slow and we zapped him. The arm and weapon fell away harmlessly. The gun was very small but the safety was right by the hammer so it was easy to put it back on. I put them back where they had been and tucked Omar in. His Blackberry phone was very new. It was right by his bed so finding that was easy.

"*Hussein will be trickier. He's awake and bored,*" I said.

"*Do we sneak or pretend to be Omar?*" Tahira asked.

It was a good suggestion.

"*Pretend to be Omar,*" I said. "*Hussein would love to be snuck up on. He chased Scott just for fun. He's a cat that guy.*"

Tahira bent down and picked up Omar's shoes. She turned them over.

"*Leather. Very chic. You be Omar with the hard feet. I'll have soft and fluffy for quiet.*"

"*My soft and fluffy friend,*" I smiled.

"*Miaow,*" she said, and swatted me playfully.

"*OK, let's go.*"

We followed the route Control had given to the stairs. My mouth was a bit dry. This Hussein dude was a soldier, and he was armed and alert. This was way different to jumping someone who was asleep.

I tapped down the stairs and came to the door. I tried it and it was locked. Damn.

"He's looking your way Sam."

I couldn't mimic Omar's voice! I extended my pinky lock picker and twelve seconds later unlocked the door.

"*Where is he?*"

"He's moved behind the door when you open it."

"*Shit!*"

"He's going to jump you Sam. You gotta let him. Tahira don't let him close the door behind Sam.

Sam? Go!"

I walked forward. I could feel him behind the door. He let me go three, four, five paces. Then he slammed the door behind me.

"Don't move!" he told me in Arabic.

I put my hands up.

"*I couldn't stop it,*" Tahira complained.

"Don't fret Tahira he hasn't locked it yet," Grandpop told her. Suddenly Hussein opened the door and pointed his cocked pistol straight at Tahira. I couldn't see this directly because I was facing the other way. I went to turn around. But he threw Tahira inside and yelled.

"Face the wall. You! Hands up! Join your friend!" The last words were said loudly.

Tahira ended up standing next to me. We had our backs to Hussein.

"OK," Hussein, said, thinking.

"Who are you? You on the right first."

"Ahmed," I said.

He was half thinking of who it might be anyway and this name seemed to be in the air.

"Ahmed who? What is your clan?"

"Walid," I said thinking quickly of the garage.

"Who is your father?"

"Ali," I said thinking there had to be a Ali Walid or three in the clan.

"On the left. Your name?"

"Farah."

"Oh Muhammed!" said Hussein, surprised he'd caught a girl.

"Farah? Who is *your* father?" he asked more slowly.

Walid was the wrong answer.

"Sayed."

Hussein's brain was doing flip-flops trying to understand modern kids.

"What the f____ are you two doing sneaking around here at three in the morning!!? Are you insane! If anyone catches you, you're dead. And why are you wearing school bags?"

"We wanted to see the Israeli girl," Tahira said.

I noticed the Israeli girl was lying very still in front of us. Sarah was awake and listening. She probably had enough Arabic to follow what was happening. I zapped her.

"*Why did you do that?*" Tahira asked me silently.

"You aren't from here are you?" Hussein could tell from her accent.

"*So she doesn't see us zap motormouth here,*" I told her.

"No," Tahira replied to Hussein.

"Why did you want to see the Israeli girl?"

"I felt sorry for her. She was on the news."

"How did you know she was here?" Hussein asked trying to hide his nervousness.

"Everyone knows. You can't keep a secret like that around here," Tahira said.

Hussein sniffed. We could tell that the lack of secrecy was bothering him. A lot of things were bothering him. He hadn't expected the news of the kidnap to end up on TV. He'd been told it would all be kept quiet and the whole thing would be over in just a few days.

"Well, I have my secrets and you have yours. Now turn around." We turned.

"OK, lower your hoods. If I have to tell your fathers you were sneaking out together I want to make sure who it is I am talking about."

We raised our hands to our hoods and both zapped him at the same time. He collapsed heavily on to his back.

"You two are so good, I just can't believe it sometimes," Grandpop said.

We went forward and Tahira took Hussein's phone.

"*Do you think we should take their guns too?*" I asked.

"They could easily kill her without one," Grandpop pointed out.

"*But with no phones, no money and no guns, they don't have much to stay in charge with do they?*" I said.

"Yeah, OK, take their guns too," Grandpop agreed.

So we took Hussein's Blackberry and picked up his gun and went back for Omar's. The guns were tiny little things.

[+]

We bent back to base and handed them over to Grandpop. He told us they were Beretta Storms made to be hidden easily. After the excitement of dealing to two tough guys we were ready to deal to Diana's too.

We decided to jump Vanya in Hungary the way we'd done Omar and Federov in Israel. Burst in and zap everyone. Vanya was sleeping with two of the girls from the guesthouse. Well, *he* was sleeping. One of them was awake, probably because of his snoring. She was about to get some sleep.

[+]

We decided to arrive outside and come through the door. It took five seconds from the time we left Renwick until all three lay stunned in bed.

"*God, he's a pig!*" Tahira sneered at the hairy man in the bed. I looked for the phone.

"*I wish I could shock him,*" Tahira said bitterly.

"*Yeah,*" I agreed vaguely, searching.

"*Ah there it is...*" I said. It was under the bed.

There was a blue flash. I jumped up.

Tahira was hurriedly pulling up the bedclothes.

"*He won't be bothering these girls again for a while,*" Tahira said happily.

202

"Tahira!…"Grandpop began sternly.

"*What?*" she replied a little guiltily.

Grandpop swallowed.

"You aren't meant to do that."

"*Why not?*" she asked remembering her anger.

"Because he won't know it was *you*," Grandpop pointed out.

"*Oh,*" Tahira realised that if she wasn't blamed someone else might be.

"*Oh no,*" she added realising where that might go.

I pulled the Nokia apart and put the sim to my omnicard. In a few seconds it had duplicated it. Then I put it back and put the phone under the bed.

"*What did you do to him anyway?*" I asked, conversationally.

"*Burnt his …*" she gestured to his groin.

"*Ow!*" I replied automatically.

We bent home. We emerged into the oil.

[+]

"*Well, I hope he doesn't take it out on the girls,*" I said.

"*Me too … But he's so evil … I get so angry when I think what he's doing to them. I just want to kill him.*"

"He is evil Tahira but killing is not the answer," Grandpop told us via the suits as we waded under the oil to the side of the pool. "Believe me, you wouldn't want to bend anywhere if you'd killed anyone," Grandpop said taking her hand and helping her out. I had to climb out by myself.

"Killing is easy to talk about but the reality is not nice. And when you hurt someone, you have to remember they will hurt someone else. Sometimes someone who is perfectly innocent. You need to be more careful," he told her.

Tahira dropped her eyes. Grandpop put his hand on her

shoulder. She looked up.

"But you are still one of the best I've ever trained."

She smiled. Then he looked at me.

"You both are. That guy Hussein. He was a professional. You handled him perfectly. Just…"

He turned back to Tahira.

"Keep a lid on it eh?"

There was a flash and Cam appeared with a travel bag. We watched as she dragged herself out of the oil. She came out and put it down in front of us. Then she opened it up revealing a lot of vegetables.

"Fresh from the Saigon markets," she said proudly.

Cam seemed very pleased with herself. Grandpop grinned at her.

"Where's Tarik?" I asked.

"Somewhere over the Solomon Islands by now. I stayed to do some shopping for dad."

"Good work Cam. I think Mariko and the girls caught a tuna this morning too."

It looked like Grandpop had appointed himself chief supplies officer to Mr Trân.

...

"Sue?"

There's no answer.

"Grandpop, Sue's asleep."

There's no answer.

"Grandpop?"

"Yeah! OK! Right! Ah … Sam, we've decided to bring her here. I'll send through a sleeping bag in a travel box." Grandpop said like he'd been reading something else.

A few minutes later a bright flash announces the arrival of a small trunk. I open it, take out the sleeping bag, and send it home. Then I pull back Sue's covers, open the sleeping bag next to it and roll the sleeping woman I've come to know so well into the sleeping bag. She doesn't even stir as I close it up. I roll her to the side of the bed, get behind her head and lift her bodily so that she's on her feet and drooping next to me. She moans, stirring.

[+]

Time seems to slow down, then the colour drains out of everything. My whole field of view folds up and distorts and I have to close my eyes. I'm falling back, unable to move, falling and spinning, and then I stop falling back and start falling forward. There's brilliant light all around me. Brilliant light and presences. My mother and my Grandmother. Dozens of people surround me, and then fade. I open my eyes.

Sue lurches awake as the lightning storm crackles around the sleeping bag. She nearly falls but I hold her in place. Waiting by the control desk, wearing a business suit as usual, Dr P is reading something on a laptop.

The lightning stops, the water sluices down, then the air blows over us and the door opens. I open Sue's bag so she can get out. Dr Prosperov switches his laptop off and gets up to greet her. Sue steps out of the bag and the cabinet. She's looking around, still only in her socks, loose pj trousers and shirt.

"Welcome Detective Constable Susan Williams. I am Dr Gennady Prosperov," Dr P says extending his hand.

Sue shakes it.

"I'm afraid you have caught me a bit by surprise," Sue says looking at me.

"That was idea," Dr P smiles and waves her over to the seats around where Grandpop now gets up and comes forward.

"Mike Kahu," he says, shaking Sue's hand.

I can see how big Grandpop is. He makes Sue look tiny.

"Sue Williams. I've heard a lot about you."

"Yes. Please to sit Detective Williams," Dr P says.

"Sam please to join us," he adds as I try to slink off. I sit down between Sue and Grandpop while Dr P sits opposite her.

"Ms Williams am afraid I have ... disturbing news," Dr P tells her.

"What now?" said Sue who was already pretty disturbed by being brought here when asleep.

"Last night the Fae engineer Hekator – you have met?"

"Yes."

"Hekator removed growth from your brain. Operation is cause of headaches, dizziness, and nausea."

Sue looks at Dr P in total shock.

"From *my brain*?" Sue bursts out.

"Yes."

She closes her eyes.

"So that's why I couldn't remember ... anything."

"It never happened. Sorry Sue," I put in.

She turns to look at me, open mouthed. But Dr P goes on.

"Situation is infiltrator Rocelli not only used hypnosis but also injected genetic mindtap. Is small virus injected via nose which grows cancer-like growth. Growth develops into means to tap memories, consciousness, planning, even sight and hearing. Your growth detected early when leaving quarantine station. Fortunately was operable."

Sue is shaking her head.

"So you guys just opened my head up and took it out," Sue asks a bit shakily.

"Opening is microscopic. But if not removed before fully grown, surgical removal impossible."

"And why didn't I get a say in this?" Sue asks directly. She isn't pissed off yet, but she's going that way.

"Exactly point of Fae Ethics Court. Court held operation must not proceed."

Dr P lets that sink in, just watching her.

Sue realises that she dodged a bullet and changes direction.

"But I might have wanted the operation, just to be asked first," Sue argues.

"Problem was informing you would inform Galactic Administration of intention. This means revealing awareness of mindtap technique. Is problem as others afflicted with mindtap – but in more advanced stage. Was essential to remove, study and analyse in order to disrupt and cure others. Fae Great Council overruled Ethics court on basis that operation in best interests of Fae security."

"*Their security?* What about me?" Sue asks, appalled that her brain was treated like a field for harvesting.

"Fae interest is Fae. Growth is weapon needing analysis. Yours is first case. Fae not a free health service to needy Earthlings," Dr P says bluntly.

Then he shrugs.

"But privately Hekator wanted to help."

Sue looks around at us.

"Wow...I don't know what to say. Just over a week ago I was a perfectly ordinary person and now you guys have brought your little war inside my skull."

"Sorry Sue," I say, automatically.

Sue takes a deep breath. Dr P continues.

"Is risk for any who know of Fae. All knowledge is valuable, but whole planet's safety relies on our security. So Ms Williams, afraid I must insist you now make a decision," Dr P says softly.

"What decision?"

"Decision needed last night but interrupted by discovery. Decision to join this group or lose memory of us," Dr P says.

"What right now?" Sue asks, shocked.

"No, no, no, no," Dr Prosperov assures her. "Of course not. We are civilised people," he assures her.

"After dinner," he smiles.

Sue checks to see if he's kidding. He isn't.

"Oh... ah that sounds a little bit better." she says vaguely. "But ... why do you want me?"

"You have adapted very quickly. You have police knowledge. And Sam's recommendation carries much weight. Is excellent operative."

Sue looks at me grinning my head off. I try to look serious.

"Can I find out a bit more about what I'd be getting into here while I think about it?"

"Is no longer reason to prevent," Dr P smiles.

"Cool," I say happily.

"Sam, please to guide guest," Dr P says to me, getting up.

"But I don't know my way around," I whisper to Grandpop.

"Scotty and Ashley are upstairs," he tells me out the side of his mouth.

Dr P has gone over to the poles.

"Suggest starting with this facility Mr Kahu."

"Right-ho," Grandpop calls out, as Dr P's disc slides up the pole toward the light.

So Grandpop takes us on a tour. Sue's fascinated with the set up. She meets Control who is the same as ever. We dial up her house in the briefing rooms and go through it. She even checks out her car which is waiting for her at the garage. We show her the changers and the new speeder bay which is still empty.

I show off the new suit. Then we come up the poles into the greenhouse.

She really likes the look of Hastings Hall. We come to the back of the house and find Mariko and Gunter in the pool with Zoe, Bernard and Patience. I notice Mariko seems a bit rounder about the tummy than I remembered her being. We stay and talk awhile.

Sue asks what it's like having to stay in the background while the kids did everything. Everyone smiles.

"Scott's the same, Sue, " Zoe says. "They think things just happen by themselves."

So they fill her in on what they do. I have to admit it's news to me. There's a lot of stuff to do with running the house, but they also analyse our intelligence and do their own research. I hadn't realised they monitored us and the others we watch over so closely. Sue comes away impressed.

We go inside to the café. Mr Trân, Mitra and Ali are chatting away while cooking. They give us some fig loaf to try, made using new figs from a tree in the garden. It's delicious. Sue is relaxing a lot. Then we go through to the library. Here we find Tahira, Scotty and Ashley. They have a bunch of books open.

"What's happening guys?" I ask.

"Homework," Scotty moans.

"Then cleaning," Tahira says to me.

"Same as normal," Ashley says, not even looking up.

"What's the school like?" I ask.

"Small and poor," Ashley replies. "S'like a bigger version of Aotea. But finally, ah'm not da only black person dhere! Dey got Aboriginals here as well."

"Is it friendly?" I ask.

"Yeah, sorta, but dhey all seem bit depressed really. Dhere's talk o closin' down da school."

"Doesn't sound like much to look forward to," I comment.

"Believe me, it ain't," she agrees.

There's a pause.

"Where are Cam and Tarik?" I ask.

"Cleaning. Zhey finished early," Tahira says still reading. "Zhey think zhey have a lead on Cam's muzzer."

Mrs Jones came out from the doors at the front of the building where I hadn't been yet.

"Samuel. How lovely to have you back with us. You can help Tahira with the cleaning."

"I'm meant to show Sue around," I mumble.

"I think she'll be safe with me dear," Mrs Jones smiles.

I feel a bit funny about letting Sue go, but Mrs Jones walks off with her talking quickly. When she's gone I sit down with the others. They just carry on as normal. I feel this huge sense of total relief. Finally I just grab Tahira around the neck and gave her a kiss on the cheek.

"Sam! Go away!" she complains, pushing me off, but smiling while trying to write.

Then I get up and go around to Ashley. She puts her pen down, faces me, grinning, and gives me a lovely, huge hug. It feels so good we hold each other for nearly a minute. Then we sit back. I have a few tears in my eyes. Without looking up Scotty says.

"Don't kiss me bra, you'll smear me lippy."

I burst out laughing and I throw a cushion at him instead. Then we have a humungous cushion fight. We're just getting into it when Mrs Jones comes back in, leading Sue. She just stops and looks at us, and we stop and sit down quietly.

"C'mon I will show you our jobs," Tahira says.

So we set off to do our cleaning. We have to vacuum the front block. It's like the guest level at Renwick and it's where Dr P has his office and rooms. Tahira knocks on the door. Dr Morozov opens it. She's not as pencil thin as she had been, but she seems warmer. Maybe that's why people call her Katya, more now.

"Dr Morozov is OK to vacuum?" Tahira asks.

"Yes. Irina is awake," she opens the door wider.

Irina is playing with her blocks. Dr M smiles and goes to close the door again, then stops, looking at me.

"Sam, I am happy you have re-turned," she says, kindly.

"Thank you Dr Morozov. I am too," I reply.

And smiling to herself – perhaps for having practised being warm – Dr M closes the door.

We vacuum together down the passages, stairs and the main entry hall. Hastings is grander than Renwick. Apparently it was built as some sort of spa over a hundred years ago but ended up as an expensive home that spent most of its time deserted. There's a big dining room, a lounge with a grand piano, and a computer room full of screens where Drs Morozov and Gursoy work. Tahira's right. There's also lots more brass – particularly on the rooftop observatory.

We chat about Sue, school and what's been happening lately. They are still working out the tricky business of getting our identities sorted out. Technically everyone is someone else at the moment. Control has created fake Australian identities for us using the same trick we'd used for Nguyen and Cam a year ago. Luckily para.no.ID never had a hand in that one.

Tahira says everyone is working carefully to identify Para.no.ID. So far they've found two members have died and another four have suspected mind taps. Three are missing. One Norwegian, one Indian and someone in California. Administration

Cyberminds are operating somewhere on Earth mimicking parts of the internet. They can easily pretend to be our technology but they watch everything much more closely. All the old internet gateways had had to be abandoned because it's possible they're compromised, so the guys went back out laying worms and spraying dishes again to rebuild our gateways into the net.

Tahira says Cam and Tarik are following a lead about a woman taken by pirates and sold into slavery in Thailand that seems to match the description of Cam's mother. The trail's complicated because she's moved a lot, and there's a hint she's been sold as a mail order bride to some German. Cam and Tarik are getting quite excited about the progress they're making.

We do a lot of polishing, as we always have, while I tell Tahira about Sue and what's been happening with me. I finally decide to admit what I've been thinking to Tahira.

"Do you think I'm stupid trying to fix up Aunty Liz with Sue?"

"I zink you are trying too 'ard," she says polishing.

"That's sorta what they said," I admit.

"Oo?"

"Sue and Aunty Liz."

"Zenn zay are prohbably right," she looks at me and goes back to work. I try to justify it.

"But ... well they just seem alike. You know? Sue is sorta ... I dunno ... a bit staunch. She likes to party. And Aunty Liz ... Well she does too. But underneath they are both really caring and gentle."

"You 'av to be patient. Zink how long it took Dr Gursoy and my muzzer to become engaged. Zey need time to get to know one anuzzer."

"But do you think I'm just completely wrong?"

213

Tahira shrugs.

"Per'aps it eez worth a try. People are zo unpredictable. Especially when it eez you trying to predict women, Sam. You are especially useless."

"Gee thanks."

"Av you seen Emma?"

"Not lately. I need to go back to her soon."

"Zat may not be possible Sam. *Zey* may be waiting."

"Well, I have to talk to her somehow."

"Per'aps you need to scan 'er?"

"Scan her?"

"Yes. For taps like *zey* have placed on Nathan."

That idea made me worry.

"Has Hekator developed a cure yet?"

"Not yet... But ee will. Ee is so clever. Do you know what ee 'as been giving us?"

"No, what?"

Tahira puts her rag down on the floor next to where she was kneeling.

"Zis."

She puts her hand over the rag. About 15 centimeters above. Then she frowns. The rag twitches slightly and jumps just a little. It's the smallest movement but it definitely was not a thin thread. Tahira relaxes.

"Zhat's all I can do at ze moment. Tarik, Cam and Scotty can do a bit more. But 'ekator says we will slowly develop ze telekinesis."

"Can I do it?"

"Were zhou sick in ze quarantine?"

"Yes."

"Zhen zhou are a week behind us."

We keep up our cleaning until Mrs Jones comes by to inspect it. It reminds me, I was meant to check the gang's cleaning of Grandpop's old house. But there isn't time now, so I go down to dinner instead.

For some reason I'm surprised how popular Sue is.

She and Zoe seem to be great mates, Patricia also seems to enjoy her company. Ken and Mariko find her amusing, Nguyen smiles a lot, but then, he often does. Mrs Jones and Grandpop obviously like her too. Mitra and Soraya are a bit cautious, while Bernard and Ali Gursoy seem uncommitted.

Ashley, Scott and Tahira are friendly, Tarik and Cam, a little distracted. But the real surprise is Dr Morozov who seems like a different woman around Sue. When Sue says she liked vodka Dr Morozov wanted to get some out until Dr P pointed out that she's breastfeeding Irina and Sue is recovering from brain surgery.

But the person I'm really watching is Aunty Liz. She's laughing with the rest of them but seems strangely shy. I watch her very hard and the reading comes to me. She's scared to hope. She really likes Sue, but she wants to be sure and take her time. Suddenly she looks at me and to my surprise *she* looks away, embarrassed by what I've seen.

Dinner goes on for quite a while. I notice Dr P go over to Sue and speak to her quietly. She smiles and nods. He smiles and pats her on the back before going back to sit with Dr Morozov who's feeding Irina in her high chair. Irina seems to like squeezing her food as much as eating it.

Dr P gives it a few minutes and then stands and bangs his glass. Even so it still takes a little while for everyone to stop laughing.

"Have brief announcement. Detective Susan Williams is to join team here at Hastings Hall. Detective Williams has been recruited after helping Sam since evacuation. Am thinking will make useful contribution to operations and community. Detective Williams please to say something." he says and sits down.

Sue stands up, looking around shyly.

"Umm Hi! I'm Sue Williams. I'm ... well, I sort of *am* a cop ... actually I'm probably meant to arrest Dr Prosperov for something."

Dr Prosperov smiles and holds out his wrists. Everyone laughs.

"Don't worry I don't think he's actually broken any laws really plus he's my new boss so I don't think arresting him would be a great career move," she says laughing nervously. People laugh with her. She waits for quiet.

"You know a fortnight ago my world was so different I hardly remember how I was part of it..."

She stops and smiles, remembering. "I was a cop, I was trying to keep my relationship with my partner together, I had a bunch of kids who had got themselves in trouble to look after and investigate. And then Sam showed up."

Then everyone suddenly looks at *me*! I felt shy.

"I got given Sam because he was the only witness to what had happened to you. And when a group this size goes missing it's a big deal. We were pretty sure you were all dead but we didn't know how or why. But I knew Sam was different because he just seemed so in control. He wasn't scared or abusive like most of them. He was just holding back. So my job was to get him to talk."

"Well fu ... far out! The first thing he tells me is my lover is

dumping me. That didn't go down too well, I have to tell you!
Then when I go home I find out the little bugger is right. She
had dumped me! Moved out and broke my heart into a million
pieces."

"Then … I don't know what I was doing … getting drunk or what
… But I swallowed too many sleeping pills. And who appears
out of nowhere having run away and taken a bus to save my life?
Sam bloody Kahu!"

It's getting a bit warm and I want to sneak away.

"Then what does he do? He starts looking after *me*! He makes
me go ride roller coasters and talks to me and he starts telling
me stuff. Then his super high flying lawyer turns up and he's
staying in hotels and going shopping and I think well that's the
last I'll see of him. But no! Suddenly he wants my help to run
away from his lawyer and he starts telling me all this crazy stuff
about UFOs and God knows what else."

"So I start to think like … maybe he's mad. So I'm straight up: I
tell him I think he's crazy. So he says let's go to Renwick and I'll
show you my spaceship. And I say … Ohhhh Kay."

Everyone laughs again looking from Sue to me and back.

"Anyway, we go to Renwick and it's all pretty straightforward.
He takes me underground. He shows me a shitload of gold
… then we see the cave-in. I think, 'poor kid'. Sam's got post-
traumatic stress. Then we meet up with Emma. I think, she's a
nice kid. I'll see if she thinks Sam's crazy too."

"And then … then … just like he says … this fu … this fricken
great flying saucer shows up and chases me down a dark, wet
cave!"

"I'll tell you what, I stopped thinking Sam was crazy and started
thinking maybe *I* was. We dodge the saucer and then he shows

me *his* flying saucer. Then he flies me home with it! Man-oh-man was I having to rethink a bunch of stuff!"

"So he starts telling me this story about you guys ... and this time I start listening real hard. But I need to take care of myself. Do the washing, get my car fixed, vacuum, so I go home. Next thing I know Sam's on the phone telling me this guy in my house is an alien agent. And so I run out and he hunts the guy down from the air like some sort of airforce pilot. And I'm starting to think 'what the hell have I got myself involved with here'?"

"So then I go to work to check out a few things and find what Sam's telling me, does check out. Then his ex-lawyer's on my phone telling me if I don't invite him to dinner I will be in more trouble than I can possibly imagine ... and now I am starting to imagine quite a lot."

"And that's when I met Tarik and Cam for the first time. And if Sir Michael could scare me with vague threats you two ... you were seriously scary. I mean you guys looked *mean* ... and when you're a cop you're trained to take control of crazy situations. You tell other people how things are going to be. And now I was on a ride and I didn't know how to get off."

"Well, we ended back at my place. And I did what I always do when things stack up, we had a party. I met Hekator. By this time I was pretty sure I was like Alice falling down the hollow tree. I had reached the bottom."

"And after that it's just been about listening to Sam tell me about what you've been doing. It's just been mind blowing. And he's told me so much about you I feel like I've known you forever. You're just like he described you."

"And now I'm here. It's been great meeting you all and you've been so welcoming and friendly I feel at home with you already.

I feel like I've known you all, all my life. The idea of going back to where I was two weeks ago just seems unthinkable. I just have a feeling I'm meant to work here with you all. I hope you don't mind putting up with me."

Then she shrugs and sits down. Everyone claps. She even gets kisses and hugs. Dr Prosperov stands, clapping.

"Our newest team member poses special challenge. Question is 'what to do with past lives'. I am thinking is helpful if old identities persist to prevent investigation by media and authorities. Is distracting Administration from new identities. Needed is plan for Detective Williams to find old identities. Then we must all scatter, and vanish."

"Second Sunday since Renwick disappearance in three days. Also is first Sunday since Detective William's disappearance. Is best if Detective Williams solves case by this time. Planning to begin tomorrow. Is all."

And he sits down again. Grandpop sneaks over to me.

"Sam, you and Sue have to go back to Auckland."

"What? Why?"

"We need to buy more time for Hekator to find a cure for the mindtap. Sue's synthetic brain is asleep at the moment and will stay that way until tomorrow but she can't stay here and we can't risk leaving her alone."

"Right."

"So what you have to do is take her home and distract her."

"How?"

"Up to you. Where are you with our history?"

"Just starting 2008."

"Well, there you go...there's heaps in that. Tell her about that. In fact while you're about it think about how they got onto Nathan.

Maybe Sue can work out how that happened. We need to close it down whatever it was."

"But won't that feed our mission through to the Administration?"

"Good point. I'll have a word with Hekator and see what he thinks."

"OK."

"Good lad."

"Grandpop?"

"Yeah?"

"Can I stay in my suit and do a few visits?"

"Who to?"

"Back to the old house and to see Emma and stuff."

"OK, but talk to Control. I don't want you getting carried away and into trouble."

"OK."

"And Control wasn't happy with you beating up the gang either."

"Sorry," I say, feeling a bit ashamed.

"*Control* wasn't happy. *I* was stoked! As far as *I'm* concerned you saved me a job. They needed their butts kicked. I thought you did great," he grins, punching my arm lightly.

"Thanks Grandpop," I smile.

"But you better go easy or Control will close you down, eh?"

"OK."

"Well, I'll go tell Sue she has to go back for a while. You've got... half an hour, OK?"

"OK."

Grandpop sidles off.

"Lucky bugger! No cleaning for three more days," Scotty says.

"Why?" Tahira asks grumpily. "He can come back."

"Will you?" asks Ashley.

I hadn't thought about it but I wanted to get back to normality.

"Sure," I decide, and then thinking about it.

"Honestly I *like* cleaning with you Tahira." I tell her. "It's relaxing."

Tahira smiles at me with those big brown eyes. Tarik makes a sucky noise. Tahira viciously elbows his arm, still smiling at me. Tarik groans silently clutching his arm.

"So what are you guys doing?" I ask.

"Looking after Nathan," Scotty shrugs.

"How's that working out?"

"It's tricky because we can't let him recognise us," Ashley says.

"Where is he?"

"Florida. He thinks he won a surprise holiday to Disneyworld. *They* know he's in Florida but they have no reason to suspect we set it up. When Hekator sorts out this mindtap though we'll pick him up."

"Is our tag in him still working?"

"Yeah."

"And what about you guys?" I ask Cam and Tarik.

"We fink we got an identity for Yen's mail order 'usband. Ee's Swiss. We fought 'e was German, yeah? But we gotta copy of 'is passport from the Thai marriage registry an' 'e used to be from Zurich. E's a geek," Tarik says, rubbing his arm.

"Do you know where he lives?"

"We know where 'e used to live. Trackin' 'im down is more of a problem. But we know where 'e was workin' and we know where the pay records are."

"Cool."

"And I am checking back wiz Jeanne, Sarah, and Khadiyeh,"

Tahira tells me, without me asking. "And wizzout a cover eet is 'ard on ze nerves."

"Well, be careful eh? I'll come if you need me," I tell her.

"So what have you told Sue about us?" Ashley wants to know.

"Everything. And she soaks it up too. She might look all shy and cutesy but she remembers everything and she can be hard when she wants to be. She's a natural detective."

They all look at me.

"And..." Tarik prompts.

They wanted to know as much about her as she knew about them. So I tell them about Sue. It doesn't take long and I realise I don't actually know all that much about her. But just as I'm finishing Grandpop brings her over.

"Gotta wrap this up Sam. We're over time as it is."

"OK."

We say goodbye. I give Rewa a special goodnight hug and get one from Aunty Liz as well. Then Sue surprises us both by giving Aunty Liz a hug.

"Thanks for lending me your nephew. He's a great kid and he's totally changed my life," Sue tells her.

"Yeah, he did that to me too," Liz jokes.

She's nervous but friendly. They part a bit awkwardly and we go back out across the lawn to the jumpstation with Grandpop leading the way. Grandpop gives me a hug, and Sue a kiss on the cheek, (which is a surprise) before we bend space. And then we're back.

[+]

Sue goes over to her drum kit and starts to play for about five minutes. She's pretty good. I lie on her bed. Finally she stops.

"You know, I've started to realise something," she says.

222

"What's that?" I ask, sitting.

"Basically they beat you, didn't they? I mean having to burn down your house means you guys lost," she says, getting up from the drums and hopping into bed.

"Yeah, big time," I have to agree.

"So what you're really telling me is a story of how you almost failed."

I hadn't thought of that.

"I guess I am, really. Though it didn't seem like that. And yeah, they got us, but apart from Nathan they still don't really know what we are doing or why. So it wasn't a total fail. Just a kick up the bum."

"A hard one."

"Yep," I nod.

"So what we really need to understand is how they caught you. And it has to involve Nathan, right?"

"Yeah," I agree.

"And Ashley thinks Nathan tagged her because he was the only one who could have tagged her? Right?"

"Yeah," I nod.

"But she doesn't know for sure?"

"I guess not," I shrug.

"Hmmm it always pays to keep an open mind. But my idea is Nathan was hypnotized."

"Yeah. Musta," I agree.

"OK, but that must have been recently or he would have done it before."

"Yeah, I guess."

"But who would have had access to Nathan lately?" Sue asks.

"I don't know. Ashley never said anything was unusual with him.

223

He was just an ordinary kid. Hung out with his friends, went to school, all the usual," I tell her.

"OK. But do we know who got to him?"

"No. But someone must have recognised Ashley," I say.

"Yeah, but how? And who would tell that this one black girl with a hoodie and schoolbag among all the others could teleport, read minds and all the rest of it?"

"They'd have to have seen Ashley do something unexpected."

"So where did Ashley operate?" Sue asks.

"Europe, Africa, North and South Americas. All over the place."

"And where did she cross the Administration?" she checks.

"Well, she didn't really. She crossed the Bruderschaft."

"When?"

"A number of times but the big fight was in France in a tiny village called Elan in the Champagne-Ardennes province, not far from Belgium. A lot of stuff came together there at the end of 2008. That was when we got Hathaway arrested by the Administration for breaking the non-intervention treaty."

"Arrested?"

"Yup, they took him away."

"Who did?"

I pointed up.

"Do *they* do that?" Sue asked.

I nod, "*They* have rules too. Hathaway and his friends had broken most of them, so the Administration acted. They rounded up lots of them. It was a big bust."

"And Ashley was there?"

"We all were. It was really complicated and weird too because Jeanne, Diana and Sarah all got in trouble with the Bruderschaft, although they never knew each other. Even more

224

weird it was Khadiyeh in Yemen who told us they would."

"Khadiyeh? How could she do that?"

"Umm... yeah well, Khadiyeh is ... well she's ... she's ..."

"What?"

"She's a prophet."

"You mean she predicts things ... like Dr Prosperov does."

"Not exactly..." I pause, a bit embarrassed.

"Well, what then?" Sue persists.

"She's a prophet like in the Bible. She's visited by angels, or whatever the hell they are."

"What?" Sue almost spat.

"Seriously. Like in the Bible. It's really scary. I don't like thinking about it to be honest."

"Sam you're getting weird on me again," Sue warns, her face a picture of disbelief.

"It's not *my* fault. It's the world, it's a weird place."

"So this Yemeni girl. What did she do?"

"She prophesied stuff. Dr P believed it. Raman believed it. It helped us find the others."

"Oo-kay," Sue says, doubtfully.

"This is the problem, Sue. The stranger the things we deal with, the stranger things get. Dr P says his whole life has been about more and more strangeness."

"Yeeah, look, just so I can keep things at a level that a simple detective can cope with, can we just focus on how Nathan can be *logically* linked to you guys. I would say the best solution is the school. For him to be hypnotised like I was, someone would have to catch him in a place he felt secure. That's where he would have let his guard down. From what you say, that wouldn't have been his home. That leaves the school. I would

225

say he was visited by an adult from outside the school sometime in the past few weeks or so. The school will have a record of it."

"Grandpop," I say out loud. "Are you getting this?"

"Sure am. Tell Sue she's brilliant. How would you like to join Scott, Ashley and Tahira in making a midnight visit to Columbia Heights Multicultural Institute?"

"Love to..." I say.

Sue looks uncertain.

"What?" she mouths, silently at me.

"But can Sue join and watch?" I ask out loud.

I can hear the good humour in his voice.

"I'll check with Hekator, but if she's meant to be sleeping, why not? It'll be good training for her."

Sue looks baffled. I fill her in.

"We're organising a raid on the school. Grandpop thinks you're brilliant. He wants you to join him on the desk to watch."

"Really?" Sue smiles.

"Yeah," I grin as a bright flash signals the arrival of a box carrying a sleeping bag.

Sue's pretty pleased with herself as we get ready.

[+]

We bend into the cabinets at Hastings, and again go through the lightning, water and wind. As we do so there were three more flashes as the others return from wherever they had been. We all head over to the desk where Grandpop is waiting.

"OK, well this is pretty simple. We're going into the Columbia Heights Multicultural Institute to break into the school office and work out who's been visiting in the past month. We did this once already to find Nathan but all we got was the enrolment and academic records. Tonight the special focus is on visitors, especially psychologists, careers advisers, police and priests. Anyone who could get Nathan alone for a while. We'll start with names but we need to be able to follow up to see if we recognise them or find any links back to the rest of the Bruderschaft gang. We need to check his school medical records too and we especially want to get any old security camera material."

"Remember at some point this person saw Ashley. That means they either saw her directly or on a camera. So also check school newsletters for pictures that may have Ashley in them. Take USB keys so Control can search the data. It's one in the morning there so no lights. Anything you want to add Sue?"

"Umm, no thanks Mike."

"Cool. Let's go."

I feel a bit funny doing a mission with Sue watching. So far I've only told her about them. Now she can us do one for herself. As I head for the cabinet I hope I don't end up looking dumb.

[+]

But as soon as we arrive at Nathan's school I forget about her. We open the office and the principal and deputy's office. Then me and Tahira go to the medical clinic. I start the computers while Tahira opens the file cupboard.

We go through the files looking for Nathan's. Finally we find it. Where all the others are big and fat, Nathan's file is so thin we can't find it at first. It's pretty obvious someone else has taken whatever was in there.

While Control copies the computers while we check the nurse's desk.

This Mrs Sanchez is a messy person. She has a picture of her cat on her desk. We check her physical diary and copy the scraps of paper she writes notes to herself on. We notice a card holder and copy the business cards she has in it. Then Tahira notices there's a pen holder and clock branded with "Edumed". We look through her personal things but apart from chocolate we can't find anything of interest.

After fifteen minutes we bend to the security office because there are too many doors on the way. The video surveillance system is impressive. There were terabyte drives for the archives, all neatly labelled. Grandpop sends through a box, and we load them up to copy at base. We switch on the security system and plug in Control so he can erase any recordings of us.

That was when things got "interesting".

"Disconnect! The Administration is running this!" Control shouts.

We pull Control's USB key out of the security machine as fast as we can.

"What do we do?" Tahira asks Grandpop.

"Hang on I'm waiting for Control," he replies.

There's a pause.

"Disconnect the machine. We have to do this offline," Control says.

We pull out all the cables at the back that we can find.

"Tarik and Cam are coming guys. Leave it. Go to the school newspaper room," Grandpop tells us.

Control feeds us the pathway. It's just down the hall from the office. We're a bit nervous about plugging in Control's USB key now but he tells us to go ahead so we plug it in and boot the Apples up.

We discover there's an archive device so we send it back to Control in a box. While we're waiting Ashley and Scotty come in.

"Office is done. But I reckon the principal's place would be worth a look," says Scotty.

"Maybe we should tag her," I suggest.

"You got her address?" Grandpop asks.

"Control should," Ashley suggests.

There's a pause.

"OK, we're taking a look," Grandpop replies.

There's another long pause broken by a flash as the box comes back with the archive in it. I plug it back in while we wait.

"Guys you'd better come back here. We're reconning the principal's apartment," Grandpop says. We fold and spin away into darkness.

[+]

After the lightning, rain and wind again, we come over to the control desk to find Sue exploring the apartment on the big screen. Grandpop's behind her. She smiles at me as I come over.

"This technology is fantastic," she says. She looks like she's having great fun.

"Almost as good as CSI eh?" Grandpop jokes.

The others smile a little, but Sue's busy and doesn't notice. She explores along the corridor some more and into a lounge.

"Well, this woman isn't here. It's half past three in the morning. There are no toothbrushes in the bathroom. The house is neat and tidy. Frankly, I don't think she's here very often. So what do you want to do?"

"Webs and flies," Tarik says, certainly.

Cam nods. We know this drill.

But I have a bad feeling about this one.

"Can I suggest something," I say.

Everyone looks at me.

"Let's not bend in. Let's get them in on their own."

"Why?" asks Tarik.

"Well, I got ambushed a day ago. And Control got ambushed a few minutes ago. They infiltrated the school security system so until we know this principal is *not* involved I think we should treat her like she is."

"I agree," Grandpop says in the darkness behind Sue.

"She's on the tenth floor. The lift is locked," Sue says.

"No probs," says Tarik. "We'll climb around the outside. C'mon lets get our creepy-crawlies," he tells Cam. They go to the discs and ride them out of sight.

"Well, I don't reckon we'll have much else to do tonight. You two may as well go home." Grandpop tells us.

"Awww, I feel like we just got started," Sue complains good humouredly.

"Well, you might have, but these kids have to go to bed. It's late and it's a school night. Sam should be going to school too." Sue looks at me.

"Sorry.It's just such a fantastic set up here. I guess I got a bit carried away," she admits.

"Dat's OK. We do too sometimes," Ashley tells her.

"Tarik could you bring a screen so Sue can stay in touch," Grandpop says.

A short while later Tarik and Cam are back riding the discs.

"You gonna stay and watch?" he asks me.

"I'd like to," Sue says.

"Yeah, me too," I add.

"OK. How do you want to go?" Grandpop asks them.

"Bend dive from one klick. Sam, watch this!" Tarik said. "You're gonna love these Lanas."

They go to the cabinets then wink out. We turn to the screen.

It's a dark night in Washington DC. Two flashes appear in the rain clouds but there's no thunder. Our view moves up to Cam and Tarik who have their wings out, their gray skins blend in with the skies above and streets below. They slide through the sky easily in wide spirals as they circle the apartment block. It's taller than most of the buildings nearby which are only three to four storeys.

Silently Tarik and Cam turn about and then come up on the apartment from below so that they climb at the last moment, losing forward airspeed as they do so. They flap a little as they land on the flat wet roof of the building, but then like huge gray moths in the night, flatten their wings and blend in. Without the green circles you couldn't see them. It's lovely to watch. Already I can see how much better the Lanas are than our old suits.

"How will they get the flies in?" Sue asks.

"Aircon," I reply.

Quickly Tarik and Cam climb the sides of the building, then set to work on the aircon units like the professionals they were. It isn't much to look at, but Sue is watching their careful movements closely.

"That was such a good bend dive," I tell Tahira, silently.

She just smiles. We're both looking forward to getting back out there again.

Finally Tarik and Cam are finished. The flies are on their way. They reconnect and reseal the aircon, take a last look around, and then fold into nothing. The flash of their arrival follows almost immediately.

"And that's the way we do that," Grandpop tells Sue, as Tarik and Cam put up with the lightning crawling over them.

"Time for bed," he adds, handing Sue the sleeping bag.

"Thanks for including me," Sue says.

"*You* are very welcome," he smiles at her, and just for an instant I realise that he sees in her the same potential partner for Aunty Liz that I do. It was the first time I had seen Grandpop seem happy that his oldest daughter was a lesbian. Sue doesn't know what to do with that so she turns to me and tells me to take her home. I high-five Tarik on the way out of their cabinets.

"Wicked jump," I tell him.

But Cam stops.

"Come back soon, Sam. I don't like you being apart from us," she says.

"I will," I promise her, and then duck into the cabinet where Sue is getting into her bag.

Sue pulls the sleeping bag up around her. I seal us both up and the control room folds to a line, spun and turns through a world of presences before blasting back into Sue's bedroom.

[+]

It's really dark. I feel tired. I help Sue out of the bag and then switch her light on. I'm still in my Lana. I can stay in it for a few days before it will start to feel grungy. But Sue chucks me out of her room so she can get changed and puts her old bathrobe on.

"Sam?" she says, as she re-opens the door.

"Uh-huh?"

"Why did you think that principal's apartment was a trap?"

She jumps onto her bed and sits there crosslegged.

"Dunno. It just seemed a possibility. You get a bit paranoid after a while. It's the only way to keep safe."

"Oh."

"How's your head?"

"Killing me," she admits.

"Take a Panadol."

"I will. I just feel awake still. It's … I dunno … I'm just buzzing about joining you guys I guess. The idea of working in a place where there's no bureaucracy, the technology is amazing and the people are so friendly it's like … Oh … Well, it's sooo different. You have no idea."

That's true. I don't.

"So you're pretty stoked about it?"

"Yeah," she smiles happily to herself.

There's a pause as she looks at me smiling.

"You know Sam … and this may sound a bit weird given I'm 28 and you're 14 but I reckon you're the best thing that ever happened in my life."

Wow. But then Dr Prosperov was definitely the best in mine and all I was doing was introducing her.

"Even though you had to have brain surgery to remove an alien mindtap?" I check.

Sue grins to herself.

"Rachel was harder on my poor little brain than this," she says. "Sometimes I didn't know up from down. She had me twisted around her so bad I hardly knew myself. Ever since she left I've just been unwinding from one weird world into … well, another weird world," she laughs.

"But your weird world is so much bigger and better than hers ever was," she adds.

I yawned. Even though my sleep had been confused by the previous night at Hastings Hall I seem to be synching with the others. Finally Sue notices I'm zoning out.

"Sam, you need to go to bed. You're drooping."

"Yeah," I agree fuzzily.

"C'mon."

Sue gives me a toothbrush. Then I go to bed. Sue stays up. I was vaguely aware of her making a phone call but in no time I was in the dark corridors of the Columbia Heights Multicultural Institute except it wasn't. It was underground.

I'm walking the corridors with the others. We're looking for something but we aren't sure what it is. The corridors twist and turn with the doors blocking one or other of us so we have to take different paths through the maze. In the background I can hear this strange unearthly singing. It makes you feel confused. Finally I begin to become aware me and Tahira are getting closer to the middle.

Then I turn a corner and enter a theatre. It's all dark with a copper bathtub on the stage. I walk into the middle and then realise that sitting on the couches facing the stage are some adults.

"It iz good to see you for real zhis time Sam," Inspector Du Croix says.

"You see Inspector. They are drawn in spite of themselves. Soon you will have them all," Hathaway tells him.

"And I will have my bath," sighs Mrs Huuygens, wearing a gold lamé dress.

Suddenly I'm upside-down and hanging over the bath. I can't move and right by my throat is the thinnest, sharpest length of piano wire.

"Sam!" calls Tahira. "Are you alright?"

She's entering the theatre. I can't warn her. I can see the infiltrators smiling; watching me on stage. The others are following after Tahira. I want to yell at them to bend out, or run away but I can't. And then I wake up.

CHAPTER SIXTY SIX: LITTLE FINGER

My suit, which has kept me warm all night, is cooling to wake me. For a moment though, I lie there looking at the gray morning. In theory I should be with the others getting ready for school – although they would have two more hours in bed because of the time difference with Tasmania.

I don't really want to go back to school but I really miss Rewa, Aunty Liz, and the others. I'm tired of this adventure. I just want to go home.

I hear Sue get up. She seems to be quite busy. I get up and go around to her room. She's pulling on a tracksuit. She jumps when she sees me.

"Haven't you heard of privacy? Or knocking," she asks grumpily.

"Sorry," I say and walk out.

So she's a bear with a sore head.

"I just wondered how your head was?" I ask from the hallway.

"Sore. But I'm going for a run."

"Can I come?"

"Ohh I dunno ... Oh, OK, but don't talk. We're probably going to spend all day with you talking at me again. I just want a little space."

"OK."

I change my suit to look like a tracksuit as well.

She puts on her trainers and picks up her keys. We go out into the chill morning air and she locks the door. Then pocketing the keys she turns on her heel and takes off at a quick lope. I have to keep up, she isn't taking any notice of me. I give her a fifteen meters and follow.

I don't bother trying to read her mind. I can feel the tension. She's running as a way to relax even though she feels like crap. I decide to just leave her alone. I'm only coming at all in case *they* try to grab her again. Even so I decide to let her get ahead so she can feel free of me.

To pass the time as I run I call up Control. I'm curious to know if the files we copied last night had given him any clues as to who had recognised Ashley and then hypnotised Nathan.

They did. A man and a woman from DC child welfare had visited Nathan at school three weeks ago. They had signed in as Mel Thomson and Andy Crane. Mel and Andy were certainly not Bruderschaft infiltrators because we had monitored them when they visited Nathan's mother at home before. But given the timing my guess was this pair were really Administration shape-shifting biobots. Nathan wouldn't have known the difference before they suddenly hypnotised him. The real Mel and Andy would have been hypnotised so they wouldn't know they never met Nathan that day either. So the question of *how* they had got to Nathan was easily answered. The problem was not *how* they got to Nathan but *why*?

Why, of all the six billion people on this Earth, did the Administration pick Nathan? They had to know Ashley was communicating with him? They had to know who Ash was. And they had to know who *he* was and how to get to him. On those more important details Control had no answers. If we didn't know who had spotted Ashley and connected her to the Fae and to Nathan there was no way Nathan could ever return to Washington. He would always be at risk of being caught by the Administration again and so would we.

My feeling was that there was something odd about the school which we should investigate, starting with a thorough reading of the principal. Unfortunately it was too early to suggest this to anyone at Hastings Hall because it was five in the morning over there and they would all be asleep.

Control could tell me that Hekator was interfering with the signals he was getting from Sue by simulating growth problems in Sue's brain. The result was they were only getting some blurry physical feedback to do with her situation and comfort, but nothing from memory or planning centres. My hope was *they* were backing off now hoping we would accept Sue and take the bait. What I didn't want was for *them* to decide to pick her up again.

As I run I think about how Sue's brain is transmitting to Hekator's copy of her brain which in turn is transmitting to *them*. It kinda creeps me out to think that a copy of Sue's mind might be trapped inside Hekator's fake world. It sounds like a kind of horrible dream. It made me start to wonder how you'd ever know if you *weren't* trapped in some fake reality rather than reality itself. What would that be like? That makes me think about how I could know I *wasn't* already in an artificial reality? But thinking about that just does my head in so instead I decide to focus on Sue as she comes to the top of her street and turns onto the main road.

She isn't feeling great. The headache from the surgery had been joined by the irritation that came before her period. Tahira was the same and I'd got used to her monthly grumpiness. But Sue handles it differently by pushing herself through exercise. She drives herself against her own limits stretching out as the road climbed again. I was impressed by her single-mindedness. But I also know, from reading her, she has to be left alone to deal with it in her own way, so I just lope along behind her, letting the suit bounce me from foot to foot, letting her draw ahead.

We run for about an hour. Sue's back is darkened with sweat. She's averaging sub-six minute kilometers over a hilly course which is pretty good considering. Finally, I find myself back at the bus stop where I'd first got off to come to her place. We're ten minutes out. Five. And then Sue is under the carport, gasping, and pulling out her keys.

Her neighbour's coming out as I roll up.

"Hi Sue? Where have you been?" he calls.

I slow down and walk as he continues.

"Some of your cop mates were 'round asking about you," he says, as Sue sits gasping by her front door.

Sue stands up, stretching.

"Hi Mark. Yeah, I took Sam, here, up to see his people. It was a bit of a wild goose chase in the end, but at least we sorted it out," she tells him, as I arrive.

Mark looks at me suspiciously. I know what he's thinking but I ignore it.

"Oh, right, but you may want to talk to that guy Kevin you work with. He seemed a bit worried," Mark says, getting into his car.

Sue grins and waves as she gets out her keys and goes in. I find her drinking out of the kitchen tap in a rather unladylike way. I realise I'm hungry. I already know there isn't much to eat in the kitchen. I was just thinking about Renwick when I realise I can whip back to Hastings for breakfast.

Sue pushes past heading for her bedroom.

"Sue? What would you like for breakfast?" I call.

"Uh I dunno. Just find yourself something," she says.

She goes into her bedroom, grabs some stuff and then heads into the bathroom and closes the door. The shower starts to run.

[+]

I close my facescreen, set my Lana for Hastings Hall, and fold away to nothing. After the decontamination I come out into an empty Control room. Thanking Control I ride a disc up to the glasshouse.

It's about six in the morning here in Tasmania. It's sunny and cool. A morning that seems nice to be up in. I'm surprised to find Mariko in her dressing gown, up and poking around the plants. She looks a bit distracted.

"Hi Mariko, How are you."

"Pletty tewibal if you want to know," she answers looking unwell.

She inhales deeply, and then suddenly grabs her sides and chucks into the flowers.

"Are you sick?" I ask.

She wipes her mouth slowly. And I suddenly realise she's fat because she's going to have a baby.

"Sick of it. Yes," she mutters to herself.

"Are you OK? Should I get Gunter or someone?"

"No ... I'll be OK. What are you doing here anyway?"

"Getting some breakfast."

She winces, and waves me away. It seems even the idea of food makes her feel ill. I leave her and jog over to the Hall. Ken is in a hot pool reading the paper. It looks like he had been running this morning too.

"Hi Sam," he says, without looking up.

"Hi Ken."

I go in. Mr Trân has been baking his usual delicious pastries. Bernard and Zoe are at breakfast with Patience in her highchair. I ask what Scotty's doing.

"Sleeping Sam. Just like you would be if you had school today," Zoe smiles. Ay, I have to admit that would be true.

I help myself to pastries while Mr Trân makes Sue a latte and a hot chocolate for me in paper cups. He puts it all in a bag and I set off back to the jumpstation. On the way I pick a pretty white flower in the greenhouse then pack everything into a travel box and bend back to Sue's place with it.

[+]

The shower's still running as I set everything out for breakfast and send the box back. Then the shower stops. I just had everything ready when Sue stomps back into the kitchen with a towel on her head. She stops looking at the table.

"What's all this?" she asks, surprised.

"Breakfast ... from Hastings Hall."

She looks at me for a moment, and then smiles.

"Sorry for being a grump ... I just ..."

"I know," I interrupt. "It's OK. Look I got you a coffee."

She grins at me and sits down. I join her.

"If I eat like this every day I'll be as big as a house in a month," she says happily.

"Is it good to be back in your own home?" I ask her.

"Yeah. Sort of. Although it feels like something I'm ready to leave behind me now. The whole place reminds me of Rachel and I want to move on. Go to Dr Prosperov's place and get started with a new life."

"You'll be the only one who has anything of their own with them," I say looking around.

"How do you mean?" she asks, biting into a pain au chocolat.

"We all lost everything in the fire at Renwick. Furniture, keepsakes, money. The lot."

Sue looks around at her things.

"I hadn't really thought of that before ... It's pretty rough really." she says, frowning.

"Yeah. We depend on Dr Prosperov and the Fae totally."

"Hmmm," she says. "Maybe I should put my stuff in storage instead."

"Grandpop probably wishes he had."

"So has he learned anything from last night?"

"Yeah. Control thinks Nathan's welfare case officers were replaced by shape-shifting biobots. We've only seen them once but we know they've got them. So that's the Administration side explained. But the real question is how they linked Nathan to Ashley. There's a lot of suspects and no leads on that one."

"Oh Good! Something to get our teeth into then."

"Yeah."

"So how many infiltrators do you think there are in the world?"

"Old ones? Probably only a few thousand. Newer ones. Maybe five hundred. That's not counting Asia of course because we haven't started our mission there. We know there are others in China and India we haven't found yet."

"What's the difference between the old infiltrators and the new ones?"

"Well, the new ones were like Hathaway and Rocelli. They only went back to the 1890's. There were a lot of mysterious airships seen back then[†] and we think there was some kind of settlement programme."

"Wasn't that at the time of those meteors you investigated in the beginning?"

"Yeah, I think I said before Hekator believes a ship was destroyed and the bits fell to Earth. He's not sure where it came from or why yet, though."

"Yeah, you told me about that before and it's interesting."

"Why?"

"Well, either it was an accident, or it was on purpose. If it was on purpose it suggests that someone changed their mind about welcoming these newcomers but was too late."

"How do you figure that out?"

"They came here to infiltrate not to invade, or we'd all know about it. They must have come here because they were attracted by someone or they would have gone some place else. But if it wasn't an accident someone – it could be the same someone, or someone else again – learned something that made them violently opposed to the new arrivals. But if what you say about the Administration being able to take infiltrators out when they want to is right, it wasn't the Administration. They could have stopped them anyway. So it had to be one of those who had originally attracted the newcomers in the first place."

I stare at her awestruck.

"Are all cops as clever as you?" I ask, taking a bite of my croissant and wondering whether I've badly underestimated her. Sue smiles.

"Well, at least there's one person who still thinks I should be a detective," she says.

"Because this squares with some things Frau Müller told us."

"Who is Frau Müller?"

"She was how Diana and Elena ended up in the deep network."

"Deep network?"

"Of the Bruderschaft."

"What is the deep network?"

"Well, I told you how the Bruderschaft women need young blood and bone to have babies."

"Yes."

"Well, they still do today, nothing's changed."

Sue gulps.

"That sounds very creepy Sam."

"It's even creepier than it sounds."

"Are these the new infiltrators or the old ones?"

"We think they are mostly old. We haven't found any new female ones yet. That doesn't mean there aren't any. Just that we don't know where they are, and, of course, we don't exactly go looking for them because they're bloody dangerous."

"But your point is that the old Bruderschaft women are still in business and there's a network to supply them with blood and bone?" Sue asks.

"Yeah ... Well, we busted up what we found of one network at the old Abbey of Elan, in Champagne, France. That was why Mrs Huuygens was so pissed off with us."

"Huuygens. She's the one married to the Virion manager in Belgium. The good looking biobot, right?

"Yep."

"But who is, or was, Frau Müller then?"

"Well, I hadn't got to her yet. She's part of Diana's story. She kept Diana and Elena as maids and knows Hathaway, Mrs Huuygens and Von Streicher. She also knows Father Rocelli who was involved with Sarah's kidnap and came across Jeanne in DRC."

Sue's eyes flick up to mine.

"Rocelli was involved with Sarah Kogan's kidnap?"

"Yup. Hathaway too."

"Shit."

"What?"

"So you have three kids in the entire world and both you and the Bruderschaft have had something to do with them all."

"Yeah," I say defensively, "except Khadiyeh and Eduardo in Manila,"

"But that's still three out of five in one point two billion. Either you're after the same thing or they know what you are doing," Sue says firmly.

A sick feeling opens up in my stomach.

"But why haven't they told the Administration?" I ask.

"Aren't your kids part of destroying the Galactic Center somehow? Maybe they see some common ground?" Sue suggested.

"Yeah well ... I don't know."

Some of the things Von Streicher had said were starting to weigh on my mind too. He'd wanted to know why we were interested in Nathan. He couldn't help but know we were interested in Diana. She had been the "main course" of the blood ceremony we'd interrupted at the old Abbey of Elan. And how was it that Jeanne ended up briefly with Father Rocelli until we'd freed her in DRC's capital, Kinshasa?

Von Streicher hadn't asked me about Nathan because he had *no* idea. He'd asked because he wanted to *confirm* what he already knew or guessed. But Sue's still talking.

"So if Lucky and the Fae can work it out, why not the infiltrators and whoever they might be helping them?"

I look at her.

"If you're right, this changes everything," I say, shaking my head. I also couldn't help thinking that people as brilliant as Dr P must have realised this already. But Sue has a happier suggestion.

"Sometimes you only realise things when you look at them backwards. It's certainly made me realise a few things about Rachel."

"But if they know our mission they can predict us," I point out.

"Only if they have realised it. If they didn't they would have been as surprised by you, as you were by them ... And I think you have the edge in terms of technology."

I think back to Dr Prosperov/Lucky in Belzer, Liechtenstein fighting off whatever it was that was beating me up. Maybe Lucky was more powerful than that cold rainbow thing. They had certainly looked pretty worried when I'd spilled my guts and told them about him.

"But if they know now ..." I start.

"You can expect things to be different," Sue nods.

"We have to talk to Dr Prosperov," I tell her.

Sue thinks for a minute.

"Yes, we do. What's the time?"

"Umm it's six thirty over there."

"Will he be up yet?"

"Probably not. He tends to work at night and sleep in."

"OK, so tell me about this Frau Müller then."

"Well, we didn't meet her until May and a whole bunch of stuff happened before then."

"Like what?"

"Well Sarah and Khadiyeh especially. Sarah's dad Uri affected

Jeanne without knowing it through his trafficking. Khadiyeh changed our whole outlook. Jeanne and Nathan got into trouble and both Ergenekon and Sinaloa tracked Tarik and Ashley down and showed up at Renwick which put the pressure on us well."

"But how does this help us work out who spotted Ashley?"

"I don't know. We might not have seen whoever it was that spotted Ashley with Nathan."

"No, you might not have. But it may be possible to deduce who they are from what you do know."

"Really? So what do you want me to do?"

"Well, you'd better keep telling me the story. But I have a feeling that right now the Administration knows you've got Nathan in Florida for a reason and is using him as bait to try and get you guys again once and for all. The Bruderschaft will be bending over backwards to help them, too, because you are really the only force which can stop them."

"OK. Ah ... well, shall I go back to Sarah?"

"Yeah if that's where it picks up. But try to stick to the main points."

"OK," I say, not knowing what that means.

"Umm, well a whole bunch of stuff happened I didn't find out about until a bit later so I'll give it to you in the order it happened rather than the order I found out about it, OK?"

"Sounds fine to me."

...

OK. So at about the same time we were stealing Hussein and Omar's guns and phones, Control watched a unit of Belgian federal police raid Uri Kogan's hotel room. Control already knew he wasn't there because Scott and Ashley had dropped flies so we could hear what was being said. They caught an old Ukrainian migrant worker Uri had given his room to so long as he claimed to be him – something all the guns in his face very quickly made him think was a very bad idea. He babbled away in Ukrainian and bad French. The cops didn't know what he was saying but they did realise that Kogan had given them the slip. An hour later, at four in the morning Israel time (and five in the afternoon our time) Hussein's phone was called. By this time Control had registered its Sim on Verizon's network in the United States. Control answered it with a brief "Yes" in Arabic and then recorded instructions in French. The caller wanted Hussein to video cutting off one of Sarah's fingers and then to transmit the video and post the finger to her grandfather, Michael Semovich. The caller rang off but not before Control had traced the call and voiceprinted the caller. The call had come from the National headquarters of the Belgian Police! But, of course, because we'd taken his phone, Hussein never got the call. In fact Hussein and Omar woke up to a pretty bad morning. They had no phones, no guns and after Omar had found an Internet café and logged-in, they discovered no money either.

Hussein kept talking about me and Tahira in a way that annoyed Omar who thought Hussein was freaking out. Meanwhile they were in danger of becoming famous. The TV morning news in Israel was still running the story of the kidnapped girl with the new twist that a reward was expected for her return. No details of how much the reward would be were made public but then the politician Shev Komenski ruined it by saying on breakfast television that he didn't think any reward should go to the *Arabs* who had kidnapped or hidden her.

Gunter explained that this was a dare to Michael Semovich to come on TV and declare that the reward *was* open to Arabs. And Semovich was famous for avoiding publicity. It was obvious Komenski was trying to keep the situation alive as long as possible for his own purpose of inspiring hatred between Arab and Jewish Israelis. Oddly in this situation he was actually helping *us* because there was no way the Palestinian women would come forward in a situation like this.

Meanwhile Chief Inspector Yigal Gur had been getting his team to interrogate the two Ukrainian linesmen who had witnessed the shooting of Federov. They had dug out their records and were giving them a real hard time. Apparently they were linked to the famous Israeli mobster David Khader[†] who had previously employed them in his restaurants and their immigration status was dodgy. Gur was insisting the linesmen try harder to identify the gunmen or he would send them back to the Ukraine.

Sarah herself seemed to have taken heart from our late night visit. She knew Hussein and Omar were hassled. She seemed less afraid and a bit more hopeful. The two local women watching Sarah had changed their attitude a lot too. They seemed a lot less harsh and very worried that Hussein and Omar were going to take off, leaving them to deal with Sarah and her shady relatives or Shev Komenski with no money to show for it.

We were hoping to find Uri when he called Semovich to explain his escape. Control would be able to back-trace his call. We expected Uri would probably want to know if the kidnappers had made any new threats. As it happened, they had.

At six in the morning a man called Semovich and told him, in French-accented English, Uri's dodging Belgian police had sealed Sarah's fate. Now, unless Semovich paid up ten million Euro and handed over Kogan in four days he would receive a "token gift" in the mail to let him know they weren't to be messed with. Semovich responded with vicious threats of revenge but the man laughed at him and hung up. That call also came from the same man in the headquarters of the Belgian Federal Police.

During the day (but overnight for us) Ashley and Scotty were on standby to track down Sarah's father, Uri Kogan. When Kogan finally did call his father-in-law, Michael Semovich, at ten, he got a bollocking. They argued for ages about what to tell Alisha. This was great for Ashley and Scott because it allowed Control to trace the cellphone Uri was using in Luxembourg. Scott and Ashley followed up and found him in a cafe wearing dyed hair and a false moustache. They watched him all day, mostly in cafes making calls.

He moved often and he kept changing Sim cards and networks. He had at least four which he rotated regularly. That meant it took longer for Control to identify all his different telephone identities. It was also hard for Ashley to work in Europe because she was so easily noticed in countries mostly full of white people. To avoid being noticed she had to stay out of sight under camouflage to keep watching Kogan. They still managed to get close enough to tag him though. Scotty bumped Uri and put a sticky tag on Uri's leather jacket while pretending to play with a soccer ball.

However by the end of their day (our night) they had tracked him to a small hotel tucked away in a quiet part of town. Finally we had tracked down one of the world's most tricky arms dealers.

Meanwhile in Israel Omar and Hussein had spent their day trying to get back what they'd lost to us. They bought new phones and emailed a numbered hotmail address saying they had changed phone numbers for "security reasons". It was a dumb excuse but covered up the more serious problem that they now had no guns.

They weren't worried about Sarah, or the women they had employed. What they were worried about was the heavy duty Hariri crime family who were strong on the other side of Umm al Fahm† and had allied with the Abdel Khader† gang, one of Semovich's many Jewish mob enemies. If the Hariri's tried to steal Sarah and take over the kidnap, Omar and Hussein would have nothing to fight with.

Hussein was also worried that word of Sarah was getting out on the street as me and Tahira had suggested, so they threatened the women helping them, telling them that they would get no money if the gossiped. Omar and Hussein were beginning to get that they were as much strangers in Umm al Fahm as Sarah was. They were professionals not locals. They're only link with Umm Al Fahm were Omar's father's cousins, the Walid's. It had only been agreed as a base because Umm al Fahm is a hard place for Israeli Police to go to without starting a riot with the local Palestinians who would join to resist a common enemy. What they hadn't considered was that the local Palestinians themselves might not welcome a high profile crime in their town.

It was not until six in the evening (or five in our morning) that Omar finally got the call ordering the amputation from Belgium that Hussein was meant to have got twelve hours before. We couldn't hear what was being said to Omar because we hadn't tapped his new phone yet but we heard him stress the importance of their being paid before they did anything.

The conversation was in French but we weren't sure whether Sarah understood it or not. It went around in circles and ended badly. Omar then complained hard-out to Hussein in Arabic about the unreasonable demands of their employer. Our fly picked them up talking about whether they should cut off Sarah's finger. They even found a big kitchen knife but they agreed that before they risked getting caught posting body parts their employer should pay up. They decided to give them two days. If they weren't being paid properly by then, they would kill and dump Sarah, and escape Israel.

By eight in the evening their time (or seven in the morning, ours) the big Russian who had masterminded the grab of Sarah, phoned to say he was coming with cash to swap for Sarah's finger. There was nothing we could have done. It was all too fast. As soon as he put down the phone Omar explained to Hussein in rapid Arabic. They chased out the women, grabbed Sarah, who screamed until they smothered her under a pillow and cut off her left pinky with a heavy kitchen knife. Then they dressed the wound with some skill. They slapped and punched Sarah hard if she made any noise above quiet whimpering. When the Russian arrived an hour later they swapped packages.

Hussein and Omar counted their ten thousand US dollars from a shoe box. The Russian checked out Sarah's cut off pinky, ignoring her crying. When everyone agreed everything was OK, the Russian left. To put Sarah to sleep they force fed her vodka until she passed out.

As I said we didn't find this out until later because we were distracted by Soraya and Mitra flying out to Israel that morning.

251

They had to be up early to get the ferry across to Auckland in time to get to the airport by midday. Tahira and Asal went with Mariko in Gunter's old Mercedes to the airport to see their mum and grandmother off.

Mariko later said Soraya and Mitra had seemed a bit nervous about leaving their children but Tahira had almost shoved them through the gate to get them on their way.

It had now been decided that the three of us (Scotty, Me and Tahira) would fly our speeders to Israel together. I think Mitra and Soraya felt that a boy and a girl together would be unseemly but that two boys would somehow cancel each other out. Tahira thought their calculations ridiculous.

Even so neither of the Khadem girls was the same after Mitra and Soraya had gone. Tahira was a bit quieter than usual and Asal looked a bit sad, so Rewa kept her company and they went to the beach to play mermaids with Mariko in their suits again.

Meanwhile Scotty and Ashley came back for a team catch-up. It was good to see them again. They said working from a safehouse was hard. Partly because you got sick of being in a suit and partly because it wasn't as much fun in Austria during the winter as Renwick in the summer holidays. After a while the dark, cold and snow got boring.

We then had a briefing from Control and it was only now that we caught up with the situation in Israel. We were all shocked by way the kidnappers had cut off Sarah's finger. We had known they were tough but we had always thought we would be able to do something. Now we realised that there were limits when things started happening quickly and when knives were involved they could happen very fast indeed.

Grandpop decided that because we needed to be ready at a

moment's notice he needed us to work in three shifts. Scotty and Ashley would be noon to nine in the evening Israel time, Cam and Tarik were ten at night until four in the morning (the middle of the day in New Zealand) and me and Tahira were four in the morning until midday (afternoon until midnight New Zealand time). We had to be ready to go at anytime to stop them killing Sarah.

It was all very gruff, but then Grandpop suddenly lightened up by saying we probably wouldn't need to do anything and it would be mostly waiting around. We talked about Sarah and Uri. We wondered about Sarah's wound. Grandpop said that unless the wound got infected – and they had made sure it wouldn't – it would heal. Tahira and Ashley wondered if the Fae might help Sarah but nobody else thought they would. Sarah would be marked for life. That was just part of being kidnapped by murderous thugs.

We wondered whether the finger would make a difference to Sarah's father, Uri. We wondered whether the Belgian Police had intended to arrest Uri or just kill him. But most of all we wondered who this guy Sergeant Oliver Xavier was and who he was working for, because it obviously was not the Belgian Federal Police. We needed to get inside the Belgian police headquarters and find out.

"I know, I know. Webs and flies. Webs and flies," Tarik complained.

But Tarik and Cam were the morning "go" team for Sarah so they couldn't do it, and Ashley and Scott had just finished their evening shift and were due to go to bed. So guess who was left? Me and Tahira.

We said goodnight to Ashley and Scott who were starting to

yawn, while Tarik and Cam decided that if they were going to have to be in their suits they may as well enjoy the summer and join Rewa, Asal and Mariko out in the sparkling, bright sea. Which left having to bug the Belgian Federal Police while they had fun – and we were a bit grumpy about it.

Control showed us around Xavier's desk. He shared an office with three others so it was impossible they weren't in on the kidnap. It was ten at night in Belgium but the office was still occupied. Another officer – a middle-aged, heavyset, white guy with curly brown hair, was reading something with his feet on the desk, leaning back in his chair. From time to time people passed the open door. Sometimes they exchanged a few words, other times they just passed by with a glance inside. Bugging this place was going to be hard.

Hekator had given us a new bug. It looked like a strip of sticky tape but it picked up sound vibrations and GPS signals and passed them back to Control. It was amazingly hard to see when pressed on to any surface. It didn't reflect the way sticky tape does, it was just sort of transparent. This was what Scotty had stuck on Uri's jacket. Our plan was to stick it under some desks. That was if we could get there without being noticed.

The best way in was to bend into the elevator which was just twenty meters down the passage. But there were at least a dozen offices on the floor as close as Xavier's and there were still police working in all of them. Sneaking in wasn't really going to be an option.

"So let's look at this," said Grandpop looking carefully at the hologram of the man reading.

"You're two kids, so you're out of place. You're darker than they are. So you're out of place again. And if you speak Persian, Tahira, you're completely out of place again. So what if instead of trying to be sneaky you go loud instead."

"Go loud?" we asked.

"Yeah. So like Tahira storms out of the lift shouting angrily in Persian and you, Sam, follow trying to calm her down. You go into the office and yell stuff he can't understand and stay there until they either chuck you out or until they find a Persian to talk to you."

Tahira looked from Grandpop to me and back.

"Umm what am I angry about?" she asked.

"I dunno maybe you want to report something. Maybe you think human traffickers have ... have killed your cousin."

"What?"

"Or something. They promised to smuggle him into Britain and it's been a month and he hasn't called. You say he's dead."

Tahira was looking doubtful.

"Zat iz ridiculous," Tahira told him looking superior.

Grandpop looked a bit put out.

"I thought it was quite good actually," he mumbled.

"*Ee* iz my cousin," Tahira said pointing me.

"And eet iz my older *sister* zey 'av killed," she said grinning, her eyes flashing.

Grandpop smiled and ruffled her hair.

"OK, you got it. Now how do you feel about doing it there?" he said pointing to the hologram of the office.

Tahira looked at man reading and shrugged.

"If eet doesn't work we weel just knock eem out and vanish," she shrugged.

"Well try and be a bit sneakier than that," Grandpop said.

"Sam weel need to practice some Farsi," she added.

"OK. No rush. Don't go til you're ready."

So we went into the corner and practised phrases like "They won't listen" which sounded like "Ou-na goosh ne-mi-dan; "You're going to get us in trouble" which was "to da-ri ba-raie ma mosh-kel do-rost mi-ko-ni"; "C'mon let's go" which was "Bi-a be-rim" and stuff life that. Even with the suit and Tahira helping it took me an hour to get used to the rhythm and music of Tahira's language so that she was happy. We practised on the holodeck with the Belgian detective still reading whatever it was that he was so busy with, just beside us. It wasn't quite like being there but it wasn't bad.

It felt a bit like doing heavy homework. The building was like a school too. It was old and looked like it dated back to the seventies but had a very fussy cleaner. The lino was very shiny and the place was spotless but there was just this feeling of neglect. It wasn't hard to imagine why cops up against the world's meanest killers might find it easier to join them.

Finally we were ready to go.

Tahira walked around the floor, getting herself worked up, as Control waited for an empty lift to come up. Suddenly bang! We were gone.

[+]

There was a flash and I found myself facing a Schindler's lift sign. I punched the sixth floor quickly and a second later Tahira took a deep breath and started shouting.

"They *must* listen to us! Those bastards have taken Najva. Maybe they still have her."

The doors burst open. Tahira ran.

"Don't try and stop me," she yelled back at me. "It's our only chance."

"You're going to get us in trouble," I yelled chasing after her.

"They have to listen. Najva may be *dead*. We have to do something!"

Tahira ran. We burst into the office, startling the man reading. Tahira ran up to him. Grabbing him. "You! *You* are a policeman? You can find my sister! They said they'd look after her but she hasn't called. Mum is worried sick."

I tried to pull her away.

"They won't listen. C'mon let's go."

She elbowed me off violently in the head and I fell.

"No! No! The police have to help us. These traffickers! These criminals! They have taken my sister. She may be in terrible trouble!"

The detective had no idea what was going on. He stood shushing Tahira saying.

"Hey ... Hey ... what are you doing in here. What's all this about? What's going on? Do you speak Flemish or French? How did you get in here?"

"They won't listen," I repeated from the floor.

Tahira blurted out another torrent of Persian allowing me to bug the first desk. A number of figures appeared at the doorway and came in.

"I can't understand you. Speak French!" the detective complained loudly.

"You're just going to get us in trouble," I told Tahira.

Then she rounded on me, shouting, scolding and slapping at me.

"She's a feisty little bitch isn't she?" one of the cops smirked.

"Yeah, but how did they get in?"

I pointed at them laughing.

"They won't listen," I shouted.

Tahira spun on her heel and launched herself at them calling them appalling names in Persian, a picture of fury. They were so taken aback I got another desk bugged. The detectives were just about to slap Tahira when a commanding French voice filled the room.

"What the *f__* is going on here?"

A man entered, still wearing a thick black leather coat and scarf. He was in his forties. Tall, greying brown hair with a drooping moustache and cold gray-blue eyes. Tahira stopped and stared at him. So did I. *We couldn't read him.* A moment passed in which we weren't sure what to do. Then Tahira recovered.

"They took my sister! They took her away and she hasn't called. They said they could get her into England but it's been two months. Why won't anyone do anything?"

It would have been better if she'd said this in Persian but the arrival of the biobot had confused Tahira so she had blurted all this out in French.

"*You were speaking French!*" I let her know silently as the detectives looked at her.

"What's the matter?" Grandpop asked.

"*This guy is a Biobot.*" I told him.

"What's this girl doing here? Why are there children in here?" the biobot demanded as if Tahira was a specimen in a jar.

"Please sir, they are organised criminals these people," Tahira began, "They transport girls like my sister for lots of money and smuggle them across the borders."

The biobot looked around.

"Sergeant Galliard get these children downstairs and take their statements."

"This is the one who called Omar and Semovich. The voice

258

matches," Control told us as Sergeant Galliard, who was the man whose reading we had interrupted, came forward to round me and Tahira up. We walked past the Biobot. I dared to glance up at him. The look I got back was full of angry suspicion. I was damn sure he knew we weren't ordinary kids, just as we knew he wasn't human.

We walked out into the corridor. Behind us the biobot was telling everyone to go back to work. Sergeant Galliard pushed us along to the lift.

"So you speak French after all Missy? What was all that nonsense before about then?"

"It is my cousin's fault. He comes with me but he says nobody will listen. He doesn't want me to come up here but I ran in the elevator and he followed. He says we get into trouble. I am so angry with him I forgot the language I am speaking."

"Sure," Galliard said as the lift opened.

"And you got a swipe card too?" he said as he herded us into the lift.

"We follow people. It's easy."

The lift doors closed.

"*Time to go,*" I said silently, getting ready to stun him.

"*No! Not yet!*" Tahira replied.

The numbers counted down the floors.

"So," she asked Galliard. "Who was that man giving orders?"

"You're a nosy, little brat, aren't you?"

"I have seen him before."

"Where?" He asked suspiciously. He was thinking "on TV".

"He visits a woman we know."

That was enough. Sergeant Galliard wanted some gossip that could be handy to get his way with his boss. The name that popped into his mind was Specialist Chief Inspector Francois Turneau.

"*What* woman?"

"Just a woman," Tahira shook her head. She caught my eye. I nodded. The numbers had counted down far enough. I hit him with the amnesia beam just as the doors opened. I ran out, Tahira followed.

"Thank you," she said to the Sergeant who stood blinking in confusion. The doors closed on his confused face.

Luckily the doors on the way out had buttons. We went straight for the exit, walking as we had always been told to do, as quick as we could. The entrance seemed to lead to a car park. But just as we were about go out a policeman called.

"Hey! You kids!"

We turned. He was very tall and blond and had just come in the entrance.

"Where are you going this late at night?" he asked, seriously, bending over to us.

"My cousin is waiting for us in his car outside. We're just going to him," Tahira said smiling a smile that could have lit several rooms.

"Oh, OK. But it is cold. Come back in if he is late. We're here to help," he smiled, straightening up. He meant it too.

"Thank you," Tahira said.

I followed her out.

"There are cameras watching guys. You need to keep moving," Grandpop warned us.

It was ten at night and the narrow street here was quiet. The police building was set a little off the street into a kind of car park surrounded by buildings. It was tempting to head behind the building we'd come out of away from the street into the shadows.

"Go to the street, guys. The other way is covered. Take a left and the right away from the main road," Grandpop advised.

We dashed out and ran to the corner. It was a strange area with low-rise flats, crummy old buildings, houses with gardens and a cathedral poking out not far away. We walked quickly down a driveway and vanished.

[+]

We had been so focused on getting away we hadn't had time to deal with the Biobot we had just encountered so we were a bit spooked when we came back. We both felt relieved to be in the oil pool again when we arrived.

"*His name is Turneau, Francois Turneau,*" I called.

"*That's the name Galliard had,*" Tahira confirmed.

"I'm searching for him now," Control replied.

"But there is slight problem," Control added." It seems the Belgian Police employ blind specialists for bugging missions[†]. Most of them speak numerous languages. Tonight it happened that one who speaks Farsi was nearby and caught some of your performance. He has told Inspector Turneau that Sam was definitely not a native Farsi speaker."

We came out of the oil pool.

"Well, I think he knew that from just looking at me, to be honest," I told Grandpop.

The only reason I might pass for a Persian, Arab or anything else was if nobody looked too closely. Close up, in good light, the differences were not hard to see. I'm darker than Tahira for one thing and our noses are way different. Grandpop looked at me over his reading glasses.

"Probably. But what we need to know is why is this Biobot shaking down Semovich and trying to grab Kogan? Is he working for someone else? Do *they* need money? What do *they* want with Kogan? To kill him or what? It's suddenly got a bit mixed up around here," Grandpop said shaking his head.

"Maybe we should tag him," I suggested.

"I dunno Sam. I'm nervous about those guys. Hathaway was dangerous. He tried to kill Scott. With regular people I know what I'm dealing with, but with them, I don't know what they'll pull on us. I'll contact Hekator and see what he says."

"What are ze bugs telling uz?" Tahira asked.

"Not much at the moment," Control said. "But I followed Turneau back to his office. He is about to lock it for the night. I can't watch him too closely because I suspect he will notice my interference pattern."

"Do we go back?" I asked Grandpop.

"We'll leave that to Tarik and Cam. It's better for the spider and the flies than a direct attack. He may have a secret camera in there."

"So what do we do now?" I asked

"Join the others. You don't want to miss the whole summer," Grandpop suggested

"Shall we bend dive?" I asked Tahira.

"Of course," she grinned. So we did, and it was excellent.

...

"Yeah OK," Sue objected.

"But what you're saying is that a Biobot was the mastermind behind Sarah's kidnap?" Sue asked.

"Yes. But he was getting orders from the Bruderschaft."

"What about?"

"Well it turned out to be because of Uri's fleet of cargo planes. He had a fleet of Antonov AN-12 ex-military cargo planes which he used for his trading in Africa. He brought in drugs, weapons and ammunition and took out diamonds, gold, coltan and orphans – usually girls. But of course we didn't know that yet.

"Why did the Bruderschaft want planes?"

"They were testing a new bioweapon. Guess who was behind that?"

Sue thought for a moment.

"Uh ... Hathaway?"

"You got it."

"So let me get this straight. Hathaway organised this Belgian police biobot to hire the Russian to hire the Syrians to hold Sarah?"

"Yeah."

"Why such a long chain of command? Why not just do it himself?"

"It took us a while to work out what had happened. First off the CIA were keen to stop Kogan supplying arms to the Sudanese government as it built up towards occupying Dafur instead of UN peacekeepers[†]. They asked Hathaway to make something happen to Kogan's planes but the CIA didn't want to know what. Hathaway learned from Turneau that he was holding a Russian Israeli mafioso on drugs charges so he got Turneau to organise Sarah's kidnap using his influence over the family. The initial plan was just to get Kogan arrested and taken out that way. But when Kogan escaped the Belgian Police, Hathaway (or it might have been Rocelli) realised Kogan's planes were an excellent resource for their own interests. So they convinced the CIA to fund their plan to buy Kogan's planes to channel aid instead of arms. But to make sure it worked they planned to use Kogan's ransom money to pay for his own planes. That meant they could keep the CIA money for their own project. It was quite brilliant really. It was another success for Hathaway because he got Kogan's planes for what seemed like not much money increasing his reputation with the CIA. He and Rocelli already had a good reputation, anyway. They knew people and their way around."

"That's ... yeah, OK, that's pretty evil. But how do you know this?"

"We watched him do it. But when we got Du Croix and the Administration to pick up Hathaway in Elan, France later on we thought the case was closed. The Bruderschaft link to the CIA was shut down when Hathaway was arrested and sent to the Center for processing. Maybe we were wrong."

"How did you get Hathaway anyway?"

"Well, that was sort of where quite a few things came together. Diana, Jeanne and Sarah were all linked to Rocelli."

"How did Rocelli come into this?"

"Negotiations with Kogan but then later on with Jeanne and Diana. They were preparing for a blood bath."

"The Catholic Church or the CIA?" Sue asked, confused.

I laughed, "No, the Catholic Church doesn't do blood baths. The Bruderschaft. Rocelli and Hathaway are Bruderschaft."

"What sort of bloodbath? A massacre?"

"No, it really is a bath of blood. It's one of their processes so their women can get pregnant. We think that's what Countess Elizabeth Báthory was doing in the sixteenth century when she killed all those girls in Slovakia†. Blood really does have life extending properties[†]."

"Ugh!! that's *disgusting*."

"Yes, and it's even worse in reality than it sounds. That was what we rescued Diana from and how we got a whole bunch of Bruderschaft arrested by Du Croix and the Administration." Sue thought about that for a moment.

"So Hathaway was arrested by Du Croix?"

"Yeah Du Croix sent him down. It was a big roundup."

"But Hathaway had to have friends inside the CIA. So whoever he worked with could *still* be there."

"Yes, or one of the other American intelligence agencies like the Defence Intelligence Agency or the State Department. We know it was American and the CIA is the biggest but it could be one of the others."

"OK, so the connection with Sarah via the planes makes sense. She's just an unlucky means to a different end. But Rocelli's connection with a girl from the Democratic Republic of Congo, two girls in the clutches of Eastern human traffickers, and a Washington school? How does that work?"

"I really dunno."

"Hmm keep going while I think."

"OK."

...

CHAPTER SIXTY SEVEN: TRANSFER TO HAIFA

The operation to rescue Diana in Hungary took a while to set up. Control had scanned *Kisalfold*, the paper of the border cities of Goyr, Sopron and Moson[+] and decided it was hopeless looking for anyone to report Diana's story because there was a crazy law limiting crime reporting in Hungary[†].

Apparently the Government there thinks if there is no news freedom it could get rid of crime. Of course what it actually meant was that criminals (some of whom worked for the Government) are protected from being reported. So instead Control picked an experienced bilingual Hungarian-Czech freelance journalist named Hanna Szakats who covered Eastern crime and women's issues for the Austrian paper Der Standard and a Hungarian website called Atlatszo which specialised in investigative reporting.

She lived in Vienna which despite being in Austria was just over the border. Gunter tipped her off about Uncle Vanya's place and she started digging around. Gunter warned Hanna not to talk to the cops because we weren't sure who was straight. Hanna also doubted Uncle Vanya hadn't paid some official or policeman. However she did visit Uncle Vanya's, posing as a pushy salesperson for an Austrian tourism magazine. Gunter said she was chased off pretty firmly – especially after she'd taken pictures for her fictional magazine.

The day after Sarah's finger was hacked off we carried out a raid on Uncle Vanya's again. This time we were after the credit card slips of his customers. It wasn't hard. All we had to do was bend in, open up a lever arch file, flip through them, and bend out again. We printed copies and put them in a box which was sent to Scott and Ashley. They put them in a shoe box and left them outside Hanna's door. Gunter then called her and warned her not to contact the names yet because they would warn Uncle Vanya.

Ken and Patricia moved just over the border from Austria to Sopron, Hungary, pretending to be tourists. Their real job was to work with Ashley and Scotty finding cops that could be trusted to raid Uncle Vanya. Ashley and Scotty had to steal some medical morphine from the Sopron Elizabeth hospital so that Patricia and Ashley could pretend to have found it and hand it in to the local drug squad. What the cops didn't realise was the quiet girl by the loud black American nurse's side was reading their minds.

They picked a black haired, handsome, young, drug squad detective named Mika Szabo who was completely straight and had a reliable team. Gunter tipped him off one hour before the courier bringing the drugs to Uncle Vanya was due to arrive. He didn't mention the girls because we weren't sure that Szabo's colleague, vice squad boss Paul Osvath wasn't a client of Uncle Vanya. But Gunter did make up a story about weapons. Hanna was also told to watch out for police that day.

The result was that Sergeant Szabo raided Uncle Vanya's the night before we relocated to Israel. Scotty had come back to Renwick for the flight the next day so Ashley had to watch the raid by herself. She reported in the next morning that the raid had been brilliant. The drug courier had arrived about eleven in the morning. Ten minutes later Szabo showed up with six police cars. Not far behind them was Hanna Szakats with a photographer using a huge lens.

They caught both Uncle Vanya and the courier with their pants down. They were dragged away handcuffed, half-naked and swearing as they slipped on the snow and were driven off. The girls, including Diana and Elena, were given a little more time to gather their stuff. It was an hour later that Ashley saw them driven away in a van.

We watched Ashley's view seven hours later at briefing when we woke up. Gunter reported Hanna had discovered that the girls had been sent to a women's prison because they were mostly illegal immigrants who would be sent back to their homelands. The fact that Diana (who was only thirteen years old) was among adult prisoners was part of the scandal Hanna was going to stress to sell to papers in Vienna.

The success of our work made it a pretty happy briefing. Then Mitra and Soraya came on and announced they had arrived at the beachfront villa in Caesarea which Dr Prosperov had rented for them. They gave us a little tour using the notebook camera. It looked great. It was right on the beach behind some dunes with a view of the sea with a high wall, a big pool, lots of fabulous rooms and a big fireplace.

They'd had a little trouble getting into Israel because their places of birth in their Australian passports were Iran. For some reason the Israeli Customs seemed to doubt Australian passports. They were not too sure about the difference between Australia and New Zealand so when Mitra and Soraya seemed to be able to speak reasonable English and describe Baha'i rituals they were let through. They picked up a car at Haifa International airport and then drove to the villa. It was night but they were looking forward to the arrival of Asal soon.

Now that the moment had come to go to Israel Aunty Liz became a bit nervous about bending in a sleeping bag. She had also packed one of the big transport trunks with enough stuff to keep a family of ten going for a month. She had to be stopped from packing a huge supply of food. Grandpop pointed out she had been eating Mr Trân's Palestinian and Israeli dishes for the past week so she couldn't say she wasn't going to like the local stuff.

Finally after packing and unpacking and checking everything at least twice the trunk was sent through. We could even see it appear with a flash in the villa. Then it was time. She came up to me and gave me a big hug.

"You look after yourself and these others, boy. Stick to the plan and don't get lost," she said, and hugged me tight. I told her I *couldn't* get lost but she wasn't interested in the technicalities.

"See ya later big brother," Rewa smiled. I hugged her.

"See ya soon Sis."

Tahira gave Asal a big hug too. Then looking very nervous they all went downstairs and got into their "sleeping bags". Cam and Tarik were still the morning "go" team for Sarah so they were suited up ready to bend Asal and Rewa to the villa. Mariko was also suited for Aunty Liz. They took hold of the handles and then folded away, only to appear as flashes in the villa.

It was their first sleeping bag rides so they were looking pretty dazed as Mitra and Soraya got them out. Asal was crying and hugged her mother. Rewa and Liz gave each other a hug too. But when they saw us on the screen of the little netbook they gave us big smiles and waved. After a few words they were all running around the villa with Rewa and Asal bouncing around like mad things even though it was ten at night over there.

We had to go. Me and Tahira took over from Tarik and Cam at two as Sarah's "go team" and it was going to take four hours to fly to Israel in the speeders. We got the ground clothes and equipment on and went into the speeder room. Ka-rea-rea, Tahira's speeder Shaheen, and Scott's Inkwazi, were on the launch rail. Grandpop and Gunter fussed around us as we got into them. Mr Trân had given us a plastic bag of goodies and a water bottle to take with us. We made toilet stops then all got into our speeders. Grandpop came along the line checking us and slamming the hatches down.

As the interface came up I found myself feeling really excited. Our first big flight around the world.

"Blend camouflage on," Gunter reminded us from the desk. The doors in the old gun emplacement at the end of the tunnel slid open revealing a circle of bright blue.

"Bearink 060 to altitude 3000 meters, 1g acceleration, at 3000 turning 100 degrees east, zhen inertialess to field intensity factor five. Follow the vaypoints and you can't go wrong. Haf fun kids. Launch in five, four, three, two, one. Go."

The tunnel blurred past me and the blue circle got bigger until I burst out into a sunny morning on Aotea Island. I rose up rapidly, the bright green island dropping away beneath us in the brilliant blue sea as we climbed for ten grand. I held back letting Scott and Tahira form up in V formation behind me. It was a fantastic day to be flying.

We were so blended-in we looked transparent. I led everyone in a curve to the right sweeping 260 degrees over ten kilometers. That way we came around over Renwick three kilometers below. We could see over the ridge of the island on to the pretty blue Auckland harbour, Rangitoto Island green and empty on the right, the harbour busy with ships, yachts and small boats far below us. It was time to kick it.

"*Inertialess at 15 degrees elevation to 40km and 4,000 knots,*" I called, "*in three, two, one.*"

Three blurs sped for the boundary of space, leaving the city far behind in a swirl of cloud.

We cruised along for a while, looking at the blue-black horizon, seeing stars above and the amazing spread of colours below us. After fifteen minutes Australia was in sight. It stretched forever, all red orange and brown below us, shrouded in its own special glow. It would take another half an hour to cross.

"*Sam?*" Scott called.

"*Yeah mate?*"

"*I'm totally stuffed, bra. I can't keep my eyes open. I'll tell Inkwazi to follow you, OK?*"

"*Yeah, OK.*"

"*Thanks,*" he yawned. "*It really is so lekker and warm in here.*" Tahira said nothing but she left her position alongside Scott and edged up alongside me but about 50 meters on my right.

"*Do yhou zink Diana will be OK in zhat prison?*" she asked generally.

"*I dunno. She seems to have a pretty rough time no matter where she is. She just has a hard life.*"

Tahira said nothing. She didn't speak again until we were about halfway over the great desert continent.

"*Do zhou ever wonder if we are on the good side?*"

"*Yep.*"

Tahira sighed.

There was another long pause. Then she asked, almost in a whisper.

"*What would zhou do if we weren't?*"

"*I dunno,*" I answered. "*I ... I ... never got that far.*"

"*Me too,*" she muttered.

We said nothing for a long time. Australia slipped by beneath and then suddenly we were over blue again. We had been flying for almost an hour. I felt fine but I checked with Tahira in case she wanted to land. She didn't, so we headed out into the wide blue Indian Ocean.

We passed the time playing music and chatting. Scotty was fast asleep and Inkwazi was just following along about 50 meters behind us. After an hour we were starting to notice a brown haze to the north or right of our flightpath. It was enormous, stretching across the horizon from east to west[†]. We wondered what it was. Control said "pollution". It was a bit scary how huge it was.

Another half-hour later we were starting to get hungry. Our bodies were saying it was lunch time even though the light was saying dinner time. We were scheduled to land in the Maldive Islands, south-east of India. The islands were warmer than the sea so, even though it was dark, we could see them thirty kilometers below us. Still, it was too high and we were too fast to properly check them out, so we did "the elevator" – a manoeuvre you can only do when inertialess – that involves instantly stopping and then dropping, in our case down to two kilometers. We sat there. Three almost-transparent craft hovering over the lights of the capital Male, just two kilometers down and two kilometers away. An aircraft, its lights blazing, was on approach to the airport island beyond but they couldn't see us. Scotty was still snoring. The weather was fine. Outside it was twenty five degrees Celsius on a lovely night.

We didn't really want to go to the crowded capital. We just wanted to find a quiet beach somewhere, so we started cruising north. The ocean turned out to be quite large so we picked up the pace to three hundred knots. But as we got further north we came up on so many pretty islands we had to slow down to make a decision. We argued a bit over a couple but I was just getting more and more hungry. Finally I let Tahira choose.

It wasn't completely uninhabited. There was a resort on the other side, but we liked the beach. So we flew low, picked out a site in the dunes behind the beach and landed. Scotty was still asleep as we popped open the tops. The air was warm and smelt of the sea. There was a fantastic sunset out over the ocean back where we'd come from so we settled down to eat our lunches and watch.

It was different not to be wearing suits. You realised how much the suits kept us from the temperature, and the breeze, and the feel of a place. You felt freer but also more vulnerable.

"Zis is exactly what my muzzer was against," Tahira sighed.

"What?" I asked surprised.

"Me and zhou alone on a beautiful beach at sunset."

I pulled a face.

"Why?" I asked, confused, taking a bite of my Ciabatta ham roll. Tahira shrugged.

"Zhey sink it ees not nice for a boy and girl to be alone wizzout chaperone. It iz the same everywhere among zer believers of Islam."

"But you aren't Muslim," I pointed out.

"But zhey grew up under Islam. Zhey do these things out of 'abit," suddenly she frowned.

"It is important when we go to Iran that zhou are my couzin and protect ze family honour."

I thought about it for a while.

"That's weird," I said softly.

"It is the zhe way zhings are for millions of women," she shrugged.

"Its not exactly fair is it?"

Tahira laughed.

"Zhou sound like Scotty! With his 'is it'."

But then she went serious again.

"No, of course it isn't fair," And then she added to herself.

"And it must change."

We sat for a while watching the last intense slice of orange fade from the sky. Then we went back to the speeders and loaded up. A moment later three short, stubby craft lifted away into the starry sky above the Indian Ocean.

We weren't that far from Iran. About thirty to forty five minutes. We flew up in formation, and went inertialess. We went to thirty kilometers again but idled back to 3,000 knots. Cloud was starting to thicken at multiple levels. Up where we were, it was clear, but there were impressive swirls which stretched out in all directions.

As we started to cross the Arabian Sea we began to pick up a huge mess of radio signals. Radar, radio, up and down the spectrum from the Navy ships below. We called it in to Control.

"That's the 5th Fleet of the US Navy and elements of allied navies. They patrol the Straits of Hormuz to keep the Iranian

Revolutionary Guard in check[†]."

There were planes flying too. Fighter jets, air command jets, sea patrol planes. At thirty kilometers we were safely well above all of them. If Scotty had been awake I might have been interested in going down to have a look at them but he was still asleep. Instead we flew over it all and crossed into the quieter airspace above Sistan and Baluchestan, Iran.

Iran was covered in cloud. Tahira pointed out that it was winter, so bad weather could be expected – especially in the Zagrob mountains in the north above Teheran.

"Yeah, but Tahira we aren't seeing Iran. All we can see is clouds. They look the same wherever we fly."

"Zhen let's elevate to four kilometers, speed five 'undred."

"OK."

"Three, two, one," she called.

It was like falling out of bed into a completely different world. From the calm majesty of the boundary of space we were suddenly tossed into the black confusion of a cloudy snowstorm. Chaotic winds made the speeders wobble slightly as we pressed through murk. I couldn't see a thing. Luckily there are no mountains to hit five hundred metres above the Kaluts Shahdad desert but we were flying completely blind. To see anything we would have to go to active sensors and there was no point being invisible with active sensors. Everyone could see the radiation we'd emit – even the Iranian air force. We may as well light up a spotlight or paint New Years greetings on the side of our speeders.

"Tahira I am not getting much of a view of your country this way," I told her.

"I know."

"And to be honest I'm not that keen on landing and going out on a dark, snowy night dressed like this in any country."

"*I know,*" she said.

She was disappointed but she could see it was stupid to keep going.

"So what do you want to do?"

"Arc to Haifa, maximum altitude thirty kilometers, velocity four thousand?"

"Just what I was going to say."

We were going to fly an arc to a maximum altitude of thirty kilometers at four thousand knots.

"Three, two, one..." she called.

And we were out of there.

The last part of the trip was only fifteen minutes. We accelerated inertialessly but then turned it off to become warp invisible. The place was alive with signals: Iranian and American as we crossed Iraq; Syrian; and finally Israeli airspace. It was strange to think we were following the route missiles might fly if there was a war between Iran and Israel. We were even warhead shaped. It was good that the warp camouflage wrapped all the Israeli air defence radars around us. We knew that behind those radars were missiles and even laser beams[†] waiting to knock down anything that came in as fast and high as we were.

It was two in the morning local time when we arrived. It was good that Control guided our speeders in because we would never have found it working from directions. As we got low enough for safety we dropped warp invisibility and switched to inertialess. The result was that three transparent pods flew up to an Israeli suburb by a beach at four thousand knots and instantly stopped. We were one hundred meters short of the deck. Then using just antigravity we manoeuvred around to land.

Aunty Liz was waiting for us in the darkness wearing a woolly hat, with a blanket wrapped around her and a cup of something hot as the three speeders lay down on the deck in a line beside the pool. We popped our hatches and came out. It was strange to be in another country without a suit. The first thing we noticed was that it was bloody cold, so we raced inside, leaving Scotty, who was still sleeping peacefully. The fire was burning low and the lounge was lovely and warm as well as very styley. We followed Aunty Liz to the kitchen where she made us instant hot chocolate from packets she'd packed.

At two o'clock in the morning we were meant to take over from Cam and Tarik so we called in on the netbook. But Grandpop said nothing much was happening down the road from here at Umm Al Fahm in the middle of the night and said it would be better if we got tuned-in to Israel time. He suggested we got some sleep even though we were wide awake.

"*How*?" I asked.

"Your Aunt will show you," he said and signed out.

"Hekator's made some sleeping jelly beans for us," Liz told us," They work instantly. Rewa and Asal were out like lights even though it was only midday for them. I'll show you to your rooms."

It really was a very nice villa. There were six rooms with Tahira and Asal sharing, and me and Rewa sharing. There would be one spare because Scotty was still in his speeder. I could see Tahira angling to get it but Aunty Liz was strict with us both, making sure we were in our pyjamas and in our beds before giving us the jelly beans. I picked a black one, crunched and sucked and the next thing I knew Rewa was bouncing on me to wake me up.

Everyone else was already up. It was ten in the morning. I felt surprisingly good. Scotty had already left for Austria. The Khadem's were taking everyone except me and Tahira for a tour of Haifa.

Tarik and Cam now had Sarah's night time cover from ten until six, while Scott and Ashley had the morning, and we had the afternoon again, but in a different time zone. That meant we didn't have to go on duty until the afternoon. But always concerned about their daughter Mitra and Soraya insisted that we call in to Renwick for an update.

It was late at night. We had missed a whole day of news on Sarah. But so far nothing much had happened. The finger had been delivered. Sarah's grandfather and mob boss Michael Semovich was beside himself with fury. Some leaders of Israel's underworld had realised they needed to get onside with Semovich before he suspected them of involvement and started a war neither side needed. Others had not come to pay their respects to Semovich and were now suspects. We couldn't get what was said at those meetings, but they were grim. There was no laughter.

Sarah's father, Uri Kogan, had actually been sick when Semovich told him about recieving Sarah's finger. He made all sorts of stupid threats but when Semovich told him what the Israeli police had learned from tracing the kidnapper's calls back to the Belgian police he shut up fast. Kogan knew he had nothing he could use against a corrupt police official in a country as important to him and his diamond trade as Belgium.

Semovich told Kogan bluntly that he expected him to put up the ten million, given he had deserted his own daughter by running in Belgium. Kogan answered nervously that he needed more time to get that sort of money together. Semovich had a fit. He seemed to have a pretty good idea of what Kogan could sell, trade or withdraw. A number of buyers were mentioned. Kogan was clearly not happy when the conversation ended.

Semovich was in such a bad mood he called up his daughter and told her about the finger. Alisha was devastated but Semovich blamed her for leaving her daughter in Kogan's care while she pleased herself. He insisted she pay for the ransom as well. Less wriggly than Uri, Alisha, just fell apart in tears, promising she would give it all up for Sarah.

Meanwhile Inspector Yigal Gur had got a bite. One of the linesmen was cracking and was ready to identify the gunman he'd seen. Gur was telling them horror stories of what Semovich would do to them if he released them and told Semovich they weren't cooperating. They knew they were safer talking to a policeman in a police interrogation room than tied up in some mob dungeon with an angry Semovich.

It wasn't long before a deal was sorted out and the linesmen identified the Malka brothers as the killers of Ivan Federov. Now Gur had something to work with because even if he didn't know where the brothers were, he could easily find people who did, and the threat of Semovich's anger was proving a very effective way for the policeman to get the usually staunch mobsters to break out in a sweat.

Meanwhile in Umm Al Fahm Sarah was not all that well. The shock of the finger combined with the stress of being held was getting to her. Hussein and Omar were getting pretty ropy as well. The women who they had relied on to guard Sarah had

been appalled to discover her finger cut off. When she was just
a rich Israeli bitch they had been happy to cackle at her and give
her a hard time. But now they were feeling sorry for the teenager
who was the same age as their own oldest children. They were
also feeling sorry for themselves. The second payment had
failed. Hussein and Omar were berating them for gossiping and
were not paying them either.

We read (from the holodeck at Renwick) that the women, Raina
Iyad and Nujood Salah, were getting worried. They could all
see how this whole thing could end up falling on them and their
families while the Syrians were safely back over the border. The
Syrians were paranoid the Hariri family were going to jump
them and Hussein and Omar still didn't have any weapons
because they had been too embarrassed to mention the fact to
the Russian, Ivankov.

They bickered over when and how they should get out and what
they should do to get rid of Sarah. The Palestinians whispered to
Sarah in Hebrew that none of this was their idea and they would
just as soon let her go. The Syrians, noticed and got angry. We
left them to their bickering because Dr Prosperov came on
the holodeck. He was in his office and, although it was late at
Renwick, still in a suit.

"Situation in Israel is dangerous. Am thinking is best now
if payments to Syrians resume. They very nervous of local
criminals. If must abandon operation they will kill Sarah.
Therefore operatives need suits while on watch prepared to bend
in to rescue Sarah with maximum firepower."

"If rescue is necessary parents insist operative safety is more
important than Sarah Kogan's. To repeat *our* safety is more
important than girl's. Therefore if bend necessary, Control

will place you *behind* guards and not between Miss Kogan and
guards. To succeed you must react quickly."

We could tell Dr Prosperov had lost this argument with the
parents because he was stressing it. With our diamond-skin
armour we knew there wasn't much Hussein and Omar could do
to us if we stood in front of them and all they had was knives and
so did Dr P. But obviously the parents had made him promise
this would be how it was done and he was anxious that we were
warned so we could still save Sarah if need be.

Me and Tahira pointed out that we didn't have suits and
didn't go on duty until three in the morning Renwick time.
Dr Prosperov said he would send someone to take us back in
sleeping bags. We wondered if flying the speeders all the way to
Israel had been a big waste of time.

The Khadems and Kahus didn't leave for their day trip to
Haifa until Mariko burst into the lounge in a flash of light with
two sleeping bags for us. Mitra and Soraya wanted us safely
chaperoned by Control before they left. We got into our sleeping
bags and were folded and spun back to Renwick.

[+]

But when we arrived and had been dragged out of the
jumpstation oil bath Mariko announced she was going back
to bed and left us to get changed into our suits by ourselves.
I couldn't help thinking how dumb these adults were as I got
undressed. Here we were, *both* getting completely naked on
opposite sides of the thin changing room wall without any
adults around *anywhere*. But *of course* we weren't going to *do*
anything, I thought as I got into the drawer. "What did they
think we were?" I asked the red light in the changer. "Animals?"
In a few minutes we were both in our suits and in the briefing

room watching our parents and sisters driving along in the Ford Territory towards Haifa. We wished we could fly the speeders while wearing a suit but back then the two designs weren't compatible. It was frustrating. Officially Scotty and Ashley were the morning "go team" but they had gone to Zimbabwe. They were showing each other their home countries.

"Come with me to Teheran," Tahira suggested.

[+]

I didn't have anything else to do so I agreed. Tahira zoomed in on an alley she knew. It was deserted. The whole place looked pretty cold and bleak. Even so I followed her to the jumpstation and off we went.

I was amazed how big and busy Teheran was. Cars everywhere, people, even though it was cold with snow. It was easy to get lost in the crowds and we did. Our outfits blended in perfectly. Nobody noticed us. We went to icy parks (that were pretty but empty), shopping areas rich and poor, and monuments and mosques. I had always associated Iran with wild-eyed religious nutjobs. That didn't describe any of the people we met. They were very cool, very styley and many were friendly. The kids looked the same as kids back home. We got some pistachio halva barnieh, which were sort of honey doughnuts, and sugar coated almonds. With Tahira confidently leading the way and my suit translating both signs and voices it was very easy to be relaxed in a city that might otherwise have been too big and a bit strange. The only thing you had to watch was the crazy drivers. Tahira showed me how you crossed the road while these maniacs sped around you. No wonder she had nerves of steel!

Two hours went fast. But after a while I was finding the whole thing too much. I just wanted to have a break, but Tahira had just got started. She wanted to show me *everything*. After another hour of being dragged about, nearly run over, and told to admire things, I pointed out we were on duty in Israel in an hour. She was having too much fun to pay attention. Gradually we started to bicker. I said I'd had enough. She tried to coax me like a little kid, promising sweets and presents for Rewa. I tried to get through to her, but she talked over me. Then I lost it, and we had an all-out row in English in a street, watched by passers-by and shopkeepers, and Tahira stormed off. I went in the opposite direction and found a doorway and went back to the villa in Israel.

[+]

I felt like a dork, being angry and hiding in an empty house. I knew Tahira thought so. She was still in Teheran and still mad with me. I wondered if she would go find her family in Haifa to complain about me and everything would be split into Khadems versus Kahus. I knew if I went to Aunty Liz she'd tell me off. I needed someone to talk to but Grandpop back home was asleep. I suppose I could have crashed Scotty and Ashley. But I knew they needed me like they needed third legs and I wasn't sure they would back me up. Maybe it was being in Israel that made me think of the only Israeli I had ever met: Mordechai Ceder. I wondered if I could find him again. I asked Control if there was a landing zone near the top of Mt Carmel.

[+]

He gave me one and a moment later I was stepping out from the bushes on the path that led down to Elijah's cave. There were spirits everywhere in a jumble. It was so confusing like thousands of people muttering at once, even though there was no-one there. I was actually about a kilometer from the Baha'i gardens where I had met Mr Ceder but it was closer than the path we had used when we'd had the bikes.

It was not a nice day. The rain was light but cold. The clouds swept low overhead. Most people would be indoors – probably including old Mr Ceder. The path led up to the cable car and the Stella Maris monastery or down to Elijah's cave. A guess, a hunch, led me down to Elijah's cave. I went past the old World War Two forts that reminded me so much of Renwick. I followed along the dirt path which followed the edge of the steep brush covered bank but gave a good view of the city centre with its ranks of apartments, rising up to taller office buildings, behind which were lines of blue and white container cranes. The rain was making the path muddy and cars below in the city even had their lights on. It was starting to come down in gray curtains.

Of course being warm myself none of this bothered me. Even so I hurried down the path and eventually found myself coming up on a square building set into the cliff with a level path around it, surrounded by trees. It seemed well used. As usual ghosts milled about. Elijah's cave was both a tourist attraction and a religious place.

I felt a bit shy going in, but it didn't cost anything[+]. There were just a few priests who noticed you. There were a few visitors inside. One or two American tourists. There was also a small information area that explained how Elijah had defied the court of King Ahab and refused to acknowledge his Philistine Queen's priests of Baal. I still felt like I didn't know what to do, or why I was there. I went further in thinking I was mad to imagine I would find Mr Ceder there. But as I went into the back of the cave who should I find praying but Mordecai Ceder.

I waited for him for a while. After ten minutes I was starting to

get a bit peeved. I was sure he knew I was there. And then I felt
a strange feeling stealing up on me. It was a feeling that the cave
was alive and had been breathing for three thousand years and it
would outlast me by another three thousand. It was like being in
the presence of Morganne. You felt small but appreciated at the
same time. Mr Ceder appeared to be finishing. He got up and
still facing the shrine at the rear of the cave came back to where
I was standing.

He was now wearing a coat and a hat. Both had seen better days.
Still without saying a word to me he drew me back out to the
entrance. The rain was now intense.

"Where's that pretty friend of yours?" he asked me in Hebrew.

"In Teheran," I replied in English, not wanting to be reminded.

"Good for you," he said, considering the rain.

That wasn't something I had expected to hear.

"Sometimes the pretty shiksa like that, needs a boy to stand up
to them. Otherwise they take you for granted. So good for you."
He drew a folding umbrella with a floral pattern on it out of his
pocket, pressed a button, and the tiny umbrella popped out. It
looked completely hopeless for the amount of rain.

"Oh well. Nothing for it," he sighed, and stepped out into the
rain. I followed along after him. He walked almost as if I were
some figment of his imagination.

"I thought you weren't religious," I asked.

"I'm not, officially. But it's a good place to listen to God when it's
raining. Elijah, he knew that too. And you have to watch your
health, especially at my age."

I just tagged along. It irritated him.

"So what do you want Sam?"

"Dr Prosperov said there was no Jewish group in Russia the

Bruderschaft would want revenge on. He said it was an excuse."

"Who is Dr Prosperov?"

"My boss. He's Russian. Born Jewish. About the same age as you."

Mr Ceder didn't seem bothered at all.

"So who's right?" I asked following.

"Why ask me? I just told you what *they* said. The only people who could explain their insane logic is *them*. I can't."

I was surprised. I had expected him to have more information. I fell behind, then caught him up again as we went down some steps. He was hurrying because his trousers were getting wet. I decided to ask him about the strange girl and the flood.

"I had a dream ..." I started.

"A dream you had. How unusual to have a dream at your age."

"There was a girl ..."

"At your age there usually is ..." he laughed.

"In a desert. I think she was real. And she could see me."

He kept walking, but he was listening.

"And you want from me, what? Psychoanalysis?"

"No ... I ... how does God speak to us in dreams?"

"That is between you and God."

"Well, that's no help," I grumbled.

"How should I know how God talks to you? I'm not even sure how God talks to me ... if God talks to me at all, and I'm not just mad."

I padded along beside him as we walked along in the light cold rain. He seemed nervous.

"What's the matter?" I asked.

"You ... you make me nervous," he admitted.

"Why?"

"How did you find me?"

"I dunno, I just followed my nose."

"Exactly ... you bring danger. It's all over you. And at my age I don't need any, thank you."

"What sort of danger?"

"The dangerous kind. How should I know? Look Sam, you are a good boy. You talk to your mother, rest her soul, but you can come and go as you please. There are forces at work ... And they are here ... They are in many places ... but they are here too ... And, because of the way you move around ... They know you. They watch you."

A chill crept down my spine that the warmth of the suit couldn't reach. It had never occurred to me bending might attract attention before. But Mr Ceder was still talking.

"I don't have the same protection. I'm just an old man."

"So what you're saying is 'leave me alone?'"

He stopped, looking around. There was no-one there. It was a path among trees at the bottom of a steep hill. It was raining.

"Maybe later when you have resolved this thing with them, but not now Sam. I am too old to face them again."

He looked sorry, and fakely encouraging, but also very tense. I had a million questions I wanted to ask him but I could also feel his fear. There was no point pushing him further.

"OK. Sorry to trouble you Mr Ceder."

There was an embarrassing moment as he turned and made off. After half a dozen steps he turned back to me, under his flowery little umbrella in the rain.

"I think your friend Tahira may have learned to stop treating you like a doormat now," he smiled, then about to turn, added "... don't act like one either."

And then he walked off quickly down the path, through the trees as the sheets of rain cascaded down.

I walked back a bit thinking about what Mr Ceder had said. He hadn't contradicted Dr Prosperov, but you never knew what that was about. His warning about bending had bothered me because it was a surprise. Maybe even Hekator was unaware of the risks. Hekator had said there were entities in dimensions we had no idea of. Mr Ceder didn't have any idea about the girl in my dream. Once again I had more questions than answers.

[+]

I stepped off the path and bent back to the villa. Tahira was already there. She looked grumpy. The silence didn't last long. She said I was self-centred. That was too much. I yelled at her. She yelled at me. We were going for it. It went on for, maybe ten minutes. She was going to throw things but thought better of it. Then Control grounded both of us. Now our suits were just heavy, without extra power or any of their normal capabilities. He told us he'd only restart them when we started behaving and were ready to make up.

Boy, was that annoying! Worst of all was remembering these suits, which we found so fantastic, had originally been designed for Fae kindergarten children, and Control was treating us exactly as if that was what we were.

So in order to win over Control we stopped shouting at each other and bitched quietly instead. The funny thing was the role of Mr Ceder. He wasn't there, of course, but he'd told me to be staunch, and thinking of him, I was. And the weird thing was, it was working! Tahira tried everything. When anger didn't work, she tried tears. When tears didn't work she tried faking sympathy for me. I told her to stick it. Finally she yelled

"What do you want me to do Sam? F_____ you! To beg or something. Because I won't."

"I just want you to stop playing me. Stop the games! Stop the power trips. Be straight with me. Listen to me like you respect me, not like someone you can manipulate all the time. I've put up with it for too long."

There was a silence. She seemed a bit shocked. Finally she bit her lip.

"I do respect you Sam."

"Good. Well just listen to me then. If I say I have had enough just be straight. Accept it. I didn't say I never want to go to Iran again. It was fun. But I couldn't take in 5,000 years of Iran and everything Iranian in one go, OK?"

"Persian."

"Persia ... whatever. Just listen to me like I listen to you."

She knew she owed me. She also knew she needed me. We also needed to get these limp suits powered up again. She thought for a moment. I started to read her.

She looked up warningly.

"Don't ... I ... it's ... I will tell you."

Then she sighed and began, talking to the floor with her chin on her hand.

"My mother says I always have done it. Even as small girl ... My father was easiest. He always gave in to me. My mother, never! " she looked up at me.

"She sees through me, and she hates it. She used to punish me. Sometimes I make my father fight with her about me. When my father won, my heart was full of wicked delight. I felt like screaming with laughter. But mother always got revenge. Sometimes I plotted to kill her. I was only six, I had no idea what nonsense I was thinking," she said, then turned back to the floor.

"And then when the Guards came for my father and we must run I realise nothing was game anymore. Making people do what I want is useful skill. I found my tricks worked on other men. First just my uncles and then others in network. They were so stupid. So easily read, so easily charmed."

She broke off. Then she looked away red faced.

"Until I tricked myself! I didn't know ... that Turkish taxi driver. He ... Well ... I didn't expect he would *really* do *that*. My mother just told herself I was lying. That I was at it again."

She looked back at me again.

"The driver was frightened of being accused – he had family and other men in network would kill him – and we were frightened of being betrayed to police. I just learned to do it better. I became meaner and hated them all the more."

She was only thirteen but looked so much older than me. At least sixteen. She sighed.

"Raman and Ishtar told me this would happen. They said it was like looking at pretty girl with pimples. I didn't want to believe them. I thought I was too clever."

"Well you aren't," I interrupted the self pity before she got into it. "And don't feel sorry for yourself either," I added.

She looked at me angrily. But I was already there.

"You were doing it *again*. Trying to play for sympathy," I warned her. Then I made a jump.

"Maybe that's part of the reason you're stuck on Tabika. You *can't* bend her to your will. You can't wind her in. She can see you coming and plays you straight back and it drives you crazy," I added.

Now Tahira looked shocked. Partly because I had mentioned her darkest secret when Control was listening, but mostly because she hadn't thought of that before.

"Do you really think that is all it is?"

"I don't know," I shrugged. "I'm not you. All I'm saying is your way of looking at people might work against you. If you showed them a little respect the world might seem a different place."

For some reason I felt Mr Ceder was nearby. I almost looked around for him. I suddenly realised too, that it was a lesson he had had to learn himself after relying on his own manipulative skills to survive the war. I started to wonder whether he had somehow possessed me. Or whether we were both possessed by the same thing.

"I do respect," she said tossing her head. She was still angry.

I wanted to tell her to prove it but that would only start her off again. So I changed tack.

"Good. Then I don't have a problem."

"Me either," Tahira said, looking more like she really did.

We sat there for a moment. Then our suits came back up.

"You must both eat. Then you may bend. Your blood sugar is too low," Control told us.

I started to realise I wasn't just annoyed with Tahira. I was starving. We ransacked the kitchen and found bread, cheese and biscuits. All the stuff everyone had told Aunty Liz she didn't need to bring. It wasn't like the food we usually had at Renwick but eating anything felt so good. After that we felt more like normal again.

Tahira got up.

"OK ready to go?" she asked.

"Go where?"

"Umm al Fahm."

"Why?"

"Because if we have to take out the Syrians Sarah may end up running through the streets and we need to know more about where she might end up."

I couldn't see anything wrong with this thinking so we asked Control for a landing zone.

[+]

A few seconds later we were climbing up a scrub covered slope under some trees and found ourselves looking out over the highway below and onto a bare section behind us. The rest of the town was to our right further down the hill. We weren't too far from the block where Sarah was being held as this was the hills on the outskirts of the town.

We walked out from the brush, each thinking about our fight and feeling a bit sore.

"Next time we should have a separate LZ," Tahira observed.

"Why?" I replied, thinking this was some new bitchiness.

"Because how does it look? A girl and boy walking out of bushes together?"

She had a point, though that was the last thing on *our* minds. Hussein had already told us off for being together. It just didn't look right here. We crossed to the street and walked down the hill that would pass where Sarah was. There was nobody around here much. It was a housing area and everyone was out.

As we got closer to the building where Sarah was being held, things were getting busier. There was a man fixing a car, women gossiping, and some plumber with a van doing some work on a nearby house. It wasn't exactly busy, but it wasn't empty either. Unfortunately, unlike Teheran, we couldn't blend into the crowd because there wasn't one, so we had to walk past. But a bit further on we came upon a small group of boys playing with a soccer ball against a wall in a small parking lot between buildings. There were also some girls watching, and talking. The boys were dressed like we did normally but the girls had trousers under their skirts and scarves over their heads. Tahira fell in with the girls while I watched the boys. After a while the boys started to talk to me. I had to open my mouth but let the suit translate. They didn't want to know much. Just what my name was, and which soccer team I supported. I picked one from their own thoughts. Soccer teams were obviously really important to these guys.

There were four families. Ali was ten, and his little bro Rashid was eight. They were the Hashims. Then there was Mahmed who was nine, and his big sister Alima who was eleven. They were Abbas. Little Yosef was seven with two sisters Alena aged nine and Nabilah eleven were Iyad and lived in the building Sarah was being held in. And finally there was Adnan and Rana Salah who were eleven and eight. They lived there too.

We realised at once that the Iyad and Salah kids already had some idea about the girl prisoner in the basement and the strangers in the house from their mothers who were the Syrian's helpers.

The kids were not only neighbours who knew each other well but also vaguely related. They were waiting for even more kids to join them. The Iyads had an older girl, Latifah, aged about 15, and the Salah's a son, Khalid aged 16. They weren't home from high school yet.

Tahira and the girls were chatting like mad while we kicked the ball around. I liked Ali and Rashid at once. They just liked to

293

play. I passed to Yosef a lot. Adnan was a bit pushy and tried to boss everyone and Mahmad did what he was told. Adnan was used to being the oldest boy so he was annoyed to discover Mohammed (as I called myself again) was a year older. He was good at soccer and determined to show he was better at it than me, which he was. It didn't bother me but his aggressiveness was annoying.

Meanwhile Tahira had been asked where we were from. She said we were from Jordan and had come to visit our Uncle Hussein who was staying nearby. The girls were surprised at this and wanted more detail. Tahira said our mum was Hussein's sister Mirim (which actually was his sister's name). They asked her how long we were here for, to which she replied a few weeks. When asked where we stayed, she said 'in town'. I could only listen in while we played.

Tahira played them beautifully. She told them our father had divorced our mother and thrown us out with nothing, and that we were hoping Hussein's special job would help us get back on our feet. She told them the special job was a big secret. It was their big secret as well so both sides dropped hints until is was clear Tahira knew their secret. This of course only made the other kids curious.

After a while the teenagers came back from their school. Latifah was with two friends and they went inside. Khalid was by himself. He joined us boys playing. He was sort of like their coach and he got everyone doing drills. The boys liked him even though he was no sports jock. He included everyone – even me – and was encouraging. Then he left us, noticing Tahira and shyly asked her about herself. He was smart but small and very shy. The other girls teased him about his new girlfriend, his confidence vanished and he went inside.

After half an hour the rain that had been going off and on became too heavy. Everyone ran off leaving us on the empty wet parking lot. We decided to walk down to the middle of town. The talk with the girls had gone well and Tahira was in a good mood.

"*You were really good,*" I said.

"*I thought you didn't like me doing that.*"

"*Not to us. But to them I don't mind.*"

"*Why not. What's the difference?*"

"*You don't have to live with* them."

"*I don't have to live with* you *either,*" she said snottily.

She was just being a bitch. I didn't rise and let her think about what she'd said and what bullshit it was.

Umm al Fahm turned out to be quite a big town. As we got down the hill the density of the housing increased and as the density increased the quality also went down. Houses were piled on houses all the way up the hill like a big pile of people. There were a lot of people. Plenty of kids, and now teenagers coming home from school. There was graffiti, and rubbish, traffic and people walking. Cars were all over the narrow streets, and the damp air was still thick with fumes. It didn't help that there were also fires going and the place smelt of the charcoal and coals the town was named after because Umm al Fahm, means 'mother of charcoal' in Arabic.

We walked down the main drag toward the centre of the small city. People were shopping for their evening meal. The shops looked cheap and a bit crappy. You could tell nobody here earned a lot of money. But you could also tell this was a town with a sense of its place in the world. It knew it was the biggest Arab town in Israel and it was also clearly not part of the

Palestinian territory on the other side of the fence on the other side of the hill. According to what we'd been told they didn't want to be part of the Palestinian West Bank territory either[†]. Nobody took much notice of us. We went through the crowds feeling pleased with ourselves.

"Sam? Tahira?"

It was Control.

"What are you doing? You can't bend to Sarah's assistance from a crowded street and that is your main task," he said quietly.

It was the lack of emotion in his voice which made it worse. We realised how dumb we had been just following our noses. We turned around at once and walked back the way we'd come.

It was starting to get dark. We had to put up with a heavy rainstorm and cars, their lights blazing, swishing water at us as we trudged back up the hill. All the way we were looking for a quiet alley to go into and bend but there seemed to be people everywhere. You couldn't get away from them.

Finally we walked up and stood outside the block Sarah was being held in. Something roused our curiosity. We focused on the inside. The Russian was there again. His name was Chaim Ivankov. He had a brother Yohav being held for drug smuggling in Belgium. He had been given these two Syrians to work with by Turneau in Belgium because they had no record in Israel and could pose as Jordanians although they had previously worked for the Syrian secret police.

The Syrians had no idea how close to the Hariri family they were and no knowledge of the Malka brothers who had carried out the snatch of the girl. All Ivankov knew was that Turneau had picked these two turkeys to guard the girl because he didn't trust local interests not to get worried about Semovich – which was a reasonable assumption as Semovich scared people.

The Malkas had had no idea who they were snatching. They had just gone for the quick money. Yohav and Chaim's wives had been happy to transport the girl to the Syrians.

Inside, they were talking, and it seemed that Hussein and Omar were feeling better. Ivankov had given them new guns as well as their money. He also had news. Semovich had agreed to pay up and the money would be paid as instructed in two days. Hussein and Omar felt good. They thought they would get a million Euro each. We knew the cold Russian was playing them. Ivankov knew they would be betrayed and get shot. Turneau had hired them because they were disposable.

Poor Sarah was lost and alone in her misery. Grieving over the aching wound where her little finger had been.

We stood in the rain as it got dark, reading, listening to the souls inside. Then while we were lost in our trances Hussein suddenly pulled open some blinds in their first floor flat. He looked out the window and saw us standing there. He recognised us at once. Two creepy, faceless kids in hoodies wearing school bags standing in the dark, outside in the rain. His mind flashed like lightning and he dashed for the door.

It took us a moment to realise what was going on. Then we ran up the road as he came sprinting out of the apartment block into the rain. He yelled at us as we ran behind the half-finished house. He was so fast. We were running for the bank that looked over the highway when he reached the corner of the unfinished house. He was fifty meters away.

"Stop! Stop or I'll shoot!" he yelled.

We had almost made the lip of the bank when there was a bang. He *had* fired! I spun in mid run and fired back. Blue lightning slashed in the rain, the light flashing in his shocked eyes, but I was still twisting in midair and just for once the targeting was out. A puff of smoke on the wooden framing of the house. The blue flash vanished but remained a line scratched on the back of your eyeball you only saw when blinking. I landed and leapt over the edge of the bank.

[+]

Hussein stopped running and advanced catlike. But when he got to the last place he'd seen us, pistol ready, we were already back at Renwick.

FLIGHTS

Map data © Google 2016

CHAP+ER SIX+Y EIGH+: MUDDLES

We took a while to get used to having briefings just before we went to bed. That was because we went to bed just when Renwick woke up in the morning. We had to bend to Renwick, get changed out of our suits and then join Grandpop, Tarik and Cam, with Mariko and Mrs Jones. Scotty and Ashley stayed where they were in Austria. Tahira and me were still angry with each other but nobody mentioned our fight. We weren't even sure if Control had told Grandpop, who treated us as normal.

"OK," he started, standing in the old Renwick briefing room talking to the six of us, but aware the others were watching, "so the situation in Hungary is that Elena is now going through heroin withdrawal and having a pretty rough time. Diana feels very alone and scared. So far however nobody seems to know what to do with them. Dr P says we have about a week to go before anything happens there. Ashley and Scott see if you can find ways to get them into Austria."

"In Israel Sarah is still in danger but Tahira did some particularly good work last night and started the local children off snooping on Hussein and Omar. I want you two to keep that contact up. Dr P says those kids are the solution to the whole situation. Semovich has a few days to make the payment. The

299

instructions haven't come through yet. Uri is meeting some people in Luxembourg who want to use his aircraft. We need to know what's happening with him so Sam and Tahira, see what you can do. The end is in sight for Hussein and Omar, so they will sit tight. It's now we need a crisis that makes Sarah want to hide from her dad so we'll be working on that. In the meantime we will keep the 'go' teams operating just in case."

"The Israeli police are making progress. It looks like Inspector Gur will have reeled in the Malka brothers pretty soon. That will lead him to the Russian, Chaim Ivankov, that Sam and Tahira identified yesterday. Gur's going to have to be either quick or sneaky though, because otherwise his link to the Syrians will be gone and he'll have no link to Sarah."

"Meanwhile in DRC, Scotty and Ashley? I'd like you guys to go check out Jeanne. She seems to be moving from the refugee camp, taking advantage of the peace to go home. As we know she doesn't have a home to go to. I want you guys to shadow her. Ashley, best if you have a suit, and Scotty you cover them both from the air."

"Cam and Tarik. Dr P has a new kid for us to look for. He lives in Manila, the Philippines. He's a Filipino orphan about nine. His name is Eduardo. He lives with half a million others somewhere in the Tondo slum and works the rubbish tips and sells stuff to people in traffic jams. It's not much to go on but it's important we find him this year."

"Sam and Tahira. When you aren't in Umm al Fahm during your mornings it's time we looked at Yemen. Somewhere there is this girl Khadiyeh. Dr P thinks she's from the north-east in a large province called Haudramaut. OK, so it's enormous and I know that's no help at all, but I need you guys to get a feel for the place. Start by flying over it in the speeders. Later we'll try the suits on the ground when we have some idea what we're talking about."

"OK, I just want to say something about private trips and interests. This includes trips to homelands especially Scott, Ashley and Tahira, but you too Sam and Tarik. I don't have a problem with you doing this except when you go anywhere you might be recognised. You are not to go to your old homes or neighbourhoods. We can't have anyone who knows you wondering how you have returned."

"I don't mind you spending a couple of hours a day doing what you want but don't forget you're being paid serious money, and the Fae have a lot riding on us too. Control doesn't just talk to us. He reports to Morganne, and she has told her council that if we don't deliver on Dr Prosperov's promises this whole thing is over. So don't muck it up, OK?"

That had everyone thinking.

"Right, so that's it! For you guys in the North it's time for bed. Sam and Tahira I've got some stuff for you so please wait a mo." We said goodnight to Scott and Ashley. Grandpop gave us some stored value credit cards loaded with Shekels, US dollars, Saudi and Yemeni rials, for our Omnicards to copy. Then he sent Cam and Tarik off to work the night shift at Umm al Fahm and took me and Tahira aside while Mariko hovered in the background. "OK you two," he said, looking down at us, "everyone who works together gets pissed off with each other sometime, but you two have a responsibility to the others to sort out your stuff. No-one else needs or wants to be involved. It's up to you. One thing I *will* tell you though is you need to start thinking about when you eat. There's nothing like hunger for turning a small niggle into a screaming row and you are being asked to look after yourselves more now. I want you both to plan your meals and make sure you eat good food, not just sweets, and drink clean water. We don't need you sick either. So far you guys have had training wheels on. Now we're taking them off. Don't fail now. OK that's it. Look after each other. I know you guys can do this."

We both felt a bit like players in a game taken off by the coach and given a pep talk. It made us realise how we were being challenged in a new way, and it wasn't something we had thought about before. Then Mariko bent us back in our sleeping bags.

Our parents knew we'd had a fight but didn't say anything. They just made us get into our PJs and brush our teeth as normal. We went to bed both thinking about what Control would tell Morganne about our fight. It was getting a bit embarrassing. But I soon forgot all about it. That night I found myself in the little painted house in the dry valley again. It was dark. My mother and father were fighting. I was meant to be asleep with my brothers and sisters. I was to be married, my father said. He had found a rich husband for me who would take me off his hands. My mother said I was too young. My father said the man would not touch me until I was older but I would live in his house. I could see out the window to the stars with moonlight shining just out of sight. Somehow the stars were moving like they were painted on cloth. My heart was racing. This business with the marriage was nothing. The voices below were nothing. The sky was drawing me. It was splitting. The unbearable light! "*Samuel*," a girl whispered in thoughts like Tabika in my head, "*I see you. Find me.*"

I woke up, gasping for breath, my own heart pounding in my

chest like I had run a race.

It was a still night in Caesarea. Rewa was snoring quietly. In the distance I could hear a helicopter. My heart was still beating strongly. I slipped out of bed. It was cool but not cold inside. I walked into the living room. The clock in the kitchen said 3:10 a.m. Out on the deck lay the sleek shape of Ka-rea-rea. Gradually I began to calm down. A plan, an idea, an inspiration – I don't know what it was, was forming.

I crept back into our room and put on my ground clothes, Qi the watch, omnicard, umbrella, MP3 translator, sunglasses, and cellphone. Then I slipped out onto the cold, dark deck and awoke Ka-rea-rea. He expanded, opened, and I got in, closing the hatch behind me. I got myself sorted, then lifted slightly off the deck and slid away silently into the dark sky under blend camouflage. I put five hundred meters behind me, then engaged inertialess and rose into the starry sky like a blur.

I shot up to 20 kilometers and then turned south-east, headed for the Red Sea. At 90,000 feet the sky was lighter, and to my left the sun lit the arc of the bright glowing horizon. I switched from inertialess to invisible to make extra sure I passed the surveillance radars unseen. I soon crossed to the sea leaving Israel's radar behind me with Saudi's coming up. Ten kilometers below me passenger planes leaving Mecca, probably at the end of the Haj, were crawling along over the mat of soft cloud as I flew high above the coast. I could see all the way to the Nile river in Egypt: a cloud line in a huge, orange-brown land.

The flight to Yemen took twenty minutes because I was looking around. All the time the sky in the east was getting lighter on the horizon. There were no clouds up so high. Just the high, clear, pale blue. I kept wondering what I thought I was doing. I was also sure that I was being guided. I just felt something was telling me to fly now.

The airspace over Jedda and Mecca was full of signals but I soon left that behind me. I switched off warp invisibility but stayed transparent as I began approaching north-western Yemen.

That was when I picked up radar scatter from two aircraft also flying from Saudi Arabia towards Yemen below me. It wasn't the sort of radar you got from ordinary passenger planes. When I looked I could see they were small and camouflaged. These were military jets.

I could have ignored them, but I didn't. I dropped warp invisibility and went inertialess, then elevated down to fall in behind them a thousand meters back, still very hard to see because of my adaptive camouflage. They were doing Mach 1.2 at 6,000 feet altitude. They seemed light and fast, and kind of cool, even though they were way slower, and less manoeuvrable than Ka-rea-rea. I learned later they were F-5E Tigers from Khamis Mushayt airbase. They flew on for ten minutes when they began to climb. I flew after them wondering what they would do. They levelled out, then their noses went down in a shallow dive. At that moment the sun broke over the horizon. The planes were flying angled down toward a mountainside. It was dark against the sun. I wondered what would happen next. I don't know why I didn't get it. They came in at Mach 1.5 and both released bombs as the sun lit up the hillside. I was shocked as I saw those black shapes released from under these cool looking planes. And instead of following the planes I followed the bombs. They had a horrible inevitability about them. And now I could see the sand coloured walls of the village perched on the sand coloured mountainside. There was a small mosque and a lot of houses with smooth earth coloured walls. The bombs were heading straight for them. It was like a nightmare. I wanted to zap the bombs but my weapons were designed for people or electronics, not a simple mechanical impact fuse. I was almost next to them and then I realised these things were going to explode and I stopped dead still and they accelerated away from me. I could see the people below. They were headed for the mosque for dawn prayers. They hadn't heard the planes flying in one and a half times faster than sound.

The black shapes seemed to slow down in time. Then there was this huge black cloud of dirt as the bombs hit a house or a building and everything and everyone inside was blown to pieces. I just hung there horrified. There was nothing to see below. The dirt and dust was hiding what had been destroyed. But I could see people running and others getting up from where they had been.

I wondered who these people were and why these Saudi jets had just killed so many of them. Surely they couldn't be a threat. Then I saw tracer arcing up from a machine gun. It was just firing into the sky as if it might ward off further attackers just by making an arc of light in the dawn that the jets had sped into, invisible against the blazing sun.

At first I just watched it because it looked magic and then I realised that this tracer was deadly too, and I was in range. I elevated up ten kilometers leaving the village, and its dead and injured below. The sun seemed to fill my vision. Somehow it was then that I realised how harsh existence was. How non-existence ate at it all the time like some dark vicious animal always hungry, always tearing away at it. And the sun, in its brilliance seemed the opposite of this nothing. An opposite to the waste, the needless death I had just seen.

I felt like chasing those Saudi planes and taking them down. I knew I could. But I also felt that it wouldn't change anything. The planes would be replaced. Even the pilots could be replaced. What was important was what motivated these men to bomb that village? I had no idea. But unless whatever idea made them do it was stopped, they would keep on trying to kill no matter what I did.

I flew on, feeling a bit strange, as the mountains gave way to a vast sandy desert. This was the Empty Quarter again. I was only a few thousand kilometers south of the Wabar craters we had visited six months before. It felt different to be speeding along above the dunes, feeling so small. They just seemed to go on forever, and not being able to bend home meant, if, for any reason, I ended up down there among them, it would be bad news.

I was heading for Tarim. For some reason I felt drawn towards that city. I had no idea why. It just felt important. Soon the desert was again replaced with rocky, rugged looking mountains. I knew Khadiyeh was among them somewhere. I could feel it. But where exactly I had no idea.

And then I was there!

Tarim, nestled below in a canyon was the dark green of the palms and fields of lighter green. Then you noticed the mud-red squares and rectangles of the buildings, which climbed up the sides of the canyon walls, all reflecting the bright sharp sun coming up in the east. I circled around, dropping height, looking around. A tall, white spire stuck out above the palms drawing attention to the white building below. You didn't have to be too bright to work out this was a mosque[†]. The dawn prayer that

Tarik and Ali Gursoy did, would be going on about now.
I hovered around about a kilometer up where I was invisible.
I knew Khadiyeh wasn't here. But I also knew she would come
here some time. I stooged about getting a feeling for the place.
But something was calling me down the canyon toward the west.
I flew along at about four hundred kilometers an hour watching
over the sparse fields of green and sandcastle buildings until I
picked up air traffic. There were light planes ahead.
Qi told me we were over Saiyun. The thing that got me was
how tall the mud-brick buildings were. They were all three to
four stories. It made the place seem quite modern. I kept flying
towards another city which felt like it was drawing me in. It was
called Shibam. For some reason I knew something was going to
be important here.
When I got there I couldn't believe it. Dead in the middle of a
huge canyon was a city on a relatively small block with a wall
around it. But what was amazing was it was six to ten stories
high, all made of mud[†]. I flew around it gawping like an idiot.
There were scooters, cars and trucks moving around down there.
It looked like a little bit of New York in the middle of nowhere.
Once again I knew Khadiyeh wasn't there but I knew she would
be in the near future.
I decided to elevate back to 20 kilometers. I flew around a wide
circle seeing if I could pick up anything on Khadiyeh. I knew
she was somewhere north-east of Tarim but I lost the trace
whenever I tried to get close. I was sure Scotty would be better at
it than me. I was also pretty sure if I didn't get home soon I'd be
missed so I turned back and, climbing to thirty kilometers, sped
back to Israel.
The radar was again obvious as I slipped through it. But again I

was invisible, then I dived down to one kilometer and flew back
to the villa.

When I landed on the deck I noticed movement inside. I opened
up and came in to find everyone sitting around a travel bag of
Mr Trân's baking. As I walked in everyone turned to look at me.
"Where did you go Sam?" asked Rewa, mouth full of chocolate
pastry.

"I flew over Yemen."

"Where's Yemen?" she asked.

"Bottom of the Arabian peninsular."

"Why?"

"Someone asked me to find her. But I couldn't."

Then I had to tell everyone about the dreams I'd had. Tahira
looked very surprised.

"She 'as come to me also," she announced.

She had had one dream. The house she described was the same
as my one. There had also been the same black snake. Khadiyeh
had also shouted "flood" in Arabic, but she had also told Tahira
she could be a guest at her wedding. Given she was only eleven
Tahira had thought this meant the distant future. My latest
dream suggested it was a lot sooner.

Everyone was a bit freaked by this. None of the kids we had
looked for so far even knew we existed. This one not only
knew about us but was *calling* us. It was even stranger than
everything else we did. Tahira obviously wanted to talk to me
about it separately. She looked a bit worried. There was still a bit
of rawness between us where we had fought but there was also a
lot of common interest, and it had to be said, concern. She had
probably also noticed I was holding back the detail about the
bombers I had seen.

Our briefing was after breakfast at eight. Once again Mariko
had to bend by to pick us all up. It was good to see all the
others again in the Renwick briefing room. Cam and Tarik were
finishing so they reported first.

They had been to Manila and said finding a kid named Eduardo
in a city of eleven million was pretty much impossible. The
slum in Tondo was huge and walking through it was pointless.
Eduardo could be anywhere. They made sure they began in
hotels and ended their tours in churches. They said there was
an expectation of miraculous things in Manila which suited
vanishing in a church.

In Hungary Scott and Ashley said they had been looking at ways
for Diana and Elena to escape. The problem was the people who
seemed to have the routes into Austria sorted out were the same
people who worked with Uncle Vanya. So if they escaped they
would end up in the same mess they were in before.

They had also been back to North Kivu. Ashley said Jeanne had
indeed left the refugee camp and was headed west around Mt
Nyiragongo towards her old home in Masisi. So far the main
hazards she had faced were the Indian UN troops who she had
avoided. However the FDLR were ahead in the hills and that
could be a serious problem. She had about two days of food on
her and was only moving during the daylight with quite a few
others who wanted to escape the awful conditions in the camp.
Ashley said people on the road were as much driven by hope
as they were desperation. She did, however, have a bit of news
which was rather sad.

"She ain't ever gonna find her parents. Dey're dead. I seen 'em
haunting her, 'long wid her lil brother. She's holdin' em all to
her. I'm not even sure dey *want* her to live. I got a pretty bad

feeling about dis walk."

"How are you getting on with following her?" Grandpop asked.

"She's seen me alright. She's unsure o everyone at da moment so she's not reaching out, but she knows I'm dere. Gettin' my clothes right was hard and I still git noticed. She tinks its *good* ahm aroun coz ifn we're attacked by soldiers dey might get *me* stead o her. She's still tinking like she 's in da CNDP."

"Get a bit closer. Be friendly. Not too close, but act like you see her as someone like yourself," Grandpop suggested. "I think you might be right about this walk getting worse. But remember we aren't here to make her comfortable. We're here to save her life and help her learn."

"How about you Scott? How are you going?"

"Well, it's no fun keeping chips fo Ash in a speeder for long. There's no food, water or toilet. I can stay for three hours at a time at most, but I have to keep going home. That leaves Ash on her own."

"It shure is nice having you dere though, dawlin. You know dhat if ah get jumped its da bad guys that will be goin' down," Ashley smiled at Scott, who just nodded.

"Once Egypt's up and running you'll be better served Scott," said Grandpop.

"When is that happening?"

"A month apparently."

"OK Sam..."

"Umm Mike," Ashley interrupted.

"Yep?"

"When was you goin' to tell us, Jeanne's pregnant?"

There was a shocked silence. Jeanne was only a year older than Ashley, Tahira or Cam. There was no way *they* wanted to have a baby. Grandpop sighed, stood for a moment thinking, then took off his half-moon glasses.

"OK," he sighed, "Look, even if this pregnancy lasts, this baby dies."

There was a howl of complaints from the girls.

"I know ... I know ... I know," Grandpop went on. "It's sad and awful but as you guys know babies die in this part of the world all the time. And yes, losing her baby will break Jeanne's heart." Even Grandpop seemed a bit bitter about it. There was a silence. Then Grandpop filled it.

"The Jeanne of the future had no children. Dr Prosperov says it's one of the reasons she worked so hard to help mothers," he said quietly.

It was hard thinking that the little baby, put inside her by one of those stoned, selfish soldiers under threat of beatings, would be born like little Patience, defenceless and cute, full of hope and trust, just like Patience, but die, betrayed by those meant to care for her and her mother. It made us all really angry.

I wasn't mad at Grandpop, or Dr P – it wasn't their fault. Yes, we could save Jeanne but then all the others exactly like her would keep on losing their babies instead. It made us angry, not at anyone in particular, but at the world. At the men that made and destroyed babies and didn't care. And at God who made a world where such things happened.

We moved on to me and Tahira's report in a quiet and angry mood. Tahira mentioned the kids around Sarah's place and our run-in with Hussein. Then I mentioned what Mr Ceder had said about bending and that both of us had had dreams about Khadiyeh. Dr Prosperov suddenly came on the screen and asked us more about them. He was very interested and made us tell everything. Then he said he would talk to Hekator and disappeared again.

Grandpop reported that Inspector Gur would probably arrest the Malka brothers that night. That meant there would be open warfare between the Malka and their friends, and Semovich and his friends pretty soon. The link with Chaim Ivankov would become known and everything would depend on whether Ivankov was caught by Gur or not. It was essential that Ivankov got away.

Grandpop summed up saying that we were running out of school holidays and needed to make progress on Sarah, Jeanne and Diana while we could. In the meantime, he said, our parents had been pointing out that we also needed a bit of a holiday, so he was planning some missions for us which were just for fun. Dr Prosperov had also been looking for more treasure ships we could work on.

That lightened our mood a bit. It was true that we had missed out on summer this year and none of us were that keen to head back to school without at least some chance to enjoy ourselves. Even so we got changed feeling that no matter what we did we would always have the weight of the world on us. I came out of the changer and found Tahira waiting. Scott and Ashley had gone back to Hungary.

"So what do zhou want to do now?" Tahira asked.

"Get our omnicards and go to Iran I guess," I said.

She smiled warily at me.

"You sure?"

"Yeah. Hey I *like* Iran ... sorry Persia ... but in small doses, OK. One, maybe two hours, tops."

"OK. You know, I haven't been to Isfahan. How do you feel

about that?"

"I dunno," I shrugged. "Guide me."

"And what about lunch? Paris nice with you? I know great bakery."

"Sounds fine."

"I'm not manipulating you?"

"No you aren't. You can't change my mind because I haven't made it up yet."

I smiled.

"What?" she asked defensively.

"Nothing. You're just cute."

"Now you're manipulating *me*," Tahira said impatiently.

"No, I'm not. I don't want anything. I'm just saying."

She smiled warily at me.

Then we talked over landing zones with Control and soon we were gone.

[+]

To be honest we had a good time. I remembered everything I liked about Tahira. It helped that she was as curious as I was. It was cold but still, and the sunlight was pale and yellow. We managed to tour around the great mosque. It's a stunning place! We went to some other religious buildings but we also bent out to look at some of the ancient Persian ruins as well. Two hours went by in no time.

Then we went to Paris and ate too many cakes. We went to look at the shops but after a while I started to get bored. We found ourselves on the Champs d'Lycee.

"*Why don't you get Emma a present*?" Tahira said looking at all the pretty fashion.

I looked at her hard.

313

"*What?*" she said.

"*I can't tell her I went to Paris,*" I pointed out.

"*You could say Ashley got it.*"

"*Who will enjoy looking for this present more, me or you?*" I asked.

"*I just thought you'd like to get the girl who ignores you and went off on holiday with that dishy David guy a present,*" she said sourly.

"*Tahira be honest. You love this stuff. It's you that wants a present. I'd rather get you a present than Emma, anyway. That would be honest.*"

She looked at me.

"*Would you really rather get me a present than Emma?*"

"*Of fancy French stuff for chicks, for sure. It's got you all over it. Emma would rather have a ... a kite-ski or something.*"

"*But ... does that mean you like me more than Emma?*"

"*No. Well, yes. But in different ways. I like you as my best friend. Emma's different. She's my idea of hot.*"

"*I'm hotter than her!*" Tahira said annoyed, knowing she was.

"*Well, yeah but ... not to me ... You're sort of ... I dunno ... Sort of ... well, you're too complicated ... she's ... she's relaxing. I don't have to think with her. It's easy-as. No drama.*"

"*Do you really think I'm too complicated?*"

"*Tahira you are hot. But I'm just a simple country boy from Northland. I'm not like you. I'm not hot either. I'm just me eh? I don't like fashion or fancy places. I just like swimming and stuff.*"

Tahira put her arm through my arm as we walked past all the fancy shops and cafes. Our suits still looked Iranian and people were looking a bit grumpy at us – especially the French ghosts.

*"You are a lovely boy Sam. And you are cool in your own
way. But you are right. We like different things. We see things
differently. But I like that you make me be honest with you. I
got so used to being dishonest with everyone I forgot how to be
honest with even myself."*

"So you don't mind me calling you on stuff?"

*"I don't like it. But it's OK. I mean, I know you aren't attacking
me. You do it because it's good for me."*

"Good."

"But be nice."

"OK."

"Where are we going now?"

"Umm al Fahm?" I suggested.

"What about Yemen?" she countered.

"I dunno. Where would we start?"

"Where did you go?" she asked.

"Town called Tarim."

"Well, why not there. We have to get used to going there."

"Oh, OK but let's go back to Renwick to check it out first."

"OK."

So we did.

[+]

We spent a bit of time looking around Tarim before we found
a good landing zone. It was tricky because there were windows
on everything. But after half an hour we had it sorted so we
appeared in the dusty city in a flash of light. The spirits of Tarim
were proud. They watched us distantly and didn't seem to want
to move into the brilliant light of the day.

We were both dressed as boys. The suits simply couldn't do the
skirt part of a Yemeni abaya. So we were boys with hoods and

school bags. It would look pretty odd, but if we kept moving it wouldn't be too bad.

It was hot and dusty after midday prayers in Tarim. We were glad the suits kept us cool. Most of the people on the street were men, but the black shapes of women, usually in pairs, also moved about. There was no doubt the people here were poor. Bad teeth gave it away, and some were pretty dirty. But they were also tough and proud. There was a surprising range of skin tones too, ranging from very dark to quite light. That was great because we didn't stand out so much.

All the men had an Arabian dagger on their hips. Quite a few carried an AK47 or 74. These weapons were all decorated although we couldn't spend time looking at them without attracting attention we didn't want.

We came into a shopping area. The shops were at the bottom of taller buildings so the light filtered down through the mud and white coloured buildings and under dusty awnings. There was all sorts of stuff there. Stuff for homes, cooking, medicines, food. There were even brands I knew, just with Arabic writing on them. All sorts. The shopkeepers seemed to spend most of the day talking to each other. Some men drifted around and seemed to have nothing much to do but chew leaves. This was qat. Those guys were slightly dreamy, slightly confused, but not especially dangerous. We kept moving and tried not to look at anyone, as if we had a job to do

It was Tahira who noticed it. A quiet shop that seemed to have no one in it. In scratched and faded gold lettering it said in Arabic, "Abdullah Karim Perfumer". I don't know what drew her to it. There were none of the brands she wore. In fact there weren't any brands at all.

Tahira drifted to the window. It seemed dark and cool inside. The walls by the window were pale green with flaking paint, but toward the back there were heavy wooden shelves full of bottles and flasks. We pressed closer up to the window. It seemed strangely magical. The liquids in different colours looked mysterious and special. We were fascinated.

I looked at what the suit captured later on and I'm still not sure how he did it. One minute we were looking at an empty shop and suddenly there was a blur and a white shirt was in front of us. We looked up at a dark, narrow face with a pointed beard and surprisingly light brown eyes looking at us from beneath a white turban. He was clean, with eye makeup, and angry. We could read him but we could also tell *he could read us.* Worse, he was stronger than us. Tahira gave a short quiet squeal, and we both backed away and ran off up the street. Some of the men sitting around looked up and laughed. When we looked back, the man at the window was laughing too, but when he saw us looking back he turned and dropped a blind. We kept running until we found an opening into the bright white sunshine of the street.

We stopped, panting, watching the scooters and pickups, and battered cars, honking and shoving past on the main road, exhausts belching in the pounding heat.

"*That was scary,*" I said.

"*Very,*" Tahira replied.

"*I've never seen* that *before.*"

"*Me either.*"

"*Did you feel him just boring into us?*"

"*Yes.*"

We caught our breaths and walked away down the main road.

317

CHAPTER SIXTY EIGHT: MUDDLES

"This place feels strange," Tahira said.

"Yeah, it does," I agreed.

"It's too quiet."

"Yeah."

"Everything's hidden."

I thought it before I said it, so I knew Tahira agreed already.

"Otherworldly," I suggested.

"Mmm."

"Do you think he was like that Belgian guy in Virion," I asked.

"Paul Maartens?" Tahira shook her head. *"No Maartens was different. He was a sponge. Soaking everyone up, blending in and hiding. That guy, back there, wasn't hiding."*

"So you don't think he's one of them, *then?"*

"No. I think he's ..." Tahira began, and then stopped.

A Toyota pickup painted white and blue with guys on the back wearing berets and carrying AKs was coming toward us up the road. Tahira was looking at it. Then she pulled me into an alley.

"Quick!" she said.

I followed after her. I looked back just as I left the street to see the men in a blue uniform jumping off the back, one had his eyes on me. He looked very similar to the man in the perfume shop. I raced after Tahira into the dark shadows of the alley which stank of sewerage. There was no-one around.

"C'mon! Renwick!" she said, and folded into nothing.

I followed.

[+]

I found myself in the oil of the jumpstation. Tahira was trudging out.

"Police," she explained without looking back.

I followed.

"*What made you think they were after us?*"
"*I don't know. I just got this feeling.*"
"*There's something going on there, isn't there?*"
"*I think there's a lot going on there. Secrets within secrets.*"
I had to agree.
"*It'll probably be better when we can come back at night.*"
"*I think you're right.*"
We had a midnight snack in the kitchen at Renwick. Mr Trân had started leaving stuff out at night knowing we would be coming and going while the house slept. It was funny being back at Renwick. You could feel the ghosts again in the dark – a cold and unpleasant sense of resentment. We ignored it and chatted softly about Israel. Then we tidied up and went back to the jumpstation. Ashley and Scott had arrived.

They told us that we should wake up Cheeky because Uri was meeting his potential aircraft customers in one hour in a crowded café area in Belgium and there was no way Ash and Scott could bug them without being spotted. They had been checking out Luxembourg but given up and had a quick tour of New Orleans instead. Then they had also gone to North Kivu. Jeanne was making good progress and had gone about twelve kilometers today. She was still living on UN food biscuits. So far nobody had bothered her and it had been sunny. She was in a good mood. But Scott had been scouting ahead and found some FDLR soldiers manning a "toll" which was nothing more than robbery. So Jeanne was moving into trouble.

We talked about her having a baby. The girls thought Jeanne was probably looking for her mother to help her. Given her mother was dead we thought we'd need to find her some kind of help ourselves. The girls especially thought having a baby so young and without any help at all could be dangerous if anything went wrong with the birth. It wasn't something they would want to do. Still, we guessed we still had a few months before we had to worry.

We went back upstairs and woke up Cheeky. It was weird going into our apartment in the middle of the night knowing Aunty Liz and Rewa were visiting the Sea of Galilee at the moment. Cheeky didn't like being woken up but he was quite happy to tuck himself back in my pocket.

The ghosts gave us a start on the way down the stairs but we only had to think "Mrs Jones" and they backed off again. Control found a landing zone inside a church which had a bell tower tourists could visit and a view of the rendezvous café on the other side of the Place d'Armes square in Luxembourg.

[+]

We flashed into the off limits office downstairs. It was sort of old fashioned, cheaply lit and a bit poor. The church too had its spirits. There were old church men there who did not seem to like us at all. We unlocked and re-locked the door and climbed the stairs fast to get away from them, and joined the tourists in their padded jackets, hats and gloves, who also made the trek up the narrow stairs toward the top.

When we got up there into the chilly air we wished we had a camera with us so we could pretend we were there to take pictures too. The two younger American women and the French man who was guiding them were taking pictures, giggling and being dumb.

We looked across the square to the cafe Ash and Scott had told us was the rendezvous. The meet wasn't for another fifteen minutes. It was cold but not freezing. The pale sun was shining.

The bare branches of the trees hid us but you could still see through them. Most of the tables were empty although six groups of tourists still sat outside. They were all wrapped up, either in puffy jackets, leather or dress coats. One man even had a hat and leather gloves. All of them were smoking.

I didn't want to get Cheeky out too soon because it was cold and being small he would feel it quickly. The American women next to us were chatting stupidly in English about their friends while the French guy twisted them around his fingers. I couldn't believe how dumb these women were being, just because the Frenchman looked good. Tahira and me chatted vacantly about what we could see.

Finally the others went down the stairs again, leaving us alone for a few minutes, as the time for the meeting approached.

"What a creep," Tahira muttered.

"Who?"

"That Marcel back there. He was just using those two."

I looked at her meaningfully.

"I see what you mean. It just isn't very nice is it?" she agreed looking out at the view.

"No."

"I wonder where Uri is?"

Two men had taken a table. With the suit's vision we could see them easily. The first made us gasp. It was Hathaway looking as fit and relaxed as if the car crash in Finland had been nothing. The other was a priest. He had black hair, dark eyes and darker skin than the blue-eyed, blond Hathaway. They sat down, clearly used to one-another, looking around.

Uri was a little late. He even stopped to buy a newspaper from a dispenser. I had to throw Cheeky out fast because we could hear some more people coming up the stairs. Cheeky was very pissed off, but he flew into the square toward the tables where Uri and the two men were shaking hands.

We missed Rocelli introducing himself for the first time. We were more focussed on Hathaway because we didn't know what Rocelli was capable of. But back on the tower things were complicated by an old couple who came up onto the lookout with us. They were German and talked a bit to each other about what they could see.

Cheeky landed and started looking for crumbs around their table while the men gave their orders to the waiter. Then they began to talk.

Hathaway said they represented a group of EU humanitarian organisations and were authorised to negotiate a six figure deal to lease four of Kogan's aircraft for a two year period for operations into Dafur in Sudan and parts of Central Africa. Kogan did not leap straight into business and tried to look unrushed and prosperous. He said they must know something because so far the peace had been holding but they had been very busy lately in that area lately, so he expected something would be happening soon, creating more demand for his services. He said that for two years of exclusive lease they were at least one digit short and seven, but more likely eight, figures would be needed.

Hathaway smiled and said that because the aircraft were needed immediately he was prepared to offer one million Euro in advance and one million per quarter for the two years. Altogether it was a total of eight million Euro.

Kogan pointed out this was only one million per plane per year. Hathaway replied these old planes could be bought for less than two million each anyway. Kogan countered that anyone could buy a forty year old airframe in poor condition, the problem was flying it. His planes had experienced crews, maintenance schedules and made a good profit which meant they generated him considerably more in revenue than they cost to operate. He suggested Hathaway buy his own planes and find out the hard way the real costs for himself.

We didn't dare probe anyone in case we alerted Hathaway but it was pretty obvious this was idle haggling before lunch. Hathaway didn't seriously expect to buy out Kogan's air fleet for eight million and was just winding him up to see how desperate he was. We noticed they went through a bottle of wine and Kogan was smiling and didn't seem the slightest bit stressed at all.

Lunch arrived and Rocelli took over. He asked Kogan whether the aircrews could be relied on to be discreet. Kogan found that funny but said nobody was more discrete. Rocelli said there was a need to transport aid into Dafur but in some cases they also needed to transport a "select" number of refugees and staff to places where immigration complications could be avoided. Kogan told them this was routine for his crews. But he added such discretion and professionalism was why his service was so expensive.

Rocelli began a long discussion about the effects of starvation among the people of Dafur which was pretty awful but didn't seem to move Kogan or Hathaway much as they chowed down on their expensive lunch. Kogan asked whether the passengers would be disruptive or not. Rocelli said they would probably be grateful. Kogan laughed and jested that the fall from the fat into the fire always seemed cool. Rocelli said nothing. It was obvious though that an appeal to Kogan's better nature would fail because he just didn't have one.

Now the real bargaining began. Kogan asked whether four machines were really needed for two years. His point was that two years was a long time and circumstances could change. He added that worked hard over a short period the planes could move a lot of people or stuff pretty fast but this would affect their maintenance schedule and availability.

Hathaway conceded that the main need was probably from February to March and that six months later the circumstances could have changed but they would need four aircraft. Kogan next asked whether the aircraft would be facing risks from ground fire, anti-aircraft missiles or air forces. He said if an airforce was involved he wasn't interested. Hathaway tried to play this down while Kogan pressed him for exact destinations. Hathaway muttered about the Chad-Sudan border. They talked about this for a while.

Finally Kogan came down with his offer "because this is such a worthy cause," he grinned at Rocelli who looked grumpy. Fifteen million for four aircraft for three months, ten in advance, with an option to negotiate a further three month extension for another five million for two aircraft. Hathaway responded ten million for four aircraft for six months, five in advance with an option for a six month extension for two aircraft for five million. Kogan just shook his head and pointed out they were not the only customers in the area. Some governments needed supplies shifted into the area without question. The Sudanese and Al Qaeda were good customers and also needed supplies no questions asked. Hathaway pointed out these were supplies to kill the people he and Rocelli were trying to save. Kogan said he made no moral judgements he just tried to get the best price for his services.

Rocelli pretended to complain to Hathaway that they were making a pact with the devil. Hathaway pointed out that if they outbid the arms suppliers for the transports they would achieve the double benefit of achieving their own goals and denying the enemy resources for evil. Both Kogan and Hathaway looked like they were enjoying themselves. Rocelli just looked pissed off.

Now the deal making began to get serious. Hathaway and Kogan were swapping numbers and conditions at a huge pace. We got confused partly because they were moving so fast and partly because Rocelli had shifted his attention to Cheeky and he had to keep flying back and forth from a tree nearby losing sound in the process.

Finally they began to get to agreement. Kogan would get two million per month for four planes for six months. He'd get another eight million on completion for a total of twenty million. Rocelli said he would need approval as this was much more than had been contemplated. But they shook on the terms of general deal and split up.

"*What do they want planes for*?" Tahira wondered.

I couldn't imagine.

We called Cheeky in. The poor little guy was freezing and curled up in my pocket and went to sleep.

[+]

We went back to Umm Al Fahm again and went down the hill to chat with the neighbourhood kids to see if they had any news. Alima Abbas and Nabilah Iyad immediately began asking Tahira more questions about her "Uncle" making it fairly clear they had heard a different story to the one Tahira had told them, although they didn't mention their mothers at first. Latifah arrived without her friends and she reminded them their mothers had warned them to keep quiet.

The boys just wanted to play soccer again so I had an easy job. Khalid, the older teenager, came up the hill but seemed embarrassed by Tahira being there again and went inside, rather than play with us or join the girls. It was about four thirty when Hussein arrived back at the apartment in a beaten up old Toyota.

The warning call of "car" was given in Arabic the same way it was in English back home and we moved out of the way while he parked. It wasn't until we had started playing again and 'Uncle' Hussein was walking through the park that he recognised me among the others. He looked around suddenly at the children and then glanced over to the girls chattering away spotting Tahira.

"Greetings, Uncle Hussein," I called out loudly in Arabic, pretending to be happy to see him, and so I could warn Tahira as well. I could see him remembering the bolt of lightning I had shot at him the previous night and noticed he was starting to feel nervous. Tahira waved as well. Hussein smiled thinly, waved, but walked quickly to the apartment. It was clear to the other kids he knew us, and he wasn't keen on us. The gossiping increased. Now Tahira mentioned the "rich girl".

The Iyat girls and the Salah kids looked very nervous about this gossiping. But Tahira said "her Uncle" was a bit worried Sarah's father wasn't going to pay and instead rely on the Israeli police to raid Umm al Fahm instead. She said the news said that the men who had been in the kidnapping had been caught. This wasn't quite true yet, but we knew it would reported soon.

Tahira acted like the money we had been hoping to get was not going to come, so we were going to leave in case there were problems later. That made the local kids angry saying that was all very well for us but what about them? Tahira wound them up brilliantly, telling them it was their fault, then we left to go up the hill. They shouted at us a bit.

We had to go quite a long way to get out of sight to find a place we could bend back to the villa in Caesarea. By now we were hungry again. We called Control and we met our parents in Nazareth for dinner. Then it was back to Renwick for briefing.

[+]

I was getting really tired by now because I'd got up before dawn to go to Yemen so the briefing is a bit of a blur for me, to be honest. Yigal Gur had arrested the Malka brothers on suspicion of murder but they weren't talking. The police announced the arrest for murder of the bodyguard, Federov, but not kidnapping. The problem was the Malka boys weren't scared of Semovich. They just kept denying everything and saying they wanted their lawyers.

The politician Shev Komenski however was demanding the army help the police in the recovery of Sarah Kogan. He had been told to shut up by Semovich but Gunter said the political opportunity was too good. Komenski wanted an excuse to drive the Arabs out of Umm al Fahm anyway. Whether they were hiding Sarah or not didn't really matter to him. He just wanted the army to drive into Umm al Fahm and flatten everything.

Meanwhile our flies in the apartment block in Umm al Fahm revealed arguments in the Iyat and Salah families. There was a lot of stress about their involvement in the kidnapping. Some said it was a deliberate setup organised by Komenski. Others said the Syrians should be kicked out and sent somewhere else. The fact they had guns made this impractical but there was a lot of impassioned talk. Then there was the suggestion that maybe the Hariris should take over the kidnap because at least they would have the locals' interests at heart because they lived in Umm al Fahm too. But Khalid, who was the same age as Sarah, pointed out all of them would probably kill Sarah and asked whether they really wanted her blood on their hands.

That turned into two arguments. A practical one: that if she was killed Semovich would certainly take his revenge; and a moral one that Sarah was a victim who had already suffered a lot from having her finger cut off. The talk went around and around and was only interrupted by the arrival of Omar. The tension between the Palestinian families and the Syrians was enormous. Tahira noticed Khalid, who was small and serious seemed to be most hostile toward the Syrians.

"He thinks he can be a hero. Maybe we can help him," she whispered.

Two calls changed the situation in Haifa. Uri got a call from Hathaway that the twenty million Euro deal for his aircraft was on. Meanwhile Semovich got a call from Turneau that now the kidnappers wanted twenty million Euro for Sarah. Semovich exploded it wasn't possible to raise twice as much money so quickly.

"Then we shall have to cut more from the girl to reduce your expenses," Turneau jeered cruelly.

"Shall we say two and a half million per limb? You can save ten million by the end of the week. Perhaps the lot if she dies. I shall have my people make arrangements."

Semovich, a man known himself for his cruelty, gave in. But he demanded one more day to raise the money. He knew Kogan and his daughter couldn't raise it by themselves. Now he would have to pay too, and he was angry.

He called Uri in a cold fury. When Uri was told that the ransom had doubled he couldn't help noticing that the amount the kidnappers were demanding was the same amount as he was making from leasing his planes. Now he too wondered if Hathaway wanted his aircraft but didn't want to pay for them. But for both us, and him, that raised the question. What did Hathaway and Rocelli *really* want his aircraft for?

YEMEN INCIDENTS

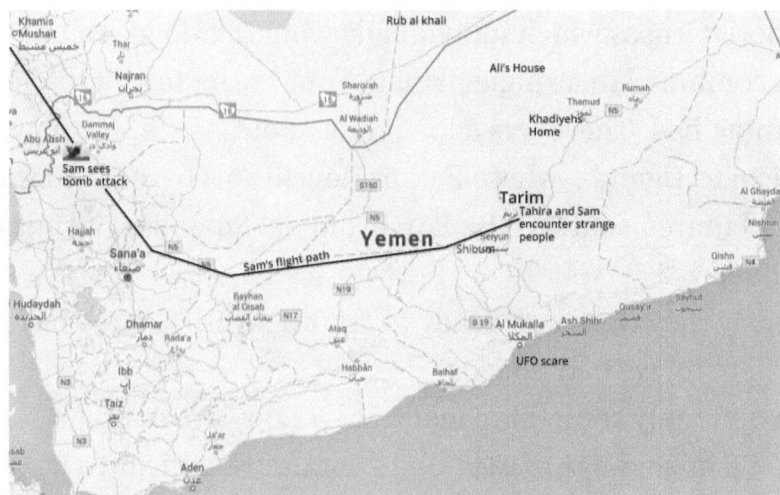

Map data © Google 2016

CHAPTER SIXTY NINE: LIFE OR DEATH

We hadn't been near the Virion factory at La Louviere, Belgium for a months. The danger posed by infiltrators like Paul Maartens and Hathaway made us a bit shy of the of the place. Our parents told the Fae that if they wanted to get more information they could do it themselves with more powerful technologies than we had. But it turned out the Fae weren't so keen to do that either, so Control had simply listened in on the factory's communications and left it at that.

Between bugging Turneau, Virion and Mrs Huuygens, Control discovered they were working toward something they called "co-agent candidates 21 and 22." Control believed that they were both viruses which individually wouldn't do much but which combined in a single patient would react together to do something bad. There was a lot of talk about Africa. Hathaway had been to Uganda, where Father Rocelli was based, and the pair had toured southern Sudan, Ethiopia, Somalia, Uganda and Rawanda.

Obviously they were now ready to start deliveries, but what of, and where to, we had no idea.

It was definitely something made at La Louviere but that covered a huge range of medicines, vitamins, and anti-viral doses. The database had thousands of customer organisations on it. But after the Cherensky operation the factory computer had been stripped of anything that even hinted at the infiltrators. So we guessed they needed to deliver a lot of something but what it was, and what it would do, remained a mystery.

There was only so much that Control could find out about candidates 21 and 22 without samples and even then Hekator would really be needed to work out what the Bruderschaft were up to. But we weren't too keen to bust into their warehouses and steal anything when we didn't know what we were looking for or what the infiltrators were capable of. For all we knew they might also be able to jam our bending like the saucer had tried to do to my suit in Greenland, and we didn't want to find *that* out the hard way. So we decided the easiest way to find out what was happening was to bug Kogan's planes. We also wanted to bug Kogan himself as he was slippery and might shed his leather jacket.

The planes were registered in the Ukraine. There was an office at Ras Al Khaimah airport in the United Arab Emirates and another in Nairobi. The planes were flying all over the place. Sudan, Chad, Ethiopia, Somalia, Yemen, DRC, Congo, Libya, Saudi, Ukraine, Moldova. There was no doubt Kogan's business was profitable. Losing four planes worth of income to ransom was going to hurt.

Bugging the planes took Cam and Tarik about an hour once Control found them. Uri was a bit trickier. He was absolutely furious about the increase in the blackmail demand. He couldn't sleep, and didn't. In the end they had to amnesia him before injecting the trace.

The next day Uri flew back to Israel and visited Michael

Semovich who was already playing host to Uri's ex-wife, and Semovich's daughter, Alisha. He told them of suspicions regarding Hathaway and Father Rocelli. The other two were less convinced. Semovich said the payment conditions had arrived and he was determined to track the money to the kidnappers and take revenge on them.

The conditions had been quite specific. The money had to be deposited in the account of Transocean Enterprises. The company was registered in the United Arab Emirates and Semovich said the Israeli Police were trying to get the UAE police onside, but he was not hopeful. There was not much trust between them. Kogan was to arrange the payment using his own UAE based accounts at the Arabian Bank and his Hawala contacts.

Control explained Hawala are just businessmen in different cities who have debts with one-another. If a client gives a Hawala in one city some money, the Hawala calls his mate in the other city, who pays out to whoever the client has asked to be paid. At some point the two Hawala sort out their total differences. The system relies on trust so all that it needs are phone calls and paper records. This also makes it hard to intercept using technology[+]. Kogan used this Arab system all the time to move his money around because Governments couldn't police it.

But Kogan also had other tricks up his sleeve. He had contacts at the UAE bank who could at least get him details of the account they were paying into. That made Semovich happy because he wanted to, in his words. "find and kill these c____".

Semovich was frustrated that Inspector Gur had so far made no progress in interrogating the Malka brothers and refused to release them, so his men could grab them and torture the information out of them. Uri Kogan said he wanted to make sure they got all of the kidnappers not just some foot soldier left behind. Alisha said the main thing was that Sarah was returned to them. She pointedly said she wanted Sarah to live with her when she came back. Under Michael's glare Uri could only agree.

Control told us the account the ransom was to be paid into was the same Transocean Enterprises account that was being used to pay Omar and Hussein. Grandpop said this was probably to make sure Semovich followed the money to the Syrians. It was possible Semovich was meant to catch them or be distracted pursuing them into Syria.

Meanwhile in Umm al Fahm the Syrians were unaware of the net closing around them and were feeling much better. Ivankov had told them the payment would be made within 48 hours. Then they could ditch Sarah and slip back into Jordan. From there they would be back in Syria in another day. They even told Sarah that so long as her father paid up she would be going home within two days. If not, Omar drew his finger over his throat. Sarah was confident. She trusted her father. Everything was moving quickly.

Dr Prosperov came down to the briefing room to talk to us. As usual he was wearing a business suit. He seemed full of energy. "Tomorrow ransom handover must fail. Money must vanish. Dr Morozov has arranged swap of special information with para. no.ID group. In return Control will provide short term access to the New York Stock Exchange computers via bugs placed last year."

"At same time operatives to be prepared to prevent attack on

Sarah. Am suspecting is best if Syrians pursued by Israeli police from place other than Umm Al Fahm but successfully escape. Will require luck and good timing. Any questions?"

"Umm Dr Prosperov?" asked Ashley.

"Yes?"

"If da twenty million Euro is sent, but don't arrive, where does it go? Does it just disappear?"

Dr Prosperov smiled.

"No, Ashley, we steal it," he said looking pleased.

We all looked at each other. Suddenly we were bank robbers.

"All sides criminals. You are expensive. House is expensive. Money must not reach, but we must save Sarah. Why not?" Dr Prosperov smiled wolfishly.

"Won't they be able to trace where the money goes?" asked Scott doubtfully.

"Sure. Goes to Russia. There it," Dr Prosperov wagged his head as if weighing something up, "disappears."

His eyes twinkled with fun. It was kind of catching.

"We develop tactical plan. Tomorrow night local time money is moved. Will arrive and then vanish. When kidnappers check next day is gone. Sarah must know ransom has not been paid and escape. Syrians too must escape to draw Israelis. Is much to do while you sleep. We meet again at 6 a.m. Israel time."

That gave us 30 hours until the payment failed in the middle of the night. After that it would be three, maybe six, hours before the Syrians would get the call from Turneau. Now we had eight hours to sleep which we did in our suits. Cam and Tarik, being still based in New Zealand, would work while we slept.

We woke early the next morning in Israel.

Mr Trân had sent goodies through again so we sat around the

table looking at the TV which we had wired up to the netbook linked to Renwick while pigging out. Dr P was talking.

"Mission for Scott and Ashley is to cover Jeanne. Is entering dangerous place. Suggest to come back to Renwick. Next is mission for Sam and Tahira. You must tell local children that Omar and Hussein have been told to ... ah ... hurt Sarah. "

He was noticing Rewa and Asal gathered around the screen. We hadn't even told them about the finger yet.

"Am thinking perhaps is good time for Rewa and Asal to join in meeting with local children as creates distraction. Mariko will bring sleeping bags."

Rewa's mouth fell open. Asal squealed. They were so excited.

"After contact in Umm al Fahm operatives to return to villa. Is all for now," Dr Prosperov said and vanished.

Aunty Liz and Mitra were smiling. They obviously already knew about the plan. The girls were hyper and Rewa was "Omigodding". I exchanged a look with Tahira. We weren't impressed.

"If you can't calm down I won't take you anywhere," Tahira told her sister coldly in Persian, "this isn't a game."

Asal scowled darkly at her older sister. Rewa caught that something was going down.

"We can't take you unless you can act natural," I told them both, "so calm down. Like Tahira said, this isn't a game. Sarah's had her finger chopped off."

They didn't know this. They also didn't know that Turneau had threatened to save Semovich money by amputating Sarah's limbs one at a time and we didn't want to tell them. They were horrorstruck enough by the finger.

"Really?" Rewa gasped.

We nodded.

"And now they are planning to kill her," Tahira added.

"We don't just go off to have fun in these suits you know. We go to stop people being killed," I told them.

Rewa and Asal were looking a bit scared now, which was good because the last thing we needed was them deciding to be heroes around Hussein. Quickly we explained what we had to do. They both chose Palestinian names. Asal became Nima, and Rewa became Nahlah. We were telling them about the local kids when Mariko flashed in with two bags.

"Two spies to go," she said playfully.

They got into the bags. Ten minutes later Control called me and Tahira back to help Rewa and Asal bend back to Haifa. While we were there Control updated us on the situation in Umm al Fahm. He'd chosen a new landing zone some distance away so we would have to walk back towards the house where Sarah was from the east. It was just below a military Kibbutz.

[+]

We bent in. The spirits were grumpy but we ignored them and walked down the hill closest to the West Bank border with the pale sun reaching down the slope casting big shadows in front of us.

The rain had gone and now it was just a bit misty and smoky. Morning in Umm al Fahm was kind of the same as morning everywhere. People were on their way to work, eating breakfast, radios and TVs were on. Because the houses were so crowded together families were always talking to each other, a bit like back home for me.

We formed pairs with Rewa and Asal in front, and me and Tahira behind. Rewa had gone from very excited to very nervous

and Asal was much more natural. I had to remind Rewa that you
had to think before speaking in case you blurted out in English
and ruined our cover.

We'd all learned some basic Arabic like "mu-ha-bah" (welcome)
and "shok-erah" (thank you) but of course our suits gave us
a perfect translation of what was going on around us. Asal,
speaking three languages, was relaxed, but Rewa with only
one (and being a chatterbox in it) was anxious that on her first
mission she'd ruin everything.

But it turned out not to matter. We just walked, passing the
crowds of hurrying or chatting adults, who simply let us by.
It wasn't until we got to the bottom of the hill that we spotted
some of the kids we knew.

Ali and Rashid Hashim passed by with barely a word said.
They were a bit surprised by Rewa and Asal but said nothing.
Alima Abbas said "hello" to Tahira a bit shyly and asked about
Rewa and Asal who just said their names and smiled as Tahira
explained they were all leaving now because our "Uncle" was
leaving. But Alima wasn't the kind to be nosy. That job fell to
Latifah, Nabilah and Alena with Yosef, who were walking with
Rana and Adnan.

They formed a little gang who stopped us, asking where we
were going and who Asal and Rewa were. It was tricky at first
because there was so much going on. Alena wanted to talk to
Asal and Rewa because they were the same age. Rewa was so
nervous she couldn't speak at all, but Asal did pretty well and
covered for her. Tahira clinched it by reminding us all what
"Uncle Hussein" had said about talking too much about "the
job", which explained Rewa's nervousness and made them even
more curious. I pretended to move the younger girls on so they

wouldn't tell, while Tahira stayed behind to spill the beans.
She did a magic job. I asked Control to shut off the girls' link
(they were chatting to each other anyway) but I listened-in to
Tahira as we walked up the hill. At first Tahira pretended she
didn't want to say anything. Then she let more and more slip
until finally she blurted everything out. "Uncle Hussein" and
"Uncle" Omar had been told to get a chainsaw in case the girl's
family didn't pay. She started crying and getting shaky, telling
them a horror story about sawing Sarah up which was probably
pretty close to the truth.

The locals were shocked but said she was crazy, so Tahira
pretended to be hurt and ran off saying at least we wouldn't have
blood on our hands, and the Israelis would come after we left
anyway. We waited for her as she ran up the hill. Khalid came
out of the house and joined the others. They obviously told him
what Tahira had said because he turned to look at us, thinking
about whether or not he should chase after Tahira to confirm
her story. He thought the better of it and joined the discussion
among the other kids as they set off to school.

"*Great work, Tahira,*" I told her.

The girls wanted to know what was said. I told them it was too
horrible for them and they believed me. Tahira gave me a happy
grin and we ran back to our departure zone. As we left the road
to head off into the bushes I looked back. Hussein had come out
to his car and, even though we were about two hundred meters
away, spotted us. I knew at once he was bothered by the fact
there were now four of us instead of two. But we scampered off
into the bushes and we were gone.

[+]

Back at the villa Rewa and Asal were on a bit of a high. Rewa kept saying she didn't know what to say. Asal was a bit quieter. We told them they'd done well, because they had. They hadn't done anything dumb and Tahira had played her part perfectly. Tahira and me had to stay on duty in case something happened with Sarah but Mitra, Soraya and Aunty Liz were planning a trip south to Tel Aviv and Jerusalem. They suggested we go outside and explore an Israeli beach while they got sorted, so we all went down to the beach even though it was cold and windy. I couldn't help thinking how good the weather probably was back at Renwick. We were missing out on fantastic swimming weather kicking around on a boring winter beach in Israel.

Tahira pointed out that we were getting even less of an interesting view of the Holy Land than Rewa and Asal who were at least seeing the sights, while all we saw was a poor Arab town in some hills. Suddenly we got a call from Scotty.

"Guys we may need some help. The bus Ashley's on with Jeanne has just been stopped."

"What's happening?"

"It's scary," Ashley reported. *"Some FDLR soldiers have come on the bus. They're pointing their guns and they're drunk. They want a woman to help one of their women who is having a baby. They are ordering all women and girls off the bus. The boys and men are terrified they'll be shot. The girls and women are scared they will … just getting down now … they're ordering us over to … oh!"*

"Ash?" Scotty demanded, sounding worried.

"They shot a boy who tried to sneak out with the girls. He's wound … oh God! They killed him! They just shot him dead! He was …" Ashley was crying.

"Are you OK Ash?" Scotty asked.

339

"*No I'm not. They're taking us somewhere,*" she replied.

"*Bend out if you have to Ashley,*" I said.

"*It's...I'll stay. They're leading us into the bush. This isn't looking good. Scott are you there?*" she asked nervously.

"*Yeah, but I've got to go active to see you Ash, the trees are too thick. I don't think I can cover you.*"

"*You just stay there and talk to me,*" she said to Scott.

"*Can you give us a landing zone, Scott?*" I asked.

"*Yep. Hang on ... OK.*"

"*OK. We're...*" I was telling her, when Tahira interrupted.

"*We can't go from here!*" Tahira said, grabbing me. "*Look at all the windows!*"

It was true the whole neighbourhood could see us, if they were looking. We needed to move into the brush. We ran up to the girls.

"*We have to go. Ashley's in trouble.*" I explained.

"*Can we come?*" Rewa asked.

"*No. Rewa, It's really dangerous,*" I said angrily. "*They might shoot you.*"

"*They might shoot you!*" she replied, showing her fear. I was touched but determined.

"*They won't. Besides you don't have any weapons. Stay here.*"

"*Please Rewa, stay with Asal. Go tell everyone where we've gone,*" Tahira said.

We ran into the Mediterranean brush and the world folded.

[+]

A few seconds later we were lying on our stomachs in the North Kivu bush listening to the sounds of our breathing, our heartbeats, and some muttering in the distance.

"*OK Ash, Sam and Tahira are here. They're about fifty meters away to your left,*" Scott reported.

"*Sam, Tahira,*" he said to us, "*the women are in a clearing with three guards. An older woman has gone on to the camp. Close in a bit to see what you can see. Sam go south-east. Tahira go north-east along the stream bed.*"

You couldn't see much. The trees were tall and there were a lot of bushes. The stream was small and barely there at all. Scott had located all the guards he could detect which meant at least we knew how far away everyone was. There was a sound of laughter. My suit was in adaptive camouflage so I was pretty hard to see but I was paranoid about making a noise. I pressed through the bush scared of snapping a twig or swishing the bushes.

"*Nothing much hap...*" Ashley began.

There was a bang bang bang so loud you'd swear someone had put firecrackers in your hair. It was followed by a man giggling. The whole forest seemed to be listening.

"*Hey you! What's the matter? You not toilet trained or something? You filthy animal!*" a man yelled in his French dialect.

There was another bang, bang, bang followed by insane laughter. Another soul released. It was like a drug to this guy. He was addicted to killing.

I had crept around so that now to the right, about twenty meters away, I could see the gunmens' camp. They were a mixture of tents and brush shelters. Further away to the right were the women and girls from the bus where Ashley was. In front of me a group of five men and boys, soldiers in camo aged from about fifteen to thirty, were smoking weed, drinking and giggling. A cry of pain pierced the quiet.

A big, fat woman in a blue print dress with a scarf on her head came out of one of the tents and went back to join the other bus women, followed by two soldiers with their AKs over their shoulders. They looked pretty amused too.

"I've got you covered Ashley," Tahira reassured her.

The woman and the two soldiers went up to the women where Ashley was sitting not far from Jeanne.

"The lady wants someone to help her with the birth. Some of the older ones offered, but the soldiers said "no". I think they're planning something bad for them. Jeanne has volunteered. They're pointing at me. Oh Christ! They want me to help. Oh shit! Oh F____! I've got to go."

"Tahira come back to the camp to cover Ash. F____! I wish I had a suit now," Scott swore.

"If you have to, come down, Scott. Waste all these m___f____s. I swear I won't complain," Ashley said shakily.

I saw the older woman, Jeanne and Ashley enter the tent. One of the men with the AKs looked in, then came out to join the others. He was tall and thin with bad skin and a scary soul.

"He's told us if it's a boy we can all go. If it's a girl he'll kill us and everyone on the bus," Ashley said.

The lives of a dozen people now hung on a fifty-fifty chance. The injustice of that appalled all of us.

"How are you?"

"I'm f____n scared. And I have a suit. Jeanne and this lady ... Mama Amina ... don't ... This woman is ... she's in a lot of pain."

She was screaming again, we could hear her. The men by the fire seemed to find it funny.

"We need help. Do we get Control to wake Mike?" Scott asked.

"I don't need Mike, I need mum,*"* Ashley cried.

"Your mother is being called Ashley. Remain calm you are not in any immediate danger," Control said.

"*Easy for you to say*," Ashley muttered.

The men had moved away from the fire and were moving purposefully towards the women and girls from the bus.

"*Oh no!*" I realised what they were going to do – right in front of Tahira!

"*Hey Tahira! Come over here*?" I suggested hopefully.

"*No*," she said grimly.

"*But we can't take them all out.*"

"*Why not? The first one that tries anything will get it burned off.*"

I thought, oh shit, here we go.

Then I noticed a couple of AKs were still where the soldiers had left them by the fire while cleaning them. A crazy idea came over me.

"*Hang on*," I said and ran out to the fire, keeping low.

"*Sam! What are you doing*?" Scotty yelled.

I wasn't noticed. The soldiers were too distracted with their new idea, and my adaptive camouflage was very good. I grabbed a gun, there were some bits which they hadn't fitted after cleaning it, but I didn't have time to worry about them. It was heavier than I expected, and ran back into the bush with it. This time my luck ran out. There were shouts of alarm behind me. I didn't have a lot of time.

I remembered watching Grandpop preparing "his friend" and did the same. I flicked the safety off and it was set to full automatic. I just cocked and pulled the trigger. Nothing happened! Now they were running at me. One was aiming. I grabbed the magazine and it came off in my hand. It hadn't been pushed in! I shoved it in, my hands shaking. Cocked and pointing it high enough to avoid hitting anyone but low enough to make everyone take cover, and pulled the trigger. I gave it a two second burst. The gun was deafening and hard to control with the barrel rising as I fired. The smell of ammomia got up my nose. I was glad the suit dampened the noise.

They all hit the dirt. I turned and ran.

"*What's goin on?*" Ashley called, worried.

"*Distraction,*" I grunted.

I ran through the bush. The first bangs started up behind me. They made your whole body go rigid. The bullets started ripping into the bush. I ran on dodging behind the trees. Then I stopped and slumped against a large tree breathing hard with a stitch. I was pretty sure they weren't going wait like in our games back home. These guys wanted to own me. I switched the gun over to single shot. I could see one of the leaders barging into the bush after me. I fired at him. Then I ran on as more bangs rang in my ears and bullets tore up the trees around me.

"*It's working great Sam! You're doing well.*" Scott told me.

I was too scared to be pleased with myself. I kept drawing them after me, stopping to hide and then fire.

I fired about seven more times before I heard the click. The magazine was empty. I couldn't afford to let them get close. Those AKs were dangerous. I kept hold of the gun and dashed further back into the bush, dodging left and right. They were moving fast behind me and obviously realised I was out of ammunition. The only thing left was to out run them, which fortunately was something I *could* do. I ran on and on, getting further away. I was getting tired and stressed out.

"*I need an LZ, Tahira.*"

"*Come here,*" she said.

I dropped the gun because it couldn't be bent anyway and was there in a flash.

[+]

Tahira had moved back from the bus women and their one remaining guard towards Ashley and the unguarded camp. I flashed into the dark behind the camp and hid behind a tree. There was a scream from the tent.

"*Ashley are you OK?*" I asked.

"*Mom's online. She's helping. She says this woman Mama Amina is obviously a midwife.*"

"*Who was screaming?*"

"*It's her. Birth hurts you know Sam.*"

I didn't know.

"*Imagine crapping a rock the size of a grapefruit,*" Ashley said.

"*Ow,*" I admitted.

"*And Jeanne has to do it too now, thanks to these bastards,*" Tahira said next to me.

"*But the baby won't be that big, Jeanne's way smaller,*" I reasoned.

"*Babies are the same size regardless,*" Tahira said grimly looking out for soldiers coming back.

"*But she's not much bigger than you, how will ...*" I wondered.

"*With pain, Sam, with much pain,*" Tahira told me bitterly. "*She is too small and there will probably be tearing,*" Tahira said.

"*Oh! You mean ... down there?*" I asked, appalled.

"*Yes.*"

I thought of Rewa and felt ill.

"*Jeanne needs help,*" I said.

"*She may have found it,*" Ashley said. "*She's watching all this*

345

very carefully."

There was more screaming.

"Contractions are three minutes apart. She's almost four fingers open," Ashley reported.

"What does that mean?" I asked.

"It means she has almost finished opening and will soon be ready to push the baby out," Ash said.

"You see women do all the real hard work while you risked your life to save those bastards from a little stinging," Tahira said sourly.

"I was getting them away from here," I argued.

"I could have taken them all out."

"But how do the hostages explain that?"

"Who cares?"

"They do."

"Sam they just want these bastards to suffer for killing them and threatening them. They don't care how, so why not?"

"But how are they going to make sense of it? What are they meant to tell their mates? That if you're on a bus being kidnapped by evil bastards and you're real lucky, some Persian chick with a ray gun will appear in a flash of light and burn the bad guys' weiners off? What do they learn from that?"

"Not much, but the bad guys get an education."

There was another scream.

"But that's just random!"

"Sure, look at it from their side. I say one less rapist is one less problem for the women here."

"Tahira look around. There's always one less rapist here. These guys kill each other as casually as we say 'hi'. Killing and raping goes on all the time. But if weird stuff follows Jeanne

around she'll be looking for the weird stuff to save her all the time."

Tahira said nothing but I knew she still wanted to zap the guards. She was looking out for them.

"Howsit Ash?" asked Scott.

"Intense. Real intense. They talk to me but I have to pretend to be mute. This mother, Clarissa, is one tough cookie. The baby is on its way."

"If it's a girl we get all of them," Tahira said. She glanced at me fiercely, questioning.

"Right!" I agreed. *"Then, we have no choice."*

"They'll be back soon," Scott warned us.

There was a long scream, almost like a shout from the tent. It was a different pitch. It wasn't someone being tortured anymore it was someone doing something painful.

"It's coming..." Ashley let us know.

Me and Tahira tensed. The first shadows of soldiers could be seen in a line coming back through the trees. I could tell they were in a grumpy mood.

"If we can line them up, they won't be able to shoot back," I pointed out.

"No. Stay here. We can't risk a fight near the tent," Tahira warned me.

That was right. I stayed.

There was another scream.

"There's a head! It's coming! It's coming! God, this is amazing!" Ashley told us. Her fear forgotten, she seemed totally fixated on the baby.

"The men are back," I warned her.

They were moving back to the firepit. They seemed a lot more serious now. I watched them closely, trying to pick them up and read them. They were worried I'd been a scout for a Mai-Mai group who had been hassling them lately.

The next scream ended with the deepest, most base cry I ever heard anyone make.

"*It's born! It's born! There's a baby!*" Ashley called, laughing and crying.

There was a tiny cry. Tahira moved like a panther ready to take down the men who were now looking back at the tent.

"*It's a boy,*" Ashley whispered. "*He's all wrinkled up. His eyes are closed.*"

We looked at each other and relaxed. The commander moved over to the tent. Jeanne met him at the entrance and announced the news. He pushed her aside and went in. There was a long and scary silence. Then he came out, grinning like a madman, cocked his weapon and fired in the air.

"My son is born!" he yelled to the others.

The other men cheered and also fired as he came over and they congratulated him like he'd actually done something. They stayed there celebrating for long enough for it to get pretty boring. Finally, they brought out Mama Amina and, Jeanne, her young assistant, and laughed and smiled with them, though they were still plainly terrified. Ashley had had enough. She'd been last out and in plain sight of the astonished mother, Clarissa, vanished back to Austria.

Invisible overhead, Scott was already gone over the horizon heading the same way.

We watched the soldiers, in a party mood, get everyone on the bus and let them go. They were friendly and helpful, although a boy and two men who had been on the bus were now rotting in the undergrowth. It was amazing to think if this child had been a girl these happy men would have set about murdering everyone they just helped. When the bus had finally gone we bent back to the villa in Israel.

[+]

Rewa and Asal had gone south to Jerusalem with Soraya, Mitra and Aunty Liz. We were still the "go" team for Sarah but it was quiet. It was kind of nice to be alone together in the villa after the extremes of death and birth in North Kivu. I could still smell that place and it smelt of fear. My own fear.

We tried to watch TV for a while but that didn't feel right. I felt a bit dumb thinking it but I really wanted to play with my old toys. I thought Tahira would think I was being an egg so I said nothing. But then she suddenly said.

"I want to go to my room in Renwick."

She said it to tell me she wanted to be alone. But I knew what she was thinking about. I nodded.

"OK. I'll be in mine."

She smiled weakly at me. Then stood up.

"Let's go then!"

And we did.

As we passed through the place where our dead were, I felt this strange feeling of being in a place where souls came and went. But I also got a strange feeling that this place was visible like a kind of zoo and that it was watched by strange beings I could not begin to understand. Like ants in an ant farm vaguely aware of the people watching them.

After all of this my room in the middle of the night seemed strange. It was my room and not. It was clean and new. Most of my stuff was still back in the Hokianga. My room back there was full of scratches, holes and marks. I knew them all. Here I was in the quiet darkness in my place, but not my home. It made me feel strange to be here, alone in the dark. Safe but not relaxed. I looked out the window. The light of the moon was on the bay and the headland where the lighthouse stood, dark and empty, was black in the glow of the moon on the water. The sea was loud.

[+]

It was weird. We both flashed onto the ground at the foot of the lighthouse at exactly the same time. I walked with Tahira down the hill in the warm night without saying a word. The beach at night was dull. The blackness of the sky, even with the mess of stars above us, seemed depressing, like death. We crunched across the beach retracing steps we remembered so very well. Finally we came to the slit of darkness in the rock. A darkness that seemed as closed as any door.

As we had that night, Tahira went first, her suit suddenly bright with a friendly warm orange light. I followed with the same colours.

Tabika's cave was a bit of a mess. It seemed as if a very high tide had come in and stirred it up. All the vines Tabika had planted had long ago dried to brittle rope. We moved deeper into the cave to the place we had known to be Tabika's bed. A raised area of rock, above the sand, covered with a springy plant that had died but which still seemed sprung. We both sat down on it with the shadows deep in the rocks around us.

"What does she mean to zhou?" Tahira asked me.

I wasn't sure. I sighed and lay down. Tahira did the same.

"I dunno. Safety. Danger. I felt she cared about me. She wanted me to grow up with her. She wanted it to be an adventure full of excitement, but caring too," I said to the roof.

Tahira sighed.

"Yes. Exactly."

I lay there for a moment. Then I reached out for Tahira. I wrapped my arms around her and pulled her close inside the thick strong, rubbery skin of the suit. She came to me and held me too. And when I kissed her – and it was a full-on snog not some dainty smack – she kissed me back as strong as I kissed her.

We kissed for quite a while. We dulled our suits to dark red. We were both pretty turned-on, but, of course, we were wearing our suits so we couldn't really do anything. The smell of the sea was amazingly strong and the rhythm of it reminded us of the interruptions of the outside world.

I didn't feel the slightest bit ashamed, nor did I care at that moment about Emma. I was kissing Tahira to express my deep feeling of trust and caring for her, our need to make up after all the bickering, and just because we both needed to kiss someone right then. It was like closing a door on all the hurt, and all the viciousness we had seen in North Kivu. It may sound weird but whenever my thoughts went back there I found myself kissing Tahira all the more hotly, as she did to me.

She rolled me on my back and lay on me, kissing me, her weight pleasant and her lips and tongue hot and playful. But slowly, very slowly the need in us, went out like a tide and eventually Tahira rolled off me and lay there.

For a long time there was silence.

"I can see now how very easy it would be to make a baby by accident," she said.

That shocked me. I hadn't gone that far. I looked at her.

"*What?*" she asked, seeing my surprise.

"*Make a baby?*" I asked.

"*By mistake ... I don't love you Sam.*"

"*I know but ... a baby?*"

"*You can't tell me you weren't turned on,*" she told me.

"*Well ... no. I was. Actually I still am,*" I admitted a bit hopefully. Her chest rose and fell in a very nice way, but she looked away.

"*I was,*" she said. "*Very ... I still am. But it is not for you Sam ... nice as you are,*" she said looking at me. "*It is for me. I could have done that with anybody. Anybody who cared for me I suppose. I just needed gentleness after that awful place.*"

"*I did too. I kissed you, remember?*"

"*Yes and I am glad you did. I didn't want to kiss you again and find myself alone.*"

There was a silence filled only by the sea.

"*Why don't we love each other?*" I asked her, not sure that I didn't.

"*Maybe we do, but it is a different sort of love ... A sideways love. We love but each knowing we are destined to love someone else. We are more than friends – I trust you more than anyone I have ever known Sam – but we are not true loves.*"

I took her hand and squeezed. She squeezed back.

"*I really wish you hadn't mentioned sex,*" I said, again noticing the pleasant curve of her chest. It felt like a warm poison in my veins.

"*Come on. Maybe we need to have a fast swim to calm you down,*" she said, sitting up making her suit go pink.

I tried to calm down but it wasn't until we were under water in the dark, swimming at high speed in the world of sound in the sea at night, that the poison vanished, replaced by sheer fun and exercise. We swam around for an hour and finally beached by Renwick at about two in the morning.

"They'll be out of school by now," I told Tahira, thinking of Israel. *"Better go back to the jumpstation."* So we bent there to avoid going by the door.

[+]

"What if Sarah escaped early?" Tahira asked as we went into the empty briefing room.

"I dunno. Control, what if we got Sarah out before the money exchanged?"

"Then she would go straight to her father," Control pointed out.

"Yeah and can you imagine how she'd be with those kids now. She thinks Palestinians are on the same level as cockroaches. She'd just piss them off," I said.

"Yes. It's true. I just wish we could avoid a last minute rescue. I hate all this violence," Tahira replied.

"Yeah," I said thinking about it. *"We really are stuck with a last minute rescue aren't we?"*

"Hmmm. There is no way around it. Unless Omar and Hussein think Uri hasn't paid, she will never find out."

"So there's nothing more we can do?"

"No. Where else shall we go then?" she asked changing the subject.

"Let's go see Scott and Ashley," I suggested.

"I was just thinking that."

"I know."

"Where are you guys?" I called them.

"*In Ingolstadt having hot chocolate. It's snowing.*" Ashley replied. She seemed a bit down.

We looked at each other, grinned, got the LZ and vanished.

[+]

The house in Ingolstadt was large, made with plenty of polished wood. It was set near some pines some distance from town by itself. The fireplace was made of stone and large. There were pictures and strange ornaments on the wall, like crosses and plaster things. It all seemed rich and chintzy at the same time. Scott and Ashley were slouched on the large rug. Ken was fiddling with a guitar on the couch, trying to do a complicated bit of music, while Patricia was in the kitchen making something with flour. She seemed very happy.

"Hi guys," said Ken, still playing as we arrived. "How's Israel?"

"We wouldn't know. We haven't seen much of it, except for a cheap restaurant in Nazareth," I told him

"Y'all want hot chocolates I presume?" Patricia asked.

"Yes please," we both said as we watched the TV.

We sat around and watched some German cartoons.

Patricia brought over the hot chocolates and started braiding Ashley's hair. The cartoons got violent. Ashley grabbed the remote and switched to some family comedy. Ken and Patricia couldn't understand a word but it didn't seem to bother them.

"How are *you* guys?" Ken asked us.

"OK," I said.

Tahira nodded.

Ken sighed.

"Well, you're tougher than I am," he muttered.

I thought about that.

"We just saw it. Jeanne had to live it. If anyone's tough it's her,"

I added.

"But what does it do to her?" Patricia asked.

"What does being kidnapped and having your finger cut off do to you?" asked Scott. "All these kids are in serious trouble. We're just helping out," he added.

"And for Sarah the world will change forever early tomorrow morning," Ken reflected, grimacing as he got the chord wrong. He put the guitar down.

"They'll check the money first thing. Then they'll get mad and ... well you guys are gonna have to stop them fast, or they'll take off more than just a finger."

"Well that's cheery news," Scott said sarcastically.

Ashley's head went down.

"I dunno if ah can keep doing dhis," she said quietly.

Suddenly there were tears running down her cheeks and she was shaking. Then she just broke and started sobbing. She kept saying "sorry...I'm sorry," but she couldn't stop. Patricia hugged her.

I felt sorry for her. She'd taken the harshness of the situation in North Kivu full-on and she was the gentlest of all of us. I'd expected it, but I didn't know what to do. Ashley seemed to be in shock, shaking and sobbing silently.

"Why do they have to hurt people like that?" Ashley blurted out to her mother.

We could all see that as a nurse in New Orleans Patricia had seen more stuff than we could even imagine. She had no answers, only scars. We all wanted to reassure Ash but we hadn't been in that tent balanced on a knife-edge between birth and murder, life and death, love and cruelty. We had nothing to offer. I almost wanted to hold Tahira's hand but I knew that that

snog in the cave would always be a one off. Our little secret way
to cope.

"Guys?" Ken suggested quietly.

He led us out to the door and we went outside onto a veranda. It
was snowing gently, soft flakes swirling down out of a darkening
sky. Being completely warm in our suits, apart from the chill on
our faces (which was soon gone when we sealed up) the falling
snow drew us outside. We made snow angels and threw snow
balls at each other for a while. Then we started making snow
sculptures of each other.

After a while Ashley came out and Scott, who didn't have a suit
and was getting cold, went in. We played with Ashley instead.
We made avalanches out of ourselves by rolling down the bank
and then discovered we could toboggan on our stomachs like
penguins.

Finally we ended up in a big heap, laughing, at the bottom of the
hill. We gave Ashley a big hug each and came back with her to
say goodbye. Then we went back to Israel to wait for the others
as it was getting late.

[+]

We tried to watch Israeli TV again – with the benefit of being
able to understand Hebrew – and that was sort of interesting for
a while. Tahira could relate better to the stories than I could and
I just ended up feeling a bit homesick. Tahira glanced over at me
looking out the window.

"Now you know what it's been like for the rest of us," she said
and turned back to the screen.

It hadn't really occurred to me why she had gone crazy in Iran.
That was it. She was finally home. It was why Scotty and Ash
were going back, why Cam was in Vietnam and Manila. I had

known they wanted to go home but I hadn't really understood because I hadn't experienced it myself. Now I was and it was surprising how strong it was.

We got a call on our suits. Aunty Liz and the others needed help. There had been a shooting at a Jewish seminary in Jerusalem. The suspects were Palestinians from East Jerusalem who unlike those in the west didn't need IDs to cross the border so now there were checkpoints everywhere[†]. Aunty Liz and the girls had to be bent out because they had no identity cards or passports. If they were caught they'd be answering questions in a police station all night.

It took a while but Control found us a landing zone. Tahira took the girls while I went back to Renwick and sent a sleeping bag to Aunty Liz. It meant we all ended up back at Renwick again just as the sun was setting in Israel and rising in New Zealand. Mitra and Soraya still had some questioning at checkpoints even though they had good passports on them.

We went upstairs and spent the morning with Mr Trân, helping him with cleaning up. Then slowly everyone came down. First were Bernard and Zoe with Patience who was holding on to things and standing. Then Dr Gursoy and Tarik after dawn prayers. Mrs Jones and Grandpop were next. Grandpop gave Rewa a big cuddle and me a hug. Cam came down followed by Mariko and Gunter. We all had a big breakfast and a chat.

The house was getting ready for Newroz, the Persian lunar New Year. The plan was for a big reunion party when Mitra and Soraya, and Patricia and Ken came back. Mariko and Gunter were planning to have a wedding on Okinawa during the Sakura or cherry blossom festival but they were also planning another wedding here first. I was starting to really look forward to coming back.

At the same time we all felt this enormous sense of being ready to act. Very soon Omar and Hussein would learn the money had not come through. We were going to have to go in hard and fast. About eight that morning, Renwick time, we went down for a briefing.

"OK, so Control," Grandpop began, "How are we doing with Sarah?"

"The money is scheduled for overnight transfer from Kogan's accounts into the Transocean account tonight. However we have also established a debt transfer in the name of the Emir against the Transocean account which will take place simultaneously. The two transfers will balance so the amount in the account won't change. The bank staff will not want to challenge the Emir's transaction based on a challenge from a relatively dubious client such as Kogan and the amount involved will barely cause a ripple for the Emir who's account is in the billions. Thus when we transfer the money from the Emir to an account in his name, but owned by us in Russia, it is unlikely to be noticed."

"So when will they know the payment hasn't been made?"

"Any time from midnight UAE time. They may leave it until later but by six there will be no question."

"So how are they now?"

The holodeck came up. The Syrians looked – well, there was no other word for it – happy. They were pigging out on takeaways. They were even feeding Sarah some. They seemed to be drinking something from a flask. We guessed it was alcohol.

"So our guys are in a good mood. Well, that is good for Sarah for the moment. How is Inspector Gur doing?"

"The Malka brothers are negotiating. Information on Sarah

for a reduced sentence on Federov. They are close to a deal identifying Ivankov," Control said.

"So if Gur gets to Ivankov the question is how long will he delay giving up Omar and Hussein? Do we even know where Ivankov is?" Grandpop asked.

"Sorry, no. He's only called the Syrian's new phones and we only had the ones Turneau called."

"So overnight Gur could pick up Ivankov?"

"Yes," Control agreed.

"If Ivankov talks, the police could be on their way when Omar and Hussein get the bad news."

"Yes."

"Do we know if they have a plan to ... hurt Sarah? Or is it just a spur of the moment thing?"

"We don't know."

"Can you guys find out?" Grandpop asked us.

We all agreed we could try. After ten minutes it was pretty clear the Syrians had no plans. They just responded to orders like they had when they worked for the Syrian secret police. Murder and torture did not bother them at all but if there were any plans the Russian, Ivankov, was keeping them to himself. We reported back to Grandpop.

"So everything depends on how quickly Inspector Gur gets through to Chaim Ivankov," Grandpop summed up. He thought for a moment.

"Scotty, we may need you up early over Umm al Fahm."

Scotty looked at Ashley. Ashley looked back a bit worried.

"I think I'd better stay with Ashley," he said quietly, but firmly. Ashley smiled at him.

Grandpop was a bit surprised and frowned over his glasses at

them, quiet for moment. Ashley looked nervous. Scott didn't.
"You're a good man Scott," Grandpop said quietly. "OK, instead
use suits. Scott and Ashley are to intercept Inspector Gur. Cam
and Tarik you are the "go" team until six. Sam and Tahira you
are the back-up from four, taking over from six. You'd better get
yourselves to sleep early tonight."
Grandpop took off his glasses and pulled a face.
"Guys. When you have a mission like this, you don't know what's
going to happen and it's all on your shoulders it's easy to stress
out. The only thing you can do is remember each other. Focus on
what you *do* know, not on what you don't. You know each other.
Together you are strong."
And then loudly in Maori he called out.

"Kotahi ki reira ki Araiteuru,
(One there is Ärai-te-uru)
kotahi ki reira ki Niu-a
(another there is Niua)
a homai he toa, he kaha e aua
(may those tani-wha bring courage...)
taniwha ki Ngapuhi."
(and strength to Nga-pu-hi)

Our suits know a lot of human languages. Unfortunately Maori
wasn't one of them. I don't really speak Maori properly but, of
course, I knew this one. It calls on two famous ta-ni-wha (a kind
of mystical water dragon or spirit) A-rai-teru and Niu-a, the
guardians of our Hokianga harbour, where I grew up, to give
courage and strength to our people. It's an old spell our tohunga
(priests or druids), used in time of war or trouble to invoke

spiritual assistance, and warn our enemies we are not alone. It almost seemed to work because the others seemed to feel better even though they weren't from our tribe and didn't know what it meant.

After that Scotty, Ashley, Tahira and me all went home in our suits. Mitra and Soraya were back by now. We had ordered in takeaways for dinner. Then we went to bed about eight, knowing that we would face a big day in Israel's morning.

CHAPTER SEVENTY: THE LONG WAY HOME.

I couldn't sleep the night before we rescued Sarah. Different thoughts kept churning around in my brain. I was running from soldiers. I was kissing Tahira. Bombs fell on villages. Sarah was screaming for help. Ashley was having a baby. Mrs Jones was singing and Mr Ceder was dancing in the rain. Hathaway was eating an enormous lunch which was Jeanne, lying there patiently. He looked at me and winked.

And I remembered my dad, Ax. It was a shock to realise that crazy and bad as he was, Ax was really so very, very small. I was looking down on him from Ka-rea-rea. Sure he had some gang members with him, but compared to the FDLR madmen, they were like saints. I wondered if he realised how small he was. How small and just how lame. He was like an ant more than a giant. In fact now *I* was the giant. I was looking down on him like he was a toy. It confused me. Like everything was all wrong.

And then Tarik said Omar was being called. Omar was saying "OK", "OK" quickly, then he went upstairs to rouse Hussein who was asleep. In rapid Arabic he told Hussein they were moving the prisoner to a new place Ivankov had set up. Hussein asked why. Omar replied, there was no payment. Hussein's face tightened in fury.

"Son of a whore," he swore.

The pair got ready with professional thoroughness. Leather gloves, guns, jackets. They packed up their stuff.

"Sam? Tahira?" Grandpop asked. "Wake up, we're busy."

And suddenly the dream wasn't a dream, and I was awake in the dark in a room in Israel. Rewa was still snoring softly. The full moon was shining a cold light in the window. My head felt like someone had thumped me with a tree trunk. I was dizzy and my head hurt.

"Come back here, you need 'wake-up pills'," Grandpop told us.

[+]

We sealed up and bent in a flash of light into the oil of the jumpstation, then trudged our way out. The world just seemed to be a huge struggle this morning. I clambered out of the pool with Tahira behind me. Grandpop was waiting with pills and a bottle of water. I took mine with a muttered "thanks" as he passed on to Tahira. Then we went to the briefing room.

Shown on the holotheatre Hussein and Omar had descended on the sleeping girl. They had woken her firmly, but not roughly, with

"Good news, you are going home," they lied.

Then they had picked her up and put her on her feet. She was still blindfolded and tied by her hands. But the lie they had told had done the trick. She wasn't struggling. Hussein went outside to get the car, leaving Omar alone with Sarah.

"You see father soon," Omar reassured her. "Understand?"

Sarah nodded.

"OK, don't make trouble now or all over."

Sarah nodded her head.

"Where are Tarik and Cam?" I asked, the pill starting to clear my head.

"Outside. They've tagged the car."

Hussein threw their stuff in the trunk and then brought the car around to the front before running back inside.

"Mike. Shall we take out the car?" Tarik asked.

"We can't stop them until she knows she's been betrayed. Hopefully they'll keep that blindfold on."

"Roger," said Tarik.

"Come here," Grandpop suggested.

"On our way."

The two men walked the teenager up the stairs and out the front door to the waiting car that was standing, engine running, lights out, in the dark. Then she was outside, across the footpath and into the back seat while Hussein got in the driver's seat and Omar in the front. They ordered Sarah to lie down, then drove off.

There was a flash as Tarik and Cam arrived back at Renwick. We switched to the car bugs which was better than Control's wormhole. Tarik and Cam came in and sat with us.

"Howsit been?" I asked Tarik as he sat next to me.

"Pretty dull actually. Until Ivankov's phone call nothing was happening," Tarik said.

"What's the time?"

"Two thirty Israel time."

No wonder I had felt so bad. I was on Israel time. I'd only had five hours restless sleep.

"I think it will get pretty exciting soon," Grandpop commented sternly, walking around, watching. "You guys better loosen up. I think you're going to have to take these guys down."

The Syrians drove out onto the highway outside Umm al Fahm

and headed north through the valley along highway 65. They didn't go far. The motorway curved along with a forest to the north on the left and then came to a turn off headed north towards Jenin and Nazareth. Just a little further on was the large town of Azar.

Hussein took the turnoff and drove a very short distance up to another turnoff to a road leading to a small town. But instead of going there he killed his lights and turned left into the Tel Megiddo National Park.

It wasn't big. There was just a sorry little hill looking out over a wide plain full of fields and towns, with a forest behind it and a small town just a kilometer down the drive. After Virunga in the DRC and training in New Zealand national parks I couldn't imagine a national park being so small.

There were two more flashes in the jumpstation tank. Scotty and Ashley had arrived.

Hussein and Omar drove up a small driveway past a small building that looked like a gift shop sheltered under the trees and palms into a car park. There were already other vehicles there. A white truck with "Haifa University" written on the side in Hebrew, a white van with the same, and three black BMWs. Waiting for them was the Russian, Chaim Ivankov, holding a small briefcase.

Scott and Ashley came up and flopped down next to us on the couches, looking as tired as I felt.

Ivankov came up to Hussein, who wound down the window. "The operation is over. You are being paid out. Leave the girl and the country."

"What about our money?"

"I have it here," he passed them through the briefcase.

Another figure suddenly appeared behind Ivankov. He was tall, wearing a long black coat and a round black hat and black gloves. We couldn't see his face. Omar took the case and opened it. Then something strange happened. The case was full of paper. Blank strips of paper tied with bands. Omar was counting it like it was real money. He looked at Hussein with a small smile on his face. Hussein looked back out at Ivankov.

"Good doing business with you," he smiled. We all looked at each other, wondering what this meant.

Ivankov opened the back and helped Sarah out of the car. She seemed to think she was going to meet her dad. Ivankov helped her out and closed the door. Hussein reversed out of the car park and pulled to the right, pointed back at the driveway. The bug, was not very good but we could see Sarah, Ivankov and the pale face of the man dressed in black. Then he turned and led Ivankov up the hill and Hussein and Omar drove off happily. Control opened a wormhole and we lifted up to watch them climb up the hill. The man in black led, followed by Sarah, then Ivankov. Sarah seemed completely relaxed, as if she was about to be freed.

"Who *is* this guy?" Grandpop complained, as we watched them climb up.

"Do you want us to try and read him?" Ashley asked.

And then the screen went black. It was completely weird.

"Control?" called Grandpop.

We were just six kids and an adult in a room on the other side of the world. Control appeared.

"Something rather strange has happened. The dimensional probe is bleeding energy at a huge rate. The wormhole dissipates faster than I can focus it. The more energy I pump in, the more it leaks and I cannot break through."

I suddenly felt a strange twinge of warning about what Mr Ceder had said. Dr P appeared as a flat projection on nothing.

"What is situation?"

Grandpop interrupted Control's technical explanation.

"We've lost contact with Sarah."

"Can operatives bend?"

"I can't get energy through so I certainly can't get matter through," Control responded.

"What is radius of effect?"

"Checking," Control said. There was a silence as we sat there in an empty theatre looking at each other. "The effect extends about two kilometers around the top of the old fortress." Control said.

"Please contact Hekator. Is extreme emergency. Role of Sarah critical for future peace of Earth. She must not be lost. Mr Kahu we need information."

"On it."

Dr P vanished.

"OK guys. What do we do?" Grandpop asked us, knowing the answer but wanting us to tell it.

"Bend dive from three thousand?" said Tarik simply.

"If we lost power we would hit the ground pretty hard Tarik," I warned.

"Control is there any reason why the radius is two kilometers?" Grandpop asked.

"I don't know but Hekator has responded."

Suddenly the hologram of Hekator appeared in a sunny garden. There were two small white unicorns with shaggy fluff on their legs about the size of large dogs, both nuzzling Hekator who had an apple for them both.

"Some places have gravitational and dimensional anomalies caused by dense masses close to the surface. Others are caused by geomagnetism. That is the natural explanation. The more dangerous possibility is that it is being generated. I will have to run tests to see which is which. However whichever the case the effect requires an enormous amount of energy."

"But what would happen if the guys go into the zone?" Grandpop asked.

"Their communications and power links are based on twinned entangled masses. The energy requirement is far lower than Control's wormholes. Worst case they will still be able to bend home."

"So they wouldn't lose power?"

"These suits generate their own power. They can operate without the network. But they shouldn't lose communication either."

"So are they safe to go in there."

"Safe from this interference, yes. But if it is generated other dangers should be considered."

Grandpop grunted and turned back to us. He looked over his glasses at us.

"Guys. We need to keep Sarah safe. But there's a risk. You know as much as anyone. Who's in?"

Scotty led us all in standing.

"How do you want to enter."

"Bend dive," Scott said.

"Gotta," agreed Tarik.

"OK, let's get out there and sort this out fast. Bend dive from three clicks. Bend in if you can or land. Abort and bend out if you have to. Your safety comes first, OK?"

We all nodded.

"OK, GO!" he yelled suddenly, making us jump.

We ran to the jumpstation which was now empty.

"Bending in five ... four ... three ... two ... one."

$$[+]$$

Existence went, and then came back, and pulled us down as we
flashed into space and time three kilometers above Tel Megiddo.
It had been a while since we'd last jumped and we took a while
to get out our flight surfaces and wings and get over the panic of
falling. Still after about seven seconds we were all in position in
a big ring coming down on the top of the hill.

The first thing we noticed was it was a clear night with a cold,
full moon. There were lots of little lakes below reflecting its chill
light and you could see the plain spread out with orange sodium
lights of towns and roads all over the place. Not too far away,
near Nazareth, was an air base.

The top of the hill where Sarah was going was lit up. There were
lights around it. It seemed like a work site except there was
no heavy machinery. There was just a sandy coloured clutter
of really old looking stones everywhere. It took me a while to
recognise what was going on below me.

There were six men in long black coats, plus Ivankov. They
were leading Sarah (who now had her blindfold off) down a set
of stairs. It was hard to manoeuvre and watch what they were
doing exactly from two kilometers away while falling through
the sky. The small procession led into the middle of the lit area
where there was a raised round area of stone. Ivankov broke
away from the men in black and suddenly walked back to the
carpark without once looking back. Meanwhile the black figures
were gathered around Sarah.

I had to manoeuvre around a bit for a while because I was veering off course. By the time I was in a position to look down the others were gasping. Sarah was lying face up on the raised stone, naked on this freezing cold night. There was something shiny on her stomach. The six figures had backed off and were now standing around her. This was looking seriously weird.

"*This looks bad. Like some kind of cult. We gotta get down there, fast,*" Ashley said.

"*Pick a place,*" Scotty said.

"*I've got one,*" said Cam.

"*There,*" said Ashley.

"*Guys,*" I said warningly.

But they weren't listening. We were approaching one klick. I wanted to stall.

"*Bending in ...*" Scotty began.

"*GUYS!*" I shouted.

"*What?*" Scott said annoyed.

"*Why is she doing that?*"

"*What?*"

"*She's not tied down.*"

"*Sam, we have to go!*" Ashley said.

We were coming up on the ground very fast.

"*Go! Go!*" yelled Tarik.

Four of them winked out. A second later we saw their flashes as they appeared on the hill top.

"*Circle,*" Tahira called.

We had our wings at max and began to manoeuvre into wide swinging circle over the hilltop.

Below four of the figures had turned outwards to face my friends and were advancing towards them.

"*I can't hit them*!" Ashley yelled.

"*They're all blurry*," Tarik complained.

"*It's ... my ... head*," Scott grunted.

"*Get them! Get them*!" Cam yelled.

There was no reason we could see why they should be missing. The figures were closing fast, less than ten meters away. We pulled up into our last stall at 350 meters. We had about two hundred kilometers an hour of vertical potential energy on board.

"*Look*!" Tahira warned.

The figure at Sarah's head had picked up a large rock and was advancing upon her, while she lay there as happy as if she were sunbathing at the beach. Then the one at her feet did the same. Tahira was already on her way. Diving like a hawk on the figure that was at Sarah's head. I followed going after the one at her feet. We levelled out ten meters above the deck doing a hundred and sixty kilometers an hour.

Tahira went in and zapped the guy at point blank range as she screamed past overhead. He collapsed with his boulder falling on top of him. I did the same. It happened so fast I wasn't quite sure what had happened as I flew past. We zoomed past the hill Tahira turning east, me turning west with our falling energy so that we could turn full circle and land quickly using gravity deflection both very aware there was a town and a motorway not far away.

With two down we outnumbered the remaining figures six to four which seemed to make them pause. I turned my attention to the two closing with Tarik and Cam on the Northern side. And then something very weird happened. I couldn't seem to see them properly. It wasn't that they were invisible, I could see they were there. But whenever I focused on one they seemed to blur and be somewhere else. I couldn't get a grip on them.

"*Ultrasound*," Tarik called desperately as they closed on him and Cam.

I landed still trying to get a bead on one or the other to zap him. The ultrasound was strong possibly because they were getting a bit desperate. It certainly set off a couple of dogs barking far away in the town, but it was making no difference to Cam or Tarik who had backed away as far as they could but were still being advanced upon.

"*It's so easy*," said Ashley dreamily.

"*Why have you stopped fighting!*" Tahira shrieked at Ashley and Scott.

"*Why bother*," replied Scotty.

I looked back. Tarik and Cam were wavering, their knees unsteady. I tried to aim a blast at one of the figures. I fired anyway, feeling that something was better than nothing. Then he turned to me and it was like having your head suddenly stuck in a fish tank. I couldn't see properly, everything felt distorted and weird. I dropped heavily to the ground and hurt my knees but it didn't go away. I sagged and sat, finding it hard to lift my head. I could hear the crunch of the footsteps of the figure on the sandy gravel as he approached me, the bright work lights in the distance. Yet I felt so dozy like I couldn't get up. All the time I felt this powerful will on me, grinding me down making me feel weak and powerless. I was shivering uncontrollably. I tried to fight mind to mind but it was like a baby trying to fight a professional wrestler. I had no answer to these men. I felt nothing but dread as he approached. All my technology was useless as my mind was being pounded to jelly.

"Grandpop. They're beating us," was all I could think to gasp.
I didn't even think to bend or try to use my electric touch. It all
felt useless. We were defeated. Death could come. My heartbeat
was loud but slowing in my ears.

"Ka maté (death?)" as my heart slowed even more. Not a
welcome but a challenge. Suddenly my ancestors Te Wharetai
and Papahurihia were in my soul. There was a strange jolt. My
heart banged in my chest. The Atua I had so feared as a child
were coming. I could feel their power inflating me like a balloon.
I was breathing heavily again. My heart was beating powerfully,
like a drum. My head was clearing. I found myself kneeling in
the gravel in front of a man in a black coat.

He had been about to turn away, thinking me defeated, but
suddenly he stopped. A new wave of power drilled into my brain,
the world reeled and I fell sideways, greying. My heart had
stopped. The lights from the site were bright. But now I could
feel my ancestors. Hear the Karakia (chant/spell) of the ones
who had gone before, willing me back to my feet. Again my heart
jolted and started again. Again my head cleared. The man in
black above me was still drilling me with his powerful mind but
the closer he pushed me towards death the more help I seemed
to have. I felt the presences of my ancestors pushing back with
me against this man, and the more he tried the less it seemed to
work. I felt a strange power in my heart rising. I was sitting up.
I could see the look of astonishment on his face as unsteadily
I rose in the dark among the ancient and foreign stones of this
land, under these bright work lights and stood to face him. My
heart was not my own. My eyes were not my own. I was like
a host to a nation of my ancestors. I could see the other dark
figures turning my way, disturbed by my resistance. Now they

all began drilling me, and we were all equally surprised that I had power aplenty to resist them.

With a quick move the man in front of me reached into his coat and I found myself looking down the barrel of a big black pistol. He looked at me, head cocked to one side, slightly disappointed, as if he would have preferred not to shoot me, but keep me for study. But then his eyes narrowed and his fingers tightened. I realised he was going to kill me and I couldn't think of a thing I could do to stop him.

Suddenly there was a series of bright flashes and all the electric lights on the site sparked and went out. It was very dark. My eyes were still adjusting as the dark shape who had been about to shoot me turned away. Then his gun flew out of his grip into the darkness. There was an intense and eerie silence. I had no idea what was happening, nor did I care. As the pressure on my heart lifted so my ancestors melted away. I felt a bit better. Dizzy, like I'd been punched in the jaw, but better than if I was being beaten up constantly. I shifted from behind a wall and saw an awesome sight.

Lit by the pale moon, shimmering with a slight electrical blueness stood Hekator, Merin, Daya and Queen Morganne herself in the darkness silhouetted and unearthly against the starry sky. They were on the wall above and behind where Sarah lay. The four remaining men in black had turned and faced the Fae. They seemed stunned by the sight of them. For their part the Fae stepped lightly off the wall and formed facing outwards around Sarah.

Now the men in black were faced with creatures they did not seem to be able to dominate. The Fae were moving easily, the figures in dark coats slowly. There was no fight. No kung fu

moves or flashing beams of light. The men just seemed to wilt
like black flowers. Slowly they clutched their heads and sank to
their knees. They writhed in apparent agony for almost a minute
but made no sound at all. I found all my senses coming back to
me. It was horrible to watch what would have been done to me
being done to them. Their eyes bulged, sweat poured down their
faces, as they screamed, but made no sound. Then they fell.
I felt wrung out. My sweat felt cold. I was raw as if I'd run
for miles. My muscles ached dully. My head and heart were
pounding. Everything inside me had been stressed and now
I could finally relax. I noticed the others staggering together.
Tarik was helping Cam, Ashley and Scott. Tahira was already
back up.

Now the four Fae turned in on Sarah. The staves of Merin and
Daya flashed green and purple and the shiny round object on
Sarah's stomach flew off of her and hit a nearby wall. Then it
collapsed in on itself as if decaying, and spreading, it flared in
flame briefly and I realised it had melted.

Then Morganne and Merin looked around. Noticed us, and
pointedly ignored us. They looked up at the moon briefly, looked
at each other smiling, held hands and folded into nothing.

Daya was standing over Sarah. He stroked her hair and, smiling,
pulled her to her feet. Then he lead her to her clothes and stood
by while she got dressed. We all knew we owed them a huge
debt. We had been on the verge of total defeat.

Hekator walked over to where Cam and Tarik were and called us
to him and drew us over to the north side of the site. It was dark,
lit only by the moonlight.

"It was an artificial field so I knew you would be in trouble.
Do not feel downhearted. These ... beings ... they are not true

earthlings. By comparison you are infants and no match for them. They are a race of our enemies. They remain our enemies today, even as others of their kind have come to see their error. These ones were strong. They would have crushed that girl bone by bone and eaten her blood and marrow. It allows them to regenerate and maintain their bodies ... perhaps indefinitely."

"They are wounded and weak now. We have attacked their memories and wrecked them. They will not remember this night and it will take them some time to regain their understanding of who, what and where they are. Unfortunately we must be ruthless in these situations. We can show no mercy for we will receive none."

"I believe you have already encountered one or two of this kind. Be careful there are many more who have infiltrated your world. We shall begin work on improving your defences against their mind controlling powers. You will not always be as fortunate as to encounter these beings on a full moon when our help is so ready to hand."

Daya looked over at Hekator. Sarah stood there smiling but unseeing.

"Sarah and the other Earthling beyond will remain in a suggestive state for a little while after we leave. We suggest you use that time wisely. But now, we must return to our world. We will contact you in the near future. Rest. You have done better than we could have expected this night."

And Hekator vanished. Daya smiled, nodded and he too folded into nothing.

A breeze came up over the old fortress. Dawn was not too far away.

"That was seriously bad," Tarik said softly. His voice shook.

"We were goners," Ashley agreed.

"Toast," said Scott simply.

"What was?" Grandpop asked. Apparently he could get through now.

"We almost got wasted," Ashley told him.

There was a pause.

"How?" he asked.

"What is situation?" Dr P interrupted. His voice sounded worried. We filled him in.

"Is best if Sarah told father tried to avoid payment and was shoot out. Will send sleeping bag to transport her back. Ivankov must be told to forget everything about where Sarah has been held. Tell him you have defeated the men in black and he must inform Turneau his plan is failure."

"I'll talk to Sarah," Tahira said.

"I'll get Ivankov." Scotty said.

Tahira went over to Sarah, who stood still with a strange smile on her face looking at the moon. Tahira began talking to her urgently, as she smiled vaguely. I turned to Tarik and Cam.

"They must know we stole the money," Tarik said. "It was an ambush," he added

"How do you figure that?" I asked, worried.

Tarik spoke quickly.

"Look around. They knew we had been in contact with Hussein and Omar. They reported you, and Turneau had seen you two as well, remember. Then when the money went missing they set up a place where we would have to come where we could be defeated. The only thing wrong with their plan was they didn't know about the Fae and picked a full moon. Without them it really would be all over," Tarik said.

I felt a bit stupid. We had badly underestimated our enemies and nearly died as a result.

"We are going to have to lift our game if they aren't going to catch us," Tarik added.

"I wonder who those guys are then?" I asked.

"More like the ones in Belgium I'd guess," he said.

A box flared onto the ground by the raised area Sarah had been on.

"Why try to kill Sarah?"

"Maybe they didn't need her for nothing anymore," Tarik guessed.

"Or maybe they needed to threaten her to get us to come. Then they could hold *us* for ransom." Cam suggested.

"But does that mean they know *why* we are interested in Sarah?" I asked, watching as Tahira organised her into a sleeping bag.

"Hard to know," Tarik said.

"*You coming?*" Tahira called to me.

"*Where are we going?*" I asked coming over.

"*Back to the Umm al Fahm apartment.*"

"*What is she going to do there?*"

"*Sleep.*"

"*Lucky her.*"

We got the LZ from Control and bent.

[+]

Even as I did I wondered about Mr Ceder's warning and I wondered if the entities he spoke of included gods. The apartment we flashed into was little better than a prison but Sarah was still in her strange dazed state. We settled her down on her mattress and told her to sleep, which she did at once, almost like turning out a light. We had no idea what would happen when she awoke.

[+]

Instead we bent back to Renwick. Tarik and Cam were already there. Tarik was talking to Grandpop and Dr P. They all looked very serious. We went to the briefing room and flopped on the chairs. Cam and Tarik came to join us as Scotty and Ashley arrived. Nobody said anything. We all looked absolutely exhausted. Finally Grandpop broke off from Dr P and came over.

"Okay, well there's no point beating around the bush. That was …" he weighed his words carefully, "a f_____n disaster."

I was a bit shocked because Grandpop was not one to use the f-word around us kids.

"We took them by surprise in Finland. This time they got us back. The only good news is they will now be more frightened of us than we deserve because they didn't know about our back up. Neither did we, which shows how bad it was. They might think it was us. Dr P says there will be hell to pay with the Fae. On the other hand I think Hekator had a role in encouraging us which I would like to get to the bottom of. Anyway to cut a long story short Dr P says it's time to stop."

"We've been going hard-out since November. Muharram is almost here so the Gursoys have to fast during the day. School starts again soon. It's time to kick back and have some fun."

We sat there on the chairs. Even hearing this announcement didn't really sink in properly. We all just stayed where we were. It was true we had been so busy for so long we hardly knew how to relax anymore. I knew I was totally sick of the northern winter. I wanted to swim, play and act like an idiot. I didn't want to see any more guns, bombs or anything else.

Grandpop said nothing for quite a while.

"So what do you guys want to do now?"

"Get this suit off," Scotty said.

It was true. It was like the suit had somehow kept the feeling of cold sweat even though it was warm and natural. The fear we had felt had attached itself to the inside in our minds.

"Yeah," said Tarik. "That *is* a good idea."

Slowly one by one we got up and went to the changers. For once it was a good feeling getting out of the suits. Somehow their powers felt more like a burden now than they ever had before. And when we were changed we went upstairs and discovered a sunny afternoon back at Renwick. It was probably a bit late for swimming, but the air was bright and warm. The sea was rolling in quietly. We went outside and walked along the beach, finding sticks, and whacking thistles and stones into the sea, like back in the days a year ago when we had first met.

We climbed the hill up to the gun emplacements laughing and joking. And when we reached the top and stared out to sea we all felt this huge sense of relief and a happiness so enormous we just laughed and started throwing sheep shit at each other as if it was the funniest thing in the world.

Tarik chased Cam and brought her down in the grass then Scotty dragged Ashley on top of Tarik and jumped on her. I was laughing at them when Tahira shoved me over them and fell on me. And although we were complaining at each other we were all laughing.

Somewhere in the distance was a thumping of hooves and the snorting of a horse. We were too busy accusing each other of disgusting things when the horse approached. I was tickling

Tahira's neck with a flower when I looked up and saw Emma and Charli looking down at us from a large gray horse. Emma's glance took one second to convey disappointment and a sense of fair dos that she had been doing the same sort of things with David.

"Hey Charli, Emma. What's happening?" Ashley called from Scotty's arms.

"Why are you covered in sheep shit?" Charli asked.

We all started laughing like baboons. Charli whispered to Emma. She thought we were on drugs.

"You guys are weird," she said as she urged the horse on. We let them go.

We totally did not care what they thought. We got up and wandered along the top of the cliffs. It was so good to feel free. So good it made you want to bend dive just for the hell of it. After an hour walking and talking out we turned and walked and talked back. The afternoon shadows were lengthening but the sun was still warm as we came to the top of the hill and went down into the warm little bay where Renwick was. There was smoke hanging in the air for some reason. But when we got back to the front of the house we found the adults busy running around organising for a barbecue.

Technically this was our breakfast but we realised some of the lightheadedness we had felt was simple hunger and we joined in to help.

At about dawn Israel time we were sitting around eating Gunter and Bernard's barbecued meats and Mr Tran's fabulous salads. Slowly the yellow afternoon light went purple, the shadows from the pine trees covered the house and the bay edged towards night.

Normally I would have been happy to go to sleep but of course it was morning in Israel. I was tired but I was meant to be waking up. I'd eaten an enormous breakfast. My body didn't know what it ought to be doing. It was Mariko who decided for us. She said if we went to bed here we would wake up in the middle of the night, but if she took us back to Israel we would wake up in the afternoon. So she delivered us back in sleeping bags.

Aunty Liz and Mitra made a huge fuss of us. It was early morning in Caesarea, of course. We got big hugs and kisses like we were small. Then they said they were taking Asal and Rewa out for a last tour around the north because we were leaving in a few days. Soraya would remain behind to watch over us as we slept off our busy night.

We weren't sure whether Control had told them about the incident in the cave or not. At the suspicion we might try and get into bed together if we were left alone Tahira looked vaguely defiant about Soraya acting as chaperone, but I just felt resigned. We didn't feel the need we'd felt before anyway and we were just way too tired to do anything but sleep. Nobody said anything and instead we went to our own rooms and went to bed. Just wearing pyjamas instead of a suit was such a nice change, and although there was light pressing through the weave of the curtains and a loud bird outside I soon drifted off.

My dreams were strange. I was racing to get somewhere in Ka-rea-rea. I was miles away and Rewa was in trouble. It was a desperate rush to somewhere but I didn't know where or what that was happening. I woke up feeling almost more tired than I had before going to bed. I lay there for a while but finally I got up and went into the kitchen. I found Tahira and Soraya chatting away in Persian. Not having a suit meant I couldn't understand a word.

"You like eat?" Soraya asked me.

"Yes please," I replied.

She had hummus, cheese and flat bread with a salad. She absent-mindedly assembled this on a plate and then spoke again to Tahira. Tahira replied while she gave me the food. I ate quietly letting their talk wash over me. Soraya was thinking about the Fae, or Peri as she thought of them. I hadn't spent much time with Soraya. She just seemed to be a distant adult to me. But as I sat there reading her I realised she was no fool. She had grown up in a rich military family where the politics of the Pahlavi Shah's court was always a matter of importance. She was interested by the way the Peri queen had acted earlier that morning and was asking Tahira about it. She was also making some soup at the same time.

She made a remark to Tahira, nodding at me.

"My Grandmother asks what you thought of Queen Morganne last night."

"I was just damn pleased she showed up."

"Yes... but the way she acted after she showed up."

"Oh ... well, I dunno, she seemed to be not very interested in us, but ... well, she came."

"What about Hekator?"

"Yeah ... Well, he was a bit strange really. He encouraged us to go ... he seemed really quite keen too. He was the first to jump down and take on those guys in the black coats."

Tahira broke off with me to give a spiel to her grandmother who listened as she cut roast meat off a bone. She then said something over her shoulder and continued on while tossing the meat into the soup.

"Grandmother thinks Morganne has something to hide. She thinks Hekator doesn't know what it is, but that he is getting her close to something she doesn't want anyone to talk about. Grandmother thinks there could be trouble."

I was amazed how people could guess so much from so little, and said so. Tahira translated. Soraya smiled and replied in Persian.

"Grandmother says when your family depends on watching the smallest hints of the Shah you learn to read the clues very quickly."

I was suddenly struck by how I had always thought of old people in terms of the things they couldn't do, which kids could. They couldn't run or jump, or use computers. All they did was smile, give presents and say encouraging things. But now I could see Soraya had spent a lifetime surviving, in good times and very bad. She hadn't got so old by being stupid. It made me realise how much older than us she really was. She lived five times our entire lifetimes. She must have learned *something* during all that time.

I finished my food and took my plate in to wash it but Soraya wouldn't have me in the kitchen and bustled me out, sending us off to the living room to play. Me and Tahira found a pack of cards and played fish, and a particularly vicious game of snap. We were still concentrating when the others came home. They showed us some pictures they'd taken on the big TV screen. They had been to Galilee where Jesus walked on the sea; then they went to Masada, a fortress where the Romans had trapped the Jews and killed everyone. That started the exodus where the Jews left Israel to wander the world. But the last pictures they had taken made Tahira and me go a bit pale.

They had been to Tel Megiddo too, except that it wasn't famous for being Tel Megiddo. It is better known as Armageddon[†]. While they showed us pictures of the archaeologists gently digging and brushing through the dirt looking for clues about life and battles of the ancient past we were thinking about the far more recent battle we had fought there last night.

Rewa had found the tiny reference to the last battle between good and evil that Revelations 16:16 is supposed to say would take place there: "THEN THEY GATHERED THE KINGS TOGETHER TO THE PLACE THAT IN HEBREW IS CALLED ARMAGEDDON."

Mitra said they'd met some odd Americans who thought that the end of the world was coming and that Israel would fight Iran in the valley of Jazreel where Armageddon was. Then Jesus would come to the Mount of Olives and world government would be established in Jerusalem. She said the strange thing was these people were perfectly nice but the seemed to think Iranians were devils because that was how they made sense of fifteen words in the Christian Bible. She shook her head and shrugged.

Tahira and me looked at each other. There seemed to be something very spooky about having been involved in a battle between infiltrators and Fae on an ancient site called Armageddon. It was even more spooky when Rewa showed us the dias where it was suspected the Caananites had performed human sacrifices. It was the very one Sarah had been placed on.

It was our last night in Israel. We had a good meal and relaxed playing *Trivial Pursuit* in Hebrew for which we needed our sunglasses and music players on, so we could read the questions and answers. We looked kind of funny and laughed about it. Then when Renwick woke up we had our briefing.

We learned that Mitra had passed on a message to the Iyad

and Saleh families. Dr Prosperov would pay them to look after Sarah. This had rather changed their attitude although they were suspicious of the motives of someone who only identified themselves as "a friend". Meanwhile Sarah had woken up, terrified of nearly everyone and everything. She was scared Hussein and Omar would come back. She was sure her father had tried to save himself the ransom money by starting a shootout over her and that she had escaped only with the help of Umm al Fahm teens Latifah and Khalid. In fact they were the only ones she trusted at all.

After a lot of debate among the two Palestinian families it was decided they couldn't throw her out because she might identify them as having helped the kidnappers, but they couldn't kill her because they weren't murderers, and she had nowhere to go because she mistrusted her family. The money (which was a bit more than the cost to look after her but not a fortune) certainly didn't hurt the argument either.

They were still suspicious of Shev Kamenev who they suspected of being "their friend." They suspected he had orchestrated the whole business to gain support for his Party and his policy of driving Palestinians out of their towns and villages. But Khalid argued that so long as Sarah was not being held against her will and they could show they were being paid they couldn't be guilty of kidnapping her.

Both families noticed that Khalid was quite interested in Sarah and he was teased by everyone for it. Latifeh however was not sus' in the same way, and also seemed curious about the Jewish teenager. After showing us the clips Dr P said he believed Sarah's situation was now acceptable.

Meanwhile Jeanne had travelled to the North Kivu capital (a

crappy town called Goma) with Mother Amina and was now working at her clinic for child mothers, so her situation was better than it had been since she had been abducted by the CNDP.

That left Diana and Elena. They were due to be sent back to Moldova by train. Elena had been through withdrawal and was paying more attention to Diana again. Even so her world had changed. She had become harder and meaner. Diana no longer followed her around like a small dog. Dr P doubted that they would stay in Moldova long but said for the moment they were in safe hands and didn't need our protection. That only left the kids we hadn't found yet. Eduardo and Khadiyeh.

Some good news here was that Hekati's bases at Siwa, Redonda Island and Mt Khakoborazi were past the structural stage and almost ready for fitting out. Unfortunately it was too soon to leave our speeders in them, and bend home so we were going to have to fly back again from Israel.

Although they were still officially out of New Zealand for immigration purposes Patricia and Ken were going to bend back to New Zealand. Immigration was still taking their time processing Patricia's residency but they never checked with school rolls anyway. They could think the Robinsons were in Europe when in fact they were back at Renwick. Mitra and Soraya would fly home on a regular jet as planned. Aunty Liz and the girls would bend.

Scotty, Tahira and me were talking about flight routes home. Tahira wanted to go back to Teheran but me and Scotty were curious about flying the long way across America. In the end, however, we decided to go east again. It was partly Tahira's nagging, but also because we wanted to scope out Yemen and

Manila on the way as well. Of course poor Scott was the one who would have to stay in his speeder and watch over us because his white skin would draw attention.

He called it his "white man's burden". Ashley called it his "white man's guilt by association" although it was more us who got the guilts about making him fly.

At six the next morning local time Tahira and me set off north, from Israel. We met up with Scott twenty kilometers above Cyprus, aware that somewhere below Alisha Semovich was crying for her lost daughter. We crossed Syria and came to Iraqi airspace. This time Scott and me dragged Tahira down to fifteen kilometers to look at some enormous American C-17 cargo planes lumbering toward Baghdad from the north. We flew around them without them noticing anything. Then we spotted some American F-16 fighters patrolling the Iranian border and zoomed off to play with them.

We flew up behind them as they cruised along at about five hundred knots. It felt kind of naughty to be invisible, half a kilometer behind and just above two warplanes. Me and Scotty laughed about how bad those fighter pilots would feel if they knew we were sitting on their tails in a perfect attack position. Maybe we shouldn't have said that in front of Tahira because the next thing we knew Tahira had dropped warp invisibility and blend camouflage and was slowly nosing forward behind them.

"Tahira, what are you doing?" Scott asked her.

"They're meant to be watching out for Iranians aren't they?" she giggled.

And it was funny to watch. This tiny gray shape not much bigger than the glass canopies of the F-16s slowly crept up behind these two big war birds. After sitting pretty much on top of the rear plane she slowly edged between them and put the Iranian green and red roundel on her sides. The way the rear pilot turned his head from lazily looking to the right, towards the lead plane and then jerked around at Tahira had us pissing ourselves.

The two fighters broke formation breaking away to the left and right with lots of serious radio traffic as they panicked. Tahira simply switched her warp invisibility back on, and vanished. We caught her up. The jets were wheeling around to come up behind us again but they had lost us. We let them fly by.

"*Let's elevate down to five kilometers and head back to Teheran,*" Tahira said.

"*Oh, alright then,*" Scotty agreed.

We switched from invisibility to adaptive camouflage and inertialess and dropped instantly turning on the spot in a manoeuvre those jet jocks would have given teeth for. Then we were zipping along over the hills toward Teheran. Tahira led us lower and we ended up at no more than one kilometer altitude roaring up on Teheran, the big hillside city at the foot of the Zagrob mountains.

The air was very smoggy so we could sneak around very low above the busy traffic in blend mode. Tahira gave Scott an aerial tour, but it was too cold to walk around in our ground clothes, so after half an hour we took off south-south west headed for Oman. Once again we had to pass the US military, who were buzzing around their carriers.

We went straight past them at three thousand knots under warp invisibility and not long afterwards were over the mean-as looking desert mountains of Oman heading east towards Yemen.

We zoomed over the huge Arabian desert and on to Tarim and
then stopped about twenty kilometers up and a kilometer east
of the city. We elevated lower down into the valley and then
flew towards Shibum at about one kilometer altitude. There was
something strange about the traffic that day which attracted me
and Tahira. We didn't know what it was but we slowed down
to three hundred kilometers an hour and zoomed along the
roads only a thousand feet up. You certainly did see more of the
country down there.

Whatever it was wore off and we got a bit higher and faster as we
went further west. The other two were as impressed by Shibum's
tall mud buildings and walls as I had been, and we flew around
it for almost half an hour. Once again we felt sure something
was happening on the main road, although we had no idea what.
It was like a nagging feeling you had forgotten something.

We flew around the faintly green fields and past the palm
plantations uncertain what was holding us. But finally we
started to get frustrated. We knew we had a long way to go and it
was nearly ten Israel time, so we decided to get on with it so we
headed south to the Yemeni coast, and the city of Al Makallah.
From here we would cross the Indian Ocean back to Australia.
It was a stunning day and the water looked like gray satin spread
out below the brown hills and valleys of Yemen. There were
plenty of old freighters, but below us was an Arab sailing ship
and it was very easy to imagine stories of Sinbad and Ali Baba
actually happening in a place like this.

It was time to go. We put our noses to the sky and shot up to
forty kilometers, touching the black edge of space where you
can see the stars. Except that one of them was moving. It was
moving very fast from the north-east, where we had been before

and was headed straight for where we were now.
"Administration craft! Back to the ground now!" Control
ordered.

We dropped forty kilometers in forty seconds, which is really
scary when you see the world come up at you like that. What
really scared us, though, was that the saucer would see us
burning down through the atmosphere at three thousand six
hundred kilometers an hour and would use its pink light to catch
us, the way it had nearly got me in Greenland. There was no
escape if it spotted us. We couldn't bend without suits.

We quickly hid in the deep valleys behind Al Makallah with
warp invisibility on and all our sensors strained upwards.
Unfortunately it was very hard to see anything. The sun was
high in the sky and drowning out everything around it. Control
warned us we could not assume the Administration craft had
gone, and then Scotty spotted a brief twinkle which suggested
the saucer was still up there and reflecting sunlight.

"You are safe over ground, or under water, but over water you
may be visible. The warp invisibility field bends light around
you but it isn't perfect and the Center's technology is good. I am
afraid you cannot cross the Indian Ocean. We are going to have
to re-route you. Please stand by."

We hovered a thousand feet over a valley which did not seem to
have a single living thing in it, feeling like rabbits hiding from
a hawk. If we went any lower we could cast shadows. We were
nervous and annoyed that we couldn't move. Finally Control
came back to us.

"We have decided to route you south down the African continent
and over the Pole in order to avoid water. You will need to
follow the Arabian coast west past Aden to the Gulf and then

391

quickly cross over to Djibouti. From there south to Zanzibar and Dar es Salaam. Then directly south to Cape Town. From there across the South Pole to McMurdo Base and then north to New Zealand. Your speed is limited at this time to two thousand kilometers an hour at twenty kilometers. You will be free to resume normal secure speeds when you reach Zanzibar."

We groaned. It was going to take an hour and a half to reach Zanzibar at that pace. By then it would be lunchtime. We were so far behind schedule it was no fun anymore. But Scotty was relaxed.

"Hey, we get to fly over Africa and Antarctica. That isn't something many people get to do," he pointed out.

So lacking alternatives we set off. The trip back low over Yemen's craggy, dusty mountains was strange because of the niggling feeling we should be somewhere else. But the further west we went the weaker that feeling got.

We were flying at ten kilometers, which was right down among all the airliners. There wasn't a huge amount of traffic over Yemen, but you couldn't ignore it either as aircraft radars swept around us buzzing in our ears.

At Djibouti we turned south. The whole of Africa lay out before us, stretching to the horizon on three sides. Puffs of cloud, like some huge flock of sheep seemed to be organised into a regular pattern five kilometers below. Even at a thousand knots it would still take forty five minutes through this shortcut through the horn of Africa. We were twenty minutes in, just chatting away when new radars swept over us.

To the right and below we saw fighter jets sprinting along just over cloud level going only a little slower than we were. I immediately knew they were off to do something evil. They just looked it.

Scotty, who knew his aircraft, said they were Mig-21s. He wanted to check them out. After the Saudi bombers I had seen I wanted to shoot them down. But Control said we had to stay on our course. He said it was possible Tahira's stunt with the American F-16s had been picked up by the Administration which was why we were having to fly so slow. Tahira didn't say much for quite a while after that.

Slowly north Africa's red brick colour shifted to gray-green and then to green and we were over Kenya. You could see Kilimanjaro poking up through the clouds in the west. We didn't want to land in Kenya. The President was refusing to step down after elections and there were riots in Nairobi[†]. Scott said the rest of the country was probably fine but it didn't sound like much fun.

We crossed the coast and very soon we were circling down into Zanzibar. It was noon and we were getting hungry. I also had business at the other end to attend to and needed to land pretty soon. Control began scouting for a quiet spot we could land the speeders and look after our bodies.

The old city of Zanzibar (which looked like an interesting combination of shabby, old, and tropical) was way too crowded for us to land in safely. The beaches to the west were also very busy. But the north, where the hills were and the south, which had more mud flats, were emptier. Finally Control decided on the hills, so we nosed into the lightly forested area among the palm trees to the north.

It turned out I wasn't the only one who had to use the "bush toilet" as Scotty called it. We all jumped out of our speeders into the muggy hot air and went off in separate directions. We were all busy in our private bits of bush when Tahira gave an awful scream. It took a while for me to get sorted and by the time I got there Scotty had already rescued her.

Tahira was standing there shuddering, while Scotty, armed with a stick had finished beating off a very large spider which was crawling off into the undergrowth. It was as big as a dinner plate is round with too many large hairy legs. I was very glad I hadn't got there first because I wasn't sure I wouldn't have screamed too.

"Bird eating spiders. There's a whole bunch of em," Scotty said, pointing to a tree where the huge webs with silk as thick as fishing line hung. There was still some web sticking to Tahira. Scott looked almost happy about this.

"They're creepy but pretty harmless. You just need a stick. After all we're miles bigger than they are."

"Zhank you Scott," Tahira shuddered.

"Welcome," he said. "Do we eat here or what?"

"May as well," I shrugged.

We went back to the speeders and got out our lunches. It was mostly Mr Tran's cooking with a few leftovers from Israel. We talked about the pros and cons of working without suits. Scott was the most relaxed about it. Not surprisingly Tahira preferred to have diamond-skin armour between her and any bird eating spiders. I was willing to give it a go. Apparently Cam and Tarik were getting pretty used to South East Asia without it.

As we talked I wondered if Ashley and Tahira would pair up again while I went with Scott after the holidays. I think Tahira was thinking the same way. She seemed to want to hang with girls more now. I wondered if all summer holidays were like this. Last summer it had been Emma. This summer it was Tahira. Maybe a summer was as long as girls and boys could stand each other.

We packed up while I wondered what Emma had been getting up to with David. I wondered if she'd snogged him. The look on her face from her horse had suggested she had. Not that I could complain really. I wondered if I should ever ... Tahira looked at me. She was reading me and looked like a snake about to strike. I got into my speeder real quick to avoid her gaze. It seemed like if I ever mentioned what had happened in Tabika's cave I'd be in the deepest trouble with Tahira.

We zipped back into the sky and swung around to the south. It was one in the afternoon Israel time. Control got us to climb in wide circles. Ten, twenty, thirty kilometers up. The blue was going. The stars were coming through the thin air. At forty kilometers up we levelled out, Africa far below us, a big green and white mat far below. There was no sign of any Administration craft anywhere. Now we could pick up the pace. We went inertialess and went from a thousand knots to four instantly. Even at this speed it would still take an hour to reach Cape Town. We could go faster, of course, but then the Administration satellites would pick us up as our field intensity grew.

On the way we talked about what we wanted to do for our last week of school holidays. Mostly I wanted to swim and surf. I had decided to buy myself a board. Scott was interested in going pig hunting with Grandpop and Bernard. Tahira just wanted to read fashion magazines, chat to her cousins and help Mariko with her wedding arrangements. We wondered what Mariko would do for her wedding. Me and Scott thought it would be rad, but Tahira thought it would be beautiful.

When we got over Zimbabwe Scott asked if we wanted to check out his old home. I remembered what Tahira had said about homesicknesses and although I really wanted to get home, agreed.

We elevated down to thirty, twenty, ten, five and two kilometers and slowed from four thousand to two hundred knots. We dropped onto wide Lake Kariba and then flew up the Zambezi river toward Hwange National Park. I was fascinated. The whole area was covered in open forest and the water level was still low, so the river was muddy. It was hard to see animals among the trees and water but we spotted hippos, giraffes and some elephants. It was very bright and everything looked dusty.

We sped up a bit and climbed to find our way. Slowly the terrain went from wide and flat to hilly, with the river threading its way between high cliffs. There was little chance of seeing animals here but it was heaps of fun whizzing up the river winding our way through gorges. To speed things up we jumped over some of that and flew down to look at Victoria Falls, where the river just falls into this huge crack in the ground. It was really impressive. Then Scotty led us over to Hwange. We were a thousand feet or three hundred meters up, transparent, doing two hundred knots and silent as the wind so the animals below didn't even twitch an ear as we flew overhead. Finally we came up on a house, on top of a hill with a village nearby. You could tell it was in poor condition from a kilometer away. We circled around it, looking down. The heartbreak was just so strong, nobody said anything. Then, without a word, Scotty led us up into the big wide sky going faster and faster until we were back up at forty kilometers and heading south at four thousand knots. Within fifteen minutes we were over the sea. Nobody had said a thing.

The sea slipped by beneath us.

"I think about them all the time," Scotty told us, as if we had

been talking.

"*Who?*"

"*Thabo, Musa, Melusi and David. I spent years playing with them. Now I haven't seen them for three years. I wonder what happened to them. What will become of them. They've been cheated by everyone. They have so little left.*"

It was the first time I realised I wasn't the only one who thought about the neighbours and friends I'd left behind. Scott had never mentioned it before but he had not forgotten. We flew south for half an hour. After a while we could see icebergs and then we were over Antarctica.

We decided to go to the South Pole. It wasn't the most direct route but it was only a few extra minutes and it meant we could say afterwards we had been there.

We dropped down from forty kilometers to ten for a better view. It was just white as far as you could see. After a while it became kind of mesmerising so we climbed back up to twenty kilometers to get a better view of the whole place. It didn't do much good. It was just huge, white and dull.

The South Pole base was a surprise. It looked a bit of a mess to be honest. There was a big runway of flattened snow. A big yellow building on poles with a circle of flags next to it and a dome buried in the snow. There were crates and crates of supplies in long lines outside the big yellow building[†]. We realised that as it was minus twenty on the ice the whole place was just one giant freezer. Things left outside would keep forever.

There were a few vehicles outside driving, and figures wandering around doing stuff. As we watched a fat gray American C-130 Hercules, with four propellers spinning came around us and lined up on the runway. Vehicles were coming out to meet it. We could have stayed to watch but we were getting sick of this trip. We moved on. The ice whizzed by. The mountains came and went. The Ross Sea and the volcano, Mt Erebus, were left behind, and then we were back over the sea.

As we headed north the sun sank below the horizon and we switched time zones from late afternoon to very, very early morning. By the time we reached New Zealand the summer sun was rising, lighting the long snowy ridges of the Southern Alps that runs the length of the South Island in pinky warmth.

We raced above them at three kilometers at two thousand knots. It felt wickedly fast. We blazed past Wellington, where somewhere below Emma's boyfriend, "David the dish", lived. Then we rocketed up past the central plateau with its volcanoes and lakes and finally along the narrow sharp Kaimai range that projects into Auckland's Hauraki Gulf.

We whizzed past the distant yellow lights of Auckland just below the speed of sound. It all seemed so small. Then in the sunshine we crossed the harbour and the dark ridge of Aotea Island and belted down the slopes until we reached the old gun emplacements. Then it was along the launch tunnel and in no time we were popping the tops of our speeders inside the underground base. It was five in the morning. It was a bit of a let down because there was no-one up to meet us. Feeling slightly fuzzy after so much travel we staggered out, put our stuff in our lockers and then went upstairs.

The whole house was quiet. It was a bit spooky really. But then we heard a noise in the kitchen and went to the café to find Mr Trân baking. He gave us some hot drinks and some muffins and we chatted helped out while he kept on with his work. It was only then we realised what a huge relief it was to be back at Renwick.

...

So who were the guys in black in Armageddon?" Sue asks me. She's smoking again.

"No idea."

"You didn't check?"

"Yeah, but they didn't exactly have name badges on."

Sue finds that funny. She's far more relaxed now. The exercise and the chocolate pastries have worked. I go on.

"So all we had was the car number plates. The university vehicles were registered by the university. One was registered to an art dealer named Adam Kerkovan. Two were owned by a car leasing business. Control may have followed it up but it probably didn't go anywhere. Anyway, I never heard anything more."

"And what about Adam Kerkovan?"

"He ended up in hospital for a while. They said he'd had a stroke. He was unmarried, officially 64. We left him alone."

"So really none of it tells us anything about their organisation," she says stubbing out her third fag. The sour smell stings my nose.

"We came to the conclusion it's more a network than an organisation. They have hidden among us and they know each other. They link up but they don't necessarily organise."

"They needed some kind of organisation to get half a dozen guys on a hill in the middle of the night at short notice," Sue objects. "One guy calls two friends and they call two friends. That's seven. Maybe one couldn't make it."

"Yeah, but why, Sam?"

"What do you mean 'why'?"

"They drew you into an ambush. Didn't anyone ask how they could do that? I mean they had to know all about the payoff didn't they? They knew they weren't getting the money. So why did they threaten Sarah? If they wanted a deal with her dad all they had to do was keep her out of his reach and try again, right?"

"Yeah," I agreed, feeling a bit nervous.

"So the whole point of the exercise on the hill was just to trap you guys. There was no other good reason for it, was there?"

"Uh … I dunno, I guess not."

"So how did *they* suddenly know you were watching Sarah, and how did *they* know you would probably be ready to intervene just then?"

"Ah … uh … That's a bit spooky really isn't it?"

"Yeah. It's what we detectives call 'suspicious'."

"What do you mean?"

"Well, it suggests that Hathaway knew you had somehow become involved and was using the situation to take you out, just as you had already almost taken him out in Finland."

I have to think about this. It takes me a while to work through all the possibilities but I see pretty soon that Sue's right.

"Shit. You're right!" I admit.

She took a long draw on her fag.

"What about Mr Ceder?" she asked, blowing it out.

"What about him?" I ask, feeling a bit got at.

"Was he any different after the Fae had hammered the six on the hill?"

"No, not at all. In fact it made it worse. He wouldn't even be near me. Saw me, got up, and walked away."

"Why?"

"He was scared."

"Of what?"

"Them. Like I told you."

"So what was Virion doing? What were the planes for?"

"Well, it took a while to find that out because after we stole the money and Sarah they were all a bit ... um ... upset."

"I bet they were. So what happened?"

"Well, first Inspector Turneau accused Semovich of betraying his granddaughter by not paying. Then Semovich accused Turneau of cheating and told him now that he had nothing to lose he would hunt him down and chainsaws would be mild compared to what he had in mind. Then he hung up."

"Hmmm scary."

"Yes, very. Semovich has a rep for killing people. Nobody messes with him in Israel. Turneau had the brains to be scared because he called back later that night. He had checked with insiders at the bank and agreed the payment had been made but that it had been stolen. By now Semovich already knew that but he pointed out that wasn't his problem. Payment had been made, so where was Sarah?"

"Now Turneau looked like a total dick. He had to admit Sarah had been stolen too. There was a lot swearing in Hebrew and Semovich smashed a few things. He demanded Turneau tell him everything he knew about where Sarah was. Turneau told him about Ivankov, who was already under arrest. But he said the Syrians were missing and Ivankov had some kind of brain injury. All he knew was that Sarah had been held somewhere in Umm al Fahm."

"Did Semovich believe him?"

"Not at first. He checked with Chief Inspector Yigal Gur and asked if Ivankov had been arrested. Gur was surprised Semovich even knew Ivankov was involved. Then Semovich asked if Ivankov knew anything. Gur said he seemed to have suffered a stroke, confirming Turneau's story. Ivankov was not in good condition and his memory was so bad he didn't recognise his own wife at first."

"Semovich told Gur that the kidnappers claimed both Sarah and the money had been stolen by some unknown third party. Gur asked him if Semovich if he believed it. Semovich said his biggest fear was that they had killed Sarah by accident and were trying to cover it up."

"That just left them the difficult task of searching Umm Al Fahm, a touchy Palestinian town of 43,000."

"What did Kogan do? He must have been beside himself!"

"Yeah, Uri wanted to go into Umm Al Fahm with a bunch of gunmen, but it would have been pointless. It would look like a turf war with the Hariri gang. The only way a search made sense was for the police to go in, but Umm al Fahm is very large and Gur didn't want to start another war without any real evidence. The Government already had enough problems with the Al Aqsa Matryrs brigade in the south to start a whole new problem in the north."

"So Semovich would have hired people to go look on the quiet, I suppose."

"Yeah, he must have, but it took a long time and by then Sarah had changed, which is what we'd wanted anyway."

"And did Kogan rent the planes?"

"Oh yeah, he demanded the original payment schedule too. He felt by making Hathaway and Father Rocelli pay he was getting back at them for Sarah."

"Must have made their eyes water."

"No, they still had the original CIA money. They just didn't make any profit."

"Yeah OK … But getting back to the point, did you find out what the planes were for?"

"Yeah and it was totally different to what we thought. We thought they wanted to test fake medicines out on starving Africans in Dafur because they would have weakened immune systems. All through February and March 2008 we did missions to take samples of the stuff they were flying in and it turned out that it was mostly genuine. They really were flying in aid. Hekator tested everything: food, medical supplies, the lot. It wasn't until March that we realised what they were really doing. They were running clinics out of the planes and taking passengers in them. It was the *passengers* that were infected."

"Hmmm OK. So had they been given doses of these viruses before?"

"Yes. They were given nasal sprays. We still don't know what their plan is but they relied on bad hygiene and high death rates in the refugee camps to cover their experiment. The two viruses they called release candidates 21 and 22 were adapted forms of influenza. One was the H3N2 or so-called "Swine Flu" variant, the other was a H5N1 "bird flu" like the Spanish Flu which killed millions after World War One, including all the ghosts in Renwick House."

"Individually they just caused a slight headache and a cough but together in the same cell they swapped DNA to become worse than the Spanish Flu. They put in a brain swelling feature like the Spanish flu and like the Spanish flu worked in all climates and only hit adults. Little children were unaffected. Hekator estimated 90 percent of people who caught it would die."

"So why Africa, and why the planes?" Sue asks.

"Northern Nile Africa because lots of people were dying there anyway and there was no health system capable of advanced diagnosis. So they could experiment under the guise of bringing aid. We weren't sure about the planes but we guessed because even in a place like Dafur a clinic where everyone dies gets a bad rep with the locals. A plane comes and goes. It brings aid. Real aid people can eat and feel better from.

"Fair enough," Sue says quietly.

"And don't forget the original idea was they were getting paid for the planes. Flying around meant they could operate in Chad, Dafur, Sudan, Kivu, Ethiopia, and they would just be welcomed as bringers of aid and medicine, taking the sick away to a better place. But all the time they watched the progress of their killer viruses."

"It doesn't sound like there would be much connection between these planes with Nate's school to be honest," Sue says.

"No. Hathaway is mostly about killing people."

"So what are they doing in Washington?"

"Hathaway?"

"No, in that school."

"Patricia said the only thing that's unusual about those tests is doing them at school. In themselves the tests are routine."

"Hmmm. That's what's on the school reports but they may

405

actually do other tests. Who does them?" Sue asks.

"Ummm … there's a logo on the bottom. It's green. Hang on let me think."

I had to close my eyes. Recalling details like that takes me a little while. I have to remember and then just read it again.

"It's a company called Mediscan."

"Hmm I wonder who owns *them*?"

I asked Control.

"Healthmatics Corporation. They're a New York listed health services firm. Stock code is HMXC. Stock is up five and three eighths cents today if you're interested."

"No, not really. Your crystal ball doesn't link them with Virion does it?"

Again I asked Control.

"No … Control says there is no connection in the ownership or news records."

"Damn. That would have been very helpful."

"Of course the way *they* operate that doesn't mean anything. They network even if their companies don't. That wouldn't end up in the news. They aren't *that* easy."

"So what if there was something happening. What would it be?"

"I dunno," I shrug.

"We know they test these kids performance all the time. And we know they do blood tests. That sounds like they are looking for a connection between something in the blood and performance in their tests."

"Yeah, maybe."

"So either they are looking for something which helps or something which makes them worse." Sue reasons.

I think about that.

"It's gotta be something which helps," I say. "They've spent so much on helping them in other ways why would they suddenly give them something which didn't."

"Hmm so they are trying to create an environment which gives poor kids the same chance as rich kids but they are also testing some of them against a dose of something."

I shrug, "If you say so."

"Who's the school nurse?

"Some woman named Sanchez who likes her cat."

"She should be checked out."

"Yeah. It'll be much easier when we're with the rest of the team."

"Yeah," Sue agreed, thinks for a moment and says, "I need to get a contract from Dr Prosperov."

"Contract?"

"Work contract, like your Aunt signed."

"Oh."

"Then I can resign."

"Don't sweat it Sue. Why don't you go to work?"

"Work! I haven't even called in yet!" she says suddenly, standing up.

"Damn! I am in for such a bollocking."

"Isn't the plan to let them know you've found everyone alive and well in a new place somewhere up north?"

"That's right. Where do you think it should be?"

"Somewhere in the Hokianga isn't it?

"Why don't I know where exactly they everyone is again?"

"Because everyone's in hiding. They would only talk to you if you wore a blindfold."

"So why are *they* in hiding?"

"They say gangs burnt down the house and they are scared."

"What gangs?"

"Sinaloa or Ergenekon. They were both outside Renwick a year ago. Why couldn't they come back?"

"What proof is there either of those groups has ever operated in New Zealand."

"Dr P complained to Sergeant Smith several times last year."

"That's hardly proof."

"No, but if it wasn't investigated it'll look pretty bad."

"Smith might not have kept a record."

"Dr P complained in writing about Sergeant Smith. That's one of the reasons he didn't like us."

"Who to?"

"I don't know. Some people in Wellington."

"The Police Complaints Authority?"

"If you say so."

"Well, then that *will* be recorded."

"Yeah."

"But maybe you should tell me how these gangs did come to be on Aotea Island."

"Well, it sort of started when we got back after the holidays. It was all Ax's fault. You see while we'd been busy in Israel and Africa he'd been busy back here."

"Doing what?"

"Relocating his gang to Aotea mostly. That, and making trouble."

"OK ... OK, hang on."

She gets up, and goes to the kitchen.

"Want a drink Sam? Tea or Coffee?" she shouts.

"Tea please," I reply.

"Sugar? Milk?"

"Just milk thanks."

A moment later Sue comes out with two mugs. She gives me one and sits down on the couch opposite me, opening her cigarettes and popping one in her mouth.

"You shouldn't smoke so much," I tell her.

"Yeah ... I know but ... I won't be able to at ..."

"Anyway," I interrupt. I just decide to plough on so I start talking again.

...

Getting back to New Zealand from Israel and sleeping in was a huge relief. We woke up the next day to fantastic weather. The morning was hot and sunny. The cicadas were singing constantly.

I was in the sea in my wetsuit with my boogie board from eight in the morning until five that night. The sand, the lemonade, the barbecued sausages, and fires on the beach: it was the best! Everyone spent the day in the water. Even Dr P and Dr Morozov came out and swam around. Nothing was organised. Everyone just did their own thing. And when the long evenings came we sat around talking and listening to music from Betty, which was parked on the beach, we were all so chilled we just wanted it to go on forever.

There was no work the next day either. We swam again, and walked, searching the beaches, collecting stuff for Mariko. Then we caught some snapper for Mr Trân. Later that evening we did some bend diving to keep our skills sharp. On the final dive we zoomed down Aotea in blend camouflage two hundred meters above Renwick and dropped into the sea a kilometer from shore.

The next day Dr Prosperov and Dr Gursoy took Tarik and Cam aside and they had to go off and do something. The rest of us skydived at dawn around the world, from the South China Sea, to the Himalayas, Tibet, Iran, and Madagascar. When we weren't doing that, we were swimming in pale blue lagoons in remote islands around the Pacific like a family of porpoises. We were claiming the whole world as our playground.

Tarik and Cam joined us later. We asked them where they had been. Tarik said they had been to Turkey where it seemed that Ergenekon was planning to take-over the whole Government. They had been providing papers from Dr Gursoy's archive to authorities to help stop them.

Over the next few days first Mitra and Soraya, then Patricia and Khenbish returned. Patricia now had a work visa so she was legal. She and Ken were very cosy with each other but nobody but us kids really talked about it. Bernard and Zoe were especially welcoming to them.

The welcome for Mitra and Soraya was more low key. Dr Gursoy showed a special interest in Mitra and it was obvious she had missed him too. They went off for a walk in the moonlight at bedtime and Tarik had to put himself to bed that night. We didn't get much out of him about it. He and Cam talked a lot together. She was really good with him.

I suppose it was good all this relaxing didn't go on too long because it did start to get a bit boring in the end. But all the time we were unloading about two months worth of stress and worry so playing like this helped heaps.

Even going back to school felt a bit like a holiday. It was amazing to wake up on a fantastic sunny morning in my own bed and know the only thing that could go wrong today was Mr

Wakefield taking our class again.

We had breakfast outside in the warm sun and Mariko came to join us. We were so happy to not to be doing anything serious we were laughing and shouting like idiots the whole time. Finally it was time to go, so we grabbed our stuff and got onto Betty. We were all doing teacher imitations and laughing.

It was only when we got to the top of the hill by the church, and saw a truck and a car, with Ax talking to some guy with an orange vest and wrap-around shades, that we calmed down. I didn't look at him but I noticed Rewa did, and he glanced up and waved to her. She almost waved back.

Even that didn't spoil the trip. Mariko was playing more recent dancy music from her MP3 player and it gave us this feeling of being so cool. Maybe we should have realised that it wasn't going to last.

Our school looked so small and pitiful after so long away we almost felt sorry for it. There was the usual collection of cars and the other bus with kids in all directions. We piled out of Betty and joined the confusion. We moved as a group towards the school hall and noticed there was a bit of muttering going on as we went, but we were so chilled we didn't really care.

Suddenly a soccer ball smashed into the concrete rear wall of a classroom just above our heads. It rebounded back over us out to the field where Marshall was waiting for it. We had all frozen in our tracks half poised to take cover. Marshall and his mates were sniggering as they returned to their game. We moved on.

I spotted Emma with a group of girls on the other side of the playground. She noticed me but her gaze didn't linger. Neither did mine. I didn't really feel anything much for her at that moment.

Most of our eyes were on Marshall. He seemed to have grown and become a bit more sure of himself. None of us thought that would be a good thing. To pass the time we started reading the other kids. It was only then we started to realise that this wasn't so much about us, as about Ax.

Aotea Island was a pretty white place. There were a few Indians and Chinese as there usually are in New Zealand but hardly anyone noticed them. There were a few Maori – like Emma – but they were pretty low key too. So the arrival of Ax and his gang friends had been noticed.

They had set up a base at the motel I'd gone to confront him at, and they now had four of the six units. They hadn't done anything loud – except sing hymns – but they'd still scared everyone with their shades and gang patches. And worse everyone seemed to know Ax was me and Rewa's dad.

The bell went and the teachers rounded us up and got us all inside. The assembly calmed us a bit because everything was so familiar. Mrs Maclean blahed on about "community spirit" and then Mr Wakefield tried to get us all excited about his plan for a "school olympics" to start the year because of the real Games in Beijing in August. Somehow we found this comparison between enormous Beijing and tiny Aotea a bit funny and must have got a bit noisy because he stopped and everyone looked at us. We had to shut up. Then he went on.

Not surprisingly we ended up in Mr Wakefield's class again this year. There were a few younger kids from the previous year who were bumped up to join us. Altogether there were 25 kids in the class which was the biggest class by far. Rewa and Asal had only 15.

Mr Wakefield started by saying that next year we would face

exams which would be very different. He said this year we would
be getting ready by doing more homework. There was lots of
groaning from everyone but us. We hoped the more homework
we had, the fewer missions we would have to do. Ashley even
cheered which seemed to annoy everyone.

Then we struck a problem. Mr Wakefield got us to come up the
front one by one and talk about our holidays. We went up in
order by surname, so "Ka" came before "Kh" which meant I was
the first up from Renwick House. The others passed me notes
but I was still really nervous when I got up.

I told the class we'd been cleaning and working on the
restoration of the house. Mr Wakefield asked me if I'd been
anywhere. My brain was reeling from memories of Iran, Israel,
North Kivu, Washington and all the other places we had been,
but I just said "no". I must have looked pretty dumb because lots
of the other kids laughed. Mr Wakefield seemed to feel sorry for
me and sent me back to my seat.

Tahira was next. She was a little better than I was but she still
looked both shifty and a bit of a loser. Once again the others
laughed at her. Scotty was no better.

Marshall had been to his Uncle's place on a farm on the
mainland further south. They had their own swimming holes,
horses and caves. He'd also been driving go karts. He said he'd
driven at eighty two kilometers an hour down the straight. We
all tried not to smile at each other. He noticed our eyes laughing
and made some comment, but Mr Wakefield didn't realise it was
directed at us.

Emma said she'd been to Wellington and Takaka in the South
Island. She said Te Papa, the national museum in Wellington
was cool, and dolphins had followed the ferry across the Strait

between the two islands. In Takaka they had explored a really huge cave down the easiest bits. Some girl called out to ask if she had pashed Dave down there and she went bright red. Mr Wakefield let her sit down.

I had expected that she had pashed him, but her embarrassment still stung. I hadn't realised what a cold, yucky feeling jealousy was. I even found myself looking at Tahira but she frowned at me, and looked away, telling me to leave her out of it.

By lunchtime I felt like a complete egg. As far as Emma knew I hadn't been anywhere, and I hadn't done anything. I was so frustrated with myself. Meanwhile Emma was being asked for all the details about dishy Dave by all her excited girlfriends. Scott and Ashley were good. They took me away from it to shoot baskets.

Unfortunately it wasn't over. Emma came looking for *me*. She thanked me for the necklace I'd given her for Christmas and then asked me straight-up if Ax was my dad. I suppose I wanted to tell her *something* so I blurted out about how he'd killed mum and that he kept chasing us and we didn't want anything to do with him. She was shocked. I'd forgotten she didn't know. I must have seemed a bit angry because she backed off fast.

But it did have an effect. This bit of gossip spread quickly. One of the other non-Renwick kids asked if it was true but I just glared and he didn't hang around. All through class that afternoon Emma had a frown on her face and kept glancing at me.

After school Mariko picked us up. She was playing the same music as before but we were a bit less playful. I guess we were a bit down because even though school was nothing compared to dodging gunmen in North Kivu it was still a hassle. Mariko cheered us up by announcing we were off missions until her

wedding – unless there was an emergency. In the meantime
Lana was coming back to talk to us about replacing the
kindergarten suits we were using. She wanted to find out more
about what was working and what wasn't.

Our homework consisted of a project on the Olympic games.
We had to come up with both group and individual projects.
We could do anything. We argued around a group theme. Tarik
suggested timing the events; Ashley, the competitors clothes
and shoes. Scotty was interested in the change in different
race's domination of different sports over the years. Cam was
interested in the changing fads in athletes diets. Tahira liked
Ashley's idea but was more into the change in national costumes
at the opening ceremony. I was still thinking about Ax.

"Sam ya gotta do something, right?" Tarik complained when I
couldn't think of anything.

"I dunno," I said irritably. "I can't think of anything."

"What about our group project?" Ashley asked.

We all mulled over that. As we were Mariko came by. She
suggested we do a group project on the changing way the
Olympic games portrayed itself.

"Rike with diffelent styres of posters, ceremonies, medarls, films
and shit."

Mariko was in a good mood. She was planning her wedding
for mid February, Gunter was busy in his workshop building a
Japanese stage for the garden while Bernard was planting out a
ceremonial garden. The adults were all very excited about this
wedding. The girls were more into it than Tarik, me or Scott.
To save arguing (and knowing Mariko would help us if we
backed her idea) we agreed to it. Then we decided that was
enough homework. We were just about to rush out when Mrs

415

Jones showed up and told us the house was "filthy" because it hadn't been cleaned properly for so long. Well, it didn't look filthy to us but it was our job so we went to do our cleaning. It was just a chore, we could almost do it in our sleep.

At first Tahira and me didn't talk. We were both in our own worlds. She was thinking about buying a sewing machine and adjustable mannequin. She had a vision of herself as a fashion designer and she wanted to practice. I found myself thinking about Ax and wondering why he wouldn't just push off and leave us alone.

"Zhou draw 'im to you by zhinking about 'im," Tahira commented suddenly when I was polishing the brass, lost in my anger.

"What? How?" I asked grumpily.

"E 'aunts you. Jus like your muzzer. Zhou 'old 'im even as you 'ate 'im," she said.

"He follows us around. He has the whole country to ruin. Why pick here?" I complained.

"Exactly. E knows zhou 'av not forgiven 'im and 'e will follow you until you do."

"Well that *isn't* going to happen," I told her angrily.

Tahira shrugged and went back to her polishing. Then she snickered.

"What?"

"Is nothing."

"No, what?"

I knew already. Emma going red.

"It was funny."

"Why?"

"Zhou. Zhou looked so shocked."

416

"Did I?"

She smiled at me, nodding.

"Oh, what a dick!" I said throwing down my rag and putting my head in my hands.

"Why?" Tahira asked, rubbing the brass.

"Because I'm such a loser to her."

"Zat doesn't matter. You are sweet because you care. She cares too. Why else is she embarrassed?"

I looked at her, unconvinced.

"You really think so?"

"Zis is the problem with being psychic. We zink we know people because zhey zink zhey know themselves. But zhen zomezing 'appens – like being asked if she kissed Dave – and Emma discovers it is not zomezing she wants to make a big noise about in front of you."

"Why?"

Tahira shrugged, "She does not know. But she looked at you and you saw she was uncomfortable."

"So you think she likes me."

"I know she likes you, but zat doesn't mean much. It is competition. Is no prizes for second."

I sighed.

"I'm probably about eleventh by now."

Tahira shrugged and went back to her brass.

I looked at Tahira. She was so hot. She kept working for a while, then looked up at me, brushing her hair out of her face. Then she frowned.

"What?"

"Nothing. You just looked so good."

Her face wrinkled and we went back to our work.

"I am not a doll for your collecting," she said grumpily.

She was actually quite angry. I was a bit shocked. I was shocked partially by how annoyed she was, but just as much to realise that that was exactly how my dad had treated my mum. She was pretty. He had collected her. This thought hit me so hard I stopped working, shocked at myself. Was it so easy to fall into *his* way of thinking. Was I really like *him* after all? I felt angry with myself. We kept working for a while but the air was getting thicker. Finally I threw down my rag.

"F____! I can't do anything f____n right!" I swore. I was so angry I just walked away. I wanted to hit something but mostly I wanted to be alone.

Tahira wanted to say something but she couldn't think of anything as I left.

I went down the stairs and out the front door. It was getting dark. Dinner was almost ready. I was hungry and angry at the same time. I knew half of my mood was because I was hungry but it was helped along by a whole lot of anger. Mostly I was angry at myself but I was also angry at my dad.

A mean thought crept into my brain. I'd smash the windows in his stupid church. That would cost him, and slow him down. This idea suddenly turned itself into a mission in my head. I had time. There were loads of stones on the gravel road. I would certainly feel better afterwards. It was settled.

I crept over the drive and picked up a dozen stones and slipped them in my hoodie pocket. Then climbing quickly and silently on the pine needles I set off up the hill.

It was strange setting out to do something without Fae technology. I had no night vision, and no extra strength. I missed the claws on my feet too. On the other hand there was no

one watching over my shoulder or yapping in my head either.
It was a bit harder than I expected getting up the hill. It was
very dark under the trees and the needles were slippery. But
gradually the hill levelled out and I pressed through the edge of
the pine forest to the bushes that surrounded the chapel.

I noticed two things at once as I got to the edge of the bushes.
The long grass on the graveyard had been cut back to short
stalks, and there were lights on in the chapel.

I hadn't really planned on anyone still being there. I'd wanted
to vent my anger at my dad by wrecking his chapel. If I threw
stones now it would be no mystery who'd done it.

Then a car drew up on the other side. I couldn't see it but I
heard footsteps crunching around. There were voices, then more
footsteps. A group of four gang guys walked around the chapel
and came back out into the graveyard. They sat down on a wall
and on the gravestones. I recognised Ray, the white guy we'd
seen up in the hills, and Jason who was dad's number two.

Ray had a whole bunch of plastic bags in his pockets and took
them out to show the others. They were talking about plots,
rainfall and sun. Ray passed around a bag and they all began
to roll themselves smokes. Soon little red dots shone in the
gathering dark and I caught the smell I had known since my
earliest days in the Hokianga. The smell of weed being smoked.
It must have been reasonably strong because pretty soon they
were giggling like fools. But what they were talking about made
me feel both better and a bit worried.

I had thought Ax had followed us because he wanted me and
Rewa back, but that was only part of the story. These guys were
joking about Ax wanting to be a king. "King of the Waitemata
harbour" they were calling him. Then they talked about the real

leaders of the gang in Auckland, how they hogged all the money and power. Dad wasn't really a king – more like an uppity lord – but he had a plan to work his way to the top by dealing. Because, it turned out, he wasn't after us especially at all. That was almost a hobby.

He had come because Aotea was a perfect place to grow tons of weed and take tonnes of Paua. There was only one conservation officer and one cop. It was way closer to Auckland than anywhere up north making supply into the gang's biggest market that much easier.

They called the Aotea national park, "the estate" and Renwick "the castle". Gradually I realised their aim was to take over Renwick House! Restoring the chapel was just to show off that they could restore things too. As I focused on their loosened minds I began to get the impression that Ax was working on Aunty Nea's son, a guy they called "the prince". He was a Maori chief and businessman who used history and the law to get stuff back for his tribe. The trick was he ran the tribe like his own private business. Ax was trying to convince "the prince" that he would be a better person to look after Renwick than some Russian weirdo like Dr P. He would even pay more too. I also got the impression that they were well aware that Aunty Nea, who had helped us get Renwick, was old and could be easily encouraged to die once "the prince" had agreed to their plan. There was something else too. They called the operation "Jericho" after the siege in the Bible. They were laying siege to our castle but they themselves would not be the ones to cause trouble. They were just preparing the way for something else. Something foreign that could be blamed on all the foreigners inside Renwick. That way they could just walk in and take over

after their foreigners had driven us and our foreigners out.
I noticed a movement out of the corner of my eye, and an old
chill I knew very well ran down my spine like electricity. I
looked around. Kneeling next to me with a bayonet in his rifle
and helmet on his head was Sergeant Aroha. Beyond him were
a few of his mates. He grinned, then jerked his head in a way
that meant I had to follow. He crept into the dark of the forest. I
followed him along with the rest of the ghosts.
The pine forest was really, really dark. I followed Sergeant Aroha
as he and his men wove through the tall trunks. It was cold and
scary following them because I wasn't completely sure where
they were leading me. I tripped a few times but they waited.
Then we came to the edge of the bank and stopped. I could see
the lights of Renwick through the trees.
"*Those fullahs are doing a good job on the old chapel eh?*"
Sergeant Aroha said, lighting a cigarette, cupping his hand to
shield the flame from some ghostly wind.
"I guess."
"*But sitting on the gravestone. Not so happy about that. That's
disrespecting the dead,*" he shook his head.
He spoke of the dead as if he wasn't one of them.
"They're criminals," I replied.
"*And you with the stones in your pocket. What are you?*"
I felt a bit ashamed I looked at Renwick.
"*Hey, I threw a few stones when I was a kid too, but not at a
church. That's bad luck,*" he said.
I had to admit that it was.
"*You still friends with those patupairehe?*"
"Yeah," I admitted. I was in for a lecture. I looked at my feet.
You don't look elders in the eye, and you sure don't look ghosts

421

in the eye either.

"You be careful they don't trick you. They are famous for tricking our people eh? Maybe you should go to church instead of throw rocks at it. I always went to church. German's never got me either, eh? Machine gun jams right in front of my face. Shell lands ten feet away but doesn't go off. Sentry doesn't hear me. Don't think that would have happened if I hadn't paid my respects to the A-tu-a eh? You need God on your side, son. So don't piss Him off throwing rocks."

Then suddenly the chill was gone. I looked around for Sergeant Aroha's patrol but they had vanished. I found the whole thing weird. Sergeant Aroha's idea of God was nothing like Mr Ceder's. He was thinking of our old Maori gods really. That was why he called them Atua, which is one or more gods. But once again he was warning me to be careful of the Fae. I didn't get it. Was he some sort of guardian spirit or just some old Maori soldier, dead almost ninety years?

I felt kind of strange coming down the hill. I'd gone up to let my anger out. To throw rocks and smash my father and any resemblance I had with him. And now when I thought about it I would have been acting exactly like him, even as I was angry about it. I couldn't believe how dumb I had been.

But that wasn't how it had turned out. Something else had happened instead. I'd learned from Ray and Jason something really useful and important. And yet I was still really angry. I wanted to hurt Ax, the way he'd hurt me. I wanted to hurt him for my being like him. I just wanted to make him suffer the way he kept making others suffer.

I calmed down. I was hungry. I still wanted to be angry but I also needed to eat. So I went inside and sat with Aunty Liz, Rewa and

Grandpop.

While I ate I looked around at Dr Gursoy and Tarik, and at Ashley who was with Scotty, Patience, Bernard and Zoe. I felt sure that somehow Ax would use their histories to get at us all. I had no idea how but I could just feel it coming.

I noticed that Dr Gursoy was looking particularly thoughtful. I started reading. It was like Dr Prosperov. Everything was fast and complicated. But what it did show was that the mission that Tarik and Cam had done in Turkey was just the tip of the iceberg. There was a huge amount happening over there. Politicians, army generals, journalists and criminals were series of flashing scenarios in his brain. It was too much to keep up with.

After dinner I told Grandpop what I'd heard and read from Ax's mates. He was asking himself why I had been sneaking around outside the chapel but he realised the main thing was to tell Dr P. So we went upstairs to his office.

Dr P's new office was on the corner turret above Mariko's studio. It had a view from the heads to the east to the road up through the pines in the west. Grandpop knocked and Dr P responded with a distracted "Voyditye". Grandpop opened the door and ushered me in.

There were three memorable things about Dr P's office. The first was the cream coloured wallpaper with navy blue flecks, the old wooden writing table, the copper telescope and the Samovar. This was the Russian in him.

Then there were the flat screens. There were three on the writing desk and four others on the walls in picture frames. Sometimes they showed art but often they showed a cascade of numbers

423

from different markets around the world. This was Dr P the financier.

And then there was the workbench, the soldering equipment, the dentists chair with the odd coils on it and the little electronic boxes with lights and "Texas Instruments" or "Hewlett Packard" written on them. This was Dr P "mad scientist". And all of this was packed into a room four meters by four which seemed to crackle and hum with electricity.

Dr P, still in a suit, swung his chair around, stretched and yawning asking us what brought us to him. He seemed distracted by what he had been doing but also aware that this was a welcome break.

So I told him what I'd read while Grandpop wondered again why I'd gone up there at all. At first Dr Prosperov showed little interest but when I came to the bit about "the prince" he became quite concerned. He asked Grandpop sharp questions which Grandpop couldn't really answer. He jumped up in agitation (again showing his surprising fitness for such an old guy) and paced about.

"Had anticipated criminal interference. Compared to difficulties with primary mission is small matter. But politics is different. We start at serious disadvantage and have no assets. Have made grave error in neglecting to protect base."

"Is there anything we can do?" Grandpop asked.

"Yes, certainly. No one else here has skill in this matter. All I can offer is help. Is essential that Renwick is held. You Mr Kahu, and Miss Kahu too, must prevent Mr Stephens from gaining the support of this "prince". We must also protect Nea Te Kahukura. I fear more than a natural death is hunting her."

"What about the gangsters?"

"I have long been aware of possibility. They are no match for us," he said shaking his head.

"I don't think the parents will be too keen to have the kids fight gangsters Gennady," Grandpop warned.

"They have been beating world's toughest gangsters for four months," said Dr P pacing. He stopped and held up three fingers.

"Three times only have children been in danger: In Greenland; in Finland; in Israel. Every time involve aliens. Children faster, stronger and better armed than any power from Earth. Except aliens. Aliens serious threat."

"But the kids have to go to school. Then they are vulnerable."

"So they wear suit to school. Is not serious problem. Serious problem is political problem. Is serious because have no strength in these matters."

I couldn't help thinking that Dr P had not been very clever about being nice to the locals. If he had made more local friends then we wouldn't find ourselves so alone now. That was where Ax was clever. People didn't like his men but he was trying and that was more than Dr P had ever done. I had a funny feeling this was going to get a lot worse before it got better.

Despite Ax's plans it was hard to feel threatened that February because it seemed we just went from one party to another. The weather was warm to almost hot and there was enough breeze coming from the warm sea to stop you melting. This year the Tet festival fell on the same weekend as New Zealand's national holiday so after a lazy week of school we had a long weekend and a festival to look forward to.

The hard fasting that the Gursoys had had to do during Muhurram (which was the same as Newroz, the Iranian New Year) was well over. But they were very concerned about what was happening in Turkey where the plans of Ergenekon had been exposed and police were making new arrests every day. But even that couldn't stop them enjoying the warm weather and the feeling of fun in the air.

The result was a long weekend spent eating Mr Trân's Tet treats, drinking fresh coconut and lime juice and getting ready for Mariko and Gunter's wedding.

Gunter's mother Heidi, father Jurgen, and brother Achim with his wife Elke and their daughter Jasmine (who was the same age as Rewa and Asal), had flown out to join the celebrations. Mariko's sister Yoshi, and her mother and father, Keiko and Hiroshi Nakama, had also come to stay. This was part of the reason for suspending operations but it also meant Mr Trân was having a great time turning out spectacular food for everyone. He astonished the Germans with his pastries and amazed the Japanese with his sushi and sashimi. Of course our guests never could figure out how we had such a great supply of fresh fish and local ingredients because they could never imagine we slipped away to the local markets to buy it.

We spent the weekend setting up an outdoor stage shaped like a Japanese castle which Gunter had built in sections and arranging the boulders, walls and gardens for it. When we got too hot, or too bored, we body surfed and swam in the cove. Jasmine – who was a little shy about speaking English at first – soon relaxed and had a great time.

Ken and Patricia were now openly a couple and were often found with their arms around each other and kissing. With Ken back, the helicopter was returned from the airport and the guests got rides around the harbour. Grandpop now had some time off and hired one of the local guys to take him out fishing for swordfish. He had a great day and came back with a Blue Marlin of 150 kilos. He said he hadn't had so much fun in ages.

Tahira had a great day with Mariko working on her makeup and wedding dress. That was all kept a huge secret from Gunter. Mariko had decided to have an Okinawan wedding on Aotea. "Irts going to be lreal traditionarl Japanese," she said seriously. And when we all like "OK", wondering what that would be like, she laughed.

"Naaaaah," she grinned.

But it turned out that actually it was a bit Okinawan because we all had to do a song and dance routine from our own cultures. That meant our family had to quickly work out a Kapa Haka routine with dances and songs from the ones we had done at school in Hokianga. We also had to visit Auckland to buy costumes or material for costumes the weekend before the wedding.

The next week at school was pretty relaxed. Even Mr Wakefield realised that this weather couldn't last forever and we should be outside enjoying it. We did a lot more Olympic stuff but it fed into other lessons like maths. So we had to do races and time one another and work out the averages. Tarik showed me how and it wasn't as hard as I thought. After a while I was even enjoying it. Emma was still a bit distant, although I read that she had noticed Tahira wasn't having much to do with me.

It wasn't that Tahira was being bitchy. We were just tired of each other. We'd been forced together for months of stress and now we could have a break we spent more time with the others. It was a bit the same with Ashley and Scott.

I spent a lot more time with Scott than before, and Ashley spent more time with Tahira. But for some reason Cam and Tarik always hung out. Tarik played soccer with the guys, and Cam did chick stuff with the girls, but they always ended up back together again like there was some invisible rubber band that could only stretch so far for so long.

Tarik had definitely changed. He was still bossy and a know-it-all but he wasn't so nervous and edgy any more. And it only took a glance from Cam to make him pull his head in. He knew he could be a jerk and he relied on her to tell him when to chill. As for Cam, she seemed solid. She was looking for her mother mostly to fix her father's broken heart and she was now sure of Tarik who had put her in the place in his heart where his little sister had been.

I would read Emma sometimes when she wasn't watching. She was definitely thinking about David, but she was also worried about her father, Tama.

Ax was paying Tama a lot of attention at the moment. Friendly attention, to be sure, but she didn't trust him, which I had to admit was wise of her. She didn't like the way Ax's henchmen Jason and Wiri would come around and lean on things. She remembered what she had overheard when Gavin, the local cop, visited.

Gavin had admitted quietly to Tama he was outnumbered. Everyone knew police backup was at least an hour or two away in Auckland so trying to be being tough with hardened crims like Ax was not likely to work. He said they could easily organise a "car crash" for him and who would know the difference afterwards? It was all a bit like back home all over again.

Emma knew her dad was pretty sure the gang was growing stuff in the park but they didn't know where because it was a big park and there were only a few of them. She was worried her dad might be hurt if he found anything. Sergeant Smith had passed on intelligence to the drug squad but so far he hadn't had any interest from Auckland. They probably didn't regard Ax as a major player.

Given the situation any hopes I might have had of charming Emma seemed pretty crushed. She was scared of my dad and even though she knew *I* didn't want him around, she still resented me for bringing him to her island. And she wasn't alone.

A lot of the other kids came from families who had tolerated us only because we kept to ourselves. Now there was a new gang of strangers linked to us through me and Rewa, their tolerance was running out. They wanted their island back the way it had been, *before* that crazy Russian showed up.

Of course Marshall and his mates had to be the ones who voiced the anger of the whole community. They were too nervous that Ax might do something to them if they were too open about it.So they took it out on us in mean, and shitty, little ways. Their favourite was to put dog crap on our bags or drop it near where we were sitting. But they'd never go so far as to actually throw it at us.

Of course after they'd played that trick twice we got them back by asking Mr Wakefield why Marshall had a plastic bag of dogshit in his left trouser pocket. He loudly denied it but was shamed when Mr Wakefield made him turn his pockets out. He couldn't quite work out how we knew where he hid it, no matter where he put it. After he and his friends got three detentions in a row we started a school saying of, "good boy Marshall!" whenever there was dog poop around, and they gave up.

Back home the days leading up to the wedding were getting busier and busier, and we had more and more, to clean. It was true that after three months of missions we had let the place get a little dustier than usual. So we were stoked when Friday came by and Mrs Jones told us we deserved extra dessert for making the house cleaner than ever.

We had also been working on our songs and dances. They made me nervous. I was sure this whole thing was just going to be totally lame. But I have to admit I was the only one.

Rewa was into it, and she and Aunty Liz were twirling their poi (a little soft ball on a string) like kapa haka champions. All Grandpop and me had to do was a haka (war dance) which I'd been doing since I was six. It wasn't hard. It was just that with only four of us it was hard to get the effect you usually get with a class of twenty or so.

Dr Gursoy and Mitra had teamed up their families to do some vaguely Kurdish dances. What Tahira and Asal liked the most were the bright clothes Kurdish women wear and they had worked hard to put together outfits with lots of gold and silver in them.

Bernard Khumalo had roped Patricia Robinson and Ashley in to join him, Zoe and Scotty to learn some Matabele songs and dances. There was no way the Robinson's had Matabele ancestors (we were pretty sure they were descended from Ghanians) but from what I saw of their practices they made up for lack of skill with enthusiasm. Scotty was a surprise because he certainly played the drums really well.

That left Cam all by herself which was even tougher than anyone else had it. But she didn't seem all that bothered for some reason. I admired that about her. She simply didn't get shy.

Mrs Jones was going to sing, same as the Germans. Dr Prosperov was going to play fiddle, but we didn't really know what Ken, or Mariko's family were going to do.

On Friday night we finally got given the schedule for the whole event. Mariko had done the whole thing like a big Japanese painting combining English and Japanese words in a poster. It was really good. The times were shown with little clock faces without numbers to get past the language barriers.

The whole thing was to be like a giant performance with feasting all through the day. It was going to start at dawn on Sunday morning with drums and Mariko would dance. This was to be followed by us Maoris doing our thing. That was cool because then we'd have it over with for the rest of the day. After us was the dance of the fish-people (whoever they were). Then we would have a wedding breakfast where all the messages from friends would be read out. Then we got to go back to bed until lunchtime (which suited me fine).

At lunchtime Gunter and Mariko would come out to the festival of the flowers (whatever that was). This would be followed by the Kurds' show. After that would be the official wedding bit. Then a Japanese and Mongolian barbecue lunch during which Dr Prosperov would play for us. This would go on until evening when Mrs Jones would sing for us. The Germans would lead a lantern walk to the lighthouse and launch some sky and sea lanterns (which looked like balloons). Then they would come back to the stage for a ceremony. Then there was a bonfire and the Africans would do their thing, followed by a Mariko style party – or that's what it looked like to me.

This started a whole heap of questions. Apparently we were hosting a Japanese group the next day including a sort of priest guy, and half a dozen drummers who were staying in the hall. It turned out we kids were the fish people playing a chasing game in the fish costumes. The festival of the flowers was basically a huge load of flowers coming the next day which we would get to throw at everyone. And it was all organised.

So the next day, as expected, a minibus full of Japanese showed up. They were very professional and had themselves set up in no time. A truck with huge boxes arrived and set them down next to the stage. Another truck showed up with all the food. We didn't have that much to do. We had a few practices of our dances. Everyone was getting ready and excited, even Dr Morozov who was sick all the time. That night we went to bed early so we could get up the next morning at dawn.

I hadn't been to too many weddings before. I think one, max.
I'd been eight. They made me wear this stupid suit and sit still
in a hot church forever while the adults yakked on and the bride
cried. Then we'd gone somewhere else where everyone drank too
much and a fight started. So I guess I wasn't expecting a lot. But
this? This was the best day.

It was calm and still at dawn, and the drumming was amazing.
Mariko wore this red dress with gold and danced like a wild
thing to be the Japanese sun goddess. She was really good.

I dunno, I had felt all shy and embarrassed before that day but
there was something about doing our kappa haka routine in the
early morning with our own people around us that just swept
you along like a wave. Anyway everyone loved it and I felt really
proud. Then we kids had to put on these fish costumes Mariko
had made out of satin, silver cloth and wire, and play one of her
complicated chasing games. The idea was to collect sticks but
only one colour stick was allowed to catch another colour. We
were running around for ages. I think Tarik won.

Breakfast was huge. There was Japanese fishy stuff, there was
German bakery stuff, there was Vietnamese rice stuff, there were
eggs every which way, fish, bacon, sausages, pancakes, waffles,
and fruits and yoghurts of all sorts. Eating it all was a challenge
but I was up for it.

An hour and half later I was wondering if I might have overdone it
when I went back to bed. After a while I actually fell asleep again
and slept until about ten thirty feeling like I was in pig heaven.

When I got up again it was still a stunning day. Hot and still, but
with enough of a swell to be interesting. Well, I couldn't *not* swim
in it could I? I wasn't the only one either. Everyone joined in.
Scott had a bit of an argument with Jasmine telling her that yes,

white people do need SPF 30 in New Zealand. We all used it. Even Ashley, 'though I think that was mostly coz she liked Scott rubbing it on her back. He complained about being her "staff" which he said with a real short "a" like "stuff".

"Dawlin, you ain't no stuff." she smiled with her eyes closed from her towel, "You da Help."

I suppose that's why he poured seawater on her.

At about twelve the parents dragged us back inside and made us dress up a bit. But Mariko had said us kids could wear what we liked so long as it was bright. That was a bit hard for me because I tend to wear dark colours but I ended up in a white shirt and black trousers. Rewa wore pink as usual.

We all gathered outside where a breeze had picked up a bit. Gunter and his family were waiting on the stage. They were dressed in green. Everyone else was gathered with them in all sorts of bright colours. There was a path of shiny steel sheets from Renwick to the stage lined with flags on bamboo poles. The drummers lined the route from the house drumming like mad things while a bunch dudes were setting up around another huge barbecue in the background. The odd gust from the fire and the smell of cooking meat made your mouth water even though I was full up. Mrs Jones called us kids together and led us over to these big boxes of flowers. Our job was to throw these orangy-yellow flowers at Mariko. That sounded like fun.

When Mariko came out I was blown away. She looked like a Fae! Her whole family was wearing violet. Her dress shimmered and she had a kind of a cross between wings and a cape on her arms. As they walked the drummers fell in behind.

"Well, off you go!" Mrs Jones called cheerfully.

So we threw flowers at Mariko who was laughing and crying

at the same time. It must have been infectious because so was everyone else. The flowers ended up all over the steel.

Finally they reached the stage and Mrs Jones told us to stop. The drumming kept going, getting louder and louder as the two families ended up facing one another with Gunter and Mariko facing each other between them.

Then suddenly there was silence.

Or actually not silence but a high clear sound which sounded as if it had always been there. It sounded like a bell, slowly fading away to silence. The priest – well he was sort dressed like a Buddhist monk but not like a real one – struck the bell again, and once again its pure high tone rang out over the sea and wind. And just as it had almost died away again, he struck it again and by now all the hype and excitement the drummers had created had gone and we were all very calm, in the sun watching Mariko and Gunter looking at each other holding hands.

Then the priest guy came out and read a short poem by a dude named William Blake that went like this:

"To see a world in a grain of sand,
And a heaven in a wild flower,
Hold infinity in the palm of your hand,
And eternity in an hour."

And ended a bit later with

"God appears, and God is light,
To those poor souls who dwell in night;
But does a human form display
To those who dwell in realms of day."

And then he made a funny speech with jokes in English, German and Japanese. The jokes were mostly about Mariko and Gunter's little habits but there were also jokes about Dr Prosperov and Mrs Jones. He was very relaxed and very good.

Then he talked about how important love was in its way to bind people who came from different places and how it was so much more important than hate and separation. He also talked about how two people will always squabble and have their differences but that their families and their village must try to help them. Then he got Mariko and Gunter to make promises to each other. Achim gave Gunter a ring and Yoshi gave Mariko a ring and then they put their rings on and kissed for a while. Someone started to clap but the priest guy shook his head. Then he made the families stand up and face one another and make promises in their own languages and drink some Japanese sake as a toast to one another. Then he asked us all to make a promise and reply "we will" when he had finished. So he read out this promise and we all shouted "We will" and then everyone went nuts.

It was kind of surprising how emotional everyone was. I suppose it was kind of because we had all become very close over an amazing year and promising to stay together and support Gunter and Mariko made us all aware how strongly we had come to feel about each other. There was a lot of bubbly wine going around. I even had some, though I would rather have coke any day. Luckily there was a huge ice filled case full of soft drinks. There was another one with beer in it. Me and Tarik tried to nick some beer but Grandpop suddenly appeared out of nowhere and took them off us. I didn't like it anyway.

Pretty soon however the place settled down and we watched the Kurdish and Iranian dancing. Tarik was surprisingly good though he looked a bit embarrassed about it. Tahira got away with a lot of bad dancing by being pretty. And of course soon everyone joined in and the quality of the dancing went downhill. Nobody knew what they should be doing but there was a lot of laughing.

Finally the food started to get handed out. The Japanese were cooking fish on metal plates and showing off these amazing knife skills as they did so. Ken had also organised another of his roasts which was totally delicious. As well as all this there Mr Trân had done salads, and snacks again so we were stuffing ourselves, which wasn't hard because breakfast had been a long time ago.

After a while Dr Prosperov came out with his fiddle and played his slippery gypsy music again. Ken found his guitar and they began jamming together. Slowly the shadows grew and deepened and the afternoon turned apricot coloured. Suddenly there was this burst of the most amazingly bright clear song that we all looked around in confusion. It was Mrs Jones.

We all stood, and then sat, with our mouths open as she sang like an opera star, with no mike or anything. I didn't understand one word she said but it still choked me up and when she finished everyone wanted more, so she did a few more as the colours around us deepened.

While we were distracted by this the Japanese guys with Ken and Bernard had stoked up some fires, cleared away the food stuff and organised some speakers behind us. So when Mrs Jones's last note and died away against the hillside there was only a brief pause until there was a big bump on the drums. Then the drummers did another routine while Bernard, Patricia, Zoe, Ashley and Scott organised themselves.

I have to say theirs was probably the best of all with a drumming, singing and dancing routine that melded into a tune called *"$5,000 dollars"* by John Chibadura and the Tembo Brothers which we knew was one of Scotty's favourites. After that Mariko declared herself the D.J and was still going strong when I went to bed. We had some pretty good days at Renwick but that was the best day ever.

After such an awesome Sunday, Monday was not so good. Mariko and Gunter had gone on their honeymoon and all we had for breakfast was leftovers because Mr Trân wasn't feeling so well. Grandpop had to drive the bus to school because no-one else had a licence. He wasn't as fast as Mariko and we ended up arriving late.

Then at school Emma told me her dad was annoyed we'd had fires on the beach without a permit in the middle of a drought. She said he didn't want to interrupt the wedding but he could have. I asked who had reported us. She said she didn't know, but that was a lie. It was Ax.

She was very uncomfortable that someone she didn't like was making her dad work against us. She knew that Ax was going to pull strings to make her dad and Sergeant Smith come down on us and she was annoyed we were making it easy for him. February is always tourist season on the island so there were a lot of camper vans that drove around the place. A lot of surfer dudes came over from the mainland and it wasn't unusual for them to camp at the beach over the road from the school in their vans. They came from all over: Australians; Canadians; Americans; Germans; and British. But sometimes there were others as well. Swiss artists on bicycles, Asians out to visit their exchange student teenagers and Israelis in small tight groups. That summer there were a couple of young Israelis on the beach opposite. You could tell because they spoke Hebrew and had a Star of David flag on their van.

I didn't pay any attention to them to be honest. They had been there for a few days. At lunch break however I found Cam and Tarik standing by the fence looking out at the beach looking a bit unsettled.

"Sup?" I asked them.

"Those Israelis," Cam replied.

"The ones who drove off a few minutes ago?" I asked. They nodded.

"What about them?" I asked.

"They ain't no Israelis," Tarik said grimly.

"What are they, then?"

"They're Turks. Turks that speak Hebrew, yeah?"

I was confused.

"What....did you....?"

"Yeah," said Cam. "We read them while they pretended to take pictures of each other."

"And?"

"They were taking pictures of Tarik."

"Tarik!?"

"It's Ergenekon. They're military spies. Something has tipped them off and now they know where dad and me are."

"Why did they drive off?"

"They realised I was taking their numberplate," Tarik said.

"But what do they want? What are they trying to do?"

"They want to stop Dad's collection of papers coming out. Some very rich and powerful people in Turkey stand to lose a lot if what dad knows about them were passed to the right authorities. The whole country is in political chaos at the moment."

"Tarik thinks they will try and kidnap him," Cam said.

It made sense. It made a lot of sense.

"But that would be pretty hard wouldn't it?" I thought aloud. "I mean we're on an island and you're almost never alone."

"Depends if they're desperate enough init?" Tarik said.

He was thinking about the way they had killed his mother and sister. We walked back across the grassy playground talking about it. We walked right through a game of touch rugby and back to the classroom. Our experience of kidnapping with Sarah was not great. On the other hand nobody had ever tried to kidnap one of *us* before. As Dr P had said we were a match for almost anyone.

When Grandpop picked us up that night he didn't seem so worried. He said anyone messing with us would get what was coming to them. But he agreed Dr Gursoy and Dr Prosperov needed to be warned. I noticed he watched his mirrors more than usual but there was no sign of anyone. We joked in the bus about what would happen to any kidnappers if they picked us up in suits. It made Tarik laugh and I noticed he looked a lot less freaked than he had been at lunchtime.

When we got home we found Lana Vilenskaya had arrived. She looked as crazy but as cheerful as ever and hugged us all. She said she wanted to get our ideas for new suits tomorrow but she was just staying up to beat the jetlag and was too lightheaded to talk to us seriously now. She wasn't talking too seriously to anyone else either, but the adults made a fuss of her and made her feel at home.

During cleaning I noticed Tahira was distracted. She was

thinking about Tabika again. It was a year since we had found her in that cave by the sea. Almost a month since we'd made out in that same place. But she treated that like a mistake. I still felt torn. Emma seemed so far away and Tahira so close.

I had this strange feeling that things were going wrong but I wasn't sure how or where. I knew Ax was leaning on Tama and that was wrong. Ergenekon was lurking nearby looking for Tarik and that was wrong too. But there was something even bigger than that. Something way bigger. It was like I could feel a storm was coming. A big black one. And there was not a thing I could do but ride it out.

That night I dreamed everything was red with pain and the sky was red with blood. I was running; running in cold soft sand in an empty land where pitiless mountains stood by and the stars shone regardless of the pain and blood inside me. It was freezing and He was coming in his truck. Coming with His brothers to get me as I ran, feet locked in the soft freezing sand going nowhere, shivering, bleeding, as His headlights lit me like a frozen sun rising in the west. And I ran desperately, terrified, but stuck in the same place as a shadow of a beast that claimed to be my husband rose over me.

And then pain. More pain as I fell and His whip fell while they laughed at me. More and more and more until my screams weren't even mine. I longed for blackness. For death, but it wouldn't come. Just relentless pain until I can do nothing and even my scream is gone. Then I am taken away and through my pain all I can see is the stars watching like slivers of ice, pitiless and remote above me. And only one question is in my mind? "Why, God, why?"

I woke up shaking. I felt weak and sick as if I had a flu, but I knew I didn't. The sun was coming up and already its warm yellow rays were slanting into my room casting long angular shadows. The sea was washing along the beach and the birds in the bush were singing their hearts out. But despite that I felt a cold sweat on me that I didn't like. I slipped into the bathroom and had a hot shower.

The water and steam helped. It, at least, stopped me shaking and feeling cold. But I still felt sick and pale. I got dressed and came out only to find Aunty Liz in her dressing gown waiting for me.

"What's the matter Sam? You look awful," she said coming up to me and putting a hand on my forehead.

"I just had a bad dream," I told her.

I could see what she was thinking. She wasn't surprised. She thought we had been stressed too much over the past months.

"It wasn't an ordinary dream," I explained quickly. "It was about that girl in Yemen. Khadiyeh. Something pretty bad has happened to her."

Aunty Liz just looked worried for me. I went down to breakfast. I wanted to see if Tahira had had the same dream. I found her talking to Ashley, Cam and Scotty. They were all looking like I felt. I sat down facing them. They looked at me and read what was there.

"She wants our help," Scott said.

"Yeah," I agreed.

"Should not be 'ard to find 'er," Tahira said.

"I dunno about that," I replied.

"Why?" Ashley asked.

"Because she may not be the only power involved."

Everyone except Tahira looked confused.

"'e's talking about God. Zis old man in Israel 'as made 'im religious," Tahira smiled.

"What man?" Cam asked.

So I told them about Mr Ceder.

"Sounds a bit creepy if you ask me," Ashley said.

"Yeah, how do you know he's not one of *them*," Scott asked.

"He's not one of them. He's terrified of *them*. He doesn't even want to talk to *me* anymore."

Tarik came in. One look told him everything and he sat down with us. The others explained what we'd been talking about. When my theory came up he looked at me.

"Sam thinks God is involved," Ashley said.

"God is always involved," Tarik agreed.

"*Especially* involved," Cam clarified.

Tarik looked at me thoughtfully and a bit nervously.

"Maybe Sam is right," he said.

So then we had a big discussion about God and the world which went nowhere much until Mrs Jones joined us. We explained what had happened to her.

"This girl is calling you. That is clear," she told us. "I have had nothing. As for God. I confess I am not much of a believer. I have seen far too many terrible things to have any faith in a good and merciful God. I may be wrong but that has been my experience."

I wanted to say that Mr Ceder had seen terrible things too but I didn't want to argue this stuff with adults. We asked Mrs Jones if she would tell Dr Prosperov about the situation. She said she would.

As Grandpop drove us out to school that morning we saw a sign outside the chapel announcing it would be opened to the public in two weeks. I asked Emma about it when we got to school.

"Uh your..." she paused unsure what to call Ax," ... your father has finished. Dad says they've done a good job too. Few more Maori carvings in it than before but he won't be complaining about it."

"Don't they need to have it blessed or something?" I asked.

"I think Aunty Nea is coming out with some of the others for that. It's next week. It's just a quiet thing. I'm going with dad. You could come too if you like."

It was nice of her to offer but I couldn't.

"If it was anyone else who'd done it I'd go. But I'm not going to see anything Ax Stephens has done blessed by anyone."

Emma understood, but she seemed disappointed. I was disappointed too, but she turned with a small, "OK, well, see ya round."

I wanted to say something but I couldn't think of anything. The rest of the day I tried to think of ways I could talk to Emma but I struck out. We were just separated by too much.

The "Israelis" had gone, but Tarik wasn't taking any chances. He stuck around the school and didn't go far at lunchtime. We wondered whether we would go to Yemen that night and if so how and where.

But instead we spent the whole time after cleaning telling Lana about what we had been up to since she had last visited. It was a lot of fun, and we laughed a lot but I felt sure we should be doing something else.

And that night I dreamt again. I was crying as I worked. Still in pain. Two old women were telling me to get used to it. He was downstairs talking to evil men who were planning to kill foreigners. I wanted to go home to my mother and sisters and take care of my nanny goat but He said I was married to his family now. That I must serve Him as a good wife and do whatever He wanted. I had never known such misery.

But even as I dreamt I started thinking. How was it possible I was able to feel this? How was it possible that I – thousands of kilometers away – could receive this. And I started to wonder about Lucky – the spirit that guided Dr P. Could he be involved in this. I searched my mind seeking, almost asking Lucky to reveal himself. But I found no signs of his personality with its cunning trickery. What I was receiving felt like it was entirely from this young girl. In some ways she was exactly like us, young and basically hopeful, but in other ways she was powerfully different. She could find us and that made me wonder what else she could find.

I drifted off to sleep after that and woke to another day in paradise. This was the pattern for the whole week. School came and went without anything much happening and afterwards we showed Lana problems with the suits. It was nice having an adult who actually listened to you, like you knew what you were talking about. We often did a bend dive just to keep ourselves relaxed in the air. After dinner we followed the news, especially about Turkey, DRC, Israel and Yemen. Control gave us quick updates on Diana, Sarah, Jeanne and Nathan. Then we would pester Grandpop and Dr P about Khadiyeh.

I think it really bothered Dr P that he was getting nothing on Khadiyeh.

We all knew more or less where Khadiyeh was. She was in the north eastern corner of Haudramaut province in Yemen. The problem was "more or less" covered an area the size of Israel which was rather more than less to explore walking around in suits. Dr P wanted to get the Egyptian minibase in Siwa operational so we could switch from suits to speeders without having to fly a speeder all the way back to New Zealand. But it would still be some time before it was ready.

Meanwhile Mariko and Gunter were on honeymoon in Queensland, Australia. From there they were heading to Thailand and then on to Japan. We didn't expect to hear from them again until they reached Okinawa. After that they were going on a bit of a tour of old Japanese gardens and buildings because Gunter was into that sort of stuff. Our big loss was Mariko as our morning DJ. Grandpop just tuned into the ancient hits radio which was really dull compared to Mariko. But that weekend we all had a bit of a slap in the mouth as we started to realise our enemies were closing. And they weren't the enemies we'd been expecting. The blessing of the chapel was a tense time. Aunty Nea and "The Prince" Tui O'Reagan Tu-ka-re-re were guests at Renwick along with two others. Grandpop said it was pretty odd for all these tribal bigwigs to show up to something as minor as a chapel. Aunty Nea was nice but she was losing her grip. Where before she had been strong spiritually even if she had been weak physically, now she was barely holding it together in any department.

Meanwhile this prince guy was everything Grandpop hated about marae Maori. All the protocol and superiority. He was really fussy about everything and looked down on Mr Trân and Mrs Jones. Grandpop said it made him grind his teeth. Bernard said he hadn't seen this much self-importance and pretence since he'd left Zimbabwe.

But when Ax showed up to take them up to the chapel it was

'brother' this and 'mate' that. Aunty Liz and Grandpop went up with Dr Prosperov and Mrs Jones. They said Ax had made a long speech about the skills of Maori carpenters not being recognised (though I could have sworn the guy I saw getting out of the carpenters van had ginger hair) and the need for Maori to manage their own heritage. They said the 'prince' had sat through all of this nodding and looking like a fat, toad who had all the flies in his grasp. Meanwhile Aunty Nea had fallen asleep and was looking increasingly confused about what was going on. The Maori VIPs had all gone off with Ax afterwards and a clearly annoyed Dr P had come home and gone into his office. It was pretty obvious that if we ever ended up depending on 'the prince' for our right to be on the Department of Conservation estate we would be gone by lunchtime.

CHAPTER SEVENTY THREE: JIBREEL

Lana Vilenskaya spent three weeks with us, talking about the suits. She had done a whole bunch of drawings. She had also decided that a completely new approach was needed. She wanted to use a different power source to get rid of the school bags. But the technology involved was nothing like as simple as the kindergarten suits we had been given. The suits she was thinking about would take every bit of Hekator's engineering skill to get right and still be nothing like as safe.

She explained her designs to the whole house the night before she flew back to America. As she saw it the main benefits were the suit would adapt to us more, the armour was thicker and the power system would use antigravity emissions rather than gravity cancellation so there wouldn't be a glow.

The main disadvantage was the suits relied on continuous links with Control and sustained antimatter vortexes which could collapse with very bad results for anyone within a kilometer or so. I couldn't help wondering whether we would have bent into Armageddon as enthusiastically in these suits as we would in our existing ones. It also occurred to me that if nothing else it would increase Control's influence over us. But Lana said:

"These are suits for teenagers, which is what your children are becoming. They will be better protected in some ways but more

exposed in others. This is a risk you would run even if your
children left us now and never returned."

The adults only agreed to think about the designs and come
back to her in a few weeks. I think they wanted to talk among
themselves without us, or Dr Prosperov, listening in. Of course
we were enthusiastic but we didn't realise then how long it
would take for Hekator to make and test them.

The week after the Chapel was blessed turned out to be more
exciting than expected. At school on Monday at lunchtime some
kids came running up to Tarik and gave him a slip of paper.

They pointed to two guys waiting by a blue car smoking.

The message was in Turkish so only Tarik could read it. He said
it was an invitation to his father to talk to them.

"Talking can't hurt, can it?" I asked.

Tarik looked at me like I was mad.

"Sam, they killed me muvver and sister. The only talk they want
involves a gun."

"But where would they get one?" I asked thinking it would be
pretty hard to bring a handgun into New Zealand.

"Who the hell cares?" he snapped.

He was angry and stalked off. Cam went with him. I thought
about it, then chased them.

"Hey look mate, the guy who killed *my* mother is camped up the
hill at the chapel and just because he's my father don't think I
don't know what it feels like," I told him.

Tarik stopped. He hadn't thought of that.

"Yeah, I'm sorry Sam. It's just I..."

"It's OK," I said and told him how I'd gone to see Ax in a suit.

"You'll just have to wear a suit to school," I suggested
remembering what Dr P had said.

"How would he take off his schoolbag in class?" Cam pointed out.

It hadn't occurred to me that Dr P would make such an obvious mistake. Of course we couldn't wear our suits at school. We'd look ridiculous with our schoolbags on our backs all the time. I was a bit shocked that I taken everything Dr P had said on blind faith.

"Well, then you'll need your ground kit," I replied.

"At least," he replied grimly.

"But they won't just bust into school and grab you will they?" I asked.

"I wouldn't bet my life on that Sam," he said very seriously. It was a bit scary to think that was exactly what he *was* doing.

So we sat through the afternoon half expecting Turkish spies to burst in and drag Tarik away. But it turned out nothing so dramatic happened. Grandpop parked the bus in his slow careful way and we walked no more than twenty meters to get onto it. The blue car followed us, just as Ax's mate Ray had followed us before, but once we hit the gravel road we couldn't tell who was behind us. It was just a wall of gray-white dust. I noticed Ax's car was outside the chapel as we drove past.

Tarik took the note to his father, who took it in turn to Dr P. We didn't see either while we did our homework, or while we cleaned. I asked Tahira what she thought, but she just shrugged. We had no idea what was really going on because we didn't understand the power balances in Turkey. Obviously whatever Dr Gursoy had done had tipped some balance in Turkey and the Ergenekon network was desperate to stop the information he had from becoming public. The question was just how desperate were they?

At dinner Dr P came down and made an announcement.
"Friends and colleagues we have small problem. It appears
Turkish military-criminal network, Ergenekon, has traced Dr
Gursoy and Tarik to this house. Have agreed with Dr Gursoy
there is now no point retaining information from authorities
and would like to ask operatives to plant entire archive for
immediate discovery by authorities. Tarik has volunteered to do
this."

"However cannot expect criminals to believe no further
information is held. Therefore is necessary to make pre-emptive
action against Ergenekon agents on Aotea. Am proposing use
of operatives and Fae resources for defence of Renwick House.
This reduces risk of legal problems and provides greatest
physical protection to all living here. Are there any objections to
this mission?"

Bernard raised his hand.

"I have no objection as long as the lessons we learned in Finland
are remembered. We don't want another shooting."

"Agreed. Is good reminder," Dr P said. "Any more?"

"I think is best if speeders used more than suits. Is safer." Mitra
said.

Dr P nodded. "Yes. Is any objections to concept?"

"No? OK, Mr Kahu is up to you to develop tactical plan."

Grandpop nodded.

"C'mon you lot. Let's see what we can do before bedtime."

So we all went down to the base.

"OK," he said when he had led us down to the briefing room.

"This is what we call an 'aggressive reconnaissance'," he growled. "
So we look for the enemy, we test his strength and if he's too strong,
we beat it quick. If not, we push on and try and break him."

"So where's the enemy. We have to assume he's nearby and work out from there. So, when it's dark enough I want Sam, Ashley, Tahira and Scott in speeders flying low around this place. Tarik and Cam are going to Turkey, Sam and Tahira work up the road while Ashley and Scott start in Port Carlyle and work back. You should find them somewhere."

"What do we do to them when we find them?" Ashley asked trying to sound tough.

"Take their car and dump it in the sea. We'll see where they are before we do anything else."

This wasn't a job that bothered us at all. Compared to Hathaway or Israel how tough could these guys be?

At eight thirty, our four gray boxes slipped out of an old concrete bunker above the sea and vanished. As the light faded, turning the sky pale gray we probed around Renwick. After ten minutes we were pretty sure they weren't anywhere near us so Scotty and Ashley nipped off to Port Carlyle while me and Tahira went up the road. To get a good view we climbed to six thousand feet and cruised along at seventy kilometers an hour. We were pretty thorough checking along the way.

But it was Ashley who followed a hunch and found them first. They were at the same place as Ax and his crew. She said they were having a good time because she picked up the sounds of adults partying inside. Now we had an even bigger problem. Ax had recruited even more help in his campaign to get us out. Scotty hung around to listen in but I couldn't. It just made me want to blast everything.

The two girls flew home but I decided to switch off invisibility and go low and fast over the sea for fun. I whizzed out a dozen kilometers then looped over and flew up the ridge to the peak

of Aotea. Then I turned around and flew down at high speed.
I zoomed over Emma's place accidentally on purpose when
I realised she was slipping out her window dressed in a dark
bushshirt and jeans.

I doubled back – a small black smudge against the stars half a
kilometer above – and watched her. She was heading for the
bush track that started not far from her home. I wondered what
on Earth she was doing. So while Ka-rea-rea watched her I tried
to get a reading.

She was looking for plots of marijuana in the bush. She had
decided that if the cops were too scared to try, she would do the
job for them. It was so gutsy I smiled with pride that she would
do that.

It was also dangerous. We knew these guys were armed and it
would be so easy for them to shoot her. I remembered a case
that had been on TV about a guy who had shot a woman and
claimed it was a hunting accident. The show said lots of people
had been killed in hunting accidents and the shooters had been
let off with nothing more serious than a fine. It would be easy
for them to shoot her and claim they thought she was a pig or
something. The only thing that was keeping her safe tonight was
the fact the bad guys were all getting drunk and stoned back in
town.

I watched her for a bit longer and then zipped home. When I
got back I found most of the others had gone to bed. Scott was
talking to Grandpop and Dr P with Bernard and Ken in the
lounge when I came in. Scott said Ax had arranged to sell these
Turkish guys shotguns. Ax hadn't mentioned Grandpop to the
Turks but Scott said Ax had been thinking to himself that *he*
wouldn't want to enter Renwick in the dark against old Mike

453

Kahu, shotgun or no shotgun. Grandpop smiled at that.

Scott said what Ax was waiting for was a gang contact from Los Angeles who was due out in a week or so. That was when the real trouble would start.

I reported what Emma was up to. I was pleased how impressed the men were with her. Dr P suggested we should immediately help Emma to find every plot on the island as a way of striking back at Ax and that this would be our mission tomorrow night. I had to admit as I went to bed that night this suited me just fine.

I slept pretty well. Then suddenly I was in a room. A woman was slapping me. She was shouting that I was worse than useless and beating and shoving me as I held my arms to protect myself. The other women in the room were just laughing or shouting encouragement. Then there was a loud shout and He came into the room complaining about the noise.

All the women told Him that I had burnt his guests stew because of my dreaming. They were all afraid of Him and they blamed me because I was the smallest and least able to defend myself. Even as I cried my apologies, terrified of the anger boiling on his face I also knew his guests were jackals who had murdered some foreign women only two weeks ago and were now heroes to my husband and his friends.

Roughly he grabbed me and shouted his fury as I tried not to pee with terror. Then he grabbed my hand and yelling that if I burned his guests food he would burn me to teach me a lesson and he pressed it to the burning hot brazier. I screamed as the pain mixed with the sound and smell of burning skin. Then he threw me down on the floor and stamped down the stairs.

I was lying on the floor. I could taste blood. My lip had hit the floor but it was nothing to the pain in my hand. It felt as if the whole world was revolving around my hand with the pain in the middle of it. Even the women in the kitchen were shocked. Then they got up and started running around. Someone came to me. They took my hand and put it in a pot of water. I screamed and cried as the pain shocked through me. Then the pain stopped and the world seemed to tear open.

It was light so brilliant, so perfect I couldn't believe it. My pain was gone and in its place a joy so complete and wonderful I laughed and cried – now with happiness. The whiteness consumed everything. There was no kitchen. No women. No house. Just brilliance. And I rose. I rose up, up through the roof, up into the sky, now dark and scattered with stars. I rose higher and higher so I could see the valley my husband's house was set in, the village of his tribe, and higher to the great desert beyond. I was so high I almost wanted to join the stars. But they whispered to me.

"Not yet. Not yet blessed one. You have much to do yet."

And I looked down and I called to my friends.

"Look and you will find me. Jibreel, Sam, Tahira, Scott, Ashley, Cam, Tarik. Come, my friends, come and find me. Come now. Right now."

And then I woke up knowing exactly where Khadiyeh was. For a second I lay there my head spinning with this dream. A dream so real it was no dream. And then like some robot given an order it cannot ignore I sat up and put my feet to the floor. Slowly I seemed to come to myself. I needed to get down to the base. She had called us. My clock said almost six in the morning as I jumped up and ran out the door.

As I came out I almost ran into Ashley, who was always a bit slow in the morning. We didn't need to say anything. We just ran.

Tarik was already getting undressed as I ran in. He didn't
stop to say anything. It was the same when Scott came in. We
just jumped in our drawers and let the dresser do its thing.
Five minutes later we were all in the briefing room with no
Grandpop.

"OK, OK what are we going to do?" Tarik wanted to know.
This question stopped us for a moment to think.

"Bend dive," Scotty answered certainly.

"From?"

"Four thousand meters."

"OK then what? I just keep thinking of the last time we all
rushed in somewhere."

"Can I help?" Control asked, appearing.

It wasn't so much a question as a demand we tell him what was
going on. So we did. When we'd explained he looked stunned.

"I can only inform my makers of this. I have nothing to
contribute," he said. "I shall also inform Dr Prosperov."
That still didn't give us a plan and time was wasting.

"Look Tarik. This isn't like Tel Meggido. It was me who didn't
want to go there, remember? I had a bad feeling about it. What
I have with this is a bad feeling we'll be late. I'm going. If you
guys want to think up a plan that's fine. Let me know," I told
them, and dashed to the jump station. I wasn't alone Tahira and
the others were right behind me. We got into our circle. Our
destination was clear in our minds.

"Three, two, one, go," I said.

[+]

Time seemed to slow down, then colour seemed to drain out
of everything. My whole field of view seemed to fold up and
distort and I had to close my eyes. I was falling back, unable to

456

move, falling and spinning, and then suddenly I stopped falling back and started falling forward. There was brilliant light all around me. Brilliant light and presences. My mother and my Grandmother.

But there was another. One I didn't know and this presence seemed very big, old and kind. It began to fade. I opened my eyes. I was falling.

Below the land was dark lit only by stars and a sickle moon. There were some lights in the valley. Casually I engaged my control surfaces and wings checking around the others who like me fell from the starry night, our faces hidden by our hoods. Carefully we opened out our ring until it was half a kilometer across.

The valley below led north out to the great desert, the Rub al Khali. It was like an immense ocean of sand. In that valley was a tiny village where Khadiyeh was waiting for us.

"*Shine!*" Khadiyeh told us, her thoughts suddenly clear in our heads.

Her meaning was clear. I engaged gravity deflection at the same time as everyone else and our bodies began to glow as we got lower and cranked up the deflection.

"*She wants us to fly in,*" Tahira said.

"*Silently,*" I added.

We all knew what that meant and cranked up the deflection even more so that the Cerenkov radiation intensified and we were falling like brilliant snowflakes, slowly and gently.

As we descended the harsh landscape wrapped around us. The steep, rocky hillsides, the emptiness of the desert. This was a place where you knew nature was boss. There simply wasn't any argument about it.

As I reached the six hundred foot mark level with the top of the hill I began to flap my wings in slow powerful strokes.

The village was small. There were only half a dozen houses built into the side of the bank. The dried river valley was about half a kilometer wide so our whole ring just fitted inside it. There was barely anything growing there. On the hillsides the shapes of goats glowed to our thermal vision. There were people by the houses standing outside looking at us. They weren't angry or scared. They seemed just plain awestruck, if anything.

"*TO ME CHILDREN OF ANGELS*!" Khadiyeh yelled.

We heard both her thin girlish voice echoing off the rocks and the powerful thought in our heads. We could see her now.

She was on the road outside the houses. All the villagers were looking past her at us as she stood with her arms raised. She must have run outside, chased by her husband's mother and sisters.

We flew towards her slowly.

"*Watch out for snipers*," Tarik warned.

I had been doing that anyway. But it seemed nobody had thought to pick up a weapon. They were just watching us, stunned or fascinated, as we flew down to the small figure in brown.

"*You must carry me. Lift me Tarik. Lift me Tahira. We must go to Jibreel.*"

Even as she thought of her destination out in the desert I noticed flickers of lightning in that direction. Out in the sand-sea a storm was building.

Tarik and Tahira reached Khadiyeh's side first. Then Cam came up behind her. Tarik and Tahira held hands and Cam pulled her back so she was sitting on their hands and then all three glowed

458

brighter than ever and rose quickly into the air, while Scotty, Ashley and me hovered 50 feet above and behind them watching the crowd.

I expected someone to shout "God is great!" or "stop her!", but nobody said a thing. We rose with Tarik, Tahira and Cam and I realised that the main emotion the villagers felt was shame. They weren't ashamed of their poverty. That didn't bother them. They were ashamed that the most despised of them all, the one they had all sneered at, laughed at or beaten had been Chosen. And the strangest thing was that even though we knew *we* were not children of angels we also knew she *had* been chosen. We were just giving Khadiyeh a lift. We were as much in awe of her as the villagers were.

We rose into the air. At five hundred feet we turned for the desert and a tail wind sprang out of nowhere. Through the night's sky we were blown, suspended between the huge sky of diamond stars over the hills of sand that reached out to the horizon like a dream.

On we flew. For quarter of an hour, half an hour, a whole hour while all the time the blue flickering on the horizon drew ever closer. By the time an hour was up Tarik and Tahira were struggling. Khadiyeh was tiny; smaller than any of us, but even with the suits' strength holding their arms in position for all this time was hard. The tailwind was also getting weaker and as we got closer the thunder went from a distant rumble to cracks that sounded like the sky was splitting. More than once I wondered what on Earth we were doing.

All the way Khadiyeh "talked" to us, encouraging us not to give up. Soon we would meet her friend Jibreel. I wondered what sort of friend hung around a sandy desert in a storm. Finally

Khadiyeh pointed to a tall dune. To me it looked as good as any other out here. We flew towards it as the tailwind, which had carried us perhaps fifty kilometers, finally gave up completely in the face a strong sandy headwind.

We battled against this with the sky and stars fading overhead and lightning ripping the sky in brilliant blue flashes that roared like huge drums. Finally when we landed I thought we were possibly in the worst place in the world.

It was strangely hot. The wind was whipping up the sand around us. Visibility was dropping rapidly and there was a good chance of being fried by a bolt of lightning at any moment. Khadiyeh with a white bandage on her hand and only her black abaya for protection was covering her face, cowering away from the wind. We were standing around her, asking why on Earth she wanted to come *here*.

She just answered she must meet Jibreel. Her idea of Jibreel was as hazy as it had been of us. She knew he existed somewhere but I was starting to think she really had no idea what he was really like. The astonishment that we had actually come at all was wearing off, she was starting to doubt her convictions about Jibreel as well.

Then the rain hit us. I didn't think you could have so much rain in a desert. But it wasn't falling. It came in sideways like a fire hose. The winds were huge. And if the lightning had been close before now it was actually striking the dunes nearby in huge flashes of brilliance with thunder that you felt more than heard. It was madness to stay there.

We all wanted to bend out but Khadiyeh would be left behind. So instead we formed a huddle around Khadiyeh, sheltering her under us with our backs to the sky, each wondering what our powerpacks would do if they took a bolt of lightning and hoping it would not mean either exploding or, just as bad, being stuck in the desert.

We stayed like that for what seemed like forever but was actually only half an hour when suddenly we all felt a presence. It was behind me. We all looked up in the swirling dark of sand, rain and wind. You could not see a thing. Not even with thermal. Yet our senses told us someone was there.

Khadiyeh had to look away and put her head down because of her unprotected eyes. But I kept looking. Suddenly I saw a flame. An orange flame dancing to my right over my shoulder, followed by another to its left, and another, and another. They seemed to be forming a circle around us. Then the first flame vanished and around the circle they all went out. But I knew something was there. There were more presences. Smaller ones for sure but definitely more surrounding us. I thought I could see dark figures through the wind and sand but they disappeared back into the storm.

For a while nothing happened. Even the lightning stopped. We just continued to crouch over Khadiyeh, trying to keep her dry and warm and not doing well at either. Space began to feel different. The window of the sky seemed to flex, the ground felt strangely distant.

"*He's here*," Khadiyeh said suddenly, standing.

Instantly it was silent. The storm was gone. But instead of hope I felt an awful sadness. I realised with a shock we had come with Khadiyeh not to live, but to die. I looked up. A figure was approaching us. It was shaped like a man but more like the outline of a man around nothing. All was still and I realised everything was over. There would be no Grandpop, no Rewa, no

Aunty Liz. Even no others. I was alone. My end was here.

A figure approached us. It didn't walk, nor did it drift. It sort of just fell over us like a shadow. And we knew that we had to give up everything. All our comforts, all our fantasies, all our hopes and dreams. They were over. This was it. This was death. Hine Nui Te Po, the great lady of night, would come now to take me for her own. For some reason I imagined her like Aunty Liz, but without breath.

A cold stillness gripped our bodies and I cried. I really blubbed. I cried in grief for myself. I was too young to die. I was too *me* to die. I was too *anything* to die. It wasn't fair. There was so much still to do. I thought, "Now I'll never marry Emma". And yet here it was, without question. The end.

Yet even though Khadiyeh was as scared as the rest of us, even though her hand was causing her so much pain, Khadiyeh spoke to us. She comforted us and somehow was comforting. And unlike us, she was not afraid.

A cold I had never imagined chilled us. It was not outside like in Greenland but inside our hearts. A soft, quiet cold that numbed your whole body. Then a soft white light fell on us from above. I looked up and wished I hadn't.

It was like looking up into a wheel within a wheel. The outer wheel rotated one way, the inner the other, and in the centre an enormous chimney of light coming down to a point perhaps five meters across coming down over us. It seemed to stretch up forever and widen like a pillar of light that didn't end like when you stand between two mirrors that face each other. You felt breathless, tiny and powerless. Around the edges of the wheel coloured lights of blue and purple, pink and yellow sparkled and danced as they rotated as they did all the way up inside its length for the whole thing was revolving and sliding down towards us like a telescope extending. It made you want to run, but you couldn't. Our limbs no longer moved. Our breath was shallow. Only Khadiyeh somehow remained standing.

We all sat looking up as the tube descended around us, surrounding us in its brilliance. Now that it was over us it felt scary but also amazing, enchanting like a shiny knife. If this was an end it now felt new and exciting. We watched it, fascinated, like the smallest babies staring at a curtain blown in the wind by the window.

We reached out to touch the sides of the tube but we couldn't. As we put out our hands they just seemed to bend around the edges. It was like "straight" had been redefined within the curve of this tube. Gradually we were enveloped in the coloured sparkling lights and, despite what I wanted, I found myself thinking about everything that made me, me. My parents, my sister, Grandpop, Rewa, Clive, Tahira, Emma. My friends old and new, my fears, my hopes, my secrets. It was like having your life turned inside out and it was pretty rough. I found myself wincing away from the lights. So were the others, but there was nowhere to go. We writhed, groaning, as the truth was extracted. All except Khadiyeh who remained standing where she was, looking blissed out.

Then something very weird started happening. Everything began to turn and I began to experience things I didn't even remember. A huge plain. Herds of horses. A train. A woman with slanted eyes. A walled red city high, high in the mountains. A forest. Blue flowers. A scream from the sky and dirt flying. Screams. My baby brother. It was like pulling a string out of a plughole and finding it just kept coming out. On and on. It was life. My life. My life-stories. Life after lifetime. I was a line. The tip of a line. Turning and turning though the years, The centuries. I was aiming for something. Aiming but not reaching. It made my head hurt.

And that was when it got really scary. Because now we weren't in our suits anymore. We weren't even in our bodies anymore. I looked down and we were turning around and accelerating away from our bodies travelling up the chimney at unbelievable speed as it widened and widened into brighter and brighter light going faster and faster.

Then suddenly we were still. Or we were moving but everything was still. Nothing changed. We were no longer on Earth. We were somehow in space. Earth was below us. Around us were other lines like ourselves. Lines streaking and weaving together. The life-lines were gathering like woven threads of different colours. This was the weaving Tabika and Mrs Jones had taught us about – for real! There were millions and millions of these woven life-lines, and as we moved, or were still, we curved around the Earth, and arrived back at their beginning, entering themselves only to begin again. The lines twisted, wove and moved circling around each other so the whole thing was like a single gigantic living being; a huge snake coiling about the planet.

For some reason I could feel myself in the core of this great woven rope. Around me the others were tightly woven about me. Around me, Khadiyeh and a few others the whole rainbow of lives coiled. I felt a strange energy building inside me. I was vibrating, like a guitar string, and the vibrations were within me, spreading up and down the lines that were us. It was like music, like life running through you. I could see my vibrations spilling out into other lines, pulling them with me. I felt a soaring sense of certainty and I found the vibrations were rippling, stronger and stronger, from me and the others coursing through all the lines, getting too powerful for me to control. We began to swell with light, backward and forward until it was a huge wave and we exploded in light.

And for an instant, not even half a second, but the tiniest amount of time imaginable, we stretched infinitely across the whole universe and just for that instant we felt like we knew absolutely everything. Every creature on every world, every speck of sand, the most complex of thoughts, every possible emotion, every weird dream. For the tiniest, tiniest instant of time we were conscious of absolutely everything across a line of the entire Universe. It was like standing on the edge of an enormous cliff. My mind couldn't contain it all.

Then before I realised what had happened I was back in my body again. The storm loud in my ears. The wheels were gone. My heart pounding like it was going to bust out of my chest. Gasping for breath. Shivering and shaking madly. I was covered in cold sweat. The storm was raging around us but we were still in a clear still place in its centre.

A brilliant light appeared, like the light of bending but brighter. And I knew this was Jibreel. I had no idea who Jibreel was but he was amazing. He … it … sex made no sense to a light … was shaped like a four pointed star and big; big as a two storey house. Khadiyeh was still standing, facing it, as it shrank a little, becoming so bright you couldn't look at it. I got spots in my eyes but out of the corner of my eye I noticed the light was shrinking to become a human-like figure. It was embracing Khadiyeh who held out her arms to it. They stayed like that for perhaps half a minute, then the figure twisted and vanished in a spray of light that slowly faded. And then Khadiyeh fainted as the storm collapsed in on us again.

We covered Khadiyeh with our bodies. We were still shaken. Still cold in our bodies. And yet our hearts ... our hearts felt hot. It was like when I thought of Emma. It was hard to tell whether what we had just experienced was real or in our imaginations, or what. But one thing for sure was that it was uncomfortably close to death and we all felt both really scared and really, really happy at the same time. I almost threw up.

We lay there covering Khadiyeh while the wind lashed us with sand. The lightning and thunder seemed further away now though, and the wind was gentler as well. We must have been there for two hours because we all fell into a dreamless sleep. We were woken by Grandpop.

"What the hell is going on?" he wanted to know. I could tell he was grumpy. And at that very moment headlights came up through the storm and formed a ring around us. Men came though the storm and grabbed us shoving us into the backs of their trucks. Yelling to each other and at us in Arabic.

"What were we doing in the storm? What was the light we had made for? Didn't we know we could die out here?" They were grumpy too, but caring in their own way. An old man with a greying beard guided us into a beaten up old yellow Land Cruiser. It was a double cab. We got in the back. A younger man with clean cut dark features got in the right side in front of Scott. The older man was driving.

I felt beaten up. The truck started to move. I was astonished they could find their way in these conditions. But I read the driver and learned that storms hid their tracks making their smuggling easier.

I turned my mind to his companion and got a mental slap. I saw his dark eyes staring at me intensely in the vanity mirror and recognised something about him at once. He looked the same as the man from the perfume shop in Tarim and he was reading *me*.

FACT OR FICTION?

As a work of fiction most characters are fictional and any resemblance to any person living or dead is coincidental. Actual persons such as Colonel Laurent Nkunda are, of course, real. There are, however, some amalgalms of fact and fiction in the work. This section is intended to clarify the fact from the fiction.

Sam's "mihi" or "acknowledgements" are inferred from his approximate family origin.

Michael Sementov is an entirely fictional character who is a composite of various Israeli mafia leaders. He is contrasted with Semion Mogilevich a leader of the Russian Mafiya and number ten on the FBI ten most wanted list. His crimes have earned him the description as 'the most dangerous man in the world'. Vachslav Ivankov is another Russian Mafiya leader. For more information on the Jewish Russian or Jewish Ukrainian Mafiya refer to the works of Robert Friedman, an American Jewish journalist. The role of the Jewish community in Pre-WW2 organised crime in Eastern Europe is a fact documented by Prof. Mordechai Zalkin, an associate professor of modern Jewish history at Ben-Gurion University of the Negev in Israel.

The character of Uri Kogan is inspired by a number of arms dealers. These include Israeli citizen Valdim Alperin (who came to prominence when his shipment of tanks to the South Sudan rebels on the M.V Faina was ransomed by Somali pirates for $3.2 million in October 2008) and Russian citizen Viktor Bout whose air transport business in Africa defied numerous official sanctions. Both men have probably worked with various intelligence agencies. There are numerous contractor airlines who deliver arms covertly for various powers. The value of the AN-12's quoted in the story is based on the listed offer price of those of Viktor Bout at the time. For a useful and insightful book on the war in Dafur the author recommend's "Emma's War" by American journalist Deborah Scroggins.

The Blood libel is a xenophobic, anti-semitic claim that Jews murder children to use their blood for religious purposes. Blood libels have been perpetrated against Jews in numerous settings throughout history. One of the earliest best-documented blood libels started in Britain in 1144.

The idea for the Julia Huuygen's "blood bath" was inspired by the historical Hungarian serial killer Countess Elizabeth Bathory de Ecsed (7 August 1560 – 21 August 1614). This noble had killed and tortured at least 650 young women. The legend that she bathed in the blood of her victims is questionable.

The suggestion that the Belgian Federal Police, the Roman Catholic Church and the US Central Intelligence Agency have been infiltrated by semi-immortal sanguiphagic aliens may be taken seriously by some people. The author is not among them.

The history of vampire legends goes back to Median Persia (circa 1000 BCE). The Assyrians and Babylonians were the originators of stories of Lilith, who drank the blood of babies in Hebrew legend.

There is a scientific basis for the restorative effect of young blood. Research by Dr Amy Wagers at Havard Medical School, Professor Thomas Rando at Stanford, and Dr Saul Villeda at the University of California, San Francisco has found that the GDF11 protein in the blood of young rodents reversed aging in the hearts and brains of older animals.

The Israeli Abdel Khader gang has been associated with the Hariri crime family in Umm al Fahm according to the Israeli newspaper Ha'aretz. The Malka brothers in the story are modelled on associates of the Abergil crime family.

Telephone calls from Israel to Dubai are possible. The reverse at time of writing is not.

The descriptions of life in Arab Israel are drawn from YouTube postings, blogs, documentaries, books, newspaper articles from Ha'aretz and fiction, in particular the excellent Omar Yosef detective series by Matt Rees. The character Yidal Gur is named after the Israeli detective story writers – Batya Gur and Yigal Mossinsohn.

As far as I am aware there is no Church with a publicly accessible bell tower with a view over the Place d'Armes in Luxembourg.

While all the Manilla treasure galleons described in the text are invented the missing cargoes are not. The Portuguese Carrack or merchantman called Nau Chagas was sunk by the British in June, 1594 off the Azores. To date its treasure has not been recovered.

The interior layout and make of lifts at the Belgian federal police building at 8 Fritz Toussaint Street in Brussels is entirely imaginary. Note the building is not owned by the Belgian Police but by the state Buildings agency.

All the atrocities described as occurring in North Kivu happened. This includes the bus birth hijacking. They are all based on witness testimony, though Jeanne is an imaginary character. The actual situation was usually much worse than described here.

The Moldovan sex-slave industry is well documented in numerous official reports. The facts of the trade have been softened considerably. That a country so well endowed with fertile soil, and with such a cheap currency is incapable of supporting itself through agricultural exports is an indictment on the European common agricultural policy. The exploitation of the girls by the Bruderschaft portrayed in this story is a metaphor for the EU's bleeding of Eastern Europe and Africa through protective agricultural policy.

The tragic shooting at the Jewish seminary in Jerusalem which cost eight seminarians their lives, portrayed as occurring in January 2008 actually occurred in March.

Saudi air strikes in North-west Yemen against Houthi tribesmen (in Yemen most people belong to a tribe so nearly all Yemen's 24 million people are 'tribesmen') actually began eighteen months after the time when Sam supposedly witnesses one. While some YouTube video is available the description here is entirely imaginary. The employment of F-5E Tigers is assumed. This phase of the story is part of Sam's psychological confrontation with real violence, prior to his confrontation with his father.

The story of Khadiyeh is partially inspired by that of Najood Ali the ten year old divorcee from Sana'a, Yemen. Her story is brilliantly told in "I am Nujood, ten, and divorced" by Persian French writer Delpine Mirou. The other main influence is the Book of Elijah in the Old Testament of the Hebrew Bible..

6

CHANGELS
GENESIS
PART SIX
THE CRUCIBLE

PETER KING

A GLOBAL SUPERNATURAL EPIC

Through incisive detective work Sue solves the case of how the Changels were discovered. But the enemy have not given up either and it now seems they are preparing to launch their biological assault on the human population. As the Changels try to extract themselves from their own mysterious disappearance their enemy strikes and the teens find themselves forced to fight an enemy older, stronger and more numerous than themselves.

To get your copy visit the website: www.changels.info

www.ingramcontent.com/pod-product-compliance
Lightning Source LLC
Chambersburg PA
CBHW020920020726
47495CB00002B/265